BLACK MIDAS

ALSO BY JAN CAREW

The Wild Coast
The Last Barbarian
Moscow Is Not My Mecca
Cry Black Power
Sons of the Flying Wing
The Third Gift
Rape the Sun
Children of the Sun
Save the Last Dance for Me
The Twins of Llora
Grenada: The Hour Will Strike Again

JAN CAREW

BLACK MIDAS

INTRODUCTION BY KWAME DAWES

PEEPAL TREE

First published in Great Britain in 1958
by Secker & Warburg
This new edition published in 2009,
reprinted in 2024

Peepal Tree Press Ltd
17 King's Avenue
Leeds LS6 1QS
England

ISBN13 Print: 9781845230951

ISBN13 Ebook: 9781845233686

Supported by
ARTS COUNCIL
ENGLAND

With sincere thanks to Wilson Harris and Herbert Scotland who provided me with invaluable background material for this novel.

INTRODUCTION

KWAME DAWES

When *Black Midas* appeared in 1958, Jan Carew was almost forty years old, some years older than most of the new wave of Caribbean writers with whom he socialised in London in the late fifties and early sixties. Among the men and few women who gathered around the BBC offices to record *Caribbean Voices*, he was the dominant raconteur. Not only was he older, he was more experienced and worldly wise. Born on September 24, 1920, in the Berbice village of Agricola, British Guiana, he had worked for years in his home country, and in Trinidad, in jobs that gave him access to all segments of society and their stories. In British Guiana he had taught high school and by 1958 he had studied at Howard University, Western Reserve and in Prague.

His travels, starting at the age of nineteen, began what was to become a life of "endless journeyings". He has visited five continents: North and South America, Europe, including the then Soviet Union, Asia, and Africa, and his perceptions of the communities that he writes about are searching and his appreciation of the people compassionate. For Carew, universal literature emerges when the writer writes about his people in a "tense and heightened way that . . . reflects the problems of the peoples all over the world".[1]

Acquaintance with his later career might tempt the tagging of Carew as a "political writer", but it is less easy to decide what label to place on the tag. Certainly he has been a "revolutionary-minded" activist keenly aware of the political realities that face the Black people of the world. But his role may be best described as a sceptic of political systems and a propagandist for unity and singleness of purpose among peoples. Carew wants people to identify their own answers to their political problems, rather than to look outside for help.

In an article entitled "The Myth of El Dorado in the Caribbean Novel" (1971), Hena Maes-Jelinek observes, "For Carew, the richness of Guyana does not lie in its lodes of gold but in its people: he perceives close links between them and the landscapes in which they have been toiling and suffering for several centuries, and he thereby contributes, albeit tentatively, to the shaping of a Guyanese consciousness".[2] If his view of Guyanese consciousness is tentative it is because he regards that consciousness as rudimentary and unfinished.

But what Carew perceives as the link between people and landscape – the true lode of gold – is their storytelling, the means whereby the Guyanese (Caribbean) people construct their own histories, people the landscape and discover rhythms in the pattern of Caribbean being. It is Carew's instinct for the well-told story that shapes the very structure of *Black Midas*. At times, the work reads like a picaresque that ends only because the author and his editors have determined that two hundred and sixty pages is about enough for a novel, rather than because the work has come to a clear and final ending. This sense of breathless accumulation is confirmed by what Carew has said about the novel's evolution – that it has its origins as a compilation of the stories told him by Herbert Scotland, a pork-knocker, who was Wilson Harris's expeditionary cook in his days as a government surveyor.[3] Carew tapped into other areas of Guyanese oral history for *Black Midas*. There was indeed a gold prospector known as Ocean Shark in the 1920s, and a police sergeant (Arthur Husbands) known as Mark-a-Book at the Oranapai station in the Mazaruni.[4]

This relationship to "stories" that come out of the oral tradition is a more radical strategy than it might at first seem. It enables Carew, with self-acknowledged origins in the "brown" middle class, to find a way of closing the gap between the authorial voice and the worlds of the Caribbean majority. Amongst his contemporaries, only Sam Selvon does anything comparable in his "ballads" in *The Lonely Londoners* (1956) and *The Housing Lark* (1965). The embedding of stories within the novel as a whole gives *Black Midas* the same kind of energy to be found in such consciously postmodern novels as Rushdie's *Midnight's Children* (1981), or in the work of the Creolité writers such as Maryse Condé, Patrick Chamoiseau and Raphaël Confiant, or the Trinidadian Robert Antoni's *Divina Trace* (1991).

If what most distinguishes *Black Midas* is the democracy of its storytelling instincts, what goes with this is a tendency to subordinate character to the needs of narrative drive.

By the end of the novel, the central character, the narrator Aron Smart, is still alive, if rather the worse for wear, and very little has been resolved in his constantly shifting sense of self. No single incident has transformed him or given him a new understanding of self that will allow us to read a natural closure to the work. He remains a restless man, seduced by the bush and trapped by his capacity to become addicted to various pursuits, whether it is mining gold and diamonds; living recklessly and naively as a would-be financial speculator in Georgetown; or experimenting with multiple sexual partners. He knows that he is a man whose attachments to people and activities are at once intense – almost pathologically so – and yet fleeting. He falls in love easily and then discards those he has loved just as easily. He needs people badly and, at the same time, is quite capable of forgetting them when things do not work out. Aron Smart's self-awareness is gradual and never dramatic. He is still as stubborn, self-driven and motivated for success when he finds himself in the collapsing mine at the end of the novel as he was in his youth. Hence, as readers we are taken through this book, not so much by the revelatory patterns of the character-based novel of self-discovery, but by the qualities of each adventure – in which each episode's dramatic structure seduces us by its novelty, texture and our growing sense of its contribution to the larger mosaic. Characters like Bullah, Richard Smart, Belle and Indra return to the story, rarely changing in their essential selves, but always adding some dimension to the plot and serving as foils for Aron. Here Carew may well be responding to a truth in life that is distorted by the moral purposes of that genre of novel which is built around transformations of character.

It is this rich array of characters that adds hugely to the appeal of the work. One of the key characters is, of course, the Guyanese landscape which Carew writes about with a deep sense of passion and love. Where Wilson Harris turns this same landscape into a metaphor for the psychic development of the individual and an entire region, Carew's fascination with the space is visceral, physical and rooted in the sheer novelty of knowing a place well enough to understand it. Though the bush is treacherous and dangerous, it can be tamed by people who know it and respect it. Men can smell snakes in the air; they can find their way along dense paths because they have done it before; they can feed on this land by hunting and by making use of its resources. Carew's canvas extends from the coastal regions of the country, to the river areas where farming thrives, into the hinterland where the forests teem with life, death and tremendous mystery and adventure.

Characters are always being asked to explain their past or some incident that may have happened, and it is the connections between these anecdotes that provide the novel's structure. If the novel seeks to answer one compelling question it appears to be: "Will Aron succeed or not in life?" But then, Carew defies the easy pattern of the coming-of-age narrative: taking a character from poverty to wealth – or from ignorance to understanding – and, where necessary, allowing for that character's tragic fall.

Aron does indeed begin poor and with very few prospects, but with a community that seems committed to protecting him and helping him. When he is injured while working on the road gang, we wonder if he will ever make anything of his life. He has the good fortune of getting an education sponsored by Beauchamp, a white man regretful over his role in the death of Aron's father. Here the story seems about to embark on a narrative of success – the story of a boy who becomes educated and then grows alienated from his past because of his western education. Indeed, when Aron reflects on his first trip to Georgetown, where he successfully takes the Junior Cambridge exam, it seems that we are dealing with a standard first-person narrative of social progress such as is common in the West Indian novel:

> "Well, Shark, boy, we're back and we did it," Brother C. said for the benefit of the assembled villagers, and I suddenly realized that I hated him, and the village, and the black faces with their white eyes and white teeth shining in the sun. Mahaica was a womb out of which I had been wrenched and I did not want to return to it. Books had made me divided in myself and I knew I would remain that way as long as I lived. On the one hand, the language of books had chalked itself on the slate of my mind and,

on the other, the sun was in my blood, the swamp and river, my mother, the amber sea, the savannahs, the memory of surf and wind closer to me than the smell of my sweat. (p.51)

Here the classic themes of division appear to connect *Black Midas* to novels such as Neville Dawes's *The Last Enchantment*, George Lamming's *In the Castle of My Skin* or V.S. Naipaul's collection of stories, *Miguel Street*, among many others. But what Carew is doing – though phrases such as "divided in myself" rather throw us off the scent – is less about pursuing the themes of Fanon's *Black Skin/ White Masks*, more about refusing to pursue the goal of education in a colonial context. To be an educated man in the colonised village space of Mahaica is indeed to live with division and separation as Carew shows at greater length in his novel, *The Wild Coast* (also published in 1958). Like Huck Finn, Aron instead "lights out for the territory", and in this movement, Carew provided Aron with ample psychological grounds for his restlessness. The repeated pattern of shattered attachments, the fact that he has been constantly abandoned and retrieved throughout his life, has made him emotionally incapable of remaining committed to an individual or a settled place.

Carew tempts us with the grand narrative of success. We expect Aron to move from the overseas exams to becoming a pharmacist, before he eventually leaves the colony and encounters the world. But this is not what happens. Aron's restlessness consumes him while he is working with Dr. Ram in the mental asylum, and once he has the money to do so, he takes off for the hinterlands to try his luck as a pork-knocker. His education becomes no more than a quirky novelty that allows him to be labelled an educated man, but apart from helping him with some medical tasks and giving others, like Belle, a sense of his difference because of his occasional desire to read, it is clear that Aron's alienation from the past is not shaped by his western education, but by a more personality-driven desire to break away from past constraints.

Occasionally, and particularly in the sequences that deal with Georgetown, Carew explores the politics of colonial society, but this work does not take on the large questions that we see

Lamming contending with in *In the Castle of My Skin*, or that we see in John Hearne's *Voices Under the Window*. Aron seems destined to become a political figure in Georgetown through his association with men like Kendall and De Freitas; but instead he abandons Georgetown after being swindled of his wealth, and returns to the bush to prospect for diamonds and gold – just as he had done earlier when faced with the oppressive and exploitative actions of Dr. Ram. At one level, Carew paints a character who has all the features of the classic West Indian man who will becomes a leader of his people in the anti-colonial movement. When Aron comes back to Georgetown with his fortune, and plans to set up there, it is made clear to him that there is a great deal of vicarious desire for his success on the part of Georgetown's Black population as a challenge to the white and coloured middle-class elite.

But despite being seen by working-class Georgetown as a Black man who will break the colonial mould, it is clear that Aron's project in Georgetown is flawed both from within and from without. In the first place, his project is not concerned with breaking the colonial mould, but finding a niche within it, a niche that involves mimicry and the kind of colonisation that Aron has so far mostly avoided. Secondly, because Aron is fatally unreflective, he is condemned to live like an intruder in the white man's house he buys and his wilful recklessness with his money and with his personal relationships ensure his failure in this world. In truth, Aron is always ambivalent about this kind of success – though he has no alternative goal – so he is destined both to betray the hopes of those who look to him and to fail in his self-aggrandising scheme, easily outsharked by Kendall and De Freitas. (It's not clear whether Carew was thinking about what was happening in Guyana in the years just before the novel's publication – the break-up of the anti-colonial movement into ethnic fragments through the naked personal ambitions of its leaders – but it is obviously possible to read the Georgetown episode as a prophetic warning of how easy it would be for Guyana's nationalist leaders to fall into a mimicry of colonial power relations.)

It is Aron's saving grace – what keeps us engaged with him – that at each juncture when it appears that he is going to assume a role within the colonial order, he responds to some instinctive drive towards personal adventure and chooses, instead, to take off for the bush rather than fall into the role being laid out for him. If for Huck Finn, the "territory" is a space as yet uncontaminated by "civilisation" and its brutal hypocrisies, for Aron the bush is uncolonised space, virgin territory where he can experience the primal dawn of the pioneer. This is a powerful recognition in *Black Midas*, that for the Caribbean person so much space is second-hand. But Carew sees, too, like Wilson Harris in *Palace of the Peacock*, that the dream of virgin territory is vitiated by older desires (Donne the conquistador, Aron the Black Midas), so that Aron finds that, like his fellow pork-knockers, he is condemned to chase the El Doradean illusion, the cyclical patterns of plunder and loss.

Carew does, though, use Aron Smart to explore issues of alienation that connect with the themes that occupied his novelist contemporaries. For Carew, Aron's sense of alienation in Guyana is part of his psychological complexity. Aron represents the West Indian who is an exile within his own homeland. In "The Caribbean Writer and Exile", Carew describes the ethos of this individual: "The colonizing zeal of the European made indigenous peoples exiles in their own countries – Prospero made Caliban an exile in his. The West Indian writer by going abroad is in fact, searching for an end to exile." Carew's explanation of this almost paradoxical statement gives us further insight into the development of Aron's character: "The West Indian person is subjected to successive waves of cultural alienation from birth – a process that has its origins embedded in a mosaic of cultural fragments. . . . The European fragment is brought into sharper focus than the others"[5].

Aron seeks his identity in a number of ways – none of them successful – as his own "divided self" renders him an outcast in his own society. He is never fully comfortable among the people he relates to; he is either too educated or too uncultured. He tries to establish respectability by using his wealth as a tool. As we have seen, this creates a superficial sense of superiority that crashes as soon as the money is finished.

His sexual relationships, if examined carefully, give us further images of the dead-ends Aron chooses. There is no question in the reader's mind that Aron's alienation creates in him a selfishness that forces him to use people and at the same time depend upon them for his sense of worth.

Aron's days with Dr. Ram, the Indian doctor, teach him in no uncertain way the reality of being Black and subservient. His relationship with Indra, the doctor's young daughter, is filled with childish passion, but he slowly realises that she is using him. This revelation sickens him and begins what becomes a trend in his other relationships. He can't make Indra pay for her rejection of him because he is Black and poor, so he displaces his desire for vengeance onto his other lovers. He must possess Belle, the prostitute, because she is so intensely desired by others. For a time he can't leave her because of the intensity of her physical prowess, but he never loves her for herself. She is described as possessing the rhythms of Africa in her being, but his communion with her lasts only as long as he needs to establish himself as king among the pork-knockers. Eventually he tires of her as he tires of the Africa in himself, as he tires of doing something productive with the money he has made. He discovers that in the end he is no different from the other pork-knockers – just as ready to gamble away the diamonds and gold he has sweated for. Aron's is an economy of plunder; he makes nothing. His attitudes to the land and women elide like Raleigh's image of Guiana as a maidenhead waiting to be penetrated.[6] His brief destructive affair with a brown girl called Beryl reinforces this point.

Aron's final haphazard and quite maddening search for identity is reflected in the wild escapade of sexual relationships that characterise the Ikowan section of the novel. He digs for gold, finds some, and spends the money on liquor and women. His close companions have to steal him away in a drunken stupor to save him from the madness of his actions. He says in retrospect after his wild days in Ikowan: "During my two years at Ikowan my life lost all purpose. Perhaps it was that my life had to lose all purpose so that I could really come to terms with myself – who I was and what I was" (p. 247). He describes the advice of his fellow "pork-knockers" as "voices trying to save me from myself." In essence they reveal to him the helplessness of all his attempts at finding his identity.

Carew does not seem to answer Aron's question as to who he is or where he belongs. The closest thing the novel offers to such a revelation is a clear statement of the things that will not lead him to the answer. Aron cannot say that he has found where he belongs. He says to Pancho during the last moments in the novel: "I am going to buy land in Mahaica, a piece of land that will stretch from the sea to the forest and I'm going to grow coconuts and rice and ground provisions. I am a village boy and I know the land just like my grandpa knew it and wrestled with it all his life" (p. 255). It is the first image of production rather than plunder in Aron's head. We are forced to wonder whether this is merely another pork-knocker's dream. But Carew may have meant it to be a real hope.

Aron has learnt, at least, that his El Doradean quest for gold or diamonds is an illusive, though an addictive one. So what Carew gives us is a very sophisticated character study of a man who, while reflecting on his life, is fully aware that life happens to him. He observes that all his life, he has not made many decisions. Things happen to him. And when those things are positive, he has no ownership of them, so his attachment to them is always slight and transitory. He is constantly being rescued – by Belle, Dr. Ram, Elsa, Tanta Moore, Brother C., Mr. Beauchamp, the memory and reputation of his father, Bullah, Santos, George Kendall or Pancho. When he does make a decision, the path has already been set by those people around him. Left on his own, he has the uncanny ability to fall into a rut and remain there until someone comes and rescues him from himself. Even in his relationships with women, he is rarely the instigator or the aggressor. The women want him and seek him out, whether it is Belle, Indra, Beryl, or the bevy of prostitutes that he encounters during his two years of despondence and debauchery at Ikowan. They are women whose one characteristic is a pathological desire to be with Aron. None of them are likely to make good partners for him, but they all share one important quality – they are adventures (and like Aron, often adventurers, too), departures from the norm. They allow Carew to explore distinctly male-centred stereotypes of gender which arrive at the reductive conclusion that women are mysterious, impossible to fully comprehend and the source of both pleasure and pain for men. Ultimately, for Aron, none of the women live up to their promise, and in this sense, they are consistent with everything else that happens to him. It is perhaps only in the character of Bullah, whose deepest emotional relationships are unquestionably with men, that there is some hint that men are capable of seeing women in less stereotyped ways, but Carew is starkly honest about the limitations of male perceptions and behaviour.

At the centre of the narrative is the folk tale that Carew returned to in a children's book years later. It tells the story of a man who goes on a journey into the mountains, discovers what must be snow, determines to return to his village with the substance, and when he arrives, after a harrowing sprint down the mountainside with this soft and burning thing in his hands, stumbles, falls, and when his hand is opened, it is empty. Aron does not grasp the significance of this story when it is first told to him by Brother C., but at the end of the novel the illumination this story brings represents the cathartic moment of understanding:

> "You doin' fine, pardner," and he fixed the tarpaulin around me. I closed my eyes and listened to the river and I remembered the night when Rhodius had told me about the voices under the river. I listened, and all I heard was a single voice – Brother C.'s – and he was telling me the story of the men who had gone up the mountain, and he kept repeating the last part of the story:
>
> "When they open he hand it was empty and they keep asking he, 'How is it that you come back and you en't bring no wondrous thing to show we? How is it?. . . how is it?. . .'" (pp. 265-6)

Of course, the questions that the people ask the young man are the same questions that Aron suspects are being asked of him. The answers are not as obvious as one might imagine, even if Aron does not quite recognise that his story – his adventures into the hinterland of his country – represents the wondrous thing that he has discovered and brought for the world to see. There is, then, a twist of irony in the way that the novel ends. It begs the question: What has Carew given us? Having taken us deep into the heart of Guyana, and filled our heads with a rich array of stories and characters; having dragged us up rapids and along the slow flow of the river further and further into the forests; after letting us hear the voices of the river, what are we left with? On the one hand, Aron's hands are empty and he feels reprimanded by the fact that he has little material wealth to show for his many adventures. In this sense, Aron epitomises the pork-knocker – a man addicted to the quest for wealth, but not wealth itself. The pork-knocker is one whose perpetual state is to be empty handed, who must always return to the hinterland to find more.

The difference between Aron and the typical pork-knocker is that he has not resigned himself to this fate. He continues to expect to see something in his hand when he opens it. But he, too, realises that he has simply not been long enough engaged with self-reflection for this transformation to fully set in. Further, the futility that is implied by that final image represents something of a challenge set by Carew for himself: Where is the wondrous thing in this novel that seems to eschew the familiar paths of political awakening, educational awakening, class awakening, or economic awakening? For Carew, the great pleasure is in the stories. These stories do not have to have hugely symbolic meanings nor do they have to be tied directly to some central theme in the work. The stories treat the landscape and the culture as the subject for expansive and beautiful passages. The stories are sometimes humorous, always remarkable for their unusualness and self-containment.

Had someone said that Carew wrote this novel because his drinking buddies told him that he needed to collect these amazing stories about Guyana in an extended narrative, I would believe them fully. Carew's later fiction does become less shaped by the picaresque pattern and more structured by the larger themes one expects from the West Indian novel. The pleasure, though, of *Black Midas* is in the grace of his prose style, and the way that these stories consume our attention and keep us hungry to learn more about the adventures of the main character. What Carew may have lost in the absence of linear development in his characterisation is made up for by his ability to describe the ecology of his characters' relationships. The characters may be types, but once thrown together, they form a beautifully painted tapestry of a community in which Carew can explore the themes of selfhood and alienation.

This is a very readable book and its delights lie in the way that Carew seduces us with his storytelling. The story becomes the thing, and as we meet these fascinating characters, experience their violence, scant regard for life, sensuality and the pure joy they experience in their complex and often pathological existence in the jungle, we want to hear more, we want to know more about these people and mostly, we want to know what has happened and why it has happened. This is what Graham Greene would have called a grand "entertainment", though for a writer with as strong a political bent as Carew, we are also rewarded with rich metaphors about the experience of the individual coming out of colonialism that continue to resonate to this day.

Notes

1. Jan Carew, "Caribbean Writing", *W. I. Gazette*, supplement (Christmas 1960).
2. Hena Maes-Jelinek, "The Myth of El Dorado in the Caribbean Novel", *Journal of Commonwealth Literature* 6 (June 1971), p. 121.
3. See interview with Daryl C. Dance, *New World Adams: Conversations with Contemporary West Indian Writers*, 2nd ed. (Leeds: Peepal Tree Press, 2008), p. 36.
4. See Vincent Roth, *A Life in Guyana*, Vol. 1, (Leeds: Peepal Tree Press, 2003), p. 295; Vol. 2, pp. 36, 61, 69-70, 76.
5. Jan Carew, "The Caribbean Writer and Exile", *Komparatistische Hefte* 9/10 (1984), 23-39.
6. Sir Walter Raleigh, *Discovery of Guiana*, 1596.

CHAPTER ONE

IT was springtide and the surf was loud. If the sun plunged behind the courida trees into the sea before I reached home I would miss my Uncle Richard and my grandmother would be angry. I ran down the dusty red road towards Mahaica, my village, and the sun followed me balancing on the courida tree tops. No matter how fast I ran, the sun kept pace. A herd of cattle crossed in front of me, their bony flanks still glistening with mud from the roadside canal. A naked East Indian boy cracked a whip, startling the herd to a run. I waited until the cows passed by and lost my race with the sun. Darkness caught me on the road. When I arrived home my uncle was already standing just inside the doorway. My grandmother sat in a rocking chair at the other end of the room. A kerosene lantern hung from a rafter with the wind rocking it gently and close by on a cross-bar was Echo, our parrot. Grandmother was using a mosquito brush. The little insects filled the hut with their singing and I could see them swirling around the lantern like dust. I felt trapped once I entered the hut.

"Shark! Shark!" Echo called out, edging from one end of the cross-bar to the other and bobbing his head. My name was Aron, but everyone in the village called me Shark because I had small white teeth and a shark grin.

"Night, Uncle Richard. Night, Grandma," I said, going up and kissing her dry wrinkled cheek. I waited for her scolding, but she only said with a note of mild reproach:

"Boy, I glad you come, because you uncle only give me six shillings from you. This is all you work for this week, boy?"

"Morning! Morning!" Echo said. He had been in the family for two generations and had the right to wag his black tongue in everybody's affairs. I looked at my uncle and there was a half-smile on his face. He always wore this smile as if there was a piece of string inside his mouth tugging it to one side. His face was a smooth black and his big eyes protruded. He wasn't a tall man, but he had a way of standing still like a tiger waiting to spring, and when you looked at him for a long time he seemed to grow taller. My eyes did not leave him as I spoke, but his never made four with mine.

"No, Grandma. I work for seven-twenty this week, and that include overtime."

I had been working with my Uncle Richard's road gang for two years and he brought my pay home every Friday because once I had gone swimming with Braveboy, the neighbour's son, and lost it.

"The boy is a damn liar, Ma Smart, that is all the money he give me, six shillings," he said, ignoring me.

"I give you a five-dollar bill, two-dollar bill and twenty cent," I shouted. My hatred for him made me reckless. Grandma looked searchingly at us both, she saw us as two boys, one of whom was telling lies. She gripped the arm of her rocking-chair and in the lamplight her fingers could have been holding shadow rather than substance.

"What sort of five-dollar bill?" she asked suddenly.

"A Royal Bank of Canada five-dollar bill with a steamship on it," I replied.

"The boy is a liar I tell you, Ma Smart," he said, and I saw a chance to trap him:

"Well, give me the pay envelope and I will show Grandma where the amount was marked down," I said, and this goaded him into losing his temper. He leapt across the room and struck me down with the back of his hand.

"Down! Down!" Echo said, hopping on his cross-bar.

"You ungrateful bitch!" Uncle Richard shouted. I staggered away with the first blow and as I was falling he grabbed me and flung me through the door of the hut. He came after me and I sprang at his throat. He tore my fingers away and locked my head under his arm, cuffing my ribs until I thought they would break. I dug my teeth into his back and he released my head so suddenly that I fell on the wet grass.

"Afternoon! Afternoon!" Echo screamed.

Grandma tugged at my uncle's arm.

"Richard! Richard, you gone mad!" she said in a voice as high-pitched as Echo's.

"Leave me alone, old woman," he said, still coming after me, but she held on to his arm. He gave her a violent push. Echo pounced on his head and dug out a beakful of hair and skin. Uncle Richard howled with pain and tried to grab Echo, but he escaped and perched high on the big mango tree in the yard. Although he couldn't see Echo, my uncle hurled a stone at the mango tree.

"Afternoon! Afternoon!" Echo screamed from the safety of his perch. My grandma was moaning on the ground and I went to her. Uncle Richard stood between us and he kicked me in the stomach as I dodged past. The kick did not hurt, but I crouched up and pretended to be in agony. He walked away mopping the blood from his head with a white handkerchief.

"Afternoon! Morning!" Echo said.

There was the sound of footsteps in the darkness and the wind brought back muffled curses as Uncle Richard left. Grandma sat up in the wet grass swaying from side to side and crying out against her age and weakness until the neighbours rushed over.

"What happen, neighbour Smart?"

"Is who humbug you, neighbour?" they asked. Tanta Moore helped Grandma up and carried her inside the hut. She told her story between sobs and the neighbours tried to console her.

"Don't worry, Ma Smart. Lef that brute of a man to the Lord," they said and she cried out:

"Is advantage, is advantage! Ow, Lord, is why you make me turn weak and old? Is why you heaping travail on me grey hair?"

The wind understood Grandma's sorrow and moaned through the po-boy tree in the backyard. Grandpa returned late from his farm on the reef behind the rice-fields. He smelt of earth and sweat and his limbs were slow with weariness. He sat beside Grandma and held her hand.

"Me hear what happen, Ma Smart, and God knows if I been here I would'ave carried that Richard Dolly to the cross," he said, and he began to fret and mumble until Grandma forgot her sorrow and comforted him.

"Don't worry 'bout him, Aron; the Lord will decide it one day," she said.

Grandma stood up holding herself erect; she could have been a black sorceress from the slave days. She locked her arms across her chest and her old eyes looked inwards, capturing the image of dark things that ordinary eyes could not see. Her voice rose and fell in a high-pitched chanting:

"From this day I put a curse on Richard Dolly, that the mouth of hell should yawn under he foot all he life; that he seed should wither and die; that purgatory should breathe down he neck when night come; I curse Richard Dolly; I curse he children and he children children."

The neighbours left carrying the awe of her curse with them. I crept inside the hut and sat in a corner. It was too late to prepare dinner and my grandparents went to bed. I sat on the doorstep for a long time with Echo beside me and I talked quietly to him, but when I looked at him he was asleep with his head buried in his feathers.

I didn't sleep that night. Occasionally I dozed off but even then I could hear mosquitoes buzzing, fruit dropping from the trees where bats fed and the wind fierce and lonely, bringing the thunder of the surf close to me.

★ ★ ★

I wanted to escape from Mahaica, but I couldn't. My grandparents wrapped themselves around me and I knew no way of fighting against their feebleness. Sometimes I wished they were dead and yet the thought of living without them frightened me. Braveboy, Tanta Moore's son, had escaped. He walked to the city twenty miles away and did not return. I had been to the city once with my grandmother. It was a place with too many people whom I did not know. I knew everyone in Mahaica and the neighbouring villages.

My grandmother's eyes searched my heart at times, ferreting out my longing to be free. Old age turns people into vampires. They must feed on the young, shut them up in rooms, breathe the same air they breathe, claw at their young limbs with dried-up hands and gloat over their innocence.

Mahaica was a bowl axed out of swamps and forests on a river bank. In front of the village was the sea and behind wide savannahs. There was a wooden bridge across the river and when cartwheels rumbled over the loose planks it sounded like thunder. A burnt-brick public road led from the city through the village and across the river to other settlements along the coast. Mahaica was my prison, but I was safe in it. They said that people starved in the city, but here in Mahaica you could find fruits, catch crabs where the mangrove roots tangled by the seashore, fish in the river and the swamps and if you were rich enough to buy a gun, hunt game in the savannahs. At the back of the village were rice-fields, small provision farms, coconut groves and patches of bisi-bisi and wild-cane reeds. The low frontlands were made useless for farming by the invading salt water and here saffron, courida and mangrove grew wild.

I wanted to escape, but I was afraid of going too far from the sound of Grandma's voice. I heard it first thing in the mornings and last thing at nights crackling like dead leaves. I always thought of my grandparents as phantoms in a twilight world. Grandpa was a shadow and Grandma a wraith. They were children of slaves, the offspring of a waiting people who had lingered in forests for millions of years. They wanted to hand down this heritage of waiting, but I would have none of it. They felt time like a river running in their blood, but I wanted to feel it like passion flaring up swiftly and dying away.

★ ★ ★

After the clash with Uncle Richard I transferred to Crooked Timber's road gang, and this meant walking seven miles to and from work. Rains washed away the burnt earth and gutted the road frequently, providing steady work for the villagers of the coast.

I woke up at three in the mornings, prepared breakfast and lunch and set out for work by five. Sometimes I managed to beg a lift in a donkey cart and enjoyed jogging and rattling through the cool morning while I watched the birds: lazy cranes and gaulins, nervous cornbirds, screaming parrots and high above them all, the wild ducks black against the sky, their necks straight forward and their wings moving with a quick, steady beat. In return for a lift I had to shout sheep, cows, goats and pigs out of the way and occasionally to chase a barking dog with my akee stick before he bit at the donkey's legs. Now and then a snake or alligator lay across the road, but no one was afraid of these reptiles, since the rumble of the cart wheels was enough to send them slithering into the roadside canal. One morning I saw a huge boa constrictor crossing the road and I broke its back with my stick. It lashed out and I jumped free, first to one side and then the other, as if it were a thick piece of skipping rope. I left it twitching and helpless with the vultures already circling and the dogs standing by for their share of the kill.

Foreday morning was followed by day-clean and the sun burnt away the mists and the darkness. Traffic churned up dust-clouds which the morning dew had kept down for a while. Other workers, men and women, boys and girls, joined me on the way to work and they chatted all the way, complaining that the work was hard, that the sun was drying up the substance of their life and that the poor had nothing to look forward to but privation. The children echoed the words of the grown-ups, for childhood on the coast lasted only as long as you could not work. I had started work as a mule boy when I was six, trotting beside a mounted white overseer while he went on his rounds at La Bonne Mere sugar estate.

My job with the road gang was to water and then pound burnt earth cinders, filling up the smaller holes in the road surface. The pounding iron rose and fell and as the sun bent away, the steady thud-thud hypnotised me like drumbeats. I was vaguely conscious of the heat, the women singing and the men talking, talking . . . about the gold-mines, women or about the great ones in the city.

Crooked Timber, the overseer, sat under a big silk cotton tree by the roadside with the brim of an old felt hat shading his eyes. He looked like a black spider against the twisting silver-grey roots and every now and then he shouted above the singing and the talking and the pounding.

"Come on, there. All you think is a picnic or what!"

I walked home in the late afternoons with the noise of the pounding iron still drumming inside my head. Echo perched on a coconut tree in front of the hut to look out for me, and when he saw me in the distance he came flapping his green wings and screaming, "Shark! Shark!" and I would hold out my hand for him to alight.

He had followed me to work a few times, but he did not like going too far from home. Besides, Crooked Timber had complained that he made too much noise. He stayed with Grandma and went with her to the market by the river every day, perched on her shoulder. The boatmen liked to make a fool of Echo: they would whisper swear words to him and he would scream them out loud and Grandma would threaten to put plaster around his beak if he didn't keep a clean tongue.

Our hut was small and tidy. Marabuntas built clay nests in the thatch and large brown spiders spanned the rafters with cobwebs. At nights the lantern attracted hosts of beetles, green flies and mosquitoes, and the spiders feasted on them. The baked mud walls were covered with old newspapers and almanacs. There was one large almanac with pictures of a king and queen with yellow crowns and yellow faces. Grandpa said they were the rulers of the Empire, that even our Governor of Guiana had to bow down to them.

"Bow down? The Governor?" I asked incredulously.

"Yes, boy, the Governor is only big fish because he in a small pond, but the King bigger than a whale in he ocean," he said, and I thought that this man must be as tall as a coconut tree. One night I spoke to Echo about the King.

"Echo," I said, "the yellow-face King big like a tree, but we don't have to worry 'bout that 'cause he never going to come as far as Mahaica, boy."

Grandpa had a double-barrelled shotgun which hung on the wall over his bed. He poured boiling water into the barrel, oiled it and polished the stock regularly. He used to be a great hunter and on moonlight nights he sat on the doorstep and told hunting stories while the mango leaves sparkled and the sea wind shivered through the palm fronds. Grandma always interrupted the story-telling, saying that it was getting late. The morning after, when sleep turned my blood to molasses, I would nod and doze on my way to work and the chirping of the birds would be muted, and I would not see the sunlight drinking dew from blades of grass, the bright lotus lilies or the saffron stretching out to the courida groves.

★ ★ ★

Whenever news came through that the Commissary was about to pay us a visit, Crooked Timber would abandon the shade of the silk cotton tree and pace up and down threatening to sack us all if his boss found fault with our work, and if I stopped too long by the canal with my bucket of water he danced about with rage and threw stones at me. One noonday Uncle Richard, who was in charge of a gang a few miles up the road, arrived in his donkey cart.

"Eh, eh, nephew. I didn't know you was working for me friend, Timber," he said, grinning like a tiger after a meal. I did not answer him, but averted my eyes and continued working.

"I didn't know the boy was you nephew, Richard," Timber said.

"You mean he didn't tell you?" Richard asked.

"Not a word," Timber said.

"It is so these small-boys ungrateful nowadays. You know is me start he out on this road work? Worthless Joe Smart was he father, and he mother, me only sister go 'way to Surinam and not a soul en't hear if she 'live or dead," he said.

"You mean Joe Smart the gold king was this boy father?"

"That very Joe Smart, he did marry me sister."

"Is what breeze blow you this way, Richard?" Timber asked, because he suspected that my uncle was not just paying a social call.

"I hear the road engineer dropping down on we suddenly, boy," Richard said and the gang stopped work to listen.

"When ?" Timber asked.

"Today, so keep you eye open, boy, I hear that white man bad like a sword; the black people say he mad."

"Eh, eh, but is what all you doing? You want me to lose me work!" Timber bellowed at the gang.

"Timber, you must watch that nephew of mine, he treacherous," Richard said, and Timber looked at me as if he was seeing me for the first time.

"But he is only a small-boy, Richard."

"The boy treacherous I tell you, Timber," Richard said, and he goaded his donkey with a sharp-pointed stick and rattled away in his cart.

The road engineer arrived in the early afternoon in a Canadian Ford with big brass headlamps. He was a lean white man with a ram-goat beard and beside him Timber looked more like a black spider than ever. I noticed that the engineer spoke to Timber without once looking at him. Fetching my bucket of water up the slope, I wondered how the white man could stand there hardly noticing anything around him; he didn't even seem aware of the wind ruffling his ram-goat beard, and I felt a sense of resentment against him and a kinship with Timber. By not noticing any of us the white man was lumping us all together. I was so taken up with these thoughts that I slipped and fell and the bucket clattered noisily down. Timber was walking behind the engineer. He looked at me with fear and hatred, snatched up a rock and flung it at me. It struck me on the ankle with such force that I cried out. The engineer looked round. I tried to get up, but could not. No one came to assist me until a woman separated herself from the group of sweating black bodies, a young woman with bare arms muscled like a river boatman's.

"All you don't see the lil' boy in trouble?" she said and I understood that this was her way of defying Timber, that she was risking her job to help me.

"Well, go on, give her a hand!" the engineer said and Timber hurried to obey.

"Wait till the white man gone," he hissed as he dragged me up the slope.

"Lef' the lil' boy alone!" the woman said, raising her voice so that the engineer could hear.

They laid me down on the grass by the roadside. The engineer looked down at me from his great height and I saw that his eyes were blue like glass which you held up to the sky.

"Who are you, boy?" he asked, looking at me so hard that I felt uncomfortable.

"My name is Aron Smart, sir."

"Smart?" he said as if someone had struck him, "Smart? . . . Smart?"

"Yes, sir," I said, wondering why my name should mean anything to a deity like this white engineer. He became very agitated and passed a hand across the side of his head several times. He must have sensed the alarm he was causing because when he spoke again his voice was clipped, controlled.

"Joe Smart's son?" he asked quietly.

"Yes, sir. Joe Smart was me father," I said. Timber looked on with his mouth hanging open and the others were straining their ears so, it was a wonder they did not fall over. The engineer stood over me for what seemed to be a long time, looking down at me, but not really seeing me. He turned round suddenly and walked back to his car with Timber ambling behind him. He said something to Timber before he drove off.

From then on Timber treated me as if I were made of glass. He told the others to knock off, put me in his cart and drove me towards the chemist's shop near the river. My ankle was swollen and very painful and I was only semiconscious when Timber said:

"Me didn't mean to hurt you bad, Shark; the white man coming upset me and me didn't know what me was doing."

"Who was the girl that come to help me?" I asked.

"She name Belle, and she come from Saltan village."

"Belle," I said feeling the pain wrench at my ankle everytime the cart hit a rut and I could not say anything else because my mouth felt too dry. I knew that Belle could not work for Timber any more because she had made him lose face before the others, and I felt sorry for her.

The journey seemed to last for hours. Every time I opened my eyes the sun's rays became splinters of bone stabbing at my ankle. Timber stopped every now and then to give me a drink of water. At last we pulled up outside Brother C.'s shop and he came out and helped Timber carry me into a back room. He said that the ankle was broken and that I would not be able to walk for a long time.

"How did it happen?" he asked Timber.

"The boy twist he foot 'gainst a rock," Timber said and I felt too weak to contradict him. Brother C. put the ankle in splints and bandaged it, and Timber took me home. Brother C. did not ask for any money because he knew my grandparents.

"Neighbour Smart, me bring you boy home; he had accident!" Timber shouted when the cart stopped outside our hut. I looked around dazed. Echo sat, not between the cart shafts, but on the treetops by the roadside.

"Ow, me God! Is what new trouble you heaping on me grey hair!" Grandma cried out, hobbling down the steps and out to the cart.

"Is all right, neighbour Smart, the white man say me must pay the boy 'till he get better," Timber said.

"The white man? Which white man?"

"The road engineer, he know the boy father and he talk to he friendly," Timber said.

"Lord have mercy!"

"Mercy! Mercy!" Echo screamed from the mango tree.

"Hold you black tongue, bird," Tanta Moore said, coming out to join us.

"Tell me what happen, Timber," Grandma said and the afternoon sun broke up into white and then red splinters and I felt darkness coming from inside my head to blind my eyes.

★ ★ ★

I was ill for a long time, but Timber brought my pay every Friday. The neighbours, who took more interest in other people's affairs than their own, disapproved of my falling sick. "Why should I have the malice to injure my ankle when my grandparents were so feeble and needed money so badly?" they asked, and, like a man beating his own drum and dancing, they answered the question – "Because I was ungrateful." Timber's regular visits, however, made them curious and one Friday Tanta Moore invited him in for a drink of mauby and wrung all the information she wanted out of him. She relayed the story to the rest of the village with many additions and the news spread that I had a white "godfather". This made everyone change their opinion about my ungratefulness, and they enquired after my health as if it had always been a matter close to their hearts. Timber became so friendly on his visits that he made me feel uneasy.

"How she going, boy?" he would ask, peering at me with his muddy eyes, his spider arms hanging like dead wood at his side.

"All right," I would answer.

"You can come back to work with me any time, boy; you was the best of the lot," he would say, bold-faced and looking me in the eye.

Brother C. came round in the mornings to dress my ankle. He

was shaped like a watermelon and boasted that he had not seen his feet for ten years. I did not like him at first, he was too quiet and shut up in himself. He came, tended my ankle, asked me how I was feeling, and, after exchanging a few words with Grandma, left. He was coffee-coloured and his face, like the rest of him, was round and smooth. His neck was so short that he could not look round without turning his body. I always imagined that his head was filled with lead or some other heavy substance which caused it to sit so weightily between his shoulders that the rest of his body had grown outwards. I was surprised one morning when he asked me:

"Shark, can you read and write?" I was lying in a hammock under the mango tree with Echo perched on a branch over me.

"I can read couple words in the First Standard reader, Brother C., and I can write like when you dip a beetle in ink," I said.

"I will give you some instructions in these matters," he said. "When you're black and ignorant there isn't any place for you in this land."

"I would like to have learning, Brother C.," I said, sitting up and staring at him. His complexion was sallow and his skin so smooth, I was sure if a fly tried to light on his cheek it would slide off.

"Why you doing this for me, Brother C.?" I asked, and I thought I noticed one of his eyelids flicker, but he didn't answer my question, he just continued as if he had not heard me.

"We can start tomorrow," he said and, because the wind was blowing hard through the mango tree and rustling the palm fronds, I had to strain my ears to hear him.

"Tomorrow?" I asked.

"Yes, tomorrow. I'll come at the same time," he said.

Brother C. wheeled his bicycle out of the yard and I lay back and watched a broken sky through the leaves. The wind ploughed up Echo's feathers and he edged up and down the branch.

I told Grandma about Brother C.'s offer, but she did not seem surprised.

"Why you think he doing it, Grandma?" I asked while she sat on the doorstep shelling peas.

"All you young boy does ask too much question. You don't have no trust in the Lord? He does move in a mysterious way.

Look how Timber bringing you money every week, boy. Just count you blessings and praise the Lord."

I had an attack of fever later that day, and my body trembled with ague and the wind grew chill. Grandma sent for Tanta Moore and they prepared a brew with lemon grass in a large iron tub. Tanta Moore lifted me out of my hammock and I was conscious of her sweaty coconut-oil smell and the softness of her breasts. They held me down in the hot brew until I felt faint and heard the flutter of hummingbird's wings in my ears. I fell into a coma and dreamt of riding a donkey in a dead forest where the roots and branches of the trees were like human limbs writhing in agony. I rode out of the forest towards a black shadow and the earth suddenly opened under me, sucking the donkey and me into a well of darkness.

I came out of the coma feeling as if I had lived a very long time. Brother C. said that I had malaria and he dosed me off with quinine day after day until the hummingbird's wings whirled so loudly that I could hear nothing else for a few weeks.

I lay on jute bags on the floor of the hut and could not hear Echo or the wind in the po-boy tree or the pounding of the surf on the foreshore or my grandmother's voice. When I woke up early in the mornings a shaft of sunlight formed a roof over me. I watched tiny specks of dust dancing up and down this roof of light and poked my finger through it.

Echo's voice broke through the bandage of silence which had wrapped itself around my ears and it had the clear ring of the church bell, and one morning I sat up and pushed my head through the shaft of sunlight and the warmth and glare made me drunk.

The fever passed and my ankle was strong enough for me to limp down the steps to my hammock, but I had to do this behind Grandma's back. She was not anxious for me to get well too quickly. She was afraid that Timber would stop my sick pay before I was able to start work again. When she finally agreed to my getting up, we waited the whole day Friday, and Timber did not bring my wages.

"You got to go back to work, Shark," Grandma said, and I thought of the hot sun, the rains, Timber shouting at me, the mosquitoes and the brute-labour.

"I still feelin weak, Grandma," I said.

"Boy, is work or starvation, because you grandpa can't harvest he provisions for another two month." I walked away and Echo hopped on my shoulder.

"Shark! Shark!" he said close to my ear. I sat under the po-boy tree and picked up a handful of brown seeds.

"Pity pity, po-boy, sorry for me,
Pity pity, po-boy, sorry for me"

I sang, cupping the seeds in both hands and shaking them.

"Po-boy! Po-boy!" Echo sang.

"I don't want to work with no road gang no more, Echo," I said.

"Po-boy! Po-boy!"

"As soon as I get big enough, Echo, I going in the goldfields, and when I strike it rich I going to build an ark for meself."

I saw Tanta Moore coming back from the market with a huge basket on her head.

"Neighbour Smart, me got news for you," she called out.

"News? What news, neighbour?" Grandma asked, coming to the door of the outhouse, part of which served as a kitchen and part as a chicken-pen. Tanta Moore stood under the mango tree with the basket on her head. Her legs were wide apart under her big flowered skirt and her face was black and shiny. Grandma blinked like a marmoset looking at the sun and she wiped her hands on her skirt.

"You know me got lil' bellyache and Brother C. tell me is me time of life?" Tanta Moore said. She wanted to tell her story with full effects and she was not going to hurry.

"Yes, yes," Grandma said.

"Well, me went to Brother C. shop jus' now to get lil' medicine because me can hardly sleep with the pain when night come, and me was talking to the big-eye boy in Brother C. shop when who should come in but a long white man. . . ."

"A white man?"

"Yes, a long white man who drive up in a big car. He ask for Brother C. in a big-big voice, and when Brother C. come out he ask, 'How is the boy?' and Brother C. say, 'The boy almost better now, sir,' and when they see me was listening Brother C. ask the white man to step inside."

"I wonder if is Shark they been talking 'bout, Tanta."

"Who else?"

"Is all the Lord's work. He lef' me with this fatherless boy and now He finding a way to take care of him. Is an answer to prayer, neighbour, because morning and night when I get down on me knees I does remember the boy to the Lord, 'Jesus,' I does say, 'if the boy mother and father listen to the voice of the Devil, then don't make he punish too much because of them.'"

"But is how you think the white man know the boy father?"

"Joe Smart, Jesus rest he soul, was a man with big idea and he meet a lot of big folks in he time, but as the Bible say, 'Fool and he money will part,' and that is what befall Joe. He was me one-son and me never know how he die; they jus' send telegram to we and when me run to the schoolmaster to read it for me, it say Joe meet with accident and he dead and the news root me and the old man grey hair to the grave and only in the darkness of we bed the old man does breathe a word 'bout he son; he got the sorrow for we boy tie up in he belly all these long years. . . . Joe was a good boy; he had he ways, but he was a good boy with not a rude word in he mouth for he old mother . . . he was a good boy, we Joe. . . ."

"Children is sorrow bringer, neighbour. Look how me one-boy pick up heself and walk away, and when me go to the police the thick-neck black man jus' sit behind a table and make few scratch in a book," Tanta Moore said.

Brother C. came next morning. He spent a long time in the hut with Grandma and I never discovered what they talked about, but it turned out that I did not have to work with Timber's road gang any more, and Brother C. started giving me lessons every day.

CHAPTER TWO

OCTOBER was a month of drought. I had grown to know the village as never before. After my lessons with Brother C. I helped Grandpa on his farm. Between planting and harvesting we fought against a constantly erupting undergrowth, but even with lessons and work on the farm I had time to wander over the swamps and savannahs and along the river bank, for Grandpa never reproached me for not working hard. He seemed to accept the absolute difference between his age and my youth. It was as if his body had beaten against so many years that he was content to withdraw from the mainstream of life and to remain an observer rather than an active hustler. I told him about the things I had learnt from Brother C., and as we pulled up weeds or ploughed or watered the cassava beds I recited poems for him: "The Two Crossing-sweepers", "The Boy on the Burning Deck", "The Chieftain to the Highland Bound" and the old man listened with his eyes creased and narrowed against the sun and once he told me:

"Boy, the white man does write down all they story in black and white, but we does keep we own lock up in we belly. Time will come when we got to write down we story too 'cause if we don't write it down it going to get lost. Now all the young people going 'way from the land. In long time past days we used to tell we story with drum, but soon even the drum won't talk no more."

Grandpa said that he could smell in the air that the drought would get worse and Grandma dreamt of reefs spotted with bones. She told Tanta Moore about her dream and Tanta shouted it over her hibiscus hedge to the whole village. Grandma's dreams were taken as seriously as the word of God, and it cast a shadow over the village for a few days. But the people of Mahaica were not a gloomy people and they soon shrugged the shadow away. "What else could they do?" they asked. "The sun was too distant an enemy." If you shouted yourself hoarse it would still crawl across the sky between day-clean and night. We harvested our cassavas, tanyas, yams, sweet potatoes and peas, and stored the whole crop in the chicken-pen.

The sun burnt fiercer and the sunsets looked like broken rainbows piled high on the edge of the sky. At nights the stars hung so low they almost touched the yellowing palm fronds. On my way to Grandpa's farm, I saw a host of white roots under the shallow water in the ricefields day after day coming closer to the surface as the sun enticed them to their death. The river fed on the swamps and the sun in turn fed on swamp and river. The villagers caught basketfuls of fish in muddy waterholes until the sun dried these up, leaving the air heavy with the stench of rotting fish. Alligators buried themselves in the mud and prepared for a long sleep. The village cattle ploughed through the mud from one clump of withered grass to the other until some of the beasts died of hunger and exhaustion.

Brother C. came every day of the week and when Grandma grumbled about Sunday lessons he said:

"The boy's got a good chance, so let him take it to the full. The Lord won't be angry to see him lifting himself out of his ignorance."

Brother C. was Chairman of the Village Council, and on the Sundays that the white minister did not come from Georgetown he preached in the Wesleyan Church across the river. He came straight from church to give me my lessons, and we sat at a table under the mango tree, and churchgoers who had lingered to gossip after the service would shout greetings to Brother C., or just stand and stare. They passed by on the public road, walking awkwardly in shoes which only encased their spread-out toes once a week. Sunday lessons mostly took the form of stories from books that Brother C. read. He was the only person in the village apart from the schoolmaster who knew of any book other than the Bible. He had read the novels of Dickens over and over again and could recite whole pages from memory. He told me stories from *David Copperfield, Nicholas Nickelby, A Tale of Two Cities,* and he made the characters seem so real that I asked him:

"How did this man, Dickens, know so many people?"

"Most of them he made up, just brought them to life out of his head. 'Course you know, the world he lived in was a big world and a wide world with enough people to fill this savannah from Mahaica to Orealla," he said.

"But this woman always sitting down knitting in *Tale of Two Cities* and the wine barrel bursting and the people's heads getting chopped off, all this must have happened, Brother C.?"

"Some of it did, and some of it didn't, but all of it is long-time-past story and if he made it seem true that it happened and it didn't, then it will be true for everybody who reads it," he said, and we turned our attention to decimals and analysis and parsing.

As the drought continued the villagers tied ropes around the bellies of their cows in a vain effort to haul them out of the mud, and when the cows died on their feet they skinned them and cut off what meat was left on their emaciated frames. Dogs and carrion crows finished the job for them, picking the bones clean and leaving them to whiten in the sun. The swamp bed became a mosaic of cracked mud which the sun baked hard as stone. It was quiet at nights. No frogs sang and there were no swamp birds to pierce the silence with their hooting and purling and screeching. There were rumours that wild animals from the savannahs and forests were prowling about the outskirts of the village. A few days after, Marajin, the daughter of Persaud the fisherman, was killed by a jaguar outside her hut one evening, and the big cat hauled her body all the way to the reef behind the village.

The villagers sent for Prophet Wills, the rain prophet. He arrived one morning, a ragged black man dressed in a black tail-coat and top-hat powdered with dust from the road. He had once been a schoolmaster, but his young wife left him for another man and he went mad. He walked from village to village along the coast calling for rain, predicting the end of the world or, when floods threatened, shouting at the Almighty to cease His blessing of rain. He was treated with reverence because we all knew that his madness had given him a prophet's vision. Everywhere he was given food and shelter. He stood outside the Village Hall and raged at the empty sky and his voice was like the roll of surf at high tide. After three days of celestial conjuring, rainclouds gathered one evening. We forgot our fear of jaguars and stood outside our huts watching. All around us fireflies gleamed like chips of ice suspended over the parched earth, flaring for an instant and melting. A few large drops of rain fell, but the wind scattered the clouds leaving stars and fireflies and our empty hearts in deserts of night.

The prophet denounced us the next day. He said that God was angry with the people of the coast and not even he could stem His wrath.

I went to church on Sunday with my grandparents to hear Brother C. preach. The church was crowded with people standing in the aisles. We sat two rows from the front, behind the schoolmaster and his wife. It was dark and cool inside the church and the sea breeze dried up the sweat on anxious black faces. Brother C. wore a black suit and a green velvet waistcoat. I saw much of the waistcoat because the jacket had been tailored for him many years ago. He stood under the pulpit bracing his short legs and he spoke the language of the village, not the "school" talk he reserved for me.

"Brothers and sisters, the Lord has laid a heavy hand on we village, and today, the Sabbath Day, when I look 'round" – and he turned his head to the right and to the left as far as his short neck would allow – "I see many an anxious face. . ." And the Lord's anger took hold of him suddenly and he thundered: "The Lord Jesus flush all you out of you dens and hovels. This year the reapers are plentiful, but the harvest, where is the harvest?" he lowered his voice and his face became calm: "Outside, the wind blowing like it always does, but there en't no ricefields, no grass for the wind to lie down on. Brothers and sisters, is when all you going to learn that the Lord is Almighty? And when you don't fear Him, he does seed you bones with fear, He does bring the high-and-mighty down to their knees, He does take the sky and sweep it clean of rain, He does use you own pride like a tamarind whip to lash you. Remember the Bible story when He did bring seven lean years to the land of the sinners? All you holding you belly and crying out loud like if you was all innocent all the time, but the

Good Lord see and the Almighty know that the Sabbath does come and go and only few does grace this house of prayer. On this Lord's Day all you come and fill-up the church with you misery. You done try the false prophet and the obeah man, and when they fail you, you flock to this house of worship like cattle, filling it up with you misery. I can see the shame write on all you face this morning. You don't think Jesus can see it too?"

"Praise to Lord Jesus!" Grandma cried, swaying as if she had fever.

"Amen, praise be the Lord Jesus!" the congregation chimed in.

"The wages of sin is death!" Brother C. shouted, "and when the sinners die, when Mantop tap them on the shoulder, they does go to a place of thick bush, a place black as all you face, a place steamin' with hell-fire where a big white devil does sit on a treetop roarin' like a howler baboon day and night. Brothers and sisters, make you peace with the Lord now, this minute, kneel down and let you black hearts talk. All you been living like bisi-bisi reed swaying with every wind that blow. . . make you peace now!"

We sang a hymn and the service ended. Brother C. stood at the door and shook hands with the congregation as they filed out.

"You preach like a Trojan, Brother," Grandma said, and others echoed her praise:

"You take a big load off me chest this morning, Brother C."

"You give me heart to face me hungriness."

"You lift me spirit up like silk cotton blossom, Brother C., thank you."

Brother C. called a meeting of the Village Council when the drought was in its fourth month, when children with limbs like twigs, and swollen bellies wandered listlessly up and down the public road, and their parents sat on doorsteps waiting, waiting. I went to the Village Hall and stood by the door during the meeting. Mr. Galloway, the schoolmaster, and Gonzalez, the rum-shop-owner, sat on either side of the Chairman on the platform, while the others sat on benches in the hall facing them. Brother C. spoke about the drought and the hardship it was causing.

"The great ones in the city have forgotten us," he said, "and we must remind them that we have dry throats and empty bellies. Folks are drinking the river water and falling sick, and the children, all they can do is come to me for medicine. They don't need medicine. It's food that they need."

Gonzalez, a brown dried-up Portuguese man, stood up and read out a resolution, holding a yellow sheet of paper close to his face. The schoolmaster interrupted him in the midst of his preamble:

"Why should the government help the lazy good-for-nothing people of Mahaica ?" he asked. "If the people are hungry it's their own fault. They know life is hard, but they don't prepare for hardship; they just sit and wait for things to happen to them. If it was left to me, I'd whip the laziness out of them."

"Shut up you big black mouth!" a farmer shouted and Brother C. called him to order. The resolution was read out and passed.

The next week a lorry came from the city with food and water and old clothes, and Brother C. distributed these to the villagers. They gathered outside the Village Hall like a pack of hungry bush-hogs, cursing, quarrelling, eyeing one another and accusing Brother C. (behind his back) of keeping the best of everything for himself.

"It's a thankless job," he told me after a lesson. "The more you do for your own people the less thanks you will receive. But it's the Lord's will that the hungry should be fed."

CHAPTER THREE

GRANDPA kept guard outside the village at nights. The Government had offered seventy dollars for every jaguar killed. He built a platform in the branches of a cromanty tree, tied a lamb to a post under the tree and waited night after night. I was allowed to keep watch with him because of his failing eyesight, and as we squatted close together listening to the wind and the silences it left in its wake, he spoke to me in whispers, while I had to keep quiet.

"I'm old," he said one night, "old and decrepit. Me body does feel like if me blood turning to mud and me foot does root theyself down with every step me take. Old age got me by the throat and now and then me mind does lef' me head and fly away from me mortal body. Me does want me hand and foot to do something these days and they don't neither of them obey me. But the old age is a good thing, boy, it does box you up with feebleness, but same time it does turn you spirit loose. It does mist-up you eye, but the picture you got in you mind does get brighter. . . but there does come a time when every night you fighting 'gainst sleep because once you shut you eye you does 'fraid that it won't open no more . . . is funny, you know, the only people me does remember clear is you father and them who try to do him harm when he was a bright-eye young boy. . . ." His speech trailed off into a mumbling, as if he was not conscious of my presence anymore.

He crouched on the rough platform Indian style, with his arms around his knees. The lamb was bleating and its voice carried over the savannahs.

"That lamb sound frightened," Grandpa said. I listened and the wind seemed to be blowing stronger in the branches over us.

He sniffed and fidgeted and held his gun at the ready. I could see the dark forms of other trees close to us and hear the wind coming from the sea and trailing away across the savannahs.

"When them jaguar get old they does be full of tricks," Grandpa said. My heart was beating so hard it was rocking my body. I did not want Grandpa to know I was afraid, so I forced myself to sit very still. I looked up and saw the leaves leaning away from the wind.

"There's something over us, Grandpa," I said.

"Is only the wind gumming the leaf together," he said. I looked up again and saw a shadow between us and the starlight and suddenly it was punctured by green fires. I shouted and, backing away, fell from the platform. I heard a deep growl and a thud. Grandpa landed near me with the big cat on top of him. The gun was a few feet away from him and he was trying to reach it. I picked it up and fired and the recoil flung me backwards. The big cat sprang away and rolled over and I crept back and looked at Grandpa. His throat was torn open and his head hanging to one side with a cheek against the earth. I wanted to go and look at the jaguar, but instead I ran all the way home.

Tanta Moore was waiting for me outside the hut with tears running down her fat cheeks. "How could she have found out about Grandpa?" I wondered.

"You heard?" I asked.

"What?" she said, and I blurted out the story of how Grandpa had been killed and she held me against her and cooed to me like a mother baboon. I turned to go inside to Grandma and she said:

"Don't go in yet, mi-boy, cause the Lord call all two of them same time. Is so when old people live together long they does have one life between them and Mantop can't take one without the other going too."

I went inside the hut and found Grandma asleep on her bed and Echo said:

"Shark! Shark!" and as I drew nearer I saw that Grandma's eyes were open. I touched her face and it was cold.

* * *

They buried my grandparents in the churchyard, but their presences remained in the hut, Grandma in her rocking chair and

Grandpa in the corner near the bed with his clay pipe. I could still smell the black Brazilian tobacco he smoked before I fell asleep at night.

The villagers said God always demanded a sacrifice before He ended a drought or a flood, and it was true, for the rains came the week after my grandparents' death, and who-you birds sang in the po-boy tree late into the night. Echo ate nothing day after day. I brought him mangoes and ripe guavas and sugar apples, but he drooped on his cross-bar and left them to the ants and flies, and one morning I found him lying on the floor with his legs in the air. I buried him in the churchyard beside my grandparents.

Brother C. asked me to come and live with him:

"You're alone in the world, boy, and I don't have any family either and I feel just like if you were my own flesh and blood."

"I want to stay here, Brother C. I'm 'customed to the yard and I won't be happy nowhere else," I said, and this was the first decision I had taken in my life.

"But your grandma and grandpa are dead, boy, and they can't come back. Besides, who will look after you?"

"Tanta Moore say she will cook for me and wash me few things, and I can keep the house clean and me mother might come back one day."

"I hope you not making a mistake," he said, and he turned to me suddenly and added: "You wanted the old people to die."

"No!" I shouted. "No! Jesus know I never wanted them to die; they was all I had and they was good to me."

Tanta Moore moved in with me. At nights she sat in Grandma's rocking chair and mended my clothes while rain drummed on the thatch and I sat at a table under the lantern doing home work. I often wondered what grandma would have thought about a stranger moving into the hut. The rain fell steadily, swelling and muddying the river and flooding the savannahs, and in the late afternoons pale lightning flickered across a cloudy sky.

Uncle Richard came in his donkey cart one day. "I come to collect some of me belongings," he said.

"Which belongings?" Tanta Moore asked.

"The couple pieces of furniture in the house. The boy is a junior and he can't take care of these things."

"Chu! Richard Dolly, but you like carrion crow, man. When the old folks was alive you treat them like dirt and now you got the bold-facedness to come for what they lef' for the lil' boy. You don't have no shame, man. What happen, cockroach eat your conscience or what. . .?" I left Tanta Moore talking to him and ran to call Brother C. Uncle Richard was still there when we arrived.

"You come to see you nephew, Richard?" Brother C. asked.

"Yes; and to collect a few things which belong to me."

"Well, go ahead and take what is yours, but the minute you try to cross that bridge to the road I will have you arrested."

"The man don't have shame," Tanta Moore said.

"I know me rights," Richard said.

"Don't make botheration with me, Richard Dolly. I am executor for this property and I won't so much as see you lift a piece of thatch from the roof. Go on about your way, Richard Dolly! Go on and leave honest people alone!" Brother C. said, and Uncle Richard lost some of his bold-facedness and walked away, and I suspected that he was cunning, but not very clever and some of the words Brother C. used must have gone through his mind like drunken men on a dark night.

"I going to put a lawyer on all you, you trying to take away me birthright," he said.

"Go 'long man! Go 'long!" Tanta Moore shouted after him as he walked out to his donkey cart.

I had not seen Uncle Richard since the day he came to see Crooked Timber, and I thought that he was looking older. There were creases on his face and the corners of his eyes looked like mud on which birds had left deep footprints. Brother C. must have read my thoughts, because he said:

"Poor Richard used to trade on his handsomeness and now age showing him up. I used to envy Richard one time. When we were young together I was courting a girl and she saw him one day and the story end for me."

"Better before than after," Tanta Moore said and I thought that they were both treating me like a grown-up since my grandparents' deaths.

* * *

There were nights when Tanta Moore had visitors and she slept in her hut. She would swear to me next morning that her visitor had been her cousin's son, her sister's god-child, her nephew from across the river, and she ended by begging me not to tell Brother C. that she had stayed away.

One night her guest left early and she came and found me reading. She brought a freckled mirror near to the lantern and peered into it for a long time.

"Boy, you think I old and ugly?" she asked suddenly, massaging her cheeks, smoothing the crinkled skin on her neck and patting her rayon dress so that it sat close against her breasts.

"Why you asking that, Tanta Moore?" I had never thought of her as anything but old, but not in the same way that my grandparents were.

"Because you is a man," she said.

"You old, Tanta Moore, but you not ugly, I won't say you ugly at all."

"Old? I will show you how old I is," she said, ripping off her dress and standing naked before me. Her breasts hung down like squash, curving around her fat belly. "Come and feel this," she said holding up one of her breasts, and I obeyed hesitatingly. I had seen naked women before, but always in the ricefields, on the seashore or by the river; never inside a house. I could smell the sweat on Tanta Moore's body as she pressed my hand against her breast and moved it up and down her flesh. "That feel old and ugly? Tell me? Tell me?" she shouted. She saw the fear and confusion on my face as I tried to look away, for her body had become a wall of flesh ringing me round. She released my hand and burst into tears. "Shark, boy, don't take no notice of an old woman fighting 'gainst she age," she said, picking up her dress and putting it on again. "But it hard, boy, it hard. Life does play joke with you. You body does get all crinkle up, but inside you still hot with fire. Shark, you is a good boy. Don't tell nobody 'bout tonight, eh?"

"No, Tanta Moore, I won't tell nobody," I promised.

* * *

Brother C. fell ill. He said it was his liver. He sat in a back room near a window that overlooked the river, and the thick mangrove and alligators sunning themselves on the muddy riverbanks when the tide was low, and cranes and gaulins stepping delicately, keeping well away from the alligators. He never left his Berbice chair, and when I went to him for lessons I always found him with an open book on his lap and his eyes on the river.

"How is it outside?" he would ask, and I would tell him what was happening in the village: the ricefields were changing colour, the police had arrested Roopnauth for stealing cattle, Rosalee, Dookia's daughter, had had a baby, a shark had broken through Telford's seine near the river-mouth, Rambalee had caught a dewfish which weighed three hundred pounds, Mendoza had trapped a sea turtle and four men had to lift it into his donkey cart. Brother C. interrupted me several times:

"Speak properly, boy. When are you going to learn to use the verb 'to be' correctly?" he would say.

At the end of the lesson I had to read aloud – passages from the Bible or Dickens or just the daily paper. As I read I noticed that the room smelt of drugs and sickness. I was always glad to get outside and hold my face up to the wind. A doctor from Georgetown visited Brother C. and told him that he had to have an operation, and a horse and carriage came and took him away to the city. A few days after we heard that the operation had been successful.

"You know what wrong with Brother C.?" Tanta Moore asked.

"His liver's giving him trouble," I said.

"I thought you did know. Is what you reading all them whiteman book for? I will tell you a lil' secret. He got prostate trouble."

"I never heard about that," I said puzzled.

"Well that is jus' another way of saying that he got trouble with he manhood. He can't use the weapon that the Lord give all man the right to use," she said.

While Brother C. was away I spent the days hunting deer, wild hogs and ducks. One morning I set out across the swamps in a coreal I borrowed from Gonzalez. I had Grandpa's double-barrelled shotgun slung across my back. I followed a canal which ran along the edge of the ricefields until I came to the open swamp. There was the sound of the wind lying down on green stems in the ricefields, but the swamp was quiet. The weeds, the wild cane, the lilies, the mucka-mucka were all still under the burning sun. Now and then clouds of tiny green flies almost blinded me; they stuck to my eyeballs and burned like pepper. Governor cranes stood motionless on one leg gazing at the green waste. Far to my right, a flock of these birds was feeding in the midst of a herd of buffaloes. The buffaloes trampled wide lanes through the weeds and the lilies and occasionally stopped to gaze with gentle, dreaming eyes at their elegant companions pecking at ticks and leeches. I passed too close to a pair of spurwings, and these, the most quarrelsome of swamp birds, hopped about and chattered, and finally flew out of a cluster of small lilies, flapping their wings with quick, nervous thrusts. I always felt at peace in the swamps. I belonged there as I did nowhere else in the village.

The land behind the village lay between two rivers, and Brother C. told me that long ago there had been a watershed like a backbone running through this land, but flood waters had torn gaps into the watershed, and with every succeeding rainy season the gaps had widened. There had been trees on this backbone of land long ago, and their roots had held the earth together, resisting the floods for a while, like fingers clawing the earth for life. But the water was persistent and it chafed the earth away from the grasp of the roots, and the watershed had disappeared.

I passed a snake coiled up in a clump of grass, a young boa-constrictor with scales as bright as brass in the sun. I could have killed it with my bamboo pole, but at that moment I felt that the snake and I were one with the sun and the sky and the young grass. I saw its smoky eyes looking at me, and I was not afraid when it followed me, swimming slowly in the wake of my coreal with only its head above the weeds. A frog was sitting on a wide lily leaf and he never saw the boa until it was too late.

I liked noonday in the swamps best of all, for the sun became a dizzy fury, and if I gazed at the horizon too long the heat-haze spinning on the edge of the sky made my head swim. At noonday the sun was too bright for me to see the red and yellow of the lilies, or the green and gold of the distant ricefields, and because everything was drowsy, the trees, the birds, the reptiles, I felt more alive than ever.

I saw a mother alligator brooding over her young – a crowd of black and brown lizard-like creatures sunning themselves on lily leaves. She heard me coming and swam towards me, threshing the water with her tail. I did not know the boa had continued after me until it suddenly came up in the midst of the young alligators and swallowed some of them. The mother turned away from me and swam towards the attacker, beating the water into a muddy froth scattering lily petals and leaving holes in the solid carpet of weeds. The boa closed in for, even with a few feet between them, the alligator would have the advantage of powerful jaws and an armoured tail. The boa wrapped itself around the alligator and stretched. The young ones looked on with eyes like raindrops on the lily leaves. The alligator struggled fitfully and was still and the boa, examining his victim, peered into its mouth. The jaws snapped shut on the snake's head and the two sank to the swamp bed, both of them dead. I poled my coreal over the spot and prodded in the mud until I felt the carcasses. I jumped out and lifted them aboard the coreal, for the skins would fetch a few shillings in the market.

Tanta Moore was pounding plantains outside the kitchen when I returned dragging the snake and alligator behind me, and she did not break the rhythm of her strokes as she said:

"Eh, eh, boy, you come back early. Is what you bring? I was expecting some wild bird." I stood watching her for a while. Her legs were planted wide apart, and as she plunged the pestle into the hollow mortar, her arms and breasts and belly quivered.

"Is a snake and alligator, Tanta Moore. I'm going to skin them and make a few shillings in the market."

"Boy, you getting more robust every day," she said, and I felt very proud as I went inside to fetch Grandpa's prospecting knife. I skinned the reptiles, rubbed coarse salt all over them, and pegged and stretched them out in the sun, and afterwards I made a bonfire and burnt the carcasses.

★ ★ ★

Brother C. returned from hospital with his clothes flapping about him like an empty rice-sack in the wind. He was so thin that he could see his feet for the first time in years. I had written to him while he was away and he had sent me a copy of Kingsley's *Heroes,* which I read many times over.

Once, the story ran, Theseus, while searching for his father, had stopped for the night with a bad man who fitted his guests into a bed. If they were too short he stretched them, and if they were too tall he cut them down to size.

I thought that Brother C. had been put into this bed in hospital, because he looked taller and I could see his neck. Tanta Moore was excited about his return and declared that she was going to find out if Brother C. had regained his manhood. I never found out if she did.

Brother C. took long walks in the morning and the sun tanned his jaundiced skin. I accompanied him sometimes and Tanta Moore complained that I came back home looking like a stray child with road-dust caked on my sweaty shorts and shirt and streaking my hair and face. I enjoyed these walks because everyone knew Brother C., and we were often invited in by the villagers and offered fresh fruits and milk and mauby. I questioned Brother C. about his stay in hospital and he said:

"I couldn't eat anything a whole day before the operation, and then they took me into the operating theatre and stretched me out like a cow for the slaughter. They put an ether mask over my face and told me to count, and the ceiling above me turned to water and the doctors and nurses looked like people in a dream. I didn't know what happened after that, because I woke up in the ward and felt sick and vomited."

"You think I will ever go to a hospital, Brother C.?"

"You better pray God you never do. Ask Him to keep your limbs young and strong, and if sickness like mine creep inside your body then ask Him to call you away to the Great Beyond." I looked up into his face to catch the hidden meaning in his words, but it was set and expressionless. We walked back across the bridge and I stopped and watched at the water curling around greenheart piles and boats loaded with wood and provisions heading for the landing a hundred yards upstream.

"Come on, boy. You've got a lesson this morning," Brother C. said, and I hurried to catch up with him, and when I had done so he asked, "You think you can take the Junior Cambridge Exam next year?"

"I don't know, Brother C.," I said. I was sure that I could not, but didn't want to tell him so.

"You can do it, but you've got to work hard," he said.

He went to Georgetown for a check-up and brought back the textbooks I had to use, and my life entered a new phase, for studying for the exam was like walking through an unknown stretch of swamp in the dark. I struggled with words and intersecting lines and figures and grew conscious of myself changing while everything around me remained the same. Tanta Moore sang her hymns at fore-day morning while she prepared breakfast. Small birds twittered and sang in the trees, and big ones winged their way from the foreshore to the savannahs. Speeding cars left clouds of dust behind them to choke barefooted people on their way to work, cartwheels rumbled, and mule and donkeys hooves clop-clopped down the hard, red road, the river reached up to lap mangrove leaves leaning over it, or flowed away to the sea, exposing shiny amber banks. Sun and rain took turns to wither and flower the earth. The moon ripened and faded through its night seasons. And yet in all this there was nothing as definite as a written word or a straight line or a circle drawn on white paper. And although these things had a definite shape, they could find no place in my mind to anchor themselves. I had to feel things before they had any meaning for me, no matter how I tried, words and intersecting lines and numbers on paper left me cold.

Brother C. was determined to ram book knowledge down my throat even if it left me suspended between earth and sky like the castaway body in *The Heroes.* I wrestled with homework night after night. My pride would not allow me to give up. The whole village knew that I was involved in a contest with the white man's knowledge and I could not fail. Brother C. said that if I failed a whole new generation might lose heart and remain in poverty and ignorance in the village. One of the reasons why I tried so hard, however, was that I was growing older and casting my eyes towards the world outside Mahaica.

I studied through changing seasons, hearing rain on the thatch, Tanta Moore snoring, rainflies burning their wings on the lantern shade, beetles knocking against the walls; smelling the fresh morning wind and mango leaves bathed in dew.

I had a good memory, and this helped me to retain even what I did not understand, and for a long time there was much that I did not. Brother C. drove me without thought for my health. While I studied for the examination, he lived only to fire my mind with a desire to learn, binding his imagination to mine, living through me. The whole of that period seemed unreal. It could have been a noonday dream.

When the time came, Brother C. took me to the examination in Georgetown like a sacrifice and the whole village turned out to see me go and to wish me luck. We set out in the schoolmaster's donkey cart and the journey to the city lasted two days. We arrived in the early morning, when beggars were stirring under heaps of rags bundled along the pavements, dogs were barking and cocks crowing.

After breakfast Brother C. took me to a large school building and when a bell rang I entered a long, narrow hall, joining a procession of boys and girls. Most of them were better dressed than I was, and they chatted and laughed and did not seem as nervous as I was. A woman gave me a card with a number on it and directed me to a desk in the middle of the main hall. I sat down and my fingers were so moist with cold sweat that I could not grip my pen until I wiped them dry on my shorts. I heard the sound of my own breathing and the scratching of my pen and once, when the examiner cleared his throat the noise made me jump. I looked up and saw him standing on a platform facing me, a tall, brown man wearing a black suit and a white parson's collar. There was a yellow-faced clock on the wall ticking away the seconds loudly. Every time I looked at it, it reminded me of the sun over courida trees in Mahaica. I used to race against the sun in the late afternoon, but I had never won. The examination lasted two weeks, and Brother C. would be waiting for me at the bottom of the steps every day when I came out.

"How did it go, boy?" he would ask, and I would give him the examination paper. He was never satisfied until I told him how I had answered every question, and he would hold his head and look up to the sky and swear that I had betrayed the whole village. When he cooled off, however, he would declare that there was a bare chance that I might have passed.

"There are all kinds of stupid boys and girls sitting this exam all over the Empire, so, by the law of averages" – he liked to use this term whenever he had a chance – "a lot of them will be more stupid than you. With this, and the fact that you come from a place the examiner never hear 'bout, the Lord might put it in the man's heart to pass you," he said.

⋆ ⋆ ⋆

The morning we returned to Mahaica, it was as if I was seeing the village for the first time: the huts stood stupidly on their tall stilts, naked children played in the muddy yards, laughing and dodging between goats, sheep, pigs, chickens and ducks, palm fronds drooped, crows specked the sky, and women sitting on doorsteps shouted to one another across ants bush, croton, black sage hedges.

"Well, Shark, boy, we're back and we did it," Brother C. said for the benefit of the assembled villagers, and I suddenly realised that I hated him, and the village, and the black faces with their white eyes and white teeth shining in the sun. Mahaica was a womb out of which I had been wrenched and I did not want to return to it. Books had made me divided in myself and I knew I would remain that way as long as I lived. On the one hand, the language of books had chalked itself on the slate of my mind and, on the other, the sun was in my blood, the swamp and river, my mother, the amber sea, the savannahs, the memory of surf and wind closer to me than the smell of my sweat.

⋆ ⋆ ⋆

Brother C. came wheeling his bicycle up the narrow path that led to our hut, and his face was shiny with sweat, as if he had cycled over in a hurry.

"I see you name in the papers," he said, leaning his bicycle against the mango tree and taking the paper out of his jacket pocket very deliberately.

"My name!" I said.

"Yes; your name's in the pass list. Aron Smart (private), it says."

"Then you mean I passed?"

"Yes, sir; and you're the only one from this part of the coast." I rushed up and hugged him, and we stood laughing and thumping each other on the back until Tanta Moore came out blinking wood smoke and onion juice out of her eyes, and wiping her hands in her skirt.

"Me hear the good news from inside the kitchen," she said embracing me, and laughing and crying, "So the boy will get paper to show he know everything in the white man book?" she asked Brother C., and, without waiting for an answer, she shouted the news to the neighbours.

"I saw your white godfather couple days ago," Brother C. said, and that was the first time that he had spoken to me directly about the shadow man who had taken me away from Timber's road gang. "And when I saw him," he continued, "he said that if you passed he was going to 'prentice you to a doctor so that you can study pharmacy."

"Lord ha' mercy, the boy going to learn doctor work!" Tanta Moore said.

"But why is he doing all this for me, Brother C.? He must have told you."

"I don't know why, Shark, but he had some powerful tie-up with you father. That I know, and if you want my stupid advice take all he giving and don't ask question 'cause white man don't help you like this for nothing."

"Is true, Shark," Tanta Moore said. "Take the help and praise God and don't ask questions 'cause white people got mysterious ways."

"I sent news to him after the paper come," Brother C. said.

"What's his name, Brother C.?" I asked.

"The good man warn you 'bout this questioning," Tanta Moore said.

"His name is Beauchamp, and don't ask me another question."

In the evening, when the villagers had returned home from work on the foreshore, the road gangs, the farms and the ricefields, they brought me gifts of eggs and chickens and fruit and vegetables, and Gonzalez, the shopkeeper sent me a young she-goat. The moon rose and many who had brought gifts stayed on to gaff. Tanta Moore cooked a big pot of rice and salt pork and peas and vegetables and we sat under the mango tree talking late into the night.

After the others had gone, Brother C. told me that I would have to leave Mahaica on the following day. The doctor was sending his car for me. Some of the men had brought bush rum to wash down the food and Tanta Moore had not missed many rounds. When she heard the news, she hugged me close against her and wept, and I could smell the rum on her breath.

"You got to go, boy," she sobbed, "but me old heart heavy with sorrow at you going."

"You won't come back to the village once you go 'way," Brother C. said.

"I will come back often to see you and Tanta Moore." I said.

"You won't come back," he said. "When the young men go 'way from this place, they don't come back."

"We will keep the house and the land for you so that whatever happen you will know you got a home, boy," Tanta Moore said.

"And you can come and take over the shop," Brother C. said, and added: "But I know you won't be coming back."

The car drove up the next day. I was waiting outside Brother C.'s shop because I did not want the chauffeur to know that I had lived in a mud hut. The chauffeur stepped out, looking very neat in his white suit and peaked cap. He looked at me as if he was not sure I was the person he had come to fetch.

"Over here!" Tanta Moore said. "This is the young gentleman you come for." He grinned and his two gold front teeth flashed like a new zinc roof in the sun.

"Me name is Santos and you don't have to be 'fraid. Me working for the doc jus' like you," he said, and I felt easier.

Santos put my cardboard suitcase and the basket of fruit Tanta Moore had given me into the boot. Brother C. told him to look after me, and Tanta Moore said that if life became too hard I should come back home. Santos stood chatting for a while; then he took a big silver watch out of his fob, looked at the time, and said that we had to go.

"Jump in!" he shouted, turning the crank violently.

We drove off with the villagers shouting after us, Brother C. wiping his eyes with a large sallow handkerchief, and Tanta Moore burying her head in the folds of her apron.

"You is a big shot here," Santos said, and I felt pleased, but did not know what to say in reply.

He drove recklessly, blowing the black rubber horn and leaving it up to people and animals to get out of the way in time.

When pedestrians shouted curses after us, he only laughed and accelerated, leaving clouds of dust to choke them into silence. Before we reached Georgetown, he had knocked down a few chickens, a pig, and a dog. Once, on a lonely stretch of road, he stopped, picked up a fluttering chicken, and stuffed it into a bag. And another time I looked back after hearing a thud. The wind cleared the dust behind us for a moment and I saw a sheep dragging its hind legs. A young girl ran out and wrapped her thin arms around it, lifting it across the road.

"What kind of man is the doctor?" I asked Santos when we were driving through the city.

"How do you mean what kind of man?" he said.

"I mean, is he a white man or a brown man?"

"He's an Indian man, and as far as me know he not bad to work for. He does take he full value in work for what he pay you, but then who don't?"

"But I won't be drawing no pay. I will just be 'prenticed to him."

"You mean you going to work for nothing?"

"I'll just be learning."

"You must be rich, pardner, or jus' stupid, because nobody don't work for nothing these days."

CHAPTER FOUR

THE doctor's house was a big, box-shaped two-storeyed building standing between the villages of Eccles and Agricola where the road to Georgetown turned sharply away from the Demerara River. Over the road, almost opposite the big white house, was a cluster of mud huts half-hidden behind coconut palms, ants bush and black sage. Further up the road was the Rectory, with tall hibiscus hedges fencing it in, and flambeaux trees shading the front veranda.

Santos left me in the empty waiting-room, and went to fetch the doctor and his wife in the car. Martha, the cook, came in after a while, and looked at me.

"So you is the new boy?" she said. She was a tall, bony woman with greying hair, an unsmiling black face, and eyes always red from the wood smoke in the kitchen. She wiped her hands on her apron absent-mindedly, and asked, "What's your name, boy?"

"Aron Smart, mistress."

"Me is not the mistress. Me is just plain 'cook'; you will meet the mistress in God's good time,' she said, picking up a magazine and turning the pages.

"Is she a bad woman?"

"Who is me to condemn the better-offs and the higher-ups? Anyhow, you will soon find out, and take a piece of advice from a woman old enough to be you mother; keep you mouth shut, padlock it, and keep you eyes and ears open, and you will get along fine." She heard the car wheels on the gravel of the drive and vanished.

The doctor and his wife came in, and I stood up. He was a short East Indian with thick, black hair, and a forelock hanging over his left eye. His eyes were the colour of stale urine, and there was a perpetual air of indolence about him. His movements were languid, graceful, and his hands small and restless. He tugged at his fingers or rubbed them together when he spoke. His wife was a fat Portuguese woman. She wore a sari which looked like a bundle of silk oddments piled up for the wash. She was the first woman I met who succeeded in looking awkward in a sari. Her burnt-brick red face was pitted with large pores, her eyes were large, veined with red lines, and her mouth wide, discontented and sensuous. Her dark brown hair was tied in a bun. Despite the looseness of her sari, I could see lumps and bulges around her waist making her look as if her body had been packed with mud.

"This is Aron Smart," the doctor said, turning to her and tugging at his fingers. She looked me over, and without a word waddled away with her sari trailing on the floor. The doctor did not seem put out by her rudeness, and he continued: "I'm glad you came, Aron, there's a lot of work for you here. Has anyone told you what you've got to do?"

"No, sir; not a word."

"I promised Mr. Beauchamp that you can study pharmacy while you helped me around generally," he said, "but first you must get some man's clothes." He looked at my arms and legs thrusting out of the shirt and shorts Madoo, the village tailor, had made for me. "Santos can take you to get them, and when you come back, we'll find a place for you to sleep. Come and see the surgery."

I followed him into a bare room which had the familiar smell of drugs. There was a desk, two chairs and a crude operating table in it, and around the walls were low shelves lined with labelled bottles. The doctor sat at his desk and seemed to forget about me as he turned the pages of a file.

"You can go now, Aron," he said at last.

I found Santos in the drive, polishing the car.

"How she going, pardner?" he asked, grinning.

"All right," I said, and after a while I heard voices in the kitchen and a woman saying:

"This blasted man always bringing strangers in the house. His wife and daughter can perish, but he will pick up some castaway."

"Is only the mistress," Santos said. "She does live in the kitchen and bad-talk everybody whole day long."

Santos took me to Georgetown to buy new clothes, and I returned to the doctor's house wearing my first pair of long trousers. I was very proud of them and expected everyone to notice that I had become a man. The trip to the city with Santos gave me the last few hours of freedom I was to enjoy for a long time. I was surprised to find that the doctor had put my bed in the same room in which he and his wife slept.

"You will sleep here, Aron," he said, pointing to a bed in the corner near the door.

That night I lay in bed and listened to the wind leaning against the house, rattling the windows, shaking the doors and moaning over the canefields behind the house. The doctor and his wife slept in a wide four-poster. She had retired early and I could hear her wheezing and turning over as she slept. He came in late, stood over me for a moment, walked away and crept into bed beside his wife, and soon I heard his breathing, soft and regular.

During my first months with Dr. Ram I found that his household was divided into separate compartments, not by walls and ceilings, but by the people who lived in it. The doctor and I lived in ours, his wife, Martha and the maids in theirs, and Santos in one of his own.

The doctor worked night and day, and I remained with him all the time. I was not only his assistant, but a foil against his wife's nagging. I never had much sleep, since I had to answer the telephone at all hours. I was imprisoned by work again just as I had been with Uncle Richard's or Timber's road gang. I thought of returning to Mahaica for a while, but I knew in my heart that I did not want to. I had made my bed and I would lie on it, and yet there were times when I could not help cursing my shadow godfather for uprooting me, when the life I had led in Mahaica would seem idyllic, and I would miss Tanta Moore and Brother C.. I wrote them regularly at first, but after a few months I did not write any more, and I felt no remorse over cutting myself away from them.

My nights were constantly occupied. I stayed at the doctor's side while he attended to patients who came from the surrounding villages, police cases of people wounded in fights, emergency childbirth cases, and during his many visits to sugar estate hospitals. And what was I learning all this time? For I never had a spare moment to open a book. I learnt to prepare the medicines the doctor prescribed, to roll up lint and bandages, to fill capsules with quinine. I also learnt that in the villages the sun ruled in heaven and disease on earth, that the doctor and I were lone axe-men trying to clear a forest of disease, that my only links with life around me were with sickness, birth and death.

* * *

I remember very clearly the first time I saw a baby born. It was the month of September, and I had been with Dr. Ram since May. A small-boy came to say that a midwife wanted the doctor to come immediately. The doctor questioned him and sent me to wake Santos, for it was after midnight. A sleepy, bad-tempered Santos drove us towards the village of Mocha, six miles along the river, where the jungle pressed upon the road. The headlights flung fan-shaped arcs of light ahead of us until they caught a woman standing in the middle of the road with a lantern above her head.

"What's the trouble, Nurse?" the doctor asked, and when Santos switched off the lights all I could see was the pale white gleam of her eyes and the pale yellow of his.

"Haven't been able to get much information out of the patient, Doctor, and the husband's away and the mother's all upset," the nurse said, and there was a note of tiredness in her voice.

"Who's with her?" the doctor asked. Santos handed me a torch and curled up in the back seat. I switched it on and flashed the light across a narrow bridge, and it lit up a path which led to a mud hut.

"The mother," the nurse said, "and the whole village."

"I'll have a word with her," the doctor said, and he stepped carefully across the bridge.

The hut was set deep in a grove of trees, and a crowd of people stood outside silent as the shadows. They made way for us, and an old Indian woman stood in the doorway blinking at the torchlight.

"Me glad you come, Doctor," she said, shading her eyes.

"You is the girl mama?" The doctor spoke in dialect and his voice took on the sing-song lilt of an Indian villager.

"Yes, Doctor. You is a good man; you lef' you house this time. . ."

"Tell me 'bout the girl." The doctor cut her short.

"She is me one-chile, Doctor; all the rest dead . . ."

"Yes, yes. How much year she got?"

"She got fifteen year, Doctor."

"This is the first pick'ny?"

"Second time she having pick'ny, Doctor; first one dead in she belly. Other doctor tell she 'No more pick'ny, Teena,' but she husband is a no-good man, get drunk, beat she, now he go 'way lef' she."

"How long the girl got pain?"

"Two day, Doctor; pick'ny should come July month; now September." The door was so low I had to bend double to enter the hut. It was full of women.

"Get out! Clear out!" the doctor shouted, and there was a shuffling of feet and a rush for the door. The air was warm and thick with the smell of sweat, curry and cow-dung, and drunken flies beaded the walls. The yellow light shone on a young girl lying on the floor with jute bags covering her. The doctor spread some newspapers beside her and knelt down. The girl moaned softly, rhythmically, her parted lips exposing white teeth and colourless gums. The doctor felt for her pulse and turned round.

"Me want boiling water, Mai, plenty boiling water," he said, and the old woman's bare feet slapped the mud floor as she ran out with an iron pot in each hand. The nurse stuck a thermometer into the girl's mouth.

"Don't bite it," she said close to her ear.

"What's her temperature ?" the doctor asked when she held the thermometer up to the light.

"A hundred and two, Doctor."

"Child's in a normal position," the doctor said, moving his hands along the girl's stomach. "Come and feel," he guided my hand. "Feel the spine and the head?"

Sweat trickled into my eyes and the doctor mopped his brow repeatedly. The nurse, a young black woman with sloe eyes and tight lips, looked weary. She held her shoulders far back to keep them from drooping.

"I'm going to puncture the outer membrane, and if that doesn't work, we'll have to use an anaesthetic and forceps. Aron!"

"Yes, Doctor."

"Spread some more paper on the floor, and bring my instruments and the big bottle of Lysol. . . and see how the old woman's getting on with the boiling water."

The mother passed me at the door, rushed into the hut and clung to the doctor.

"Ow, doctor, save me one-child," she said.

"Get the boiling water!"

I fetched the instruments and the Lysol and the woman brought in one of the pots and stood it over a low fireplace inside the hut. The nurse fought to keep awake as she helped the doctor. It was all a terror-dream. For a moment the girl seemed to be very close to me, her breath misting my eyes, but with every moan she drifted further and further away. It would have been better if she had shouted and screamed, but when the labour pains seized her the same low moaning continued.

"I've punctured the membrane and the head's reached as far as the second ring, but it's stuck there," the doctor said, and then he added: "She's too young and underfed to have children." I kept mopping his brow while his hands were occupied. The nurse held the anaesthetic mask to the girl's face. The moaning stopped and I kept listening for it to begin again.

When the baby's crying broke the tension in the room, the nurse rushed out sobbing. I would have followed her, but the doctor said:

"Leave her alone. She's just overtired."

"Thank you, Doctor. Thank you, Doctor," the mother said, getting down on her knees and kissing the doctor's feet.

Dr. Ram stood up, hardly noticing the woman. He always looked the same – grey and indolent. I detected no sign of fatigue in him, while I leaned against the wall hardly able to stand. The mother stood up and her face was composed.

"The nurse going to visit the girl and she pick'ny every day," the doctor said, and he handed her a bottle of liver extract. "Give the girl this three time a day and keep the pick'ny clean. If you rub cow-dung on the pick'ny it will die, you hearing me?"

"Yes, Doctor."

"You got milk, Mai?"

"Yes, doctor, me got two cow."

"You must boil the milk before you give it to the pick'ny. You understand?"

"Yes, Doctor."

I collected the instruments while the doctor picked up the bloodstained papers, took them outside and burned them. Before we left he asked the mother:

"You got money, Mai?"

"How much, Doctor?"

"Five dollar."

"Ow, me God! Me nah got five dollar, Doctor."

"All right. Bring chicken and egg to me house; me got to live too, you know."

"Yes, Doctor."

It was raining when we drove away. Santos was nodding at the wheel and the nurse was fast asleep in the back seat.

★ ★ ★

One night as I lay in bed I heard the doctor's wife upbraiding him for being impotent, for neglecting her and her relatives (of whom she seemed to have legion), for being stingy with money, and she threatened to shame him by taking up with a black lover in the village.

"Go to sleep, Elsa," the doctor said. She continued her diatribe, listing her many ailments and blaming them all on him.

"Go to sleep, Elsa. The boy's in the room."

"The boy, chu! You got he under your wing like a tick."

"Go to sleep, Elsa."

Mrs. Ram was a diabetic and was supposed to follow a strict diet, but she had a passion for sweets and highly-seasoned foods. The doctor was always threatening to sack Martha for encouraging her mistress's indulgences, but Martha only shrugged, and when her master was out of earshot muttered:

"Who is me, a poor black woman to tell the high-and-mighty, eat this or eat the other? If the red woman want to kill sheself, that is she lookout."

As soon as the doctor woke up in the mornings he examined the chamber-pot his wife used.

"Go and call the mistress," he would say to me, for she woke up early to gossip with Martha and the maids in the kitchen. I would find her holding court, sitting in a high-backed mahogany chair in the corner away from the stove.

"The doctor wants you, mistress."

"Is what he wants?"

"I don't know. He just sent me to call you."

"You is a damn liar, boy; you on he side . . ." I never waited to hear the rest.

"Elsa," the doctor would say when she waddled into the bedroom, "you've been at it again."

"I swear to God I didn't touch anything apart from the diet."

"Then why are the ants following your urine?"

"That's the ants' business. All I know is that I didn't eat anything but what you perscribe, and if the ants following the piss then the perscription must be wrong."

I seldom had dealings with Mrs. Ram. When the doctor was out I spent my time alone in the surgery. I often heard her gossiping, for when Martha went to market she followed the maids around the house as if she could not bear to live with herself. She boasted that she was going to "bury" her husband, because her horoscope told her so. There were times when she rushed into the surgery while the doctor was attending to patients to accuse him of being ashamed of her, of not wanting to take her out with him. On these occasions he waited for her frenzy to pass, then he took her back to her chair in the kitchen. The patients looked on calmly, silently. This was a glimpse of the life the high-and-mighty led, and they were content to observe and to withhold comment until they were safely at home.

One day I was preparing bandages in the surgery. The doctor was out. Mrs. Ram came in and started questioning me:

"Aron, how much money you think the doctor does make?"

I turned on her angrily.

"I don't know. He is your husband; the two of you share that same bed when night comes."

"Where he does keep the key for his iron chest?"

"Don't ask me. Ask him."

"Nasty whore-dog! He is you father and you not going to tell."

"My father's dead. How can he be my father? I'm black and

he's Indian. You're a disgrace to be a doctor's wife; you're worse than an ordinary whore."

"I going to tell the doctor when he come; you wait and see."

"I don't care," I said and she flounced out, cursing. "I don't care!" I shouted.

I looked out of the window towards the canefields. The sun had turned the plumes above the green leaves all golden and they tossed in the wind. Why was I staying with Dr. Ram? I asked myself, when I could walk through the front gate any day and never return. But where could I go? I wondered. I was a village boy in a strange world, an orphan with no relatives but a good-for-nothing uncle. Brother C. and Tanta Moore would welcome me back, but I did not want to return to Mahaica. I had thought of approaching my white godfather, but he was a deity, not a man. I could not go to him and say, "You cut me loose from my village, and now I don't know what to do with myself." No, I couldn't go to the white man. It was better for him to remain the shadow-god that he was, and, after all, Dr. Ram was kind to me. He worked me hard, but there were times when I felt that he understood me better than anyone else had ever done.

When the doctor returned, his wife rushed into the surgery to complain. He listened, narrowing his eyes and keeping a straight face, and when she had run out of words to abuse me, she left.

"Don't worry with her, Aron," he said. "She's a sick woman, old before her time and hating it."

Very few patients came to the doctor during the cane-cutting season, for everyone had to work. The six-weeks-long harvest-time provided the only wages most of the villagers earned during the year. I was cut off from what went on outside the house, but Santos was a good source of news. It was from him that I learnt about events in Eccles and Agricola.

Santos said that the minister who lived up the road in the Rectory was very popular. He was a big, brown man with a voice as deep as a drumbeat and he had more women than King Solomon.

One morning the doctor woke me up earlier than usual and said that he wanted me to accompany him to the Baggotsville courthouse. The girl whose baby we had delivered had poisoned her husband, and he had to give evidence.

Santos and I waited outside the courthouse while the doctor went inside. A group of men and women – East Indians, Portuguese, Chinese, Negroes and Coloured – squatted on the front lawn, or lounged against the building. Two policemen stood by the door, and every now and then a short black man who wore a white suit and steel-rimmed spectacles shouted a name from the doorway.

"These people love court, eh," Santos said, slouching in the seat and tilting the peak of his cap over his eyes. "They don't have money to buy food, and yet they flocking here for all kind of stupidness." I saw that he was in a talking mood and encouraged him.

"Tell me 'bout the minister," I said. His face brightened up and he signalled me to come closer.

"I hear a story 'bout he the other day," he said, showing a row of big white teeth with the two gold ones in the centre making a shining gap; "there's a nice-looking samba woman in Agricola who is a strong churchwoman, and the story go that the parson was in bed with she the other day. He does always visit them bright-gals to pray when they husband working. That parson is a real man, boy. Well, to make a long story short, he was stroking this gal in the height of the morning when who should come in but she husband? But you think he catch the parson? No, sir, that brown man too smart. He hear the footstep and before you can say 'Jesus wept,' he and the gal was kneeling down by the side of the bed praying, and the hubby, a real maku man, come in and kneel down too. Parson didn't even have a chance to button up he trousers, so all the time he was praying, he had to turn 'way from the hubby. Yes, sir, that parson Jones is a smart one. The last one they had was a white man who used to stand up in the pulpit with he head in the cloud and the folks didn't take to he one bit. Now this new parson converting all them young coolie gal, got them coming to church in they white frock, and when night-time come, he throwing they frock over they head. . . I hear you and the mistress fetch away the other day." Santos could change his conversation suddenly, and without a word of preamble. "That mistress is a trial, boy; me don't know why the old doc does put up with she. Time was when she used to make sweet talk to me, but me don't like to graze in pasture so near home, no, sir. That is looking for trouble; can't play with you bread and butter these days. Work scarce, but woman always plentiful. What you going to do with youself, Aron; you can't go 'long slavin' like this for nothing?"

"I'm learning a lot," I said. The intimacy I had shared with Santos while he was telling his story was suddenly broken, because I felt a sense of loyalty to the doctor and did not trust Santos enough to discuss what was troubling me.

"You got a strong mind, boy. Me couldn't face that beast work you does do."

The doctor came out of the courthouse supporting an old Indian woman who was wailing in the high-pitched, heart-rending way that peasant women in sorrow can.

"Is the girl mother," Santos said. "They loss the case."

"Ow! Me one pick'ny! O-w-w-w! The las' fruit from me belly!" The crowd stirred uneasily, and an old black woman in a flowered dress and a high turban to match hobbled up and put an arm around the mother. The doctor left them and walked towards the car.

"Nah worry, neighbour, nah worry. Leave it to the good Lord," the old black woman said, and I thought of my grandmother and Tanta Moore, and knew that they would have shared the East Indian mother's sorrow in the same way. The other women gathered around and joined in with their words of consolation. I heard the short black man shouting at them to be quiet as we drove away.

"What happened?" I asked the doctor, already knowing the answer.

"She'll have to face trial in Georgetown, and they'll lock her up for life. She'll get good meals and exercise and free medical attention."

"But the baby!"

"It will live and die like grass."

"Jail will take she out she misery," Santos said. The doctor sat back and closed his eyes. When he reopened them he said:

"The husband came back to her. He didn't want the child. He worked in the canefields, and when he drew his pay on Fridays, he came home drunk and beat her up, so she killed him."

I liked the doctor although Santos was always trying to convince me that he was taking advantage of me. At first I resented his cool detachment in dealing with patients. But gradually I discovered that he had found out the secret of rationing his compassion. He was like an ant at the foot of a mountain of sorrow, and in order to survive, to continue burrowing into the mountain, he had to use his energies economically. I knew nothing about his past, since he never talked about himself.

During the cane-cutting season he began tutoring me for my first pharmacy examination. His mind was quick and alive and he compressed ideas into as few words as possible, so that what he taught me seemed simple. The books on pharmacy which he gave me to read were even drier than my Junior Cambridge ones. We did simple chemistry experiments in a small room adjoining the surgery, and I enjoyed these. He kept his books in this room and sometimes used it as a study. He had not bought any new books for a long time and those on the shelves were worn and dusty, smelling strongly of insecticide. It was a mixed collection, medical volumes, textbooks from his grammar school and university days, novels by Scott, Stevenson, Dumas, Hugo and the Brontë sisters. I did my assignments in pharmacy, and long after the doctor had retired read the novels one by one until I had read them all. It surprised me that I could put myself in the place of so many of the characters, that I had dreamed the same dreams as strangers across the seas.

After the sugar-cane harvest, Eccles and Agricola were caught up in a fever of drums. Eccles was a Moslem village and its inhabitants were preparing for the festival of Hossay, while the Negroes in Agricola were getting ready to celebrate the birthday of their prophet, Jordan. The rival concerts of drums continued night and day. The villagers of Eccles were building a tajah near the canal which marked the end of the Rectory grounds. The patients who began to trickle back to the surgery told me about it. It was as tall as a po-boy tree, cone-shaped and glittering with tinsel, small mirrors, carvings and varnished bamboo, and when the time came it would be thrown into the river to mark the death of Hosein and Hasein.

While the Moslems made their tajah, the Negroes of Agricola built a huge mora cross, for Jordan had promised to go through the whole ceremony of the crucifixion on his birthday. The drummers in Eccles beat out swift cadences while those in Agricola went in for resonant tones, thumping steady rhythms like surf. The drums worried Mrs. Ram and she complained to the doctor:

"But is why we got to live near all these heathen people. Them drums tapping inside me head whole night and I can't catch a moment sleep."

★ ★ ★

Santos told me that Jordan had been a shoemaker until one night he received a call, and left his cobbler's trade to preach. His first sermon had been delivered outside the village rum-shop. The spirit had taken hold of him and he conjured up such vivid pictures of hell that some of the rum-shop's most faithful patrons had repented and followed him. Jordan was not only a man of the spirit; he also had a good business sense. He gathered his flock around him and, knowing the art of good farming, rented land and put his followers to work. He chose twelve disciples, more for their ability as farm overseers than for their piety, and they worked directly under him. He did the praying and his followers the work, and the farm prospered. He built a low white church near the entrance to the farmlands, and his followers dressed in long white robes, the men wearing turbans and the women veils, and they lived apart from the rest of the village. Both Moslems and Christians thought Jordan's religion a bastard offspring of their own, but his sect took roots and flourished in Agricola and his disciples carried the word to other villages and to the city. Jordan had decided to make a big occasion of his birthday because his enemies were questioning his right to the gift of prophecy.

As the day approached, processions of torch bearing Jordanites passed by the house chanting hymns in the sad tones of wind in tamarind trees. And the drums continued night and day.

★ ★ ★

Mrs. Ram took to her bed. She said the drums gave her insomnia and complained of pains all over her body. Although she spoke all the time about her legion relatives, none of them ever visited her. Months after I had been with them, I discovered that they had a daughter in a convent school in Georgetown, and she only came home during the summer holidays.

Dr. Ram spent his free time reading the latest medical journals from England and America, and ordering drugs from firms in those countries. If he had the most up-to-date drugs and the Government did not, then he could resell them at a profit. He looked on money with reverence. When the last patient left the surgery in the evenings, he locked the door and took a large iron canister out of a cupboard which was built into the wall behind his desk.

"You alone know my secret, Aron," he said, opening the canister and taking out a handful of silver coins.

"You don't bank it, Doctor?"

"Bank it?" he said, pouring the coins from hand to hand. "Not me. You know what a bank does? They take your money and invest it in all kinds of things – Malayan tin, Government securities – all kinds of things."

"But they must keep some in hand."

"Yes; but it's not the same thing as having it near to you."

"But you got to die and leave it, Doctor."

"You've been reading too many books, boy," he said, shutting the canister and returning it to the cupboard.

★ ★ ★

Straining brown bodies, bright with sweat and moonlight carried the tajah towards the river on the anniversary of the death of Hosein and Hasein. As I sat looking out of the window, new presences appeared around the dazzling tower of tinsel. Masked dancers, striped like tigers, leapt and whirled and swayed, and voices shouted "*Hosein! Hasein!*" over and over again. The leading dancer wore a huge mask, and a chain trailed behind him, twisting like a snake as he stamped and swayed. The moonlight made everything unreal and it was hard to tell what was shadow and what was flesh, what tinsel, and what leaves wet with dew. The procession moved out of sight down the path by the koker and towards the river. The drumming sounded far away. I waited, and there was a great shout, "*Hosein! Hasein!*" and the Moslem drums were silent.

The master drums in Agricola continued their slow, solid rhythms waiting for every echo to sink into depths of the heart. I went to bed and the drums never stopped.

★ ★ ★

The following morning I found Santos polishing the car in the drive.

"Morning, Santos. You look heavy-hearted, boy."

"Aye, pardner, the news heavy this morning. The prophet pass on."

"The prophet?"

"Yes, Prophet Jordan. They crucify he, and now he dead."

"But they can't crucify a man; it's against the law."

"Was like this. You know he did promise crucifixion for he birthday? Well, las' night it happen. Came sundown and more black people flock 'round the church than leaf on a tamarind tree. There was a lot of hymn-singing and drum-beating and all of a sudden, the prophet burst out from the bush behind the church he and Barabbas was carrying the cross. All the prophet had on was a lap-cloth. Barabbas didn't do that much work since he hear the call, and he was sweating! To cut a long story short, they plant the cross in the churchyard near the sapodilla tree. One disciple had hammer and nail ready, but the prophet shout out, 'I don't want nail; tie me up with rope,' and they tie he up proper, and he stretch out on the cross jus' like Jesus. He didn't settle down on the cross well when some people start tantalise he, so he call on them to stone he. One nigger man throw a big rock and the prophet bawl, 'Not stone. Pebble!' Then things settle down and the disciples watch and pray and sing and beat drum. The black people in the village say that later on much bush rum pass 'round and the disciples sleep more sound than the seven foolish virgin. Rain fall and wet the prof' and dew soak in he skin and by the time they take he down, he was stiff. . . ."

"Dead?" I asked.

"No; not dead. Jus' damn stiff. You know it en't no fun getting crucify whole night! The Sisters rub the stiffness out of he, but by ten o'clock he pass on, with pneumonia. Is big weeping and gnashing of teeth and beating of gum, and the prophet body stretch out in the church. The disciples say he will rise again if they keep he forty day and forty night."

"You think he will, Santos?"

"Me don't know, boy. The prophet was a powerhouse of a man, but whether he can walk the trail back from the beyond is another story."

The doctor came into the surgery to begin the day's work, and I told him about Prophet Jordan. He looked at me and smiled.

"I'm a prophet myself – in matters like this. After two days Jordan's corpse will stink to the heavens above and the police will step in and order burial," he said.

The doctor's prophecy came true.

★ ★ ★

Indra, the doctor's daughter, came home in July. I heard her laughter before I saw her and it sounded like tajah bells. Santos was talking to her in the drive while he washed down the car. I was bandaging a boy's shoulder. He had been stabbed in a fight. I finished quickly and looked out, but she had vanished. I did not see her until late that night. I was reading in the study and she came in, barefooted, and wearing her nightgown. I stood up, pushing my chair away so clumsily, that it fell.

"You look funny," she said, stifling a giggle. "Aron, big Aron," she sang in her childlike voice, dancing around the room on her toes.

"You better go back to bed. What will your father say if he finds you here?" I said, finding my tongue at last.

"I know all about you. Santos told me."

"I don't want trouble, miss. You better go."

"You're tall and strong and not too black," she said, examining me from head to foot.

"I'll go and call the doctor."

"No, you won't, 'cause I'll run back to bed and say you were telling lies."

"What do you want?"

"Let's go for a walk through the canefields."

"You're mad!"

"It's late and they'll never find out."

"You know what you're talking 'bout, girl?"

"It's bright moonlight and they'll never find out. Let's go, please, Aron. I've been cooped up so long I want to do something adventurous." Indra was the most beautiful girl I had ever met. She had inherited the grace of the Hindus, a harmony of flesh and spirit from her father, and from her mother the ability of the Portuguese to balance restlessness of mind against a sensuous indolence of body. She did not wait for me to disagree further, but danced out of the study and returned a few minutes later wearing her school uniform and tennis shoes.

We tiptoed past the room in which Martha and the two maids slept. The walls were thin and we could hear heavy breathing. Santos' room was near the back door. If he was in, then he must have been sleeping soundlessly. Outside, the moon was high and the sky cloudless. We walked past banana, paw-paw, and cocoa trees growing amidst tall grass in the backyard. Indra held my hand and I could feel the tension in her fingers. Her palms were moist, so that her skin stuck to mine like moss to a rock. I was not afraid once we were well away from the house. The earth was soft and the grass wet with dew. Our canvas shoes were soaked and our feet made a slushing noise in them. We came to a wide canal which separated the backyard from the canefield. We scouted along its bank until I found a canoe with a bamboo pole stuck in the mud beside it. A blue-winged chung, awakened from its sleep in the reeds, rose up in noisy flight, and I thought that its shrill cries would arouse the whole village.

"Let's go that way," Indra said, pointing towards Agricola, and I obeyed, for at that moment if she had ordered me to plunge into a river full of whirlpools I would have done so. Here and there amidst lotus lilies, reeds or paragrass were alligator's eyes like bottles of fire. If the canoe went too near them they swam away with a splash, turning the still water into jagged silver. I picked a bunch of yellow lilies for Indra, and she stuck one in her hair.

"You afraid, Aron?" she asked.

"Not of the water or the canefields."

"I am. I feel all funnyish inside, as if I have lizards running up and down my belly. Belly! You know if I say that in the convent the Sisters would make a fuss. I have to say tummy or stomach."

"Tummy? I only read about that in books."

"It's English. My form mistress is English, and she speaks as if she's got guava seeds in her mouth."

The canal turned at right angles round the canefields where the high beds shouldered their way into the dark water and cane leaves curled over to gaze at their images. There was an eeriness about the moonlight and everywhere blue shadows crouched like live waiting things. I moored the canoe behind an island of reeds and we walked under the tall canes. Indra found a clear spot and sat down. The moonlight deepened her eyes and shone on her hair. We sat close together and listened to our hearts beating.

"All of us have boyfriends at the convent," she said.

"But they never let you out."

"I know; but the boys meet us at Mass. We can hold hands in the holy water for a minute. My boyfriend's name is Gavin; he goes to Queen's College and he sends me letters by his sister." I broke off a fat cane stem and gave her a few joints to suck. "Aron," she continued, "you ever had a girl?"

"No." She rested her head on my shoulder and I kept very still. The blood rushed to my head as if I were doing a handstand.

"You're frightened to touch me," she said, laughing close to my ear. "Two girls in my class, Mary and Eula, had boys when they went home for Christmas; they didn't like it. Hold me here, Aron," she said putting my hand around her waist.

"I never had a girl, but I saw the whole thing. I used to live with a woman named Tanta Moore and men used to come to her. One night I peeped through a hole in the wall. She and the man were bracing themselves close together, naked, and he was trembling, and he tumbled her into the bed and they were close together like mud when something is under it making it tremble." Indra unbuttoned my shirt and moved her fingers along my chest, my back, my stomach. I shivered and the words dried up in my throat. She rubbed her lips against my neck and her breath was hot. I held her against me clumsily, felt the deep groove in the small of her back, the curve of her hips. We explored an experience as green as young canes, and suddenly I was afraid, not of the consequences, but that I did not know what to do. We fumbled and groped and laboured. She cried out several times and laughed and whispered childish endearments until she saw a pallor creep over the moon's face and said:

"It's getting near morning!" We got up hastily and she tried to scrape the mud from the back of her serge uniform. We started back home.

"I thought I would bleed a lot," she said, "but I'm all right."

* * *

Santos found out our secret. Perhaps he had been awake when we passed by his room. He broached the subject while we were sitting in the car, waiting for the doctor outside an estate hospital.

"You got to step careful, Aron," he said.

"Step careful?"

"Yes, with the boss' daughter, man. Don't ask me how I know, because I not going to tell. You see, the doc holding all the trump, and if you make a wrong move he will carry you to the cross. You playing with fire, Aron. I been with them since Indra was a baby. That girl always had she own mind and they could never manage she. She papa worship she like how Moslem does worship tajah, but the mother, she was poison to the girl since she eye see daylight, the mother is she kinnah. I will cover up for you, but don't stick you neck out too far, because me is a careful man and I like this work."

"Santos, boy, this girl all wrapped up inside me. The whole thing happen so suddenly! And now it eating inside me like a wood-worm."

"It knock you hard, pardner, 'cause you is a book-man. I plant solid on the ground and you up in the tree-top. Look, pardner, this love business is jus' another day's work. If you line up all the woman I did love before me, I wouldn't know half of them. The thing is you musn't fool youself that you is the first person this happen to. I know this girl; she born with hot blood and they shut she up, so she got to pay them back now. She want to break out and she using you and if you wasn't there would 'ave been somebody else."

"I love her, Santos. If I don't see her for a day I can't eat or sleep."

"You got it bad, pardner, but stop going 'bout looking like a sick cow. Keep a straight face, man. You can bring she to me room and I will keep watch."

CHAPTER FIVE

THERE were times when Indra resented me, laughed at my clothes, my accent, my blackness. When her school friends visited her, she sought me out and insulted me in front of them. At other times she complained to her father that I was lazy and disrespectful.

"What have you done to my daughter, Aron?" the doctor asked. I was filling a capsule with quinine and it fell on to the floor. I turned my back to him and picked it up.

"I haven't done anything to her."

"She's growing up and it's a painful business. She gives me hell sometimes too," he said, and I could hear him rubbing his hands together.

After insulting or ignoring me all day, Indra would lie in my arms on Santos's bed at night and swear that she loved me. There were times when she went down on her knees begging me to forgive her. We spent passion the way a drunken cane-cutter who won a lottery spent money. We used up what should have lasted a lifetime in a single night. Indra was only fifteen, but she grew up into a woman in the first month I met her. The tight lumps of her breasts filled out to curve softly under my hands, her hips grew wider, rounder, and her quick, boyish walk changed as if her limbs had attuned their movements to the sway of a wild palm in the wind. She kept insisting that she wanted to have a baby, begging and threatening me night after night. Her parents doted on her, and she, with all the cunning of an ocelot, deceived them shamelessly. There were times when I heard her cowing her mother with the fire of her young spirit, and I felt sorry for the sick old woman. I suspected that she could deceive me too, but I pushed this thought away and was content to live for the moment.

One night I lay beside Indra in Santos's bed. Her head was on my bare chest and when she spoke I felt the warmth of her breath.

"My mama's bringing a young man to meet me. She says I'm a woman and it's time I was married, so she's going to arrange a wedding." I held myself very still and felt as if a cold iron had been pressed against my spine. "You don't have anything to say, Aron? You don't care. I know it. You jus' want to use me and then I can go my way." I felt her body against mine and was conscious of her animal smell filling the small room. She jumped out of bed. "You don't love me, Aron!" she said.

"Indra, you know that's a lie. I would do anything for you, anything."

"I don't want you to touch me any more. Who are you anyhow? Just a black nobody, a black nothing from some village!"

I sprang on her and held her close. She spat in my face and dug her nails into my back. I forced her towards the bed. It was like grappling with a leopard, for she was all claws and fury. She bit and clawed and tore herself free, and I locked with her again.

"Black beast! Black brute!" she hissed. I pinned her arms to her sides and forced her on to the bed. I sat astride her while she reared up and twisted and kicked, certain that her strength would give out before mine, and afterwards I lay on top of her, panting and sweating. She relaxed suddenly and began to cry.

"I don't want anybody but you, Aron; only you. Give me a baby, Aron. I want your baby."

"They can't take you away, Indra. They can't plough me out of you or you out of me. You musn't do it with anybody else. Save it all up for me, girl. When I'm working in the surgery the whole day I can smell you on my own flesh and I can feel your hotness."

"I don't want anybody but you, Aron. Give me a baby; then I'll have to marry you." We talked with our lips on each other's, and we tried to fuse our bodies into one. The wind sounded like huge bat wings flapping over the canefields and Santos whispered at the door:

"All you two better go now. I hear somebody stirring upstairs."

* * *

Indra returned to her convent early in September. There was something final about her going. She had promised to write, for we planned to run away together, and as soon as I heard from her I was to meet her outside the convent and take her to Mahaica. But as soon as she had gone I knew that the scheme was an impossible one. She would never be content with a being a barefoot village girl.

I gazed through the window at midday looking at the wind rolling over the canefields, at crows specking the sky, at cane-cutters walking in single file along the far bank of the canal with cutlasses on their shoulders and saucepans hanging from the end of the cutlasses. The doctor must have called me several times, for he walked up and shook me by the shoulder.

"What's the matter? Look, we don't have time for dreamers here," he said.

Santos warned me that evening:

"Pull a blind over you face, pardner; you giving the game 'way. You walking 'bout with a face long like the wall and everybody, even Martha, who don't see further than she nose, say, 'That boy walkin' 'bout like baboon mother when she loss she pick'ny. He fullin' up he head with too much book and if he don't look out he will go mad.' Is what you working up youself 'bout, pardner? This world full of woman." In many ways I was sorry that my romance was a secret. It would have been good for everyone to know that the orphan boy who was always at the doctor's beck and call had won Indra's love.

"It's showing on my face so bad, Santos?"

"I can see it a mile away, pardner."

"She'll never leave me, Santos. She swore that she'd marry me."

"I hope you not chasing silk cotton blossom in high wind, pardner."

"Santos, you don't like her."

"Is not that me dislikes she, but I don't want to see you make a big fool of youself, boy," he said, taking off his cap and scratching his head. He always did this when he was worried. He changed the topic. "You hear the doc get transfer?"

"Yes. He didn't tell me, but I heard him talking to the mistress."

"We going to the madhouse in Berbice," he said. "Only for six months. Then we're going to Maichony."

"That's near you home ground, pardner; you can look up the old folks."

"I would like to see them again."

* * *

The doctor, Santos and I drove to the mental hospital while Mrs. Ram and the servants travelled by train from Georgetown to the ferry at Rosignol. On the way to Berbice, I asked the doctor to stop at Mahaica. I walked up the trail to my old home and found Tanta Moore in the kitchen.

"Tanta Moore, it's Shark!"

"Well, Lord bless me eyesight! Boy, you come home?"

"I just came to see you for a minute; the doctor's waiting for me on the road."

"But how you grow up big, boy! All dress up in you town clothes. . . and you talking different too, boy, jus' like a town man. Is why you didn't send message tell we that you coming?" I looked around me and everything had become smaller, the huts, the yards, the mango and po-boy trees, even the stretch of saffron between the public road and the courida trees had narrowed and shrunk. Tanta Moore looked older, the lines on her face grooved deep, the eyes misting.

"I was busy, Tanta; never had a chance to write. Everything fine with you, Tanta?"

"Things going one-one, boy. Is the same story here; nothing don't change." She left me and bustled about the kitchen and came out with fruit and a joint of mutton. "Like they starvin' you, boy; look how you face get thin! You must nourish you body, boy. The old man will be glad to see you."

"I must go, Tanta. Stay well."

"Lord, Lord, look how we Shark growed up, eh!"

"Stay well, Tanta!"

I found Brother C. in the back room of his shop, sitting in his Berbice chair and looking at the river.

"Boy, you come back!"

"Only visiting, Brother C."

"I should know better. You won't come back. This place too small for you." He sat back and I noticed that his face was yellow and drawn.

"I saw Tanta Moore," I said.

"She talks about you all the time, even after you stopped writing. You grow into a fine young man, got you Uncle Richard's good looks without his meanness. But you can't write, boy, just a few words to say that you're alive? The day might come when you will be glad to have two old people who believe in you, who will stand by you."

"I will write, Brother C. I will write every now and then."

"What wind blow you this way, boy?"

"The doctor's been transferred to Berbice. I must go now, Brother C., I really must go."

"You will come back, Shark? Will you come back?"

"Yes, Brother C."

"Don't make it too long, boy."

* * *

The hospital compound was a pleasant one. Wide fields of paragrass and cassava beds separated it from the town of New Amsterdam on the one side, and the Canje River and walls of mangrove sealed it off from the village of Canje on the other. It was a self-contained unit, criss-crossed by red, burnt-brick lanes, which were lined with trees. The administrative buildings, wards, cottages, workshops and playgrounds were fenced in by palings and high hibiscus hedges, and about six hundred people, patients and staff, lived on the compound. We were cut off from the town and the neighbouring villages as soon as the guards closed the big timber gates behind us.

Patients were working on the lawns and flower beds. It was a peaceful scene. Figures moved about in slow motion and attendants lounged in the shade, but, as if to remind us that we had entered a world of the abandoned and the damned, voices shouted from the North Block, frenzied, daemonic voices such as I had never heard before.

"That's where they keep the violent ones," the doctor said, pointing to a stone building near the river. Its walls were overgrown with vines and I saw giant butterflies dancing against their shadowed green.

The Superintendent's house had been built near the public road and it was ringed with flambeaux trees. From the windows on the top floor I could look over the trees towards the dark amber river, the mangrove and the village.

I remember the doctor going about his duties, threading his way through a jungle of secret frenzies, his face suave, unreadable, showing no uneasiness. He was not qualified to deal with mental illness, but he was by nature kindly and had immense patience. He clung to the theory that all insanity was caused by glandular trouble, but he never tried to apply his theory, and on the whole must have done little harm during his six months as Superintendent. Patients were sent from hospitals all over the country. They spent some time locked up in cells under observation and were then certified by a doctor and a magistrate.

Once admitted, they were herded together and classified as violent or passive, sick or able-bodied, paying or non-paying. The men worked on the farm across the public road or on the island at the river mouth cutting wood, and the women weeded grass on the compound, scrubbed and cleaned the wards, and worked in the kitchen or laundry.

* * *

Mrs. Ram was ailing and more crotchety than ever. Everyone knew that she did not have long to live, but she refused to admit this to herself. Whenever she was able, she spent her time in the kitchen, and she would get one of the maids to hold up a mirror before her every now and then. Between bouts of examining every line on her face she boasted about how beautiful she used to be and the many conquests she had made. The doctor, she claimed, had been forced on her by her family, and she had regretted marrying him from the beginning. Martha, whose flesh seemed to be shrinking into her bones as she grew older, endured her mistress's daydreams, and if she caught one of the maids smiling she clouted her and drove her out. Martha was very loyal to the family. I often heard her talking to the maids about Mrs. Ram, running her down, but if the maids agreed with her, she would turn on them and accuse them of being ungrateful and upstarted, and end by declaring that she alone had the right to criticise her betters.

When we had moved into the Superintendent's house, the doctor again insisted that I sleep in the same room as he and his wife. I had always been a sound sleeper, but after Indra left my nights were troubled, and I heard Mrs. Ram wheezing and crying out in her sleep. Sometimes it was as if she were struggling with phantoms and the doctor would wake up and soothe her.

"Elsa, what's the matter, girl? It's all right. I'm here, girl."

The madness invaded my dreams, and in them I saw Tanta Moore, Brother C., Timber, Uncle Richard, locked up in the North Block, or weeding grass on the compound with their backs to me, and when I went up to them they looked up grinning insanely.

The townspeople and villagers avoided me if they saw me coming out of the gates. They believed that madness was contagious. The attendants resented the patients, who, in turn, hated them. An old warder told me the story of how a patient had found an attendant sleeping under a tree and had cut off his head and buried it so that the sleeping man could not find it when he woke up.

Our first stop in the mornings was the head office. Here, the doctor looked through case histories of newly arrived patients and those due for release. We then set out for the kitchen, the carpentry shop, the hospital for the physically sick, and the North Block.

The hospital wards stank like mudflats strewn with rotting fish. Nurses and patients alike were untidy. Light slanted down from high, barred windows, showing patients sprawled on cots or sitting listlessly in chairs, some of them in twisted uncomfortable positions. The wards reminded me of a beach strewn with driftwood. The violent patients were strapped to their cots.

It was good to return to the sunshine and the shaded red lanes, for the terror which clawed at me in the wards melted away.

I remember individual patients we met:

The young Negro in the blacksmith shop who was building an aeroplane with scraps of tin to fly to the North Pole.

The woman who, whenever she was let out, buried her face in the ground and lay there until the female attendant tore her away.

The young man in the general ward who came up to the doctor furtively and handing him a letter whispered:

"The enemy, they're all around. I want you to send this to the King. They've robbed me of thousands since I've been in here."

"All right. I'll forward it," the doctor would say and at other times the same patient would come up and ask:

"Any news, Doc? Has the King ordered them to free me?" He was an educated man and I could never think of him as being mad, for he spoke with such conviction.

Then there was the old Portuguese with a face wrinkled like a fruit-skin drying in the sun. He believed that he was an international money dealer. When he saw the doctor coming he would rush up, smiling:

"Price of steel's up, Doc. There's going to be a big war and they've got to see me. I control the steel." In the midst of his conversation he would stop and listen. "It's my secretary, Doc, the telephone," and he would hurry away.

"What was the call about, Pedro?" the doctor would ask after.

"Six millions in steel, Doc. The Belgians, you know," and he strutted around with a paper cigar stuck in the corner of his mouth.

I often saw a patient sitting on the doorstep of a cottage smoking a pipe. I asked the doctor who he was and he said:

"He's worse off than the rest; he's sane. Been here for years. He killed his wife and baby, but the family had connections and they arranged for him to come here. He's an accountant and he audits our books."

Our last stop was the North Block. This was the house of demon faces. Naked figures stood in small cells staring nowhere in particular with wild eyes, or howling like beasts. The attendants used powerful hoses to subdue those who tried to kill themselves. We invariably found them with their backs turned to the patients, looking out towards the mangrove, the river mouth, and the green island.

"This place getting you down, Aron?" the doctor asked one evening.

"I'm feelin' old, sir, old before my time. People say that if you stay here long you will get jus' like the inmates. I feel like them already."

"It's getting me down too and I feel my wife isn't going to leave it alive."

"I hate this place, sir."

"You hate it! Lord, what about me! I write the Director every week and say the place is a stinking mess. And what do I get in reply? A note saying that the Government hasn't got any money; they're doing their best." He came as near to an outburst of anger as I had ever seen him. "By the time they get around to dealing with this mess I'll be dead. And who's to blame? Every damned one of us."

We were standing in the garden with mosquitoes buzzing around us. It was ebb tide and we could hear the river swishing around piles and chafing against its banks. A piper owl was fluting a sweet song from a distant flambeaux tree, carts were thundering over the Canje bridge, and a female attendant was shouting at a patient. The doctor continued: "This is the first time since I started my practice that I feel lost. Across the way there is the prison." He waved an arm towards the outskirts of New Amsterdam. "I'd rather be in there." Stars flared in the dark sky, and lights appeared in the kitchen, the living-room, and the bedroom on the top floor where Mrs. Ram was lying in bed with a mirror in front of her, watching herself die. I wished that she would die quickly so that Indra could come home, for her letter had never arrived.

Mantop came for Mrs. Ram in the afternoon, and she wrestled with him until there was a rattling in her throat like dry locust seeds in a pod. Indra came home and she bawled and shouted over her mother's grave, threatening to throw herself in.

A week later she settled down to becoming mistress of the house. She never gave me a chance to talk to her alone, but I watched her and waited, and finally caught up with her one night in the garden. The doctor had gone into the town to pay one of his rare visits.

"Indra, you don't have any more eyes for me?"

"It's over with us, Aron. Finished." Even in the starlight I could see that she had grown plump, and yet she had only been away for six months.

"Indra, I couldn't sleep for thinking about you, girl."

"I met a man, Aron, and I'm going to marry him. He's Indian like me and Papa won't say anything."

"You were playing with me, girl, making a makuman out of me, but all the time I was the servant-boy."

"What else did you expect?" She turned her back on me and I swung her around.

"I will make you sorry for this."

"You! Make me sorry? Chu, don't talk stupidness."

I left her and went in search of Santos. I found him in his room on the ground floor. He had only that morning returned from Essequibo, where he had been visiting relatives.

"You look like thief carry 'way you mother white fowl," he said.

"The blow fall heavy, boy."

"Is the girl, eh?"

"Yes; she don't want me. She say I'm only a servant."

"What you expect, pardner? You help she become woman and since blood thicker than rum, the gal is she mother's daughter."

"I want to go 'way from here, Santos. I'm sick of being poor, crawling like a snake under people's foot."

"Bide you time and raise some cash, then you can cut adrift, pardner, make for the city or the gold-mines. The road always wide when you got the cash."

"Was the way she spoke to me, Santos, just like if I was a worm or something."

"Is why you so upset, pardner, at least you give she something that she can't forget. Once a woman throw she leg up in the air with you on top she, she can't never slant proud look down she nose at you. Jus' bide you time, man. What you got to worry 'bout is money."

The doctor returned late, and found me sitting at the big mahogany desk in the study. Nothing had been changed since the English doctor had left. The room had kept its smell of seasoned leather and dusty books. There was a brass kettle on a shelf, and faded paintings on the walls. The doctor had aged since his wife's death. His eyes had retreated into their sockets and his hair was greying.

"You like my daughter, Aron?" he asked, laying the flat of his hands on the desk.

"Who, me, Doctor? Me like your daughter? Look!" I said, holding my hand up to the light. "I was born at midnight, black and poor, like a stray dog." He ran his fingers through his thick hair, pressing his forelock down with the ball of his palm, seeming not to hear me, to be unaware of the anger in my voice.

"We don't chose our parents. Who said that? Can't remember any more."

"Mine were black," I said and he looked up at the ceiling, where a money-spider was struggling with a rain fly.

"An interesting case came up today," he said, picking up a file, and I knew that this was what he wanted to talk about all along. I was sure that he did not know anything about Indra and me. He had just been holding a blade of grass in the wind. "A patient came in this morning," he continued. "Remember Beauchamp, the man who sent you to me? I hadn't heard from him for over a year, and of all places, he had to turn up here." I searched the doctor's face. He was smiling a twisted smile like a man in pain. He was trying to let me know that I was trapped. So long as the white man was there, all powerful, then I could have broken away from him, but now he had us both in his power. There were times when I felt that he was as jealous of me as a woman with a lover. He wanted my absolute loyalty.

"I'm still going to leave you," I said.

"And go where, back to the mudyards?"

"I can work, Doctor."

"I'm all you've got, Aron," he said and when he came over and put an arm around my neck I pulled away because his fingers were as soft as earthworms.

"I'm going to leave you," I said.

"You're talking like a fool, boy. With me you can become a professional man. . . ." I ran out of the room.

I told Santos about my conversation with Dr. Ram and he said:

"You make a wrong move, pardner."

"I don't care."

"Don't talk stupid, boy. You must bide you time and keep you mouth padlock."

"Remember the white man I told you 'bout?"

"The one with the ram-goat beard?"

"He's in here."

"He never did sound too right in the head to me."

"I read his case history this morning. They say he's manic-depressive, and what this is don't ask me."

"Sound like a bush tea me grandma used to brew, pardner."

"It was all written down on the paper, said he was a mining engineer, that there was a big accident in one of his mines and since then he was never too right in the head."

"I thought you tell me he was a road engineer!"

"I told you he worked as a road engineer. If you white, boy, you've only got to look inside an engineering book and you can be anything. Remember I told you he knew my Papa?"

"You Papa must'ave catch it in he mine. Ask he. If he mad then he will talk more quick than if he sane and sober. Ask he when you get a chance."

"You've got something there, Santos."

"Madhouse is a great place, pardner; black, white, coolie, buck . . . is all the same here."

I made up my mind to talk to the white man, and waited until the doctor had gone to New Amsterdam on business. Mr. Beauchamp was a paying patient and he shared a cottage with the accountant. I found him on the front lawn of the cottage. Since our first meeting, his hair and ram-goat beard had turned white and silvery like sea-island cotton. He was tall and straight, a hollow log of bone with red, sunburnt skin pulled tightly around it.

"Who are you, young man?" he asked, and I remembered that he had put this very question to me the first time we met.

"Good afternoon, Mr. Beauchamp."

"Who are you? Let me see, you worked down the number four shaft in Perenong. . . ."

"I'm Joe Smart's son, sir. Joe Smart, you remember? You said you knew him. He was my father."

"Number four shaft . . . said he'd go down and make sure those damned Chinese didn't rob us. . . big chap with plenty of teeth. . . stupid, but he played cricket. . . always carried his gear with him when he could . . . funny with these chaps, they really take to the game. . ."

"I'm Joe Smart's son, Mr. Beauchamp. You gave Brother C. money to educate me, and you 'prenticed me to Dr. Ram. I want you to tell me about my Papa. Tell me 'bout him, please?" He stared at me and a gleam of recognition came into his blue eyes. "Tell me about my father, Joe Smart?" I asked again, but the eyes looked inwards once more and he mumbled:

"They never had a chance when the river came in on them. . ." The accountant appeared at the door of the cottage and signalled me to go away.

"He wouldn't know if Good Friday fell on a Monday," he said, "and he might get violent." I walked across the lawn towards the lane which led to the doctor's house.

"Smart! Aron Smart!" It was Mr. Beauchamp calling me back. "I've been keeping something for you," he said when I had returned.

"Tell me about my father, sir? I want to know 'bout him. My mother left me and I don't never hear a word about her."

"Wait here," he said, and he disappeared inside the cottage. The accountant shrugged and walked away. Mr. Beauchamp came back with a large envelope. "Take this, boy," he said, and, as if he had forgotten about me immediately, he looked at the sun, shading his eyes. "Used to be brighter at Perenong," he mumbled, "only the mine was dark. . . . Never had a chance when the river rushed in. . . ."

I left him standing there, muttering, and ran towards the doctor's house. Indra was picking up flambeaux blossoms and pulling out weeds in the garden.

"What's that?" she asked, looking at me and noticing my excitement.

"Not your damned business!" I shouted, and she said something about complaining to her father, but I rushed upstairs to the spare room and locked the door.

★ ★ ★

The envelope contained four hundred and eighty dollars in bank notes and a letter. I felt the notes, smelt them, held them up to the light. I had never seen so much money. I folded the notes carefully and put them into my pockets.

The letter was written on onion-skin paper. The handwriting was executed in thick and thin strokes with an ordinary pen. Before I could read it I heard the doctor and Santos returning in the car. I tore up the envelope and put the letter into my jacket pocket. The doctor found me in the study.

"I thought you were working in the dispensary this afternoon, Aron. This place must really be affecting you. Indra said you ran past her like a lunatic just now clutching an envelope."

"I brought some samples for you," I said, pointing to an envelope on the desk.

"What was all the rush about? You could have brought them over any time."

"I wanted to look up something in the medical dictionary, sir."

"We'll soon be out of here, Aron. After Indra's wedding we're leaving for Maichony. Once we've settled down there, I've got big plans for you, boy, big plans."

"I didn't know your daughter was getting married so soon."

"Yes; we arranged it. She's marrying young Sankar."

"What kind of big plans you've got for me, sir?"

"I'm opening a chemist's shop in Maichony and putting you in charge. I've ordered the drugs and equipment and you can qualify while you're there."

"How about the money side of things, sir?"

"You'll get a regular monthly salary and, living with me, you'll be able to save. I'm going to launch you out into the world, Aron."

"Yes, sir."

"You don't sound too pleased, boy."

"It's just that you took me by surprise, sir."

Late that night Santos and I met in his room. Only a piper owl, voices from the North Block, and the rumble of carts over the Canje bridge kept us company. The room was small, and a bed, a table and an ocelot rug were all its furnishings. A kerosene lantern hung from the ceiling on a piece of wire. Indra had forbidden the servants to use electric lights, although the Government was paying for the electricity. I heaped the bank notes on the table and Santos whistled with a hand over his mouth.

"You rob the doc' iron canister!" he said, going to the door to make sure that it was locked. I shook my head and laughed. "No; couldn't be the canister. Must be the pay office," he said, picking up a handful of notes and caressing them. "Jesus wept! It's the real stuff, pardner! Tell me how you come by it before I burst an organ inside me. Is how much, pardner?"

"Four hundred and eighty."

"Jesus wept!"

I told him about my meeting with the white man, and he interrupted me several times. He wanted to hear every detail.

"Where's the letter?" he asked when I came to the end of the story.

"I've been feeling it like fire inside my pocket since this afternoon." I spread it out on the table.

"Read it, pardner. Read it, man."

"It says, 'To Mr. Aron Smart.' Boy, this is the first time a white man wrote me a letter."

"When white man write you is always trouble, to take 'way you land, or send you to jail."

"It begins, 'I am of sound mind. The voices which disturb my sleep at nights are quiet. . . .'"

"But white man story peculiar, eh."

"Give me a chance to read the letter, man."

"All right. Read on, pardner."

"It says, 'Since I am the best judge of my own sanity, my claim to be of sound mind at the moment of writing can be taken as valid. I address this letter to you, Aron Smart, because we are the only survivors of a tragedy for which you bear no responsibility. You are the son of a man whom I wronged cruelly. . . .'"

"A lot of big words, eh."

"Give me a chance, Santos."

"All right, pardner; not another word from me."

"It says, 'I met your father, Joe Smart, shortly after coming to Guiana. I must tell you something about my reasons for coming although it is no direct concern of yours.

" 'I left a young wife in England. We were married the very year I sailed. Her family had been against the marriage because I had neither money nor social position, and she, under the influence of a carping, nagging mother, made my life miserable. A friend had told me about the gold and diamond rushes in Guiana, and I came expecting to make enough money in a short time to return to London and live there with my wife in our own home. I met your father at a bar in Georgetown. He had just returned from the diamond mines in the Mazaruni and was spending extravagantly. I saw him often after that, and when his money ran out he suggested that I went into partnership with him. I had three hundred pounds which I had borrowed and I invested the whole sum in equipment and stores.

"'We were lucky from the beginning. In three months we made over three thousand pounds. I sent most of my share to my wife, who had written to say that she was expecting a baby. I should have left then, but the diamond fever took hold of me. You cannot imagine what it was like for me to be suddenly released from our civilised traditions and modes of behaviour in England, to find myself in a primeval world where debaucheries and excesses were the rule. At first I was disgusted, frightened. I held myself aloof and was driven by a single purpose: to make a sizeable fortune and return to my wife and child. Our luck continued. Your father had an uncanny instinct for locating rich claims. Fate, however, gives with one hand, but exacts heavy penalties for her bounty with the other. . .'"

"Lord, pardner, let we take a drink. The white man story heavy, boy."

"Let me finish reading, Santos. If you don't want to hear the story, I will read it to myself."

"All right, man, all right."

"Where was I again?"

"The white man was talking 'bout Fate. Read on, pardner."

"It says, 'News arrived that my wife had died after the birth of her stillborn child. I was demented with grief and plunged into a whirlpool which I had so far avoided – drink, black women, gambling. . . .'"

"But is who tell the white man them things so bad ? If you got the money to do them."

"All right, all right, but give a man a chance, eh?"

"Carry on, then, pardner."

"It says, 'Your father helped me wonderfully. There were no barriers of race in the jungles. Every individual was master of his own fate as long as one had strength and cunning. Your father was a big man with a plethora of appetites. . .'"

"Chu!" Santos muttered and I continued;

"'He was quite irresponsible but he never wanted for laughter or compassion for his fellow man. He stood by me in my grief and if it were not for him, I would certainly have taken my life. He mentioned a wife on occasion, for he too had been recently married. When I met him you were a year old and he had only seen you a few times. At first I deplored his indifference to his wife and child, but after a time I understood that he was not a family man and never would be. Money was for him an alien symbol which he both loved and hated. When he had it he seemed totally committed to disposing of it quickly and in a most astonishing fashion, and having spent every penny, he returned to the hinterland to perform monumental labours to acquire it once more.

"'After the first wave of grief had passed, I applied myself to buying up more and more claims, importing machinery, introducing modern mining techniques, and finding cheap, reliable labour. The black pork-knockers were too independent and unreliable, so I contracted labour from China. I worked four mines simultaneously. The biggest one was at a place called Perenong in the Mazaruni. There, I put your father in charge of two hundred Chinese miners. We sunk the mine deep, and struck the richest vein of gold I had ever come across. It yielded over a hundred ounces in a single day. I promised the Chinese that I would release them from two years of their contract when the vein was worked out. They followed the vein under the Perenong creek, cutting through layers of sand and schist, and I never warned them of the danger.

"'Gold and diamonds make monsters out of men, drive all decency and kindness from their hearts, turn honest men into thieves and liars, good men into fiends. I betrayed your father and the two hundred Chinese when all of them trusted me implicitly. They followed the vein too near the creek bed, and the water burst through and drowned them all. What made the experience more terrible was that I saw your father drown. I was standing at the head of the mine shaft, and your father and six of his men were climbing up the rope ladder. We all heard the roar of water and the cries of terror and they started running up the ladder. They were about thirty-five feet down, so that I could see their faces clearly. Your father was a big man, not as agile as the Chinese, and they tried to pass him on the ladder as the water rushed upwards. The last glimpse I had of him, he was pulling his way up with his hands and the six men were hanging from his legs. I ran for a piece of rope, but when I returned the water had almost reached ground-level and it was seething like a devil's cauldron.

"'These are the bare facts, and as you grow older you will no doubt wonder from time to time how I felt during and after this tragedy. Part of the answer is that we English are a race burdened with conscience, while we remain suspicious of feelings and emotions. Indeed, it was difficult for me to feel grief for the loss of hundreds of men in the same way that I felt it for the death of my wife and child. I went about working the other mines for a long time and the sense of guilt which was to obsess me came upon me slowly, nibbling at my conscience over a period of years until I could find no refuge from it. It was then that I tried to find your mother. I enquired after her up and down the coast for years. It was not until the day we met by chance that I knew you were still alive, and afterwards I found out from your Mr. Cyril that your mother had abandoned you. I had in the meantime given all of my considerable fortune to various charities in the hope that the Almighty would redeem me from some part of the guilt I had to face. The money I am giving you is all I own apart from the small pension I receive. May God bless you and I pray that someday you will forgive me.'"

"That the end?" Santos asked.

"Yes. It's signed, Julian Beauchamp."

"How you feel 'bout it, pardner?"

"I don't understand all the white man was trying to say, but at least I learn something more about my pa."

"You don't think the white man is a bad man?"

"I don't know, Santos. I don't know. If he was all that bad he wouldn't go to all that trouble to find me and me mama. Me father didn't care 'bout me nor me mama either, and to make matters worse I don't remember them, don't even know what they looked like. Well, the white man come along and help me, so how can I say that the man was so bad."

"I was only asking 'cause as far as me concern if the Devil make move to help me, and me want the help, he can be Santos' friend."

We sat in silence for a long time listening to the carts going and coming across the bridge. I knew that I had to decide for myself what I was going to do. The idea of going to the gold and diamond mines had been planted in my mind since the days when I worked with Timber's road gang, and Mr. Beauchamp's letter made the prospect more exciting then ever. The doctor was offering me a safe career, but once I accepted his offer I would be tied to him for the rest of my life. Santos had told me that he had been to the mines, but he didn't have any luck. If I could persuade him to come with me, he would know about the things I had to buy, the equipment and supplies, and I wouldn't mind risking the money. I saw Santos' eyes catch fire at the sight of the money and knew that if I offered him a fifty-fifty share it would be hard for him to say no. I thought too, of returning to Mahaica and farming and taking over Brother C.'s shop, because it was a lot of money to have in a village, but this didn't appeal to me at all.

"Santos," I said, "I want to go to the mines and try me luck. You want to come with me?" He looked at me as if he wanted to make sure that I wasn't joking, and then he became very guarded.

"Pardner, that is big plunge to take. Me got me safe work and me uniform and me en't sweating meself out in no hot sun. Is lots of brute work in the bush you know. That work make plenty man old before they time."

"I will go fifty's with you, man, and I know I will have luck. I just know it, boy."

"Fifty's, you say?"

"Yes, fifty's."

"And when we will pull out, pardner?"

"Tonight, man; this very night. I will leave a note for the doc. and Mr. Beauchamp, and we can make the morning ferry."

"You take me sudden, pardner, but me will come."

CHAPTER SIX

DARK, porous clouds were sifting stars when we left the mental hospital compound, and the voices in the North Block were still. All my belongings were packed in the old suitcase Brother C. had given me. I carried it on my shoulder because the handle had broken off. "I should stop over in Mahaica and say goodbye to Tanta Moore and Brother C., but this would mean admitting my failure to qualify as a pharmacist, and I could not face their sympathy," I thought.

Santos carried his things tied up in his bed-sheets. It was the rainy season and the Trade Winds were damp and chill. The road surface was soft under our feet.

We entered New Amsterdam and it was very quiet until we turned down a lane and heard a dog pulling at his chain and barking. There were lights in the police station as we passed by and a constable at the gate said:

"All you early for the ferry, boys."

"We know, pardner, but we will catch some sleep before day clean," Santos said, speaking for the first time since we had set out.

Other passengers were waiting at the entrance to the stelling when we got there – farmers and cane-cutters from the coastal villages who had come by donkey cart and on foot. They slept under the protecting zinc roofs of the warehouses. We sat near to an East Indian farmer and his wife. They were lying on the bare earth and talking in undertones. Santos sat down, leaned against his bundle and closed his eyes, and I stretched out, using my suitcase as a pillow. I thought about the doctor. I was certain that he would not miss me until around eight o'clock in the morning, for if he woke up and found my bed empty during the night, he would assume that I was reading in the study.

Behind us, the stelling with its timber gates closed, jutted out into the Berbice River like a wooden peninsula, for the banks on this side of the river were constantly silting up, and the stelling had to be extended every few years. The sharp cry of a curlew occasionally broke the silence. I slept fitfully and was awake at day-clean when the sun crept out of the sea beyond the river mouth. There was a white mist over the water like mosquito nets suspended from the sky, billowing in the cleaning wind. This wind dried up the dew on our faces and limbs and made us shiver. We bought our tickets and boarded the river steamer as soon as the gates were opened by a black porter whose eyes were still thick with sleep. Passengers bustled aboard, porters shouted, winches rattled, and waves stirred by the wind slapped against the iron sides of the steamer. I felt a sense of mounting excitement. At last I was as free as the white cranes winging their way towards the mudflats over the billowing mists. The gangplanks were hauled away and the steamer's engines pounded like drums. I could picture Indra telling her father maliciously that he had wasted his time with me, that both Santos and I were ungrateful blacks who were bound to let him down sometime.

We travelled on the lower deck. Cars, carts and cattle were packed close in the bows, while third-class passengers crowded aft. I looked over the side and watched the water rushing by. The mist was lifting, and from mid-river I looked back at New Amsterdam with its neat buildings like heaps of cotton under the trees, its church steeples, and its saw mills with rafts from up-river stranded on the mudflats beside them.

Santos never said a word. He sat hunched in a corner looking down at the deck.

"What's the matter, Santos?" I asked, and he buried his head in his arms and did not answer. I repeated the question and he fixed me with an angry look.

"Lef' me 'lone!" he said. "For Jesus sake, lef' me 'lone, boy!"

I thought that he must either have had second thoughts about leaving the doctor or he was worried about the girl in Canje. I was not very perceptive at that moment, for I was too excited about my freedom and the thought of the gold and diamond mines. Later I came to understand that Santos disliked change. Whatever situation life threw him into, he was content to live within the limits of experience it provided, and he himself would never take the initiative to break out. I was determined that he should share my happiness and began to imitate the doctor's voice, Martha's, Mrs. Ram's, the patient in the blacksmith shop. Other passengers gathered round and, encouraged by their laughter, I turned somersaults and clung to a crossbeam like a monkey. Before the boat had reached Rosignol on the opposite side of the river, Santos was cracking jokes with a young East Indian mother who was nursing a baby from a full brown breast.

We spent three weeks in Georgetown buying mining equipment and supplies. It rained continuously, but the bad weather did not interrupt the bustle and ceaseless activity of the city. This surprised me, because when rain fell in the country nearly everyone stayed at home.

We lived in a boarding house near the Law Courts, and in the early morning I could see the statue of Queen Victoria through veils of rain. Drenched and solid, she stood before her throne gazing across a canal towards the Stabroek market, where Santos said the Dutch once sold slaves. I liked walking through the streets with Santos. They were like rivers jammed with logs, and we were pieces of driftwood. Crowds poured in and out of the large market-square, jostling, shouting, cursing, laughing, people of every race and colour on earth – Chinese, Negroes, East Indians, Europeans, Syrians, Amerindians and others, a mixture of so many races, you could not tell what they were. There were Negroes with Chinese eyes, people with woolly hair and Hindu features, white men with faces which looked as if they had been rubbed in the dust of a burnt-earth road, swarthy men with grey-blue eyes and kinky hair, blonde Negroes and pale-faced Amerindians. To me, they were either rich or poor, a few rich and many poor. The rich had the gift of silence, while the poor shouted in a ragged chorus above the sound of grinding wheels, engines, hoofbeats. Their huts and shacks could not contain them and they were always spilling over into the streets and marketplaces.

The night before we left for the mines Santos took me to a brothel. He said that this was my initiation, for the moment we left the city the only women we were likely to meet would be whores. We went early, because Santos thought it better to get in on the first shift. The girls would be tired later on, he said. We walked along the waterfront until we came to a large building with a dance hall on the first floor, and rooms on the second and third. Elsa, a former lady of the streets who had made good and become a madame, greeted us.

"Eh, eh, Santos, you en't been this way long time, boy!" She had a hard, ringing voice which matched the glitter of eyes in her sharp face.

"I been working steady, Elsa."

"You know me husband?" she asked, pointing to a massive Red Indian brown man who merged with the shadows under the staircase.

"Didn't know you was married again, Elsa."

"Get up and say howdy, Slackfoot," she said sharply, and the big man limped towards us. "Is which lil' boy you got with you, Santos?" she asked, turning to me and examining me like a piece of beef in the market.

"Is me pardner, Elsa. He en't no lil' boy; he is a educated man and he know doctor work inside out; is only that he face smooth. What kind of gals you got, Elsa?"

"What kind you want?"

"Fair-skin one."

"That will cost you more, boy. Go up to the dance hall and look 'round."

"Come on, pardner!" Santos said, and we walked up the stairs. The light in the dance hall made me blink. There were big electric bulbs hanging low from the ceiling, without any shade over them. Four sweating black musicians sat on a stage in the centre, and around them a few white sailors and a sprinkling of brown and black men were dancing. A woman came over to me when the music stopped. She was wearing a low-cut white dress, and from the way it clung to her, I knew that she did not have anything else on.

"I know you," she said, and her whole face came alive when she laughed and her teeth shone as if she had electric lights in her mouth.

"Know me!" I felt shy and confused.

"Remember Crooked Timber road gang?" she said, and the

laughter came from deep inside her. "You grow big," she added, looking at me until I felt like running away.

I remembered her. She was the woman who had come to my assistance when Timber broke my ankle.

"It's a long time since," I said, and she looked so friendly that I lost my shyness.

"You fix up, pardner," Santos said grinning. "I want a fair-skin one."

"Try Mary," the woman said, pointing to a thin Portuguese girl across the room. I was glad that I had found a country girl, because she was not so much of a stranger to me.

"What are you doing here?" I asked, and when I looked at her I knew it was the wrong thing to say. However, she did not seem to mind.

"You don't remember? My name is Belle," she said. "Buy a bottle of rum and come up to me room or madam will start grumbling. You got money?"

"Yes," I said. "I've got enough." The way her breasts trembled when she walked made my throat feel dry. Belle's room was small and neat. There was a bed, a chair and a washstand with a basin and porcelain mug on it. I sat stiffly on the chair. She gave me half a tumbler of rum and water. I drank it and my eyes watered. She laughed and took the glass away from me to refill it.

"Sit on the bed, Shark," she said. "You see, I even 'member you name. . . . You don't have to look like you in Sunday School."

"Nobody called me Shark since I left Mahaica."

"I hear that white man pay for you schoolin' and you turn a book man."

"But how did you hear that, Belle?"

"Me not like you; me does go back to the coast now and then."

"It's a long story. The white man felt he wronged my Papa, and so he helped me."

"Me hear all that too."

"You were here long, Belle?"

"Don't tell me you going to preach to me, Shark. God give me one thing aside from me blackness and I using it, boy," she said, taking off her dress. Her skin was dark as the spots on leopard wood and she smelt of sweat and cheap perfume. "Before I break meself up with road gang I rather make money this way. You want a long time or a short?"

"I rather just talk to you, Belle. I'll pay just the same!"

"Them book gone to you head, Shark," she said, pressing close to me so that I felt her breasts rubbing against my cheek. I put my arms around her and her skin felt like down on a chicken.

"I don't want you to act like if it's business, Belle."

"Is business, boy – work – every night five, ten men – C.O.D., pay as you go. Some of them, the high-and-mighty, does come and cry on top me and swear they love me, then they does pass me on the road next morning. Is just that I lucky tonight, I catch a young boy with he head full of book-story. You want a mother, Shark, not a whore." She poured another drink and it did not matter what she was saying any more. I lay on the bed and watched the ceiling dancing in time to the music from downstairs. She took off my clothes and ran her hands over my body. My blood caught fire and the rhythms of her body sucked me in. She moved like a snake under me. The passions she released in me were mature, boundless ones, and what had passed between Indra and me was children's frolic compared to this. We never slept that night. Santos knocked on the door at four o'clock.

"Come on, pardner. We got to go!"

"I didn't like that man, Shark," Belle said. "Me spirit didn't take to he one bit. Stay with me, Shark, stay! I will set you up in a house and work for you."

"I've got to go, girl."

"I will follow you, Shark; me swear that me will come after you."

"Come on!" Santos bellowed. "If every time you dip you wick you going to fall in love, then God help you!"

Belle jumped out of bed and pulled on her dress. She flung the door open, caught Santos around the waist and lifted him over her head, balancing him near the landing rail.

"Don't let me hear that kind of big mouth talking near to me," she said.

"He's my partner, Belle. He didn't mean anything by it." She planted him on his feet and he stood wide-eyed and shaken.

"Give me a long kiss before you go, Shark," she said, and with

Santos looking on, and I feeling embarrassed, she held me close and I could taste her salty tears.

"Don't forget me, Shark. I going to come and bring you luck, boy."

This meeting with Belle heightened my consciousness of other people, and suddenly I was aware that Santos was jealous of me. All along our relationship had been based on his being grown up and my being a boy, but Belle had humiliated him before me and this had cut him down to size in my eyes. I felt just as much a man as he did, and understood that in future when decisions had to be taken I would assert my opinions and stand by them.

"That woman strong, pardner. Me en't no flyweight and she pick me up like a leaf. I hear 'bout this Belle before. You going to be a killer with the women, pardner, like you is a champion stroker." He was laughing, but I knew that the laughter was not real and I sensed the tension behind his words.

We walked away and our footsteps were loud in the sleeping city. Crossing the market-square, I said more to myself than to Santos:

"Belle is a good woman. She's better than a thousand like Indra."

* * *

A light drizzle was sweeping across the river when we boarded the steamer for Bartica. The rain had been falling out to sea and the wind was driving it inland. We sailed out of the Demerara River and round the coast towards the Essequibo. The sea was choppy and the wind blew in gusts. The steamer rolled, and dug its way through angry, bursting waves. Santos was seasick, and his face was the colour of moss as he regarded the offending water with lacklustre eyes. I kept an arm around him as he leaned over the rails and he felt small and crumbled. Spray washed over bent figures on the deck, and now and then a man coughed and sputtered and vomited.

Crates of equipment piled up on the foredeck strained against the ropes which tied them down every time the ship rolled. It stopped raining and the sun came out. I saw the outline of the coast with factory chimneys pointing to the sky from the lowlands behind the mangrove swamps. The steamer settled down to a gentle rocking and Santos sat down and leaned against a crate.

We entered the mouth of the Essequibo River and sailed towards the stelling at Parika.

"I feeling empty," Santos said.

"Take a swig of this," a man said, offering him a drink of bush rum; "it does settle you stomach."

"I don't have nothing lef' in me stomach, pardner; is just a hole," Santos said, wiping the mouth of the bottle on his sleeve and taking a long drink. "That's better, but I still can't face that sea." He handed the bottle back and chatted with the man.

"Can't believe this is a river," I said. "Man, it's so wide I can't see the other bank."

"This is river father, pardner," Santos said, "twenty miles wide. Across the water is Leguan Island, and behind that is Other island."

We went ashore at Parika and while new passengers embarked we bought fruit and roti from peddlers on the stelling.

"Is good to feel land under me foot again," Santos said.

"All aboard!" a sailor shouted from the steamer.

We sailed upriver and the water darkened. Clouds massed and dispersed, but no more rain fell. Trees verged the river banks with shadows when the sun appeared. The river was so still that we sailed across an inverted bowl of sky rimmed with trees. The passengers recovered from their sea sickness and milled about the deck talking animatedly, laughing and singing. A tall, loose-limbed black man with a grin that stretched across his face perched on top of a crate and strummed a river chanty on his guitar, singing in a high clear voice:

Gal me lover letter loss.
Gal me lover letter loss.
Gal me lover letter loss.
If you find am me go give you carat stone.
If you find am me go give you carat stone.
What me mother going to say.
What me father going to say.
Gal me lover letter loss.
If you find am me go give you carat stone.

The others joined in the chorus and bottles of bush rum went the rounds. This was my first experience with pork-knockers, and their easy-going, generous ways surprised me. They were boisterous, obscene, quick-tempered, but they shared whatever they had as if life was an endless carnival.

Fort Island was the next stop. This was the site of the old Dutch capital. I saw the ruins on high bluffs overlooking the stelling. Trees had burst through the stone, toppling walls and canon, and vines and creepers were erasing all that strangers had built in their pride and left.

The steamer slipped away sailing further upriver. The sky was clear and the sun brassy. The falling tide exposed golden sand-banks, and the Blue Mountains appeared behind a sea of green. Santos had forgotten about me and was shooting crap with four pork-knockers. I found a cool spot under a lifeboat, lay down and fell asleep. Santos woke me up when we reached Bartica. We helped unload our crates, left them in the warehouse and walked through the town.

"This is a quiet place," I said, because the quiet of the forests which ringed the town seemed to muffle people's voices and the barking of scrawny dogs which slinked across yards and alleyways.

"Not quiet; just waiting. You should hear it when the pork-knockers passing through on they way to Georgetown. Man, the place does be wild. Whore and shopkeeper does grow up like tree, and the rum-shop does need police, and money does pass like fire. The town just waiting for the good times, man." I was glad that Santos was in a talking mood, because I wasn't feeling sure of myself any more. So much had happened since we left the doctor that I needed time to think it all out and arrange it in my mind.

We found an empty hut near Sorrow Hill, a graveyard on the outskirts of the town, and we slung up our hammocks after driving out the bats. I gathered wood for a fire and looked with awe at the hunched backs of mountains silhouetted against a sunset sky, for the coast was flat as the bottom of an iron and I had never even seen a hill there. Night fell suddenly and brought heavy dew and a chill that crept inside my bones. The wood was rain-soaked, and when I lit a fire it hissed and spat and smoked and it didn't blaze until Santos poured kerosene oil on it. We lit a storm lantern and left it inside the hut to keep the bats away, and we sat close to the fire munching biscuits and salt fish and drinking hot tea. A host of eyes pinpointed the path which led away from the hut and Santos said that they were the eyes of bird spiders which had come out to feed.

"I win five dollar on the boat," Santos said, and I listened to frogs calling for more rain and wrapped my blanket closer.

"Santos, you think I'll be all right in the bush?"

"The bush en't a bad place, pardner; is only people does make it bad."

"Santos, tell me 'bout yourself. You know I never heard how you grew up, where you went to school, if you married or not."

"Some old-time story is best forgot, pardner. Me grow up catch-as-catch-can and me start chauffeuring young. Couple year before you come on the scene me get married. . . ."

"I didn't know you were married."

"Is who you think me went to see in Essequibo the other day? Me wife living with me great aunt. Me live with she one year, but the woman like she wanted to tie me to the house with bush rope, so me cut loose and run 'cause me is not a stay-home man."

"Then why you get married, man?"

"Was a double-barrel wedding, pardner. The doc was working near Buxton village and me eye catch on to a samba gal and next thing me know she was in the fam'ly way. To tell you the truth, me didn't know what to do, but me mind was telling me to light out fast. Come one Saturday night when me was going to visit the gal and a friend tip me off that she father find out. But me thought that me was smart, so me go just the same. Well, pardner, me foot didn't land inside the house good when the old man brace me 'gainst the wall with a shotgun and ask me what was me intention. It didn't take me long to answer, but all the time me was thinking up scheme how just as me reach outside not even bullet would catch me. But this father was a stone-face black man with eye that don't miss a thing. When me done talking to the gal and getting ready to go, the old man was still by the door with he gun and me say, 'Go'night, father-in-law,' and he say, 'It raining outside, boy. You better stay in that room we prepare for you,' and 'though me didn't hear no rain me take the old man word 'cause a man can't argue with gun. Well, to make a long story short, they never let me out 'till the wedding day, and the old man and a big nephew take me to church and they never lef' me side 'till they hear me say 'I will,' and is so me get married."

"What happened to the child, Santos?"

"It growing up," he said, and changed the subject. "We got to get up fore-day-morning to catch the boat, pardner, so we better get lil' sleep." He stood up and stamped his feet and I saw some of the spider's eyes on the path vanish.

Santos fell asleep at once, but I listened to the noises from the forests behind Sorrow Hill – the lunatic hooting of a ooskudu owl, dew-drops dripping from leaves, the long-drawn-out howling of an ocelot.

A family of red howlers shook the earth with their roaring at day-clean. It was cold outside the hut and I ran up and down the hill to get warm.

"Come on, pardner!" Santos said, coaxing the fire to a blaze, blowing his cheeks out like a pig's bladder. Tinamous filled the silence which the red howlers had left for them. They sang to one another deep in the forest, and it was the sweetest music I ever heard. They began in a low key, and carried the notes so high and held them so long, I thought their throats would burst.

After a breakfast of turtle eggs, biscuits and tea, we headed for the stelling. Behind us, sakki-winki monkeys chattered, and toucans screamed with delight in a big mango tree.

The main street of Bartica had come to life. It was crowded with pork-knockers carrying huge loads, naked Amerindian families in single file, the men in front with wareshis harnessed to their foreheads and shoulders, and the women and children shuffling behind them, boatmen with torsos thick as tree trunks carrying broad-bladed paddles, loudmouthed, laughing women who vibrated everywhere at the same time. The pork-knockers shouted farewells to the women.

"Mary, I going to pour gold in you lap and full up you belly with joy when I come back, gal."

"Ow! Hennie, come with me, gal. You does make me feel like a king on top you throne."

The women shouted back, flexing breasts and belly-skins and backsides, and laughing raucously.

Before the sun looked over the hills we had loaded our crates aboard the *Victor P.*, and captain and bowman were standing by to push off. There were twenty-four other passengers aboard the *Victor P.* and with crates and bales piled up to the gunnels, she sat deep in the water. She was a squat, shallow-draught river boat. The Captain was a burly man, black as river water when a shadow fell on it. He was so accustomed to shouting above the noise of rapids that even when he talked ordinarily, his voice sounded like a red howler's. Standing in the stern with a paddle in one hand, and the cord for starting the outboard motor in the other, he looked as if he had never been born in the ordinary way, but had fallen there like a stone.

"Cast away, and God be with we!" he bellowed, giving the cord a hard pull. The motor sputtered, then settled down to a steady phut-phutting and the *Victor P.* swung out into the river. We sailed through still waters, parting the mists. I looked back and saw women washing clothes on the river bank. They put the wet, soapy garments on the flat of rocks and beat them with paddles. The mist swallowed them, muffling the sound of their voices and the slap-slapping of their paddles.

By mid-morning we were chugging up the Mazaruni River. The current was running against us and we took turns at paddling. We reached Tetruba Falls at noon and the bowman, who had crouched motionless in the V of the bow since we left Bartica, stood up, feet astride the gunnels, and plied his paddle right and left with swift, sure strokes.

"Pull away there!" the Captain bellowed, and the pork-knockers sang a boat-song with the paddles keeping time to the rhythm. The Captain and bowman knew every inch of the river, the shape and size of submerged rocks, and the channels between them. A quarter of a mile above Tetruba we came to the Marshall Falls, and the captain signalled us to man the lines. We jumped into a rush of water, feeling our way with bare feet from rock to rock, all twenty-six of us straining against a bow line, a bow brace and a stern line. The water on the surface was warm, but the curling, pushing water at our feet felt cool. The boat cleared the draught of whirlpools and circling eddies, and we re-embarked.

In the afternoon we came to Quapow Falls, a rock staircase

down which the water came so fast that the sun danced and dazzled on exploding suck-tides, and it sounded as if a crowd of mad children were laughing and running down the flights of rocky stairs. When we disembarked I answered the mad voices in the falls, dancing and shouting on the rocks, and Santos said:

"What's wrong? You mad, pardner?" but the others said nothing, for this was their world, and they knew how it affected strangers.

We had hauled the *Victor P.* to the top of the falls when there was a cry like an animal surprised in its sleep. A man had slipped on a mossy rock and was swept away. Without thinking, I plunged in after him. I rose to the surface, and was deafened by the shouting of the river. I saw the man ahead of me, his hands beating the swirling water and his shirt billowing. Rocks, bare legs and trees raced past me. After the first drop I went under and had to fight my way out of the undercurrents. I shot up gasping, pushed away from the sharp edge of a rock, and swam until I started gaining on the inflated shirt. I was prepared for the second drop and swam away from the whirlpools, but the third one followed before I caught my breath. The water tugged me down until I felt my knees touch gravel, and I came up with arms spread wide to avoid the rocks. I came abreast of the drowning man in the turn-tide below the fall. He tried to grab me, but was nearly exhausted and I held him off and flung water in his face until he went limp. I struggled to get out of the turn-tide, every now and then feeling for the river bed with my feet. The water moved round and round in narrowing circles in the centre of which was a whirlpool. I lay on my back and kicked hard. The sky was bluer than I had ever seen it and trees with an array of greens arched towards me. I touched a submerged rock, but it was slippery and I could not gain a footing. The water dragged at my feet, and the drowning man was so heavy I could barely keep his head above water. Instead of floating with the turn-tide, I fought against it. The Captain and bowman rescued us just in time.

"Is you first trip up this river, pardner?" the Captain shouted, as he swam between us pushing my limp charge and me towards the rocks. He was strong as a buffalo and his eyes flashed as they caught the sun. The bowman helped me on to the rock shelf, and when I tried to stand my legs felt as if water had been poured into them.

"Come on, hero!" the bowman said, lending an arm for support. The Captain laid the man I had been trying to save face down on the rock and moved his arms up and down.

"Is you first trip?" the Captain said. "You damned lucky. Don't do nothing stupid like this on me boat, man. Me is Captain and me can look after me passenger." Water poured from the man's mouth, staining the rock face. Santos was waiting for me with an anxious look, but as I drew near he grinned.

"Pardner, you got mind. Me couldn't face that river to save me mother. Them pork-knocker think you got mind too," he said, jerking his head towards the others, "but they won't say nothing. Is so bush people stay: they won't say nothing now, but they will make up song 'bout you later on."

We continued upriver. The man I had helped save lay on a tarpaulin in the bow staring at the sun. His name was James Wellington. When he came to he had said:

"Thank you, pardner. If you want extra hand to work you claim, me ready to help you," and I could see that he was not a talkative man and he had difficulty in blurting this out. We camped beside the Spanior Fall and the Captain divided us up into work parties. One group unloaded, another set up tents for the night, while the third gathered firewood. The sun crouched above the trees for a while, and suddenly it disappeared, leaving stars and bonfires and lanterns to light the darkness.

The other passengers were issued with a pint of flour, six biscuits and two spoons of sugar, but Santos and I prepared a good meal with our own provisions. The tall pork-knocker who had strummed his guitar on top of the crates after we had left Parika, struck up a tune after dinner. His name was Socket. His long neck fitted between his shoulders without any rising of the trapezus muscle, and somebody had said long ago that it looked as if his shoulders had a socket between them to fit the neck.

"How you feeling, Shark?" Santos asked, swinging one black leg over the side of his hammock and flicking a mosquito brush over it every now and then. "Me got to call you Shark from now on, 'cause you make that river look like stupidness, pardner."

"I'm all right now, Santos. Was a lil' bit afraid when we started out in the bush, but now I'm all right, boy."

"You don't see that young man is a general!" a pork-knocker lying near us said. I wanted to tell Santos that the ducking had cleared my head, that in the swift journey down the falls I had proved to myself that I was a man, that I was sure my idea of going to Perenong to start work near to the claim where my father had been killed was a good one. But the others were laughing and joking around us, and I would have felt a fool saying this to anyone else but Santos.

At three o'clock in the morning the Captain shouted:

"Strike a light ashore there!" Pork-knockers crept out of their hammocks, and, groping in the dark, kicked over pots and buckets, and stumbled over the firewood piled up around smouldering bonfires. We ate breakfast in the glow of bright fires, and afterwards, folded up our hammocks, packed our equipment, and removed the tarpaulins from the tent poles. By six o'clock we had carried the last bale over the rocky hump which bulged above the mist. The sun came out and shone on glistening cobwebs which spiders had spun across branches during the night. We started hauling the *Victor P.* across the portage while it was still cool, and by eight o'clock we were chugging upriver once more. The exercise and the thought of getting nearer to the mines loosened tongues. Everyone swore that they were going to strike it rich within the first few days of their arrival and head back to the city to live in style. James Wellington sat in the bow with his back to the rest of us. Since he had offered to help me work my claim he had not spoken to me again.

Day after day was spent loading, unloading and hauling the *Victor P.* over rapids, everyone drilled to their job by the Captain's trumpet-voice. One afternoon when we had passed Marippo Fall I sat between two crates escaping the sun and the Captain said:

"Me hear you is a book man and you study doctor work?"

"Only some pharmacy," I said. I had not learnt yet that pork-knockers like to exaggerate every detail of their lives, and if you don't do the same, then they thought very little of you. But the Captain was looking back at Marippo and he hadn't heard me.

"You notice Marippo there," he said. "Every time me pass that fall me does feel like singing. That is fall papa. More people drown there than you can count."

"Looks like all the rest to me, Captain."

"That's because the water high. Take 'way a foot of that water, and this river will carry we all to the forest of the long night. Every year that fall does claim a boatload. Last year was Capt'n Ratan. Them rock got teeth to bite near Marippo."

"Boat aground!" the bowman shouted. The Captain abused him and his ancestors while we jumped out, and, standing up to our waists in the river, pushed the *Victor P.* off a sandbank. When we were all aboard once more the Captain continued his conversation as if nothing had happened:

"Me can tell you 'bout accident on this river from now 'til never ready morning. Yes, sir. Jus' like how you know doctor work, me know me river. You can't learn 'bout this in book, you got to read every twist in the water like if is you wife' face you reading."

On the fifth day of our voyage we arrived at the foot of Parbakacsh Fall. All around us were forests, hills and sheer cliff faces striped with vines and dotted with stunted trees growing out of rock. The world around me grew bigger while I felt smaller than an ant, and more and more I felt a sense of community with the pork-knockers, who fought for life every day, and laughed and sang around campfires at night. Santos and I climbed to the top of a hill near Parbakacsh and watched the sun setting.

"This is one big country," he said, and I knew what he meant because we had been shut in on the coast, cramped between the sea and an ocean of forest.

"I want to spend the rest of my life here," I said.

"Every coast man does say so, but this place big and bad and it don't invite you to live in it. You can come and go, but you mustn't stay or it will get you."

The journey became an even swifter succession of rocks and racing water. We passed Caburi Rock when the midday sun stood over it, and the heat haze over this arching, writhing hill of stone made it look as if it was about to melt and crumble. We bypassed the Looking-Glass Fall, sailed down the Kusewayo stream, saw Topoco in the morning mist, edged around white fangs of rock at Turesi, and came to a sluggish mooring at Kamakusa. Here we reported to the police, and had our mining passes checked. I noticed that the police were all men from the coast, while the prisoners were pork-knockers. The latter looked like men enjoying a holiday, whilst the former looked trapped. There were no walls ringing the prison compound, only the forest trees and the river. Santos told me that once both warders and prisoners had left the prison during a diamond-shout.

Two day's journey from Kamakusa brought us to our destination at the mouth of the Perenong Creek. We camped in the Perenong back-dam within shouting distance of the Grass Fall. On the first night I dreamt of a journey up a river which climbed up to the sky, and the shouting of the waters began in Heaven and echoed all the way out to the sea. We saw the sun greying the ripe moon at day-clean and heard monkeys screaming. The sun burned away veils of mist to show us giant trees garlanded with lianas and orchids, and hills with russet trees and yellow blossoms breaking their green monotony. Santos knew his way around Perenong, and I was sure that there was not a corner of Guiana which he did not know. When I woke up, I saw him returning from a bath in the creek, shaking himself like a water-dog.

"I feel like some fresh meat," he said, "and me hear some marudi by the fall."

We took our guns out of their oilskin bags, and pulled the barrels through with flannel until they shone like moonlight on still water. We followed the creek until we were abreast of the fall. Santos stopped under a mora tree and pointed to a marudi in its branches.

"You take it," he whispered, and I aimed and fired. The report awoke the whole forest and the bird fell with a thud. There was a flutter of wings in the tree and a scurrying of feet across the forest floor. A green parrot snake slithered past, almost touching my feet. The marudi's mate was perched higher up and it flew away with raucous cries. "He will come back," Santos said, and he put the edge of a leaf to his lips and gave a staccato whistle. The bird returned, circled, and alighted, and Santos shot its head off. "This two can last we a week," he said, and when I picked them up they must have each weighed over ten pounds.

Later in the morning when the sun was climbing high we went to Bullah Daniel's store. It was half a mile from where we camped on the creek bank.

"Aye, Bullah!" Santos shouted from the bottom of the front steps.

"Who is that?"

"Is me, Santos, and me friend, man!" The shop was a big, ungainly building with a galvanised zinc roof and walls made from troolie palm trunks.

"Santos?" the voice said, and its owner opened the door and came down the steps. He was a short black man with a head like a knot on a tree trunk. His brows were thick, beetling, his eyes wide apart and kindly. His nose must have been broken, but even if it was it did not make very much difference, for it had a wide, low spread over well-fleshed lips and a strong chin with a deep indent in the centre. His neck was short and thick, his shoulders wide and narrowing to a small waist, and his legs had a bounce to them when he walked. "Oh, is you, Santos," he said. "So you take walk this way again."

"Yes. I trying me hand again, Bullah."

"Is who you got there with you, pardner? That boy face look like me see it before."

"Is me pardner. He study doctor work, but he come this way to try he luck with the gravel. The boy is a general, Bullah. You should'ave see how he haul James Wellington out the river at Quapow!"

"Me hear that story last night. What's you name, young man?"

"Aron Smart."

"Lord ha' mercy!" he said peering into my face, circling me and looking at me from head to foot. "Not Joe Smart son?"

"Yes. Joe Smart was my papa."

"Lord ha' mercy! Look how thing can happen, eh! Lord! Lord! Boy, shake me hand. Me never cry more than when me hear Joe dead. Me warn he 'bout the white man, but he never listen. Joe was a big-hearted man; used to take people jus' like he see them. You know, when he tell me he had wife and son me think the man was joking. Well, bless me eyesight! Joe Smart son. Boy, shake me hand again." He said all this in a rush, hardly pausing for breath. He shook my hand, took a step back, then forward, and thumped me on the back. I didn't know what to say. "Aron, boy, me going to look out for you. Have no fear. Bullah Daniels is friend worth to have – just ask anybody from here to Orealla, from Roraima to Akarai. Me got big heart for me friend and bitter one for me enemy." He was beside himself; thumping the banister, pumping my hand. "Tonic!" he called out, and a slim black boy with cross eyes came to the door. "Tonic, this is Joe Smart son, boy. 'Member me always talking 'bout the man?" The boy looked on unmoved, with his head cocked to one side. "Tonic, get some whisky out boy. This call for a drink."

"Joe Smart like he did know everybody," Santos said.

"He bound to know everybody," Bullah said. "The man was a cricketer and a lot of other thing."

We went inside the shop and stood at the counter. Tonic poured us drinks. The heat from the zinc roof made the room so hot that we all took off our shirts. Santos looked pleased as he sipped from his tumbler.

"Tonic," Bullah said, "me going to show Aron the mine shaft where he papa get drowned. Me does go there every now and then and talk to Joe and cuss the white man."

"Yes, skipper," Tonic said, his face still unsmiling. "The boat tie up by the kakarali tree, skipper." Tonic was one of those people who is born old, and looking at him you could never tell if he was sixteen or sixty. But when he moved, you could see the muscles like bush ropes coiling and uncoiling all over his body. We finished the bottle of whisky and Bullah rowed us across the creek. We walked up a steep trail to an abandoned mining camp where the vegetation was overwhelming scattered pieces of rusty equipment and broken-down huts. We picked our way carefully, avoiding pitheads which were hidden by the undergrowth. A battered water-soaked sign hanging awry from one hinge read, "BEAUCHAMP & SMART – Number Four Mine." I didn't know we had come to the main shaft, but Bullah parted some bushes and said:

"This is it, Aron." I looked down and saw water-lilies and weeds growing over a surface of water fifteen feet below me, and I thought that my father, who had been born in the mist of the Mahaica swamps, must be at peace under there. I dropped a handful of pebbles into the water, hardly realising what I was doing. Bullah took off his straw hat and held it against his chest.

"Joe," he said, "me going to look out for you boy. Is not you first lend me the money to open me shop, Joe? And you help people left and right once they had trouble and they was near you and you had money. Me going to look out for Aron. Me promise you that, Joe."

"Let we go!" Santos said. "I don't like this place. Lord! It got spirit roaming all about me."

"The bodies never came up?" I asked Bullah.

"Not one. The river and the mine lock them up. You must come and talk to you Papa sometimes, boy, 'cause he 'prisoned up there with a lot of Chinese and he can't talk they language."

We returned to Bullah's shop and between us drank two bottles of rum. By late afternoon, a crowd of pork-knockers and a few women had gathered from the surrounding districts. They drank highwine and bush rum from half-pint tumblers and paid for their drinks with nuggets, gold dust or diamonds. Two men started a fight over a woman and Bullah settled it by knocking both of them down and throwing them out so quickly that, before I realised what had happened, the two were laid out on the grass outside with the dew cooling them off. I saw James Wellington sitting in a corner, looking very taciturn and brooding over his drink.

"Aye, James Wellington!" I said, going over to him. He looked up, and his lips barely twisted themselves before he raised his mug to me and emptied it.

"Is when you starting work, skipper?" he asked.

"Couple days' time, got to get a gang together. The bush is thick as mud all over the claim."

"Me will help you get couple pork-knockers together. Me know them all, who can work and who got sweet-skin."

"Bring them 'round tomorrow. We can meet here at the shop, and me and Bullah can look them over. You know Bullah?"

"If me James Wellington know Bullah Daniels? Me know Bullah since he boxer days. . . ."

"Then you should know my father – Joe Smart?"

"Me hear 'nough 'bout Joe Smart, but we track never cross."

I told Bullah about my conversation with James Wellington, and he said that the man was a good worker, but he kept himself to himself and in the twenty-odd years he had known him he had never found out what his story was.

Sixteen men came around to the shop on the following day and we picked ten of them.

The night before we started work I dreamt that I was a boy in Mahaica again, hunting in the swamps. I walked up to a cluster of lilies, but before I reached near them the earth suddenly swallowed them. I reached the spot and heard voices shouting under the water, the voices of a man and a woman, she was scolding him and he was laughing loud. They climbed out of the deep hole and came towards me and for a moment I thought that they were my father and mother. I ran towards them calling them by name, but as I drew near I discovered that they were headless and the laughter and talk were coming from a hole in the centre of their shoulders. I ran away from them in horror, and woke up in a cold sweat.

Work started on the claim. Santos and I agreed that we would split a half-share between us, whilst the other half would go to the ten men working for us.

Bullah and James had chosen the men well. Once work began the thought of striking it rich drove us as nothing else could have done. We worked from sun-up to sun-down, sweating, laughing, singing in a naked discordant chorus. After they had heard the story of my father, the men believed that I had inherited the magic of finding diamonds. They all owed Bullah for food and other supplies, and he had warned them that the first one to cross me would have to account to him.

Pork-knockers were a strange race of men. They took hardship and danger for granted, made and squandered fortunes, left the forest with thousands in their pockets swearing never to return, but they always came back, sometimes with only the shirts on their backs to call their own. They changed, but the dream which hounded them never did. When their credit ran out in one district they moved to another. They were very smart at getting credit from shop-owners, for every one of them had an eldorado up his sleeve when they were broke. Many of them had families on the coast, but the forest had its own codes, made its own demands, and for a pork-knocker to abandon wife and children, relatives close or distant, was as ordinary an occurrence as eating or sleeping. These men were adventurers. The forests, the rivers, the mountains, the high savannahs which stretched and tumbled, raised themselves to the sky or spread flat across the heart of a continent reduced men to the size of a speck of dust. But they saw themselves as giants subduing a wide world. They were heroes of big spaces. It never mattered to them what they were; it was how they saw themselves that counted. They had a lust for gold and diamonds, because, in searching for them, they could cut loose from everything that tied men down to life on the coast. During my first month with the pork-knockers, I realised that both Santos and I had too much of a sense of greed in our hearts, of a craving for security and order, to share the pork-knocker's dream wholeheartedly.

We broke up into two gangs of six men each. Santos was in charge of one and I, of the other. After digging two pits twenty-four by fourteen, and twelve feet deep, James Wellington and I took over the jigging. He was my immediate assistant, while Woody Sam, the most talkative man on the claim was Santos'. James and Woody brought boxes of sand, gravel and clay to the tom near the creek where I worked most of the time. The tom was a lightwood box eight feet by two and not very deep. The two men mashed the contents of their boxes until a muddy liquid dripped through holes in the bottom of the tom into another large, shallow box. I dipped this thick ooze with a baler and poured it into a sieve which I jigged over a waterhole, bringing the sand to the surface. Washing away the sand, I heard pebbles chattering like teeth in ague. With a quick action I shook the sieve again and again, so that if there were any diamonds they would settle in the middle.

The first glitter of a diamond which caught my eye made me shout and sing and hop around like a chicken on hot coals. The others stopped work to hold it up to the sun, feel it between their teeth, balance it in their palms. Woody Sam broke bottles of rum over the pits before work was started again.

"This is good indication," Woody said. "When you strike diamond at four o'clock you can never go wrong. That pay dirt got much to give yet."

"Woody got something there," a man said.

"That is rass-man talk," James growled and the men did not take him up.

By the end of the week the two pits yielded ten thousand dollars worth of diamonds. There wasn't much talking and laughing in the pits, for everyone worked harder and concentrated on the job, but in the afternoons, after a wash in the cool water above the Grass Fall, the pork-knockers would take turns to walk down the trail to Bullah's shop and bring back buckets of highwine and rum. I always felt sleepy as mud in the early evening, and sat close to the campfire picking ticks out of my skin and nodding every now and then. It surprised me that the others never seemed to be as tired as I was after a day's work, and once or twice when I fell asleep near the fire a pork-knocker woke me up and in a rough, good-natured voice pointed out that if I let the dew soak into my skin I would get pneumonia. But as time wore on I grew tougher, and joined the others in their revellings at night. The pork-knockers drank hard at nights and sweated the drinks out in sun and rain during the day. The highwine was so strong that the first few times I drank it my throat felt as if I had swallowed hot ashes the next morning. The others, however, drank it like water, and talked and played cards and danced late into the night. On the whole they were a strange group of men drawn from all parts of the country, having little in common apart from the dream of striking it rich. In their drunken sprees night after night, they cursed and fought one another like wild bulls on the Llanos. But for James Wellington some of the fights would have ended fatally, but although he drank heavily, he never got drunk. There was a savage calm about him when he parted a fight. He moved in swiftly, tore the contestants apart, and if they were foolish enough to turn on him, he knocked them down with short, perfectly timed punches. Listening to the talk around the camp fire, I found out that Mannie Ray had lost two fortunes in gold; Woody Sam swore that he was going to send money to his wife, but he never did; Old Man Galloway had not seen his wife and children on the coast for twenty years; Barnes had preached and prayed his way up and down the coast until he settled down with a woman who two-timed and ruined him; Lockjaw Kirton had been a sailor on schooners in the Caribbean and his ambition was to own a ship; Dead-an-'live Morrison had nearly been buried alive during an influenza epidemic; Ruction Daniel had been a trumpeter in the Salvation Army, but he had put the white Major's daughter in the family way and had to get out of town. Of the others

I remember little save that James Wellington and Paul Slowe said nothing, and we all knew that they had too much to tell.

Santos didn't like change, but once he was caught up in a new situation he fitted into it like a mango inside its skin. In a few months he became a pork-knocker, walking their languid, lean walk, talking like them, drinking, dancing, swaggering.

Because of this change in him our relationship grew strained. On Fridays I took the week's take of diamonds to Bullah's shop. He graded them, weighed them, and afterwards I shared them out, with the men watching me like condors. Bullah acted as my banker, but Santos kept his diamonds in the pouches of a belt which he wore next to his skin. On Saturday nights we trouped over to the shop and started a spree which ended on Monday morning. One Sunday morning I faced Santos across a table near the bar. The sunshine pouring through the window near us was like grit to his inflamed eyes. He tossed down three fingers of highwine, and I said,

"Watch yourself, Santos, boy; you drinking too hard."

"Who is you to tell me how much I must drink?" he shouted, pounding the table with his fist. "Look, small-boy, go and take a swim in the river. You think because you got book learning you can act like a white man!" He leaned forward and laughed in my face and the men at the other tables looked up. I felt the blood rush to my head.

"Watch your tongue, Santos! That small-boy talk doesn't go down so good any more," I said.

"Let me tell you something, small-boy. Drink or no drink, me can teach you a lesson with one hand tie behind me back."

"Just try!" I said, and he pushed the table away and stood over me. Bullah jumped over the counter and parted us.

"Santos," he said, "me going to give you a piece of advice. Don't come inside me shop to insult me friend, pardner, and don't even let me hear you insult him outside. Me know this boy father, but you don't even know who you father is, man. Take a piece of advice from Bullah Daniels. Let this boy be!"

"Is all right, Bullah. You don't see the man's so drunk he can hardly stand." My anger had passed and I offered Santos my hand, "Come on. Shake, pardner!" He ignored me and staggered out gripping a bottle of highwine.

"All of you 'gainst me! Is why all you 'gainst me!" he shouted.

"Watch that Santos!" Bullah said, following him with his eyes.

"The man's drunk, Bullah."

"Drunk man is a case of 'mouth open story jump out' boy. That nigger-man got something 'gainst you. Watch he! Don't trust you own mother in this bush, boy, me telling you."

"You'll see, Bullah. He'll make it up with both of us."

"Aron, you jus' like you Papa. You does take people jus' like you see them. But that Mr. Santos better don't make wrong move when Bullah Daniels 'round this Perenong waterfront or me will carry he to the cross sure as river does run to the sea."

"Me got news," Bullah said later on when we were sitting in the back room.

"Sound like you heard about a claim, Bullah," I said.

"Better news than that, boy. A boatload of woman coming from Georgetown soon. News gone abroad 'bout the diamond shout in Perenong and Capt'n Rhodius bringing a boatload to pick all you clean."

"They won't get much out of me, Bullah. I've got a girl."

"What kind of girl. She don't write you. How you know she not two-timing you?"

"She can't write, Bullah."

"Then she should get somebody to write for she."

"She's a good girl, Bullah, even if she don't write."

"Well, pardner, let we drink to she: What she name?"

"Belle. Just Belle. I don't know if she's got another name."

When I returned to camp Santos was snoring in his hammock, and next morning he woke and said that his head felt as if a tree had fallen on it.

"Sorry if me make trouble with you and Bullah," he said with his head sunk on his chest.

"It's all right by me, Santos, but you must make it up with Bullah. He was lil' upset."

"Me will go and see he later on."

"Let's go for a swim, Santos," I said, and he gripped his head with both hands, and turned it from side to side and shook it.

It was before sunrise and the men were groping about in the

mist, taking down their hammocks, lighting fires, taking out pots and pans to cook, and cleaning their tools.

"Coming, Woody?" I asked when we were passing the hut in which he and Marshall slept.

"Yes, skipper, but let me haul on me trousers." The three of us walked to the top of the Grass Fall where rocks encircled quiet pools, holding back the rush of water. It was safe swimming there, but at the bottom of the fall, perae fish and electric eels often lurked near the rocks. We were a long time swimming and splashing in the cool dark water and when we came out the sun was over the trees. On our way back I saw a rainbow boa coiled around a branch which hung over the trail. Santos took my gun from me and shot it through the head. It tumbled to the ground writhing and slashing out with its tail and when it lay still I skinned it.

"Is bad luck to kill them snake," Woody said. "You mark my word. When you shoot them camoodie it means a man in the camp going to die."

"The skin will make pretty shoes for my girl, Woody," I said, but he kept muttering all the way back.

"Is bad luck. Me don't like look for trouble."

In the weeks that followed, things went back to normal between Santos and me. At nights we swapped stories about the doctor and Indra, Mrs. Ram and Martha. It always surprised me that Santos remembered every detail about these people, while to me the whole experience of living with them seemed so remote. Bullah's warning about Santos made me observe him more closely than I had ever done before. Living close to him, listening to his conversations with the pork-knockers and seeing the way he was always willing to side with them against me even in little things, I began to realise that he was jealous of me. No matter how he tried to hide it, he was envious of me, of the way Mr. Beauchamp, the doctor, Bullah, treated me. He was one of those people who needed envy to keep him alive. He let it grow on him, and enjoyed the pleasure of its poisoning his relationship with those closest to him. I could not take his easy laughter, his banter, his amusing stories at face value any longer. My eyes never left him while he worked in the pit. My suspicions had come to me suddenly, but somehow all that had happened in the past, incidents I had overlooked, strengthened the doubts I felt.

At twenty feet both pits began to yield larger stones, and we worked with a subdued excitement. The pork-knockers settled down to a routine of concentrated work. As they worked they talked about how they were going to spend their time in Georgetown, about their past experience with city women, and about the many occasions on which they had just missed striking it rich. Only James Wellington remained silent, answering questions about himself shortly, so as to discourage further ones. When he went to Bullah's shop he stood in a corner by the bar drinking slowly, thoughtfully, and after finishing two bottles of highwine, he left. I often saw him perched on a rock near the creek looking down at the water for hours on end.

On the moonlight nights the camp pulsated with music. Lockjaw Kirton played a guitar and Galloway a drum while the others improvised instruments – Fry's Cocoa tins with pebbles in them served as maracas, a cow horn with tissue paper glued to the larger end, as a saxophone, a sawn-off kerosene drum, as the bass. Another musical instrument was made by fitting a smooth, arched piece of wood around a drum. A piece of cork fitting tight to the mouth of an empty bottle was then rubbed up and down the bow of wood.

As soon as the orchestra struck up a tune pork-knockers began shuffling slowly around the fire, warming to the rhythm. The music grew livelier and other musicians joined in with mouth-organs, tinkling spoons, pieces of iron clinking together and drums. Rising above the beat of river shanties and songs from the coast was the droning of Grass Fall.

I often joined in the dancing. The rhythms were so catching that feet picked themselves up, and limbs loosened themselves, and laughter jumped out of mouths. The moonlight and firelight gave each dancer a shadow for a partner. Santos was the best dancer of us all. He moved with speed and fury, and when the music took hold of him his body was no longer flesh and bone, but fire and wind. The musicians, sensing a kindred spirit, played only for him. As he danced he became a leaf spinning downwards from a tall tree, wind rolling and racing across high savannah grass, a tongue of surf reaching up a beach slowly, before it raced backwards.

Night after night the music, the moonlight, the dancing the echoes from the fall filled our hearts with such particular gladness that if we had found a mountain of diamonds it could not have given us as much pleasure.

And when the dark nights came I listened to the noises of the Mazaruni – the ooskudo owl hooting, the death-cry of a frog caught by a snake, the hoofbeats of deer running past the camp, and the wind in the forest.

In the wet season there was the muffled droning of rain, thunder bursting inside your head and lightning splitting giant trees.

★ ★ ★

We found a forty-carat blue diamond one afternoon and immediately ordered four cases of whisky from Bullah's. The sun couldn't set quickly enough that day. Darkness fell and we ringed the camp with lanterns. Pork-knockers from other districts came to celebrate with us. The night was filled with a chorus of drunken shouts, music, and the clinking of whisky bottles against the edge of enamel cups. Towards midnight the fête ran dry, and Woody and Galloway went to the shop for more liquor. Kirton was raving drunk. He smashed two lanterns and nearly caught himself afire. Wellington, Santos and I tried to hold him down, but he broke away and ran towards the creek. I nearly caught up with him on the creek bank, but I stumbled and fell, and he plunged in. Woody shone a torch on him and shouted:

"Come out, sailor-Kirton! That creek full of eel! Come on out, man. You want to kill youself?" Kirton swam across the creek, ran down the bank and plunged in again. The light followed him as he swam towards us. He had so much whisky in him it was a wonder that he didn't sink. He was in the middle of the creek when we heard him shout. I saw his eyes big and white with terror against the dark water. The electric eel struck and struck again. Wellington ran along the creek towards a boat, jumped in and rowed towards Kirton. He reached out for him, but an electric shock flung him back. The big eel swam round and round Kirton until he disappeared. Marshall came back nursing an arm.

"Me get the shock indirect," he said.

"Me tell you 'bout that snake," Woody said. "Every time you kill one the bush does claim a man."

"You can't go before you time," Marshall said.

The news made all the drunken pork-knockers sober.

"That diamond got death in it," one said.

"Don't talk stupid," Santos said. "Mantop does fix He own time."

They found Kirton's body floating down the Mazaruni between Perenong and Kamakusa. There wasn't much left of him, and they buried him on the river bank near a spot where the body was found. We searched his belongings for letters with the address of any relatives, but there were none, so we sent them, with his share of diamonds, to the Police Station at Kamakusa.

"They should 'ave let he bones roll all the way down to the sea," Woody said. "He was a sailorman."

★ ★ ★

Pork-knockers, like sailors, sometimes live without women for years on end. During their long, lonely spells they live on past memories, telling every detail of their meetings with whores in the city, repeating the same stories so often that you come to know the women – what they looked like, how they talked, how it felt to run your hands over their flesh.

When news of a boatload of women coming to Perenong reached the pork-knockers, the camp was caught up in a fever of preparations. Stolen diamonds were taken out and examined openly, flannels, salara shirts, and bright scarves were fished out of the bottom of canisters, shoes polished and it was agreed that if there were not enough women to go around on the first night they would have to be auctioned off to the highest bidders.

Ruction Daniel, who had a reputation as a sweet-man, tried on his outfit the morning before the women arrived. He put on his two-toned shoes and suddenly started rolling in the grass howling. We were all alarmed until he pulled one shoe off and saw a macushi ant clinging to his big toe. The pork-knockers danced about and roared with laughter, and Daniel was quiet and surly for the whole day.

The women arrived on Saturday afternoon and the pork-knockers turned out in numbers to greet them at the Perenong landing. The men were dressed in bright silk and salara shirts, doeskin flannels, and scarves with diamond pins stuck in them. Their feet, widened by the constant need to grip bare earth, were locked up in expensive shoes. Santos, as one of the leading claim-holders, stood in front of the crowd, and every now and then he strutted to the end of the landing and scanned the river.

Gunfire and shouts greeted the *Sun Girl* as she rounded a bend in the river and came in sight. The boat pulled in, and the men acted like boys, showing off, jostling, shouting, making obscene antics, treading on one another's sore feet in the rush to help the women ashore. Bullah and I, with Tonic on a stool behind us, stood by the shop door. But for the natural good humour of both men and women there would have been a riot. Captain Rhodius, squat and thick-limbed like most river captains, led his charges up the path to the shop, bellowing at the crowd to make way. His laughing, loudmouthed bevy in rainbow colours followed behind, keeping the pork-knockers at bay with abuse, cuffs, kicks and ringing slaps. I recognised Belle towering above the others. A man tried to embrace her, she punched him in the stomach, and he folded up while the others laughed but kept their distance.

"That's my girl!" I said to Bullah.

"Which one, boy?"

"The tall one in the white dress. You see how she's like a queen!"

"Well, go on to her, pardner! The girl come all this way and all you doing is standing up here talking. Go on, man!"

"Belle!" I shouted, "Belle!"

"Shark! Lord bless me eyesight!"

"Belle, you came!"

"I tell you I was going to come, Shark."

"But I wrote you and you didn't answer."

"Me can't write, Shark, and I couldn't tell me story to nobody to write down for me. I get a white man to read you letter to me, an educated white man. I wanted the words to sound good. And the white man say you write good, that you know how to put word down on paper."

"Come and meet my friend Bullah. The man knew my father

and he looked out for me well since I came this way." I took her to Bullah and he laughed his deep belly laugh and embraced her.

"So you is the samba gal me boy get typee for. He tell me you was like a queen. Well, you more than a queen, gal."

"You got a lot of sweet talk in you mouth, but me like you." Belle gave him a loud kiss on the forehead and the pork-knockers cheered.

"The old man still got a lot of stuff lef' in he," one of them said and Belle's laughter sounded like music to me.

I introduced her to Tonic, and Woody Sam, and James Wellington, and Santos came up.

"You remember Santos?"

"If me 'member, Santos? Is not he bring we together?" We went inside the shop. The other women were surrounded by admirers who were vying to buy them the most expensive drinks – whisky, *crème de menthe*, champagne – fifteen to seventy dollars a bottle; an hour's, a day's, a year's work, according to a man's luck.

"Is how things going, Shark?" Belle asked. Bullah had gone into the store room to fetch a special bottle of *crème de menthe*. Santos wrapped his arms around a brown-skinned girl and kissed her on the ear. She wriggled and laughed and bit him on the cheek.

"I'm making money, Belle, but it's lonely here, gal."

"You remember me, Shark? You think 'bout me some time?"

"You will ask that, gal? I used to think 'bout you, remember how you skin felt that night, an when I thought that somebody else might be passing their hands over it I wanted to come back to you like a streak of arrow."

"Shark, you does talk some wild story, boy." She stood close to me with her breasts pouting near to my chest. I had seen a jaguar crossing a trail ahead of me one morning, and Belle had the same untamed energy under a silky skin. Her coarse black hair, her wide eyes and high cheekbones betrayed her Amerindian blood. Her face was oval with a wide forehead, her nostrils wide and shapely, sensitive to every breath and mood and her heavy lips parted easily to show teeth as white as tiger orchids. Her shoulders were wide, her arms muscular, but her hands were delicate and in her limbs was the secret fire that Negro limbs possess giving them the power to saunter sloth-like, or to explode into movement like a mad wind.

"Belle, why you picked me of all people?" I asked suddenly and she laughed.

"Shark, me know men, all kind of men, all colour, that's why me pick you, boy."

"Tell me more, Belle, that not enough?" She touched my face, ran her fingers along my cheek and round my chin.

"I will show you, Shark. Me don't spin words out like you, boy."

The shop was crowded and the spree well under way. I could sense the release of pent-up feelings in the pork-knockers' voices, their violent antics and the vibrations of their sweating bodies. Bullah had hired James Wellington to help behind the counter for the weekend. There were many fights, but Bullah never let them get too far. He broke them up before they inspired a more general anger. Belle complained that she was tired and Bullah gave us his room for the night and promised to rent us a cottage on the hill overlooking the shop. We fell asleep to the sound of drunken voices and the banging of enamel mugs.

A shaft of sunshine slanted over our bed next morning and Belle stretched and moved her fingers up and down the hollow of my back. I had drunk too much the night before and could hardly open my eyes.

"Shark, you will never be a drinker," she said.

"I know; but I'm always following the crowd."

"Let we go and swim in the river."

"Not around here, gal. Top of the fall is better."

We found Bullah sitting on the doorstep picking his teeth with an acouri thorn.

"All you sleep well?" he asked.

"Sleep like a top," Belle said and she excused herself and went inside to fetch something.

"Come sit near me, boy," Bullah said spitting expertly over the banister. "You know me see a lot in me time. Bullah Daniels had he share of woman; 'though me never marry, if me and Solomon take count me won't come off so bad. You know Bullah is you friend, boy? Well, take a piece of advice: cage up that bird-of-paradise; you got something good there."

"Like you giving he advice," Belle said from the doorway.

"The boy like me own flesh and blood, Queen."

"Shark got good ways, but if he don't look out people will take advantage of he."

"He tell you 'bout that nigger-man, Santos?"

"I was going to tell her later on, Bullah," I said, but he continued:

"That man up to no good."

"Me don't know if Shark tell you, but me spirit didn't take to he from the start. But me is a woman who don't carry malice long, and when me think that is Santos bring we together me does feel thankful to the man."

"He got plans and scheme, and he don't mean no good, Queen. Bullah Daniels see a lot of folks come and go in he time. Some of them had two face and some of them three, some of them had birdseed in they mouth and talk more sweeter than tinamou can sing. No, Queen, people can't fool Bullah no more."

"I've been watching him, Bullah," I said.

"Jus' keep on watching, boy; that Santos is a deep one. Me got a man in he gang who owe me plenty and me warn he to keep a lookout too."

"Bullah, is why you don't leave this place and settle down in town, man? You don't get lonely?" Belle asked.

"Me try to cut away couple time, Queen, but me couldn't. After a couple month me come right back. You see, me don't have a chick or a chile, and this place creep in me blood. Bullah Daniels going to stay right here, and when the Good Lord call he they can lay he bones under that kakarali tree by the waterside."

We sat in silence for a while and heard Tonic whistling in the kitchen.

"By the way, Shark, me forget to tell you, a man join the boat at Bartica and he say he is you fam'ly," Belle said.

"What kind of man?"

"Medium black with big eye; say he name was Richard Dolly. He was making up to me, asked if I didn't 'member he when he was road overseer, but I didn't 'member at all."

"Lord, Lord, he's my uncle! Well, I declare, Uncle Richard making hot-foot for the bush! His luck must have run out on the coast. . . ."

"And what is more, when the rum go to he head the night we spend in Kamakusa me hear he talking 'bout Santos."

"But I'm sure he and Santos never met. Santos would have told me."

"Don't be too sure, pardner," Bullah said. "I tell you that nigger-man deep and contrary. Jus' keep you eye open wide."

"Food ready!" Tonic said, looking at us sideways from the doorway.

"Tonic calling for food, and he is a man does get vex if he cooking cool too long."

"How long Tonic been with you, Bullah?" Belle asked on our way inside.

"Me find he wandering 'bout the street of Bartica when he was twelve, and me brought he back with me lean and maugre as a stray dog. Tonic is a good boy. He don't smile 'cause smiling does make he face all twist up and lopsided, but he got a kind heart and he's a real bushman; he can walk you from here to Roraima with he eye shut."

After breakfast Belle and I went to the pool above the Grass Fall. We spent hours swimming or lying naked on the rocks. I gathered bunches of wild flowers and covered Belle with them. Twenty yards from us the water tumbled steeply, changing from dark amber to a foaming white. We played childish games and nearly burst our sides laughing when a river fly lighted on the tip of Belle's nose or a kingfisher swooped down to snatch a fish, and a harpie eagle dived like a stone hurled from the sky and chased the kingfisher away. Belle plunged into the clear water and sat cross-legged on the white sand at the bottom looking up at me. I leaned over the rocks and made faces at her until she came up laughing and spluttering. When we were tired she sang love-songs to me, making up the words as she went along.

"Belle," I said turning over to look at her as she lay with wild flowers heaving on her stomach and a purple orchid between her breasts, "Belle, I feel good, better than I ever felt before."

"I feel clean," she said, "as if the water and the air and the sweetness of you wash away all the sweat of them man who did lie on top me night after night."

"Belle, I'll make you a queen. Look. I'll put this crown of orchids on your head. See how good it fits you head, gal. Belle, you must be an orchid and I'll be a tree and you can wrap 'round me and never let go 'till I die."

"Shark, nobody never talk to me like that. Me feel good too, boy; never feel like this before. You know, Shark, me nearly ten years older than you and sometimes it does worry me that me might grow old too quick. . . ."

"I swear I'll never want any girl but you, Belle. . . ."

"Shark, you don't know enough 'bout life and woman. . . ."

"I know you, Belle, and that's all I ever want to know."

We moved into Bullah's cottage on the hill late that afternoon and the next day I went back to work. The pork-knockers, encouraged by Santos, tantalised me about my lovesick state.

"Skipper, this typee knock you hard, man!"

"Pardner, you can't see diamond today, you head too high up in the clouds."

"Skipper, with a queen like that, me don't blame you."

Belle brought me luck. That week we found two large diamonds and I gave her the larger as a present. In the evenings I walked up the path to the cottage with my head full of dreams, and my eyes searching the veranda for Belle or gazing at the yellow daisies, the wild azaleas, the sunflowers striping parched grassy slopes in the soft afterglow. Giant moras and kakaralis flung long shadows across the thatched roof of the cottage and downhill towards the creek.

Belle decorated the cottage with ocelot, monkey-skin accouri, and baboon rugs, and bamboo curtains. The people who lived there before us, a succession of whores and pork-knockers, had never really lived there, they had merely inhabited a part of it, sheltered, cooked, ate and slept, and then they had gone their way. But Belle turned the cottage into a home, gave it the feel of a place where a man and woman could live and bring up a family.

Night after night, Bullah, Santos, James Wellington, Woody Sam and Ruction Daniel visited us. They didn't only come to drink and gaff; they came to sniff and savour the atmosphere of the coast which Belle had brought with her, the atmosphere of domesticity which they had once known and had forgotten.

We were all awkward at first, talking in voices too loud or too hushed, saying the wrong things and groping for the right ones, and I often thought of Brother C. and Tanta Moore and would swear to write and send them some money, but I never did. After a time it became easier for us and the cottage rocked with laughter and music and loud talk.

"Belle," I said one night after the others had left. "I like being alone sometimes, gal. When these people keep coming every night like this we don't have time to ourselves. I've got some books in my canister which I never even opened. You brought me peace and I can't enjoy it." She laughed standing with arms akimbo and legs apart, and she tossed her head back.

"You en't full up you head with enough book-story, boy! Is better to live than to read the white man book, 'cause what you read in the book does only make you feel good, while when you got drink and people 'round, we all does enjoy weself."

"You don't understand, Belle. When you read books, then you have more to talk about to other people."

"All them book in Georgetown put together don't have half the story that people does live. Chu! Life too short to worry 'bout white man book. Me meet enough white man in me time and they want the same thing from me like everybody else."

One night Bullah arrived early, breathing hard after his walk up the hill.

"Me got news, Shark!" We were eating and Belle offered him some peas and rice and salt pork. "Me didn't come to eat, mind you, but the queen got a sweet hand and even if me full up to me ears me can't say no."

"Is good news or bad?" Belle asked when he sat down at the table and began shovelling the food into his mouth.

"Depend on how you look at it, Queen," he said, swallowing a mouthful which made his Adam's apple jump.

"Let us hear the news, Bullah. Man, my stomach's full enough to stand anything."

"You notice Santos didn't turn up last night?" He lowered his voice and looked around. "Well, me had a man shadowing he all the way to Oronopai, and the nigger-man meet with you uncle and the two of them pow-wow with they head so close you couldn't pass grass between them."

"Like me got to take a hand in this," Belle said.

"Stay out of this gal. Bullah and me can handle it."

"The man didn't hear what they talk 'bout, but he say they talk plenty."

"Don't sound too good," Belle said.

"Santos got scheme, but me hope he know what he doing 'cause this bush big and wide and a lot of smart-man get tangle up here."

"I wonder if it's not better to go and meet Uncle Richard face to face. If he didn't want me to know he was about, he wouldn't have spoken to Belle like he did."

"Don't talk stupid, Shark. Me love you, but me won't fool meself that you is a champion schemer. When you got enemy is better if they think you foolish."

"Listen to the queen, boy. Let Mr. Santos make he move first. We can wait."

The others came later with a full orchestra, and the noise burst out of the hut and echoed through the forest. The musicians sweated under the petrol lamp, their eyes glazed, and their feet tapping the floor. Santos moved to the centre of the room and we made way for him. When the music took hold of him he whirled like a hummingbird, and Belle jumped into the ring and faced him, her shoulders shaking as if she had ague.

"Dance me, big girl, dance me!" Santos shouted and she stalked him and circled him, moving to the rhythm of Galloway's drum.

Old man Galloway saw that it was a contest in which the two dancers would fuse and burst apart, sway, and leap and spin, until the will to dance fled their bodies and left them exhausted. He was a zombie god controlling their every movement as he thumped and caressed the tight goatskin of his drum. Belle's eyes burned bright as fireflies, and her dancing had a sinuous strength to it, while Santos was all speed and grace. Insects flew around the lamp, burnt their wings on the shade, and fell in heaps on the floor. We stood around the dancers, chanting and clapping and urging them on.

The pork-knockers were mesmerised by the movements of Belle's body, and I could hear them breathing hard. The drumbeats raced like water tumbling down a fall, faster and faster. Old man Galloway stood up and circled the dancers, his body moving with rhythmic jerks, and Daniel followed him with his bamboo flute. The dancers embraced, separated, embraced again, and suddenly they parted and the two fell down laughing, but exhausted. The pork-knockers would have pounced on Belle like studs worked up to a frenzy, but Bullah and I stood over her and kept them at bay until their frenzies cooled and they crept away shamefacedly.

★ ★ ★

We worked down to the bottom of the layers of gravel in the two pits and struck rock, and we started digging new ones. With the rainy season due in a couple of months we started work on three pits instead of two. Woody Sam worked with me and I put James Wellington in charge of the third pit which was near to a kakarali tree. As soon as we broke through the katch-kaow we struck a layer of gravel which yielded so many diamonds that I could hardly hold the sieve straight as I jigged.

"Double shares today!" I shouted, holding out some stones in the palm of my hand, watching them glitter in the sun.

"Double shares and a spree tonight!" We worked in a fury.

The only sounds from the pits were the rap of shovels against stones, the thud of crowbars striking the katch-kaow, of picks biting into the gravel, the grunts of men lifting heavy boxes. The sun was directly overhead and all around us were dark islands of shadow and bright ones of sunlight. A marudi, high up in the branches of the kakarali tree under which James Wellington was working, uttered raucous cries.

"Don't dig so close to that kakarali tree!" Woody shouted to James Wellington, but he didn't even look up and I saw his shoulder muscles coiling and glistening in the shallow pit.

"I can watch out for meself," Wellington said as he passed a full box of gravel to Daniel. But Woody walked over and inspected the tree.

"Let we haul the tree down, James," he said. "These kakarali does have a big main root and they does tumble easy."

"I finding diamond like fire, man. Ask the skipper. You think

I going to lef' off now to haul any tree down. You look and see, I going to take all the gravel from 'round this kakarali root and lef' it stand up straight," Wellington said, and Woody walked away grumbling that diamonds can make sane people mad.

The marudi shrieked and flew away and a pork-knocker cried out:

"Oh, God! Oh, Jesus Christ!" We ran over to Wellington's pit; he was bent in half with the weight of the tree on his back.

"James! James, say something, man!" There was no answer. When we scopped James Wellington out blood was pouring from his eyes, ears, nose and mouth. He had been killed instantly. We wrapped his body in jute bags and carried it back to camp. I left Santos and Woody Sam in charge and walked over to Bullah's shop.

"Give me a bottle of highwine, Tonic!" I said and when he hesitated, I shouted, "Hurry up, for Jesus' sake, man!" Bullah came out.

"Eh, eh, boy. You and the queen had quarrel?" I swallowed a mug of highwine before answering.

"I killed James Wellington. . . . a hundred carats for a man's life. . . . The white man killed two hundred and one and I kill one. But this was a man like meself, a cocoa-brown man. . . ."

"Tell me what happen, boy. You eye look so wild and you face look like everything inside you draw tight. Tell me what happen."

"Is James. . . He was killed. . . He was working too near to a kakarali tree and it mashed him up. . . . Is my fault, Bullah. . . I never. . . I didn't even say a word to stop him. . . ."

"Don't talk stupid, boy. Anybody ever tell you this bush life was easy, that man does dig gold and diamond out the ground without trouble ? If Bullah Daniels tell you all the thing he see you will fill up a dry river with you crying, man."

"But he died so quick. . . died for nothing, I tell you."

"He take he chance like everybody else."

We found a letter in James Wellington's pocket. It was from his wife and it said:

> DEAR JAMES, – You been away two year less two month now and the children keep asking about you coming back

until I sick of putting them off is when you coming man for God sake write and tell me. Is always next month when the rainy season finish when the dry season start but two year short two month come and gone and next month not here yet. The good Lord make it so that the law say husband and wife and children must live together but he make it diffrent for we. James Wellington when I marry you I know you had the bush tie up in you belly but I thought I could root it out and Jesus Heself know how I try but was no use you going to live and die there and we going to live and die here. For God sake man come home and see you children face. Dorothy and Jonas going to school rain and shine and they giving me enough trouble the las money you send reach me fine for God sake James come home.

Your ever loving wife,

JOYCELYN.

We held a wake for James Wellington and the pork-knockers and the women danced, and sang hymns, and drank buckets of highwine. Because he had been a hard drinker in his time the pork-knockers poured highwine into the dead man's mouth until it overflowed.

"Drink, James, drink and make you entrance to Heaven or Hell in you cups, pardner," they said after every round. The wake lasted until morning, and when the sun was high, we buried the dead man near the spot where he had often sat gazing at the water. Bullah read a few verses from the Bible and we lowered the crabwood coffin and covered it with earth and stones. Belle and the other women bawled so loudly, crying out to Jesus to witness their sorrow, that no one heard Bullah.

"Come home and rest today, Shark," Belle said after the funeral.

"It's better to work, Belle."

"Shark, this thing upset you. Leave the diamond for a day and let the dew wash away the blood for another night."

"For God's sake leave me alone, Belle. It's my lookout if I work 'till I drop."

"The boy upset, Queen. He en't got pork-knocker stomach yet," Bullah said.

"He don't have to talk to me like I is he enemy," Belle said, flouncing away.

We went back to work and Santos broke a bottle of rum over James Wellington's pit.

"You claim one life, you not going to claim no more," he said.

We raised three thousand dollars between us and sent the money to Mrs. Wellington and her two children.

The pork-knockers found it ironical that death should cut a man off from his dreams of wealth, his friends and his family. To most of them it only meant that a man had dropped out of the carnival crowd. Death made them uneasy but not sad, for they knew the risks a pork-knocker had to run, and accepted them, for they were born gamblers.

James Wellington had meant very little to me while he was alive. He had been a silent man who did his job well. He would have gone his way after the claim was worked out and I might never have set eyes on him again, I told myself. But I kept seeing images of him in my mind. I remembered the way he had of standing so still that I had to notice him, and when he moved, he did so deliberately as if a dynamo inside him controlled his ropy muscles. Perhaps my youth died with James Wellington, and some of the romantic visions I still clung to were stripped away. His death made me see myself as I was – an ambitious, selfish individual who had been helped by many people but who had helped no one in return. This self-knowledge changed my attitude to those closest to me. I saw Belle as a woman with great warmth, generous and ready to share everybody's trouble. On the other hand, I felt somehow that she had taken to the streets not only because of poverty, but because she needed the attention of many men. Part of her love for me came from a desire to live a respectable life, but her flesh and spirit had strong cravings and I could not tell what she would do in the future. And Bullah I saw as a middle-aged man whose spirit had battered against many years. He had found his little nook and had accepted what he was. He could afford to help others because his feet were planted on the earth and nothing could uproot him.

I realised, too, that I was no better than the white man who had caused my father's death. I could have warned Wellington, but I had hesitated because the diamonds were rolling in. I knew that the white man had done this thing, and I had also done it, but I did not have his sense of conscience. I would not go up and down the coast to look for Wellington's wife and children, for in a few months time I would forget all about them. If they had been nearby I would have given them all I had in the first flush of my guilt, but I was a man who went with the tide and I seldom looked back. I asked myself: "Who is the better man, the white man or me?" and I could not answer the question.

⋆ ⋆ ⋆

Belle had to be amused all the time or else she felt caged and restless. I was able to live by myself much more than she was. She had to have company all the time, men and women to gaff and gossip and laugh. When we had to be alone together I could sense the restlessness in her, and it made me irritable, and after a while things would become strained. We had been alone all Sunday and I sat out on the veranda reading, while she came out of the living-room occasionally to look down the trail for any visitors.

"How much money you got, Shark?" she asked, and from the tone of her voice I knew that she wanted to start an argument.

"Over fifty thousand."

"Me could make that much in six months in these parts." I knew that I should not have taken her on, but the words came out before I could check them:

"By whoring about the place? I thought you told me you'd turned your back on your old life, gal?"

"If you use that word one more time, Shark, me will walk out of this house, boy."

"Which word?"

"You know very well which word me mean. You might play stupid sometime but you don't fool me."

"Stupid! So you mean I'm stupid." I was angry and didn't care how much of a row we got into.

"You talking fool-talk, Shark."

"I said you were whoring 'bout the place and it's true."

"Me warning you, Aron Smart. . . or whatever you name is, me warning you," she said quietly and the hurt in her voice made me feel bad.

"I'm sorry, Queen. I didn't mean to hurt you, gal. I need you.

You don't understand? You alone can make me feel like a proper person, not frightened to look at myself, not wanting money. . . ."

"Talk, talk talk! A lot of big mouth word! Me living closer to you than the smell of you sweat, Shark, and me can feel you changing. At first was all love-talk, but now you does get crotchety and sometimes you can't bear the sight of me. Me does think. . ."

"Don't say any more, Belle. Listen to me. . . ."

"No, Shark, me must get this off me chest. Bullah and me talk the other day 'bout you, and he say, 'The boy changing; he growing up. You got to 'low he chance to knock he head 'gainst the tree trunk like everybody else?' But me getting older, Shark." Most of this was true, but Belle had a woman's instinct to make a great ballad out of a story when she knew that I was in the wrong. She sat down heavily and continued in a low voice: "Is better if me get an old man to settle with. Young man like you with they head full-up with book-story does live in different world. The time going to come when me must make up me mind, Shark, and Jesus in Heaven know which way me will jump."

"Belle, I love you, gal. I'll die if you leave me. I need you, Belle. I love you." I knelt down beside her and put my arms around her waist. I tried to kiss her, but she jerked her head away. I held her face between my hands and kissed her eyes and cheeks, and she held me close against her and burst into tears.

"Shark, me love you too. Me love the mud you walk on."

"I'll give a big party for your birthday next week, Belle. Spread the news from here to Oronopai. We'll give the pork-knockers something to sing about."

* * *

The pay from the new pits was fabulous, and news of a shout spread all the way to Bartica. I staked out claims on both banks of the Perenong Creek, and Bullah sent Tonic downriver to Kamakusa to register my claims before pork-knockers started descending like mosquitoes. Tonic reached Kamakusa a few hours ahead of Santos. Rumour said that I was finding diamonds big as coconuts, and Bullah encouraged them because legends of my rich strikes brought trade to his shop, and life to Perenong which the settlement had not seen since Mr. Beauchamp imported the two hundred Chinese miners. Bullah said that I had made the richest strike since Pidgeon Island Brown, a man the pork-knockers sang about in their shanties. The songs said that he had found so much gold that he had roofed his house with gold sovereigns and papered its walls with five-dollar bills, wrapped cigars in hundred-dollar bills, and scattered gold dust and nuggets over the drive that led to his house. Bullah rechristened me Ocean Shark, the diamond king of Perenong, and Galloway composed a shanty:

Ocean Shark is king ah man
Is king ah man in Perenong
He throw he diamond down a trail
To light he way to Ikowan
He light he way to Ikowan with diamond.

I began to dress like a diamond king, to wear silk shirts and doeskin flannels, a white broad-rimmed velour hat, a silk scarf with a twenty-carat diamond stuck in the knot, deer- or snakeskin shoes, and a diamond ring on each finger.

"You making a fool of youself to show off on these nigger-people," Belle said, but she enjoyed the glory which was heaped on me and which she was sharing.

Santos didn't like all this because he felt that he was part-owner of the claim and the pork-knockers had overlooked him to crown me king. I walked into the shop the night before Belle's birthday and Bullah jumped up on the counter and shouted:

"Let we drink to the King of Perenong!" Mugs and glasses were raised and shouting, stamping men and women shook the shop on its high stilts. Santos was standing by the bar just under Bullah and he didn't join in the toast.

"Eh, eh, Santos," I said. "You not drinking to your pardner, man?" I was flushed and excited and wanted to pick a row with him. I had been jealous the night he danced with Belle and the thought of it still rankled.

"I will drink who I want to drink to."

"Don't talk to me in that big-big tone, boy. You come a long way. Don't forget I knew you when you were chauffeuring for twenty dollars a month."

"Is you better not forget that you was the doctor kiss-arse boy who come from a breakdown village."

"I brought you here when you didn't have a red cent to call your own, boy, don't forget."

"Is since when a dull-time king like you can bring any body anywhere!" A crowd had gathered around us, and the men and women took sides and started their own quarrels.

"You should know 'bout dull-time kings, Santos!" I shouted and the crowd laughed. Bullah came up and pushed me aside.

"You in the wrong, Shark, and me can't side with you. Is you start the row." He pushed me to the far end of the bar and whispered, "Not now, man. Don't expose you hand now."

The quarrel soured the whole evening for me and I drank heavily. Later, when Belle arrived, I stood on a table and shouted at the top of my voice:

"Tomorrow is the queen birthday and everybody's welcome on the hill. Come early, keep you throats dry and you stomach's empty, 'cause it's going to be a big-time fête!"

It was open house on the hill from early morning on Saturday. Pork-knockers stopped in on their way to work bringing gifts of whisky, rum, money, gold and diamonds, and had a few drinks before they left. Claim-holders from as far as Kamakusa had come for the fête and some of the newcomers sat on the veranda with Bullah and me all day long drinking and gaffing. Tonic and Woody Sam removed spiders, cobwebs, marabunta nests, and scorpions from the roof and Tonic caught a rat snake in the thatch. He held it just below the head, and it coiled around his wrist and arm and he took it outside and set it free. Belle hung streamers of orchids and wild flowers from the rafters, and made pleasing designs on the bamboo curtains with balsa flowers, giant azaleas, wild daisies and croton leaves. Woody took cases of drink down to the creek and, securing them with vines, let them sink to the bottom to keep cool. A few of the women had come to help Belle, and they laughed and gossiped as they cooked meat under hot stones, baked unleavened bread and prepared huge pots of rice and curried rabbit in the kitchen.

The claim-holders were all men of Bullah's generation who had either known my father personally or had heard about him.

They relaxed in cane chairs on the veranda and drank as if they were determined to consume all the drinks in Perenong before they left. Ezekiel, a big, rough-hewn man, was a famous cricketer who had levelled a hill at Oronopai to lay out a pitch.

"You don't play cricket, Shark?" he asked. "'Cause you old man used to bowl thunderbolt in he time and he could knock a ball over a mora tree."

"I used to play bat-and-ball with a coconut branch bat and a balata ball," I said.

"Must invite all you to a match at Oronopai before the rainy season. You still up to a game, Bullah?"

"How you can ask that, Zik? Last time me come you way me knock-up twenty runs before all you umpire thief me out."

"Gold price falling," Benson said. He wasn't going to get caught up in cricket talk, because Bullah and Zik had a feud which had been going on for years. Benson was a fat, brown man. The top of his bald head was sunburnt, but his face was pale and he had a bulb of flesh behind his neck. "You lucky, pardner," he said to me. "They tell me you reaping diamond like fire."

"Luck's got two faces, Ben. One will laugh with you and same time the other one's laughing at you," I said.

"You talking old-man talk, Shark," Joe Scotland said. He had once been a teacher and he still dressed like one, wearing a white drill suit and a tie.

"The boy read plenty book," Bullah said. He never missed an opportunity to boast about my education.

"I would have been a schoolmaster by now if I had stayed teaching," Scotty said.

"Scotty, man, you love woman and rum too much to be schoolmaster," Zik said, and the conversation switched to mining; the prices gold and diamonds were fetching in Georgetown; the latest shouts near the Brazilian border, where pork-knockers were finding so many nuggets in a single day that they couldn't lift the day's takings by themselves; the accident at Tumatumari, where Captain Pye's motor had cut off topside the fall and he and forty-five passengers had been drowned.

When pork-knockers got together to catch a gaff it always ended up with somebody spinning out a ballad about some awful happening in the bush. Ben tossed a drink down and cleared his throat.

"All you know a man name Tengar?" he asked, as if he expected us to know this man in the same way as we knew who the King of England was, or who Pidgeon-Island Brown was. But none of us had ever heard about Tengar. Bullah knew that once Ben started a story there was no stopping him, and he tried to change the topic.

"Me en't see Santos whole day," he said.

"He brought a gift for the queen this morning and said he was going back to camp to make preparations for the fête," I said. Ben cleared his throat louder and continued:

"This man Tengar come and work for me couple month at Oronopai and the man tell me a story that make me head buzz and me hair stand up."

"But you en't got no hair to talk 'bout, Ben," Zik said.

"Is not only on you head you does have hair. . . Like me was saying, Tengar say he was working a claim near the Arisa Mountain, he and another man. You know near them mountain the bush so thick, en't enough room between the tree trunk for a man to pass. Well, Tengar and this man was working near the river bank and they used to see the Indians coming and going opposite them across the river, and Tengar man get suspicious and say he going to see what happening. The man cross the river one bright mornin' and he never come back, so Tengar go after he. He scout up and down 'till he find a trail and follow it, and towards sundown he come to a hut. Pardners, when he look inside what he see make he belly shrink – the man was inside stretch out on the floor, but he was a skeleton, and Tengar only know was he because of the hat and shoes he find – the macushi ants did pick the body clean. Tengar scout 'round the house 'cause he know something else had to 'tack the man before the ants move in. He circle the hut and find mound all round the yard like if plenty people bury there. Night catch he, and rather than walk back all that distance in the dark he decide to stay inside the hut and see what was brewing. He sit down inside and wait with he torchlight and gun ready. . . ."

"He brave," Scotland said.

"The man Tengar 'fraid neither God nor man, me tell you," Ben continued. "He wait and wait, and he ears was cock sharper than he gun, and jus as he was dozin' lil' bit, something drop from the roof on top he head, a black hairy spider so big, that the foot reach all the way down to he neck, and cover he face as far as he chin. He try to shake it off, but it had a grip like a strong man. He know that if that spider bite he, was jus' as good as Mantop tappin' he on the head, so he took out he prospecting knife and scrape it off so quick he nearly scalp heself, and when he shine he torch on the roof there was the spider mate, big as he, and Tengar shoot it, and burn down the hut. The Indians used to make sacrifice to them spider in that very hut and now they searching all over the bush for Tengar."

Darkness had set in and the claim-holders had one for the trail before they left to get ready for the fête. Bullah arranged it so that Tonic and Woody should take turns to guard the shop. He lent them his German rifle and told them to keep a sharp lookout, because he had enough gold and diamonds in the shop to buy half the country between Morawhana and Akarai.

Four paraffin lamps brightened the hill and lit up the surrounding forest that night. The women arrived first, dressed in gowns made by the best dressmakers in Georgetown, and wearing so many diamonds it looked as if they had strings of fireflies around their necks and arms. They sported lamé, silk and satin gowns, and some of them had gold tiaras on their heads. They came from the slums of Georgetown or the coastal villages originally, and yet the famous courtesans I had read about had nothing on them. White men, sailors and civil servants had been their best clients in the city, but the pork-knockers were kings compared to them, they weren't fussy about spending thousands for one night of pleasure.

The men trouped in later dressed up to kill in silk, satin, salara or fine linen shirts, doeskin flannels, broad belts inset with diamonds, and two-toned shoes. The claim-holders wore silk scarves around their necks and diamond-headed pins arranged in the shape of crosses or hearts gleamed on the scarves.

Belle came out when the fête was under way. She wore a white sequined gown and champagne-coloured shoes. Around her neck was a half-moon necklace with a single hundred-carat diamond burning like white fire against her black throat. The musicians sat on a platform of boxes covered with red cloth and they wore garlands of tiger orchids. The women circulated amongst the crowd of men showing off their gowns, but the men commented more on what was under the rich cloth and made their bids early. Before the music struck up Bullah jumped on the platform and held his arms above his head for silence.

"Ladies and gentlemen!" he shouted joyously. "Tonight is a great night for we all. Me never thought me could be so happy. Tonight we all gather here to celebrate the birthday of the Queen of Perenong!" The guests shouted and stamped and Bullah raised his arms again. His salara shirt was open to the waist and his doeskins looked as if they had been poured like hot latex over the bulges of his buttocks, thighs, and calves.

"Ladies and gentlemen," he continued, "the queen bring we all luck, she make Perenong a place to sing about again. 'Bullah,' she say to me the first day she set foot here, 'Bullah' she say, 'me feel good luck in me bones,' and from then on Ocean Shark start rooting up diamond like fire, and now money passing from hand to hand like stupidness. And now, ladies and gentlemen, me will call on the queen she self to come on the platform."

"Speech, Queen! Speech!" the guests shouted as Bullah ushered Belle to the platform.

"Ladies and gentlemen," she said in a low voice trembling with excitement, "me man Ocean Shark is the speech-man and all me can say is be happy, have a good time, enjoy youself 'cause tomorrow. . . who know 'bout tomorrow and who care?" The applause was like the thunder of a waterfall in the rainy season and before it died the band struck up and we abandoned ourselves to a sustained, ferocious gaiety. At midnight Santos called on Belle to sing. He was in a boisterous mood, boasting about his wealth, dancing, kissing the women.

"Let we have a song from the queen!" he shouted, jumping up to the platform, and the pork-knockers stamped and cheered. Belle stood in the centre of the room and sang *Marchita* with only a guitar and a flute accompanying her. The guests fell silent as she sang. I knew she was singing only for me. Her song brought back memories of life on the coast – moonlight nights sitting on doorsteps listening to piper owls fluting, the surf pounding up beaches, dogs barking and children crying and voices talking with slow, easy cadences. When the song ended violence broke loose afresh. The pork-knockers lifted Belle to their shoulders, and Bullah with drunken tears running down his lined face, bawled, "Me never see an angel 'till tonight! Sing, Queen, sing to me and me will give you every last board in me shop." I signalled the musicians to stop playing and mounted the platform.

"Ladies and gentlemen!" I shouted, and my head felt as if it were floating up to the rafters. "Ladies and gentlemen, this is part of the queen's birthday present!" I pointed to four cases of champagne at the foot of the platform and the crowd made way for her.

"Bring a washing tub!" she said, and when Woody had done so, she slipped out of her gown, kicked off her shoes and stepped into the tub. Woody handed her an empty mug which she used as a dipper to pour the champagne over her naked body until she looked like a polished wood carving after rain. She stepped out of the tub dripping champagne and the crowd opened for her to pass, feet rooted and eyes staring stupidly. One of the musicians behind me muttered, "A thousand-dollar bath, pardner." The other women, not to be outdone, took turns to have a champagne bath. A few of them were so drunk that they splashed about in the tub fully clothed. A barbaric shouting burst out of the cottage, swelled and echoed through the forest and re-echoed over the hissing and droning of the Grass Fall.

CHAPTER SEVEN

BULLAH woke me up when my head was still heavy with sleep and alcoholic fumes.

"Shark, wake up, boy!" he whispered, and I rubbed my eyes to make sure I wasn't dreaming. "Don't wake the queen. Jus' haul on some clothes and come with me."

"What's matta, Bullah?"

"Shhhh!" He put a finger to his lips. I let one foot drop over the side of the bed and Belle moaned. I waited until she had settled down again and crept out. Outside, the cold morning air made me bite hard to prevent my teeth from chattering.

"How did you get in, Bullah? The doors were locked."

"Me climb through the window, pardner, cause the story heavy and nobody must know 'bout it, not even the queen." His voice was grim, and as he walked down the path ahead of me I saw that his shoulders were drooping.

"For God's sake tell me what happen, Bullah?"

"Somebody lash Tonic 'cross he head and rob the shop."

"You're making fun, Bullah. Thing like that can't happen here, man."

He turned around clenching and unclenching his fists.

"Me tell you it happen, boy. Tonic lie down in me bed like dead right this minute and some thiefing, good-for-nothing, whore-dog pick me iron chest clean."

"You mean the one with my diamonds in it?"

"You diamond, and me own, and everybody else own."

"You went to my camp yet?"

"One thing at a time, boy. You know doctor work, and me want you to look at Tonic."

Tonic must have turned his head at the moment when the blow aimed at him fell, or it would have cracked his skull. He opened his eyes and moaned when I touched the bump above his temple.

"He's got a slight concussion," I said to Bullah, "and he mustn't sleep." I propped him up and went down to the creek and collected some leeches from amidst the reeds, and I returned to find Bullah talking loudly to Tonic and begging him not to fall asleep. I put the leeches on the swelling and after a while he said:

"Was Santos and another man."

"Santos! You sure, boy?"

"Yes. Was he hit me, and before darkness bandage me eye me see two of them climbing up the back steps." I saw it all then. Santos and Uncle Richard had made their move. They had been scheming for a long time and the fête gave them the chance they were waiting for. It was still dark outside, although day was cleaning slowly. The two were making a getaway at that moment with a hundred thousand dollars in the pouches of their belts. Only five hours ago I could have afforded to buy champagne for bath water and suddenly I was broke. I looked at Bullah, feeling like a child again.

"We should tell the police at Kamakusa," I said.

"Police! Chu! Them police is town-man and even if they did know the bush me won't trust them." He spat the words out. "We going after them weself. The law of this bush is that when a man thief you, you must settle account with he face to face."

"But if they've got a good boat and a man who knows the river they'll be past Bartica before we make a move."

"With that amount of diamond you don't even trust you own mother, pardner. Richard Dolly boat still tie up by the landing, so they making to bypass Kamakusa overland, heading for the Cuyuni. You got to get Tonic better, then we going hotfoot behind them. They can take twelve-hour handicap. Me tell you before, Tonic know this bush like a Buck." Bullah's certainty made me feel better, but doubts still nagged at me.

"This forest big like the ocean. En't no telling what can happen. All I know is that me diamonds gone, and those two got them, and they'll be sporting the money and laughing at me before the next moon come and go." Bullah clapped a hand on my shoulder.

"Look, Shark. Me work for me money harder and longer than you. Before you Papa eye light on you Mama, me was watching me sweat water this Perenong pay-dirt, and in this bush you can murder, but you can't rob pork-knocker. Take lil' advice from Bullah Daniels, boy. Act like nothing en't happen; don't even breathe word to the queen. Me going to open the shop as usual, and when afternoon come me will say we going hunting. People know me is a hunt-man and nobody will lift an eye, and we can plant rumour that Santos gone to Kamakusa to spree. Come back midday time, and knock back couple drink, and catch a gaff. Tell you gang to rest up 'till you come back, and offer them seven dollar a day free pay. Me will say that Tonic drink too much and he fall down the step."

"All right, Bullah. I'm trusting you." I bandaged the leeches on to Tonic's head and gave him hot broth and brandy.

"Skipper, the man take me by surprise. Me wasn't. . ."

"Is all right, Tonic. Shark know doctor work and he will make you better in no time."

I walked into the morning sunshine. In the short distance up to my cottage I realised all over again how serious my plight was. My fall from king to pauper had been so sudden. I despaired of ever recovering the diamonds and thought that I would have to start all over again on a claim which was nearly worked out. At best I would end up with enough to try my hand on a new claim. It was better to think this way than to bank on catching Santos and my uncle. Bullah sounded certain, but how could anyone be, in a situation like this? Beyond Perenong was a continent of forests, rivers, mountains, savannahs. Those two could head across the Brazilian or Venezuelan borders or make a clean getaway by going north-east to the coast, and chartering a boat to the islands.

I was grateful when I returned to the cottage and found Belle still asleep. It gave me time to compose myself before facing her. She lay in bed with one hand against her cheek. What would she do? Go back to her old life? I wasn't even sure that to escape from her gilded cage was not what she wanted.

"Belle!" I called out softly, touching her cheek. "Belle!" She opened her eyes and lay still.

"You must be hungry, Shark, and look how me lying down and sleeping! Is what o'clock?"

"It's eight o'clock, Belle, but I'm not feeling hungry. I came to tell you that Bullah, Tonic and me, are taking a trip to the Cuyuni, hunting and looking up a new claim."

"All that way, Shark, just to look at claim? You en't got enough money?"

"You know how it is, Belle. You got to put aside something for a rainy day, gal."

"And who looking after the shop?"

"Woody."

"Tell Bullah me will help. Me can't bear the thought of staying here all by meself with nothing to do. Me could come with all you if it won't humbug you."

"They got some bad snake in that bush, gal. Better stay and help Woody." She made a face and said:

"Me can't stand snake. One time a coolie woman in the village say a big boa crawl inside she hut when she was sleeping and suck the milk from she breast. Since then me and snake don't agree at all; jus' to think 'bout them does make me inside go all slippery."

"You know, Tonic fell down the steps last night and he's got a champion bump on his head."

"And how he will go on that brute walk?"

"It's not too bad, and I'll have him better in no time."

"When you leaving, Shark?"

"This afternoon."

"Look out for youself. Me had bad dream. Me don't 'member what it was all about, but the dream wasn't good; that much me know." She sat up and hugged her knees and looked at me searchingly.

"You don't look well, Shark. What troubling you?"

"Nothing, gal, nothing; just the drinks and getting up so early."

"Look out for youself now; you is me one-eye, boy."

"All right, Belle. I will look out for myself, gal."

Tonic was walking about when I returned to the shop, and the bandages made him look like a white-faced monkey.

"Me ready, skipper!" he said, smiling a twisted smile.

"Take it quiet for a couple more hours, boy."

"You hear what the man say?" Bullah said when Tonic kept pacing up and down. Tonic sat on the edge of the bed and pretended to look hurt.

"You've got a hard skull, Tonic. That blow could have stunned a bush cow."

"Is he slave blood and the Indian blood," Bullah said; "them two does make powerful brew."

"You think we'll catch up with them, Tonic?"

"Sure as day, skipper. Them two got to go over the hills and 'cross the swamp. We taking short-cut and we bound to butt-up with them or me name en't Tonic."

"Me got it all plan," Bullah said, shading his eyes and looking through the window at the sun. "About ten mile from here is the hills. Say they lef' here at three o'clock, then they should reach them hill by afternoon. Them two goin' try get over them hill fast, and b'time they cross that last hill call 'Ham Nah Jai' en't going to be much breath lef' in them, and even if they got any lef' then they can't cross them swamp at night; 'part from everything else, it got some bad anaconda snake; you can smell them far off if the wind up, and you does hear them snoring like man. Halfway through them swamp is a river that does cut 'cross a reef and that is where me think we going to meet up with them two smart-men."

"I hope you're right, Bullah."

"If a snake gobble one of them, will be the richest snake in the bush," Tonic said.

"You excited, boy," Bullah said. "Me en't hear you talk so much long time. Like the blow loosen you tongue."

"I never saw a patient so frisky with such a big lump on his head," I said.

"You can chew car tyre?" Bullah asked.

"I have strong teeth. That's why they call me Shark."

"'Cause all we going to eat 'till we catch up with them nigger-men is tasso and bull. We got to move light and fast and we can't hunt no game 'cept man-game."

I sat at the counter and chatted with Woody and Galloway. I

asked them to keep an eye on the claim until I returned. We sipped drinks and gaffed until Belle came over from the cottage. I had a hard time keeping a straight face, hiding my restlessness.

"Is time," Bullah said, coming out of the back room with his wareshi already harnessed.

We stood at the foot of the front steps to the shop, ready to go.

"All you travelling light," Belle said. She sat on the bottom step with a worried look on her face. I was busy hitching up my pack and examining my rifle and I didn't look at her.

"Got to," Tonic said. "Is plenty ground to cover, Queen."

"Me feel in me bones that all you hiding move from me, Bullah. Something wrong. Tell me is what."

Bullah's eyes met hers, but his kindly black face didn't give anything away. He stood relaxed, leaning slightly forward with the weight of his wareshi, looking like an upturned triangle with immense shoulders tapering to a small waist, and legs which didn't somehow seem to belong to him. I thought for a moment that he would have told her, but he said:

"You know how it is, Queen. We after a new claim. You might think Shark got enough money, but look at me, making it all the time, piling it up. Sometime money does give a man root after he get over the first flush. For thirty-five-odd year me been in this bush, and of all the oldtimers me is the only one the Lord bless with property. When me start out me used to spend money like fire, but come the day when me say, 'Bullah, don't make fool of youself, boy, put aside something, buy a shop, the money will come slow but sure'; that is how me start – one-one, shilling by shilling, dollar by dollar. Me want Shark and you to have a good life but me want he to keep the future in mind. Look what happen to he Papa!"

"Me know all that, Bullah, but me still feel something wrong. Me know me man and he spirit en't happy today."

"We got to go, Queen," Bullah said, taking a large gold watch out of his fob. "We got to make twenty mile by fore-day-morning."

"Take care of Shark, Bullah; don't let nothing happen to he. Me had bad dream last night and me still upset."

"You're acting like if I'm still a small-boy, Belle."

"R-e-a-d-y, T-o-n-i-c!" Bullah shouted.

"All set, boss!"

"Then let's go!"

We walked around the hill and forded the river above Grass Fall. The sun was bending towards its four o'clock mooring, sparkling high above us in the treetops. Strands of greenheart and mora surrounded us in the half-dark, half-light world of the forest. The earth was red as canna lilies, and as we walked along the winding trail we occasionally crossed bright patches where fallen trees had let in pools of sunlight. Butterflies with incandescent wings hung like small lanterns in the twilight. The forest darkened and in many places the trail was overgrown. The red earth changed to white, and then brown sand. Tonic walked with quick, shuffling steps like an Indian. We passed sprinklings of wild pineapples and giant azaleas. I only knew that it was night when I looked up and saw a star through a hole in the roof of leaves. We walked one pace apart, so close that I could not tell if the noises that walked with us were made by the wind, our breathing, or the soft crunch of our footsteps on the sand.

"This is snake country," Tonic said, and the darkness boxed up his voice so that I could barely hear it.

"It must feel like this walking under a river," I thought, "for darkness has weight, it sits on top of us and every time we part it, throw it aside, it closes in behind us." Red howlers roared above the clamouring of insects, and tinamous and saki-winkies joined in. A pair of eyes, bright as fire, appeared ahead of us. Bullah switched on his torch catching the bandage on Tonic's head and, fifteen yards away, a tapir. Tonic flung his spear just as the tapir was plunging into the underbush. The spear glanced off the beast's thick hide and planted itself quivering into a tree trunk.

"Only bullet can stop he," Bullah said.

"Would 'ave got he between the shoulder if he didn't turn," Tonic said.

"And then what?"

"Could 'ave had fresh meat for days boss."

"Add twenty pound of meat to you pack and a couple pound inside you belly and you jus' as well say good bye to them diamond, pardner. How the head feelin'?"

"Fine, boss."

"Tell me if it giving trouble, 'cause once we reach the hill country is going to be rough, pardner."

"The head fine, boss."

I thought about Santos and Uncle Richard. I had to think about something real, for the forest and the darkness were too full of melancholy and weird noises. "These two must be sleeping now," I told myself. "They couldn't hold out this long without sleep. They were somewhere in the forest or the sand hills with the diamonds close against them, and the thought of what they could buy even closer. They knew we would be after them, and thoughts of escape must have knocked together in their minds all the time they were on the trail." And yet as I thought about them, it was Uncle Richard that I hated most. The man was my own flesh and blood, my mother's brother; we could have been close as spittle to a tongue. He was the one who had betrayed me, not Santos, for Santos was one of those people who could be easily influenced. And just as how I hated Uncle Richard, I knew he hated me. I could imagine him burning up inside when he had heard that I was rich, and now he was getting his own back.

"Me can feel the thought ticking inside you head," Bullah said. "You worried 'bout the money, eh."

"Not the money so much, Bullah; somehow I feel better about that part of it. I don't even mind if I've got to begin all over again. After all these years I still hate the man, and now we must have a reckoning."

"Is so fam'ly story does go, boy. Blood thicker than rum."

"I haven't set eyes on him for years, but I know that the man like a lizard; he can take on any colour or shape."

"But you tell me one time that you grandma put a curse on he, and pardner, the old people curse bad like a sword."

We were still on the trail at day-clean. The forest was thinning out and the mist so heavy I knew we were approaching water.

"Me smell a big snake," Tonic said, and we stood still while he sniffed and scouted around peering through the mist. When Tonic signalled us we moved forward cautiously. We saw the snake coiled up between the roots of a Brazil nut tree and it was hard to tell which was which except that the anaconda was snoring like a man. "He just swallow something; see how he belly swell out," Tonic said. The anaconda's head was thick and blunt while its eyes shone like quartz stones through smoke. The head was high above the rest of the snake's body, and I unslung my rifle and rammed a blunt-nosed cartridge into the breach.

"Lef' it alone," Bullah said. "Me don't want to have the mate following we all the way."

"We should hit the swamp any time now," Tonic said, and I thought he sounded tired. Bullah must have noticed too, because he said:

"We can take a rest when we hit the swamp. Is long time since me do this kind of walking." He mopped his brow and fanned himself by shaking his shirt front. "Man, the sweat deluging me. You ever hear 'bout this part of the world?" he asked.

"I heard about it all right. Woody said that he had to cross it once."

"Is not a nice piece of country to cross, pardner. Me think the Lord fashion it like this to bring man low. Them two we chasing will take a while to cross it; me can tell you that for sure. 'Cross the swamp and over them hill is Nameless River. They call it by that name 'cause once you mount them hill and reach the river you does be too weary to remember any other name. Tonic know a short-cut, and before sundown we will be waiting for them two by the river bank."

We came to the swamps and put our packs down. Tonic stretched out on the sand and closed his eyes. I had been carrying my balata pouch so long that when I put it down I kept leaning forward as if the weight was still on my back. I found a cochineal plant, cut one of its leaves in half, and bandaged it over the swelling on Tonic's head. Bullah stood over us, looking on with his forehead creased and his eyes showing his anxiety.

"It don't look too good," he said.

"He must rest couple hours. I think he's got a temperature."

"How you feeling, boy?"

"Lil' bit heavy in the head, boss, but me will be all right once me doze off," he said and his face was the colour of moss. He licked his lips and moaned softly. Bullah and I walked away and stood by the edge of the swamp. I was fighting against sleep and my eyes felt as if they had sand in them. Bullah took out a flask of bush rum, drank some and handed it to me.

"You think the boy can make it, Shark?"

"I don't know, Bullah. I don't know. He'd rather drop dead than admit he can't go on."

"That boy mean a lot to me, Shark. Me rather lose everything me got than sacrifice he for couple diamond. Is fifteen-odd year since he been with me and me grow 'customed to he ways. Look, Shark, if the worse come to the worse you will have to push on alone." I didn't answer him, because the thought of doing the journey to Nameless River by myself frightened me. I looked across the swamps, and the white sand hills rising out of the black ooze made the place look like a huge skull. We walked back towards the spot where we had left Tonic, and Bullah suddenly gripped my arm and pointed. A snake was sliding down a tree trunk not ten yards away from the sleeping boy.

"Look out, Tonic!" we shouted. He sat up and held his head. When he saw the snake he moved so quickly I didn't see when he unsheathed his prospecting knife. The sinuous body with its shiny scales tensed itself to strike. Tonic sidestepped and drove the heavy knife through the reptile's spine. The tail stirred up a cloud of dust and the rest of the body moved convulsively.

"Is a young anaconda," Tonic said as we approached.

"Me thought he had you," Bullah said, looking at the blood-stain on the sand.

"Boss, you should know that even if me cripple en't the snake born that can get me," Tonic said.

We struck out across the swamps when the sun was high and the haze made it difficult to judge distances. When we reached the hills Tonic scouted around until he picked up the two men's trail.

"They was planting they foot heavy," he said. "The walk must be wearying them."

"Look like they take the long way," Bullah said.

"The way they take, they got to cross another swamp more bad than this one," Tonic said.

From the summit of the first hill we saw growths of giant moras, amaratas, and kakaralis. Butterflies and toucans flashed across sunbeams and vanished in the twilight under the trees. No breath of wind stirred across the unbroken roof of branches and leaves. The sun was directly above us and the silence was weighted. Bullah grew restless and he climbed high up a kakarali and scanned the country around. We looked at him, hoping he would signal that he had seen the two men but he came down and said,

"Me en't even see a leaf tremble." We pressed on. The hills rose gradually and tumbled down steeply, making the descent harder than the climb. Tonic started lagging behind, and we stopped to rest and to prepare tea.

"The boy don't look too good," Bullah said, and I noticed a dark patch on Tonic's bandage. I took it off and washed the wound with lysol.

"How's she going, boy?" I asked. He clenched his teeth hard and didn't answer, and before I finished tying the bandage, he fainted. He came to quickly, willing himself better.

"Jus' feel lil' bit weary," he said.

"We staying right here!" Bullah said.

"Is all right, boss; me can make it. Is only four hour walk to Nameless River straight as a die 'cross these hill." He stood up and braced himself against a tree. Bullah picked him up gently when his legs gave out.

"Lef' the bandage and any food you can spare, Shark," he said. "Me will stay here with the boy." I knew that Bullah wasn't going any further, diamonds or no diamonds.

"I'll go on alone," I said, and the way Bullah looked at me made me feel that I had to defend myself against the accusation in his eyes. "As far as I'm concerned, it's not only the diamonds, Bullah. I've got to meet those two face to face. Santos was my friend; there was a time when we were close like brothers and I would 'ave done anything for him. And as for Richard Dolly, it's like if all the days the Lord made me see had to be blighted by this man. The angriness in me is deep and strong and, though I'm afraid, I know I've got to go after them."

A silence settled over us three – not the silence of the hills and forests, but one inside of our hearts. I was angry with Tonic that he had to fall sick, vexed with Bullah that, for all my big-talk, he knew that I was willing to sacrifice a friend's life for a sack of diamonds.

"Don't take it to heart, Shark," Bullah said. "Life got plenty lesson to teach you yet, pardner; this bush does make you like a wild beast, and then you does got to fight you way back to prove you is a man. You better get moving. Don't make sundown catch you before you reach Nameless River."

"Walk straight on," Tonic said, "and when you come to the river you will see two big mora on the bank. Hide behind one of them and wait."

I left half of my rations with Bullah and Tonic, cleaned and oiled my rifle, and set out. The two of them watched me as I walked away, but I did not look back. When I was certain that they could no longer see me I broke into a run. Whenever I looked at the sky the treetops seemed to be reaching closer and closer to the sun. The exertion and the thought of reaching Nameless River ahead of Santos and Uncle Richard filled me with a particular gladness. Every time I reached a hilltop I expected to see the river below me. I slowed down to a steady jog and could feel my prospecting knife slapping against my thigh and making a noise as if someone was running close behind me. I looked back once or twice involuntarily and, realising how tensed up I was, laughed at myself. I thought of Bullah hovering around Tonic like a mother hen with an ailing chick. He said that he was going to build a hut and nurse Tonic back to health while they were waiting for me. I had a vision of Belle sitting in the shop and talking to the pork-knockers. They were making big bids for her and she was laughing at them. I reviewed our relationship during the past few months. Something had come between us of late that was almost like hatred. I didn't like the way I depended on her for everything. It was as if she had leeched away a part of my insides and I was no longer whole. "You're like an orchid-man," I told myself; "always hanging on to other people 'till it looks like if you can't cut yourself loose and live. Was like this from your Mahaica days. In a way, this going after Santos and Richard by yourself is the first big thing you ever did on your own."

Halfway up a hillside I heard the river and speeded up my pace. I clambered up, holding my pack close so that it wouldn't rattle. From behind a tree I watched the sluggish black stream flowing by a hundred yards or so away. I figured that it was an hour and a half before sundown, and scanned the surrounding country for any signs of Santos and Richard. I saw a deer and a tapir wading in the shallows, and when a marudi chattered in the mora tree that leaned over the river, they turned around and retraced their steps up the slope of the river bank. When I reached the mora tree the two animals had vanished. I made sure that there weren't any snakes to keep me company and hid between the mora roots. The sun was falling down to the level of the treetops all too quickly. I knew that if the two didn't turn up before dark there wouldn't be much chance of catching them without Tonic to help me. I didn't have enough rations for another day, and they would be well supplied. Besides, Bullah had said that there were half a dozen well-used trails to the Cuyuni and there was no telling which one they would take. The only thing left to do once they crossed the river was to get to Bartica ahead of them, and that would mean chancing it to the Cuyuni, doing a three-days' walk on a day's ration. And even then I might not find a mining camp and a boat for weeks. The marudi croaked a raucous warning, and I heard voices coming from the trail behind the hill. Santos and Uncle Richard came into view. The sun had fallen behind the trees, but the afterglow was still bright. The relief of seeing them, and the sight of the two men in their tattered clothes, almost made me burst out laughing. I had not seen my uncle since I left Mahaica and was surprised how little he had changed.

"'Cross the river is open country, boy! We'll be in the bright-lights under a week." He had the same tight lopsided smile that I had seen on his face the night in Grandma's hut. Santos' eyes wandered around nervously.

"We better cross right away," he said.

"Man, what fretting you? You think them man got wing or what? That pace we keep up today only bird can catch we now, pardner." My uncle was talking like a man who knew his way about the bush. He seemed surer of himself than Santos was, although Santos was in better condition after the walk. I waited until they were about thirty feet away from me. They were each carrying a gun and a large pack.

"Richard!" I called out, holding my rifle steady. They stopped as if bullets had hit them, and Santos spun around not sure where the voice had come from. Richard's mouth hung open with surprise, but when I emerged from behind the tree he pulled himself together and smiled.

"Oh, is you, nephew! Is long time we en't meet, boy."

"Don't make a wrong move!" I shouted, covering them with the rifle.

"Where you friends, nephew?"

"I just want a few words with all you two. Throw your guns well away from you, then throw the diamonds. I know you got them tied 'round you waist. Move on!" I shouted, firing a shot so that it kicked up the sand between them. Santos obeyed, but my uncle flung his gun away from him and said:

"You got to come and take these diamond off me, nephew."

"I'm warning you, Richard Dolly, don't cross me!" I picked up the cartridge belt Santos had thrown midway between us. The light was fading and I kept a close watch on them. I was fumbling to open the pouches when Richard flung his pack down and sprinted towards the river. He ran, dodging from side to side. I fired low and the bullet hit him on the right thigh. He staggered and almost fell backwards, but he righted himself and plunged into the river. He was a strong swimmer, and I saw his head breaking the smooth surface as he made for the opposite bank. I stood between Santos and the river, hesitating because I didn't want to kill Richard Dolly. Suddenly I heard him scream and saw him beating the water with his hands furiously. He screamed again and again.

"The cannibal fish got he!" Santos shouted in a hoarse voice. My uncle cried out for the last time, an insane gurgling cry. The water around him was beaten into a white froth as the cannibal fish bit, and spun away, and returned for another mouthful.

"You murder he! You murder he! Oh, God!" Santos sobbed, hugging himself and swaying from side to side. Night fell suddenly and the river was still. Santos went on and on, moaning and sobbing and hugging himself. I felt he was putting on an act and never let him out of my sight. And yet, now that we were alone in the starlight, I couldn't feel any hatred towards him. But I knew that I was in trouble. I had killed Richard Dolly before a witness and might have to face a charge for murder. I lit a fire and squatted close to it. Santos' whining was getting on my nerves. He kept on and on. I couldn't believe that my uncle was dead, although it had happened before my eyes and I knew that Grandma had put a curse on him. Thoughts flitted in and out of my mind. Santos sat on the sand, alternately mumbling to himself and sobbing. I examined the diamonds in the firelight and saw that Santos must have cheated his partner and kept the highest-priced stones. Perhaps my uncle didn't know that the diamonds with flaws in them fetched better prices. I estimated that Santos had kept over two thousand carats for himself. I couldn't help thinking that if I killed Santos and threw his body into the river I could say that I saw the cannibal fish destroy both he and my uncle. I released the safety catch and aimed at his head. His eyes had the look of a wounded beast. He stared straight at me, and yet he was not seeing me, and I knew then that his reason had left him after he had heard my uncle's screams. I lowered the rifle, knowing that I could only have killed him in anger. I squatted by the fire once more and it became so eerie with a madman in front of me and a ghost behind me that I decided to head back to the valley where Bullah and Tonic were waiting. I knew that just telling the whole story to Bullah would make me feel better.

"Come on!" I said to Santos. "You carry the dead man's pack." He kept staring at the river and mumbling. "Come on!" I shouted and he picked up the pack and started out ahead of me, walking like a drunken man. I threw my uncle's gun into the river and kept Santos'.

We found Bullah and Tonic near midnight. Santos had not said a word all the way. He tried to run away when he saw Bullah, and I went after him and brought him back.

"Was a blighted day when we lef' Perenong," Bullah said. Santos picked up a prospecting knife and rushed at us, and Bullah stepped aside and knocked him down. We tied him up and left him a safe distance from the fire. Tonic was delirious and didn't know what was going on, and I told Bullah what had happened.

"You lucky that madness catch that one," he said, pointing to Santos. "En't nobody going to believe he now."

I didn't sleep at all that night, and twice I had to get up and move Santos away from the fire after he had wormed his way too close to it. At fore-day-morning we made a stretcher for Tonic, and while we carried him Santos walked ahead of us meekly. He didn't give any trouble for the whole day except that he refused to eat anything, but at sundown he became violent again and we had to tie him up. It took us a whole day to cross the swamp. The fever left Tonic and he refused to let us carry him in the stretcher any longer.

"Me feel fine, skipper," he said to me. "You got a proper healing hand." We rested until the sun cooled, but when we started out again Santos collapsed. I sat beside him all night while he raved and shouted. And while Bullah and Tonic slept through it all I wondered what had brought this madness on him so suddenly. I remembered him when he came to fetch me from Mahaica. He had been a swaggering sweet-man with a quick eye for a pretty girl, and a smooth tongue for warbling out a story. And I knew that it was a cursed day when his eye had lighted on the first diamond. I had persuaded Santos to leave the small enclosure of his easy-going life, and once he left it the secret rhythms, which reach from the earth, on which a village child is born, to his heart, had jangled themselves out of harmony.

The next morning we heard voices and the sound of gunfire and Woody and a party of pork-knockers found us.

"Is what happen to Brother Santos?" Woody asked.

"He gone mad as a thirsty monkey," Bullah said, and when he saw the men staring at Tonic's bandage he added: "the boy meet with an accident. This was a proper bad luck trip."

"Queen say that she feel in she bones that something was wrong. She say whole night she keep dreaming 'bout blood and she make we come after you," Woody said.

"We laugh at she when she start with this ballad," another man said, "but she keep on and on. 'Me mind tell me that they in trouble,' she keep saying, and she wouldn't give we no peace 'till we start out."

Santos lay on the stretcher rolling his eyes and straining against the bush ropes with which we had secured his arms and legs.

"He got it bad," a pork-knocker said.

A crowd of pork-knockers and their women came to the top of Grass Fall to meet us, and when they saw Santos in a stretcher they shouted questions all together.

"Is what happen?"

"Lord ha' mercy! Is what befall po' Santos?"

"But the man was bright as cut diamond only the other night! Is what happen to he?"

Belle jostled her way through the crowd, and when she saw me she ran towards me laughing and crying alternately.

"Shark, you well? Nothing en't happen to you? Lord, me nights was bitter with dream! One night me even dream that the earth self was crying blood." I held her close and for once didn't mind the outlandishness of her greeting. The others shouted encouragement.

"Well, Queen, now you man is back them bed spring going to talk loud!"

"You got to work up you power-house tonight, Shark!"

"Well, boys and girls, it all over now, and is good to be back. Me thought me and trouble was cousin, but in that short walk me see more trouble than in all me born days," Bullah said.

"Come and soak you throat bit before you start talk," Belle said.

"Me can do with a drink. Lord, that walk desert-up me insides," Bullah said.

I watched at Bullah as we neared the shop. He was an old man coming back to his yard. He climbed up the steps slowly, not because he was tired; he wanted to feel the wood under his feet. He entered and sat heavily on his mahogany stool behind the counter. His eyes roamed over the shelves, and I knew that he could tell how much drink had been sold since we were away to the half-pint. He even looked up at the rafters to see where the spiders had spun new webs, and the marabuntas' nests.

"Serve drinks all round!" he ordered. This was his way of reestablishing his rights as master of the shop.

We locked Santos in Bullah's room and I felt guilty about treating him like an animal, but didn't know what else to do.

"Is what really happen, Bullah?" Woody asked.

"Let sleeping dog sleep, Woody. The Lord punish the sinners and we all get back safe."

"Ahmen!" the pork-knockers said, tossing their drinks down. "Come on, Shark, or you will have to use matchsticks to prop you eyelid up, boy," Belle said.

It was good to hear the noisy green frogs singing and the ooskudu owl hooting on our way up the hill. I knew that Belle resented not being told all that had happened, and I would have no peace until I told her everything. We sat out on the veranda when we reached the cottage, and I told her about Santos and Uncle Richard and the diamonds, and when I finished she said:

"But, Shark, you don't trust me, boy? You think me would 'ave give 'way you secret?"

"I would trust you with anything, gal, but this was a case where I was frightened. I couldn't just break the news to you suddenly that I was poor."

"But, Shark, you cause me more worry by not telling me than if you did tell me the whole story beforehand."

"I won't hide anything from you again, Belle, 'cause when I do, nothing but bad luck seems to come my way. You know the thing that frightened me most was the thought that here I was with all that money tied up in diamonds, and I hadn't even taken a trip to Georgetown to spend some of it."

"In other words, you telling me that you want we take walk to the big city."

"Once I work out my claim I think we should."

"Me like the city, Shark. Me proper like the high life there, but me don't think the time ripe for you to go yet. Make up you mind how you going to run you life, where you want to live, what kind of work you want to take up. . . ."

"Work? Chu, gal! Why should I work with all this money."

"Black people too 'custom to hard work to bruck-off suddenly. Is only white man know how not to work and still live quiet and regular."

"I'm going to buy a business, Belle, and a house with so much land 'round it that not even an eagle flying near the sun can see from one end to the other. I'll buy a car like the one the white man had with brass head lamps, and a carriage with six horses. Gal, I'm going to give the black people something to sing about."

"Sound to me like you goin' make a big fool of youself. You don't know that the higher you climb up a tree the more easy the limb does break under you?"

"But why do you have to jump down my throat every time I say something? Don't you know a man's got to talk for talk sake sometimes? I don't mean all I say about living big and flying high. It's just echo-talk. I dreamt about these things since I was a small-boy and I'm just telling them to you because you're close to me."

"Me know all this, Shark, but you mean some of what you say and that kindah talk does worry me."

"Look, Belle, I've got this money. You and Bullah and every-body else say is luck why I got it, but I don't feel that way 'bout it. My mind told me to come here, and I came and found the diamonds; some people's mind can tell them right and some can tell them wrong. . . ."

"Chu! You make me sick. Whole day is talk. . . ."

"Why you picking a row with me, Belle?"

"Because you does tell me thing jus' to fret me spirit. I know what you going to do. You will go to the city and spend up all you money, then you will come back to the bush and try again. You will be like all the other pork-knocker going and coming 'till you lef' you bones to scrape 'gainst some river bed. You not like them yet, but if you don't look out, you will be. And, me, what will happen to me? Me will have to sit down and watch you changing, growing old, and same time playing that you still young."

"You're mad, Belle, mad. I'm going to start a small business on the coast and marry you and settle down. . . ."

"Me won't marry you never, Shark, although me love you with every rumble inside me belly, and the thought of leaving you does knot and tie me up. But is the Lord will. All of we got to make we bed and lie on it, is so He ordain it."

She went inside and I heard her moving about the bedroom preparing to go to bed. The ooskudu owl still hooted and tinamous sang far away. I remained on the veranda for a while watching the eyes of bird-spiders lighting up the front path like fallen stars.

"You not coming to bed?" I flung my cigarette at the spiders and went to her.

⋆ ⋆ ⋆

The fore-day-morning was warm and sultry, with thick rain clouds tumbling before an early wind. The sun only made fleeting appearances and from the heavy droning of the Grass Fall

I could tell that rain had been falling up-country. Belle's eyes looked puffed and sleepy and there was a peevish droop to her mouth.

"Is what time?" she asked, squinting, and arching her body so that only elbows and heels touched the bed.

"Couldn't be later than six o'clock, the morning air still coldish." I had perspired on the sheets and they stuck to my back and chest. Belle got up slowly.

"Lord, the air thick this morning, eh!"

"Looks like rain will be pelting down soon."

"Is morning like this does make me feel me should be back in Georgetown. This bush too dark and thick-up with mist and all kind of funny noise."

"But you're the same person who was telling me that we should stay longer. I wish to God you would make up you mind, gal! What you want to do, stay, or go to Georgetown?"

"Me think we better go 'long we way to Georgetown you know."

"Rhodius is coming by in the *Fire Plume* in couple days time, we can pack up our few belongings and go."

"Me going to ask Bullah to come with we."

"I will leave that to you, gal."

Belle stood before a small mirror combing her hair, pulling the steel comb through the frizzly, resisting mass so that her biceps muscles danced.

"Come back to bed, gal!" She pretended not to hear, and I jumped out of bed and embraced her, fondling the nipples of her breasts and pressing my hips against hers. We moved towards the bed and the bird-song outside sounded near then far away.

"Skipper, you at home?" It was Tonic's voice and I heard him trying to open the front door. I got up and dressed quickly.

"Like something bad happen," Belle said, sitting up and hugging her knees.

"I'm coming, Tonic. The door's locked." I found him on the veranda looking comical in an oversized hat and a shirt and trousers which had once been Bullah's.

"What's wrong, Tonic? Why you rousing me up this time of day, boy?"

"The boss send me over to tell you 'bout a calamity that happen last night, skipper."

"Wait 'till me get dress," Belle said. "Me want to hear the story." Tonic sat down on a cane chair until Belle came out patting her dress and arranging her hair.

"Santos meet with an accident last night."

"Lord, Lord! But look how some people does have bad luck, eh! That poor, unfortunate man!"

"This morning when me wake up he wasn't in the room, and me follow he trail round the hill, and when me reach the river me find he body between the reed."

"The poor man!" Belle said. "He hear the river calling he in he madness, and he must 'ave jump in."

"Is he in a bad way, Tonic?"

"No, skipper. He look same like when the madness didn't catch up with he, 'cept that he belly swell up. The fish didn't touch he."

"Come and eat something," Belle said. "The both of you need food in you stomach to face the dead man."

"Me can't face food this morning, Queen," Tonic said.

"I couldn't either, Belle."

"All you two jus' step inside and sit down by the table! Me en't taking no for answer this morning." We obeyed, and while she was chopping up wood for the iron stove in the kitchen, I said to Tonic:

"Santos traitor me, but rest his soul in peace; he had his good ways. Was a time when I looked on him like a brother, 'cause he helped to ease me through some rough situations when I was young and stupid."

"But he could 'ave dance eh! The man dance with me that night like he had wind in he foot," Belle said.

After breakfast we all walked down to the shop. Santos' body was laid out on a plank under the building, and Bullah stood nearby, smoking his clay pipe.

"Mantop claim a lot of folks round this settlement lately," he said, and I looked at the dead man's tight face with its grimacing mouth and staring eyes.

"But why did poor Santos have to turn mad and die so

stupidly!" I cried out, looking at the overcast sky, the trees swaying in the rising wind, Belle and Tonic looking at me as if I was mad, and Bullah puffing at his pipe stolidly.

"The Devil does take care of he own," Bullah said. "But one thing me sure of; Santos gone to the forest of the long night to join Joe Smart and Ah Ling and Tengar and River Tom and all them legion pork-knocker Bullah Daniels used to laugh and talk and drink with and he, nor none of them, en't coming back no more."

We held no wake for Santos. He had to be buried quickly and everyone felt so sad after the funeral that a fête started up in Bullah's shop. A pork-knocker from Oronopai scattered a handful of diamonds across the counter. The women's eyes flashed and thirst scraped the men's throat dry.

"Me don't feel like spreeing," Belle said. "Me think me will go home and pack up we things for the journey. You coming, Shark?"

"This thing upset me, Belle, and I want to drink away some of the upset."

"Don't be late, Shark. Me don't like staying alone on that hill with all kind of wild beast hollering in the bush 'round me." I walked her up the hill and returned to join the loudmouthed, frantic revellers. A red-eyed woman, shouting at the top of her voice, offered me a whole night for fifty dollars. Uncle Ezekiel immediately offered her sixty.

"You too big, Uncle Zik," she said, and when the shouting and laughter died down she added, "that greenheart plank you got will rupture me insides."

"Me will take you on for a hundred, Zik!" Maugre Houri, the most famous whore between Perenong and Bartica, shouted.

"All right; but me don't want no bawling when me get started," Zik said.

"Don't make I laugh!" Houri said, and Zik lifted her high above his head and walked out of the shop.

"Go on, Zik! Go on, man! Plug up that well she got!" the pork-knockers shouted, banging their mugs on the counter.

CHAPTER EIGHT

WE left Perenong early one Sunday morning. Rain had been falling steadily during the past few weeks, and the Mazaruni was swollen. The day, however, had dawned clear and cloudless, and sunlight flashed on the dark, swift water. Captain Rhodius' *Fire Plume* was moored to the landing, and the whole settlement had turned out to see us off.

Belle had had no trouble in persuading Bullah to come with us because, he said, he wanted to show Tonic what city life was like so that, when the boy grew up, a trip to Georgetown wouldn't turn his head. Captain Rhodius stood in the stern, wide-shouldered and square, looking at the women with sly, lusting eyes, and boasting about what he would do to them when he returned to Perenong. John Pye, the bowman, stood astride the gunwales near the bow, looking like he'd stood there all his life. He was a long-limbed black man with a long neck and a small head and a voice which seemed to rumble out of a cave. Belle and I took our seats in the *Fire Plume* and sat waiting for Bullah and Tonic. The sky was a hard buck-crab blue and no wind stirred in the trees. A harpy eagle soared near the sun, waiting to ambush ducks and herons on their way to the savannahs. The boat shivered like a deer with an instinct for flight. She sat high in the water, for there were only eight passengers aboard and a cargo of half a dozen bales and canisters.

"Come on, Bullah!" Rhodius shouted. Bullah walked towards us slowly as if he didn't want to forget the feel of the wet earth or the sight of the young grass striped with yellow daisies.

"Take care of everything, Woody, and if you want get in touch, send me a telegram," he said.

"Don't worry, boss. Woody Sam can manage."

Tonic came running out of the shop and when they were both aboard Rhodius shouted, "Cast away, John Pye!" The *Fire Plume* sprang away. Pork-knockers sang and guitars strummed a farewell. There was gunfire and shouting above the phut-phut of the engine. I looked back at the green bluff which was arched like the hump on a buffalo's back between the creek and the river, saw the shop and the men and women waving and thought that I would never return. The sun pressed close to the forest, and the river caught and scattered its reflections in a swirl of eddies. A flock of cormorants, so heavy that they could barely fly, flew ahead of us almost touching the water with their wings.

"They will lead we all the way to Kamakusa," Rhodius said. The *Fire Plume* rounded a bend and John Pye bellowed,

"Obstruction ahead!" The captain pulled the tiller hard over and we moved towards the shadows by the river bank, where the musty smell of dead leaves was strong. A mora tree had fallen across the river. It was partly submerged and lianas streamed away from its branches like a dead woman's hair. We edged up to the tree with the engine cut off and the propeller high out of the water. Rhodius tied a stick of dynamite to the mora roots and we headed up river, lit the fuse and waited. The explosion shredded the trunk and the river tugged away what was left of the tree. When we passed by, the trailing lianas were still above water. I settled back in my seat. Bullah and Belle were chatting with the other passengers, discussing Santos' death and the prospect of anybody finding gold or diamonds around Perenong after the rains. Tonic sat in the bow with John Pye. I had over three thousand carats in diamonds in the sack which hung around my waist. I figured that they were worth sixty thousand dollars, enough money to buy the whole village of Mahaica and still have plenty to spare. I had sent three thousand dollars to Santos' wife and a thousand each to Brother C. and Tanta Moore. I could imagine what would happen the day the postman arrived with the letter telling them to go to Georgetown to draw the money at the Post Office. They would discuss it with the schoolmaster and Gonzalez the shop-owner, and in a few hours the whole village would know and the news would spread up and down the coast and all kinds of relatives they didn't know about would descend on them with hard-luck stories.

We sailed past the Eping Creek and stopped at Inaku to take on passengers. It was the same thing all the way to Kamakusa, crowds gathered at the landings to greet us and give us a rollicking send-off. At Kamakusa, the police examined our mining privileges and searched our luggage for undeclared diamonds. Bullah spoke to the officer on duty, and he took us to the sergeant's quarters. Prisoners weeding grass and tending cassava beds stopped work to look us over curiously. The officer knocked at the door of a rough wooden hut and an irritable voice asked:

"What's wrong now?"

"One Mr. Daniels want to see you, Sergeant."

"You mean Bullah Daniels?"

"Yes, man, is me."

"Come on in, Bullah!"

We found the sergeant sitting at a table writing. He peered at us from behind steel-rimmed spectacles, he put his pen on a stand carefully and stood up.

"Eh, eh, Bullah, is why you didn't send message that you was coming, man? Is how you travelling like ordinary pork-knocker!"

"Mark-a-book, me heading city way with me friend Shark. The boy is Joe Smart son, you know. Boy, you father and Mark-a-book was good friend, used to play much cricket together."

"Me hear 'bout the boy, me hear all 'bout he – Shark, the diamond king. Boy, me hope you can latch on to money more than Joe Smart."

"And this is Shark woman, Belle, and me-boy, Tonic."

"Me hear 'bout the queen. I'se happy to make your acquaintance," the sergeant said, and his eyes took in every inch of Belle's body. He was tall and he held himself stiffly erect. His narrow, aristocratic Negro face was just beginning to show the effects of a lifetime of excesses. "Sit down! Sit down! Is what you got on you mind, Bullah?"

"Me bring heavy news, Mark-a-book. Me got to report two death to you, George Santos and Richard Dolly. . . ." The sergeant looked from Bullah to me. I controlled my expression with difficulty, but Bullah continued calmly. He gave a matter-of-fact account of Santos' death, and when it was my turn I made a statement about how Richard had died without mentioning that

I had wounded him before he tried to swim across Nameless River. The sergeant recorded what we had told him. He had known Bullah for a long time and understood that his friend wanted to satisfy the great ones in Georgetown without implicating anyone.

"The law say that me should have a witness with me when statement like this come in," the sergeant said.

"Me didn't tell you, Mark-a-book, but you fam'ly in Perenong ask me to give you three hundred dollar to keep safe for he." The sergeant's laugh exploded in the small room, banging against the walls and rebounding like fists of a mad prisoner.

"All right, Bullah. Me will get the young officer outside to sign after; he looking for quick promotion and me got to recommend he."

"So that's all, then?"

"That's about it, pardner. The good thing 'bout these two story is that dead man tell no tale." He crossed the room, opened the door and called the young officer.

"Bring some of that good rum out of the storeroom," he said and turning to Bullah, he added, "Is a long time we en't catch a gaff together."

"Long time, Mark-a-book, over a year since you come my way."

"You know how it is, pardner; pork-knockers always misbehaving theyself. Only yesterday there was a big fight at Oronopai over a woman. Words lead to blows and blows lead to stabbing, and next thing one man get kill. Me had to send off two of me men to track down the killer."

"But is why you got to hunt the poor man down? He kill a man in hot blood and by now he must be sorry," Belle said.

"Queen, sorry can't bring dead man back to life, and if everybody think like you me won't have no work." The officer brought in four bottles of rum and some cups and the sergeant poured himself a tall drink. "Here's to the queen, to Joe Smart son and to you and the boy, Bullah! If the future got more whip to crack over all you back, then laugh in future face and say, 'When me had chance to live me live big. Me had more than me share of everything and me live every minute.' Once you can say that then en't nothing to worry 'bout!" When Rhodius sent to call us we had finished two bottles and started on a third.

We left Kamakusa in the late afternoon and travelled through the night. The others slept huddled up in blankets against the chill night air and the dew. I couldn't sleep and sat with my ear pressed to the side of the boat listening to the river. Rhodius stood near me and his silhouette reminded me of a sawed-off tree trunk.

"You hear the voices?" he asked.

"Which voices?"

"The river, man, the river. This water got more talk than the tongue in Babel. When night-time come all the dead man under the river does talk." He spoke quietly, with his eyes on John Pye's shadow in the bow all the time. "They got good people and bad one under the river, and me travel up and down so often me know them all. Me travel when star was bright, when moon hang low, when dark so heavy me couldn't spit through it. The good people does say, 'Rhodius, Rhodius, don't take no chance with the power-god; Kusewayo sitting stony-still in he big chair. Steer clear of the living rock; they got tentacle-hand to pull you down. . . don't take no risk by Topoco, the green spirit of the quiet water got whirlpool to suck you in. . . don't make mistake at the Looking Glass, is time of the year for sacrifice, that water deep with hungrying for you.' But the bad ones does say, 'Come down, Rhodius. Come down, Rhodius. We will make you bones flute like weeping wood! Come down, Rhodius; the river bottom smooth and we will roll you eye from here to Macharee.' You hear them?" he said. "You hear them?" And I pressed my ear against the gunwale, but all I heard was tongueless lisping and all I saw when I sat up was starlight dancing on the rim of whirlpools.

I fell asleep and woke up when the *Fire Plume* jarred to a stop at Topoco. I could hear the water rushing by and see the outline of trees on the river bank leaning over in the thick mists. The morning wind sent the mist curling and spiralling like silky hair. Passengers stumbled ashore with a clatter of pots and saucepans and I heard their feet stirring up dead leaves as they prepared breakfast. I shook Belle awake. She was sleeping with her head on Bullah's shoulder, and she mumbled and rubbed her eyes and asked where we were. We stretched our stiff limbs and went ashore.

"Lord, me will be glad when this boat trip finish," Belle said. We ate breakfast squatting on the wet earth. The mist cleared and the sun flared up. Tonic had made friends with John Pye and he kept telling us excitedly that he wanted to become a boat captain. John Pye stood astride the gunwales and addressed us all.

"For them who don't know the river let me give you advice, once this boat gone-a-fall no man speak but the Cap'n. All you must man the paddle and when the Cap'n shout, pull, then move like you got tiger on you back. If you want to know why me telling you this or you think me making meself big, jus' look at them crosses bottom-side of Topoco."

The *Fire Plume* moved into the mainstream. We seemed to be standing still while rocks and trees rushed by. I could see the blue of the sky through thin, smoky clouds. John Pye plied his big paddle left and right as he swung the bow away from rocks. I looked at Rhodius as he manoeuvred the *Fire Plume.* He swung the tiller hard over to the right, slowly to the centre, then hard left. His sloe eyes were narrowed, his thick, muscular body tense. He was enjoying every moment of the chance to triumph over the river once again. He swung the *Fire Plume* broadside and we took the first drop.

"Pull, for Christ's sakes!" he bellowed, and like one man we paddled away from the suction of the whirlpools and the undertow. Belle suddenly started laughing crazily.

"Shut up you big black mouth!" Pye shouted, and she put both hands over her mouth and sat trembling and shaking until we cleared the third drop.

"Is all right, Queen," Bullah said. "This river does make all of-we mad sometimes."

At the foot of Topoco was the Morebisi still water, and its unbroken sheen reflected sky and trees and even dewdrops on the leaves. It was a pool of silence under which the water chafed and tugged, swept round and round, smoothing pebbles and sculpturing godheads on rocks. We continued down the rapids – Turesi, Itaki, Popekai, through the dark gorge at Tramway Hole and past Macharee. In the afternoon we paid tribute to Kusewayo, the god of stone, who sat on his rock-hewn throne eyeless and remote. We took off our hats as the *Fire Plume* rushed by.

* * *

Stars and fireflies came out to greet us the night we sat on cane chairs in a hotel balcony in Bartica, sipping rum and gaffing with Rhodius and John Pye. The town was quiet. Most of the pork-knockers had passed through, on their way to Georgetown before the rainy season. The hotel balcony overlooked a stretch of razor-grass beyond which the dark Essequibo River crept towards the sea like a thief.

"Is what you going to do with all that money, Shark?" Rhodius asked.

"I don't know. I'm not thinking about it. Right now the money's like a tree fallen across my life."

"Buy solid things, pardner," Bullah said, stirring the rum in his glass with his forefinger. "Solid things that you can sell when things bad – house, land, them is not thing people can take 'way from you easy."

"Shark got to beat up he head 'gainst the tree trunk like everybody else," Belle said.

"All right. So I'll beat my head 'gainst the tree trunk, but for God's sake let me do it and enjoy my misery without everybody pouring out a sermon."

"Many is the time the spirit move me to try me hand with gold and diamond," Rhodius said. "Me does hear plenty 'bout where to stake claim when me carrying pork-knocker up and down the river. But me know that me is a weak-minded man and if me make too much money the laziness that sleeping in me bone will wake up, and that will be the end of ole Rhodius, so me set me mind 'gainst it, and me going to sail boat up and down these river 'till me drop dead or me drown." He tossed down a drink for the road and stood up. "Got to make it up the Cuyuni at fore-day morning, so me will say good night to you all."

"Night, Cap'n!"

"Fast sailing, and let no rock stop you!"

"Don't kill youself with the girls at Perenong!"

"You coming, John Pye?" Rhodius said, and the bowman shook himself and followed his skipper out.

CHAPTER NINE

A RAGGED, barefoot crowd gathered at the entrance to the market stelling to gape at the black man who had found his eldorado. Georgetown was small, and rumours could sweep across this city like fire over dry savannah grass. Rich pork-knockers were a legend in the city. During the gold and diamond rushes they had erupted out of the colony's heartland, loud-mouthed, reckless, buying excitement with stacks of dollars, making the good times roll for a short season before returning penniless to the forest and high savannahs.

From the moment I set foot on the stelling I was living in the shadow of those others – the legend-makers whom the coast people sang ballads about. I had planned to live quietly with Belle, to spend wisely, to buy land and settle down to farming it, but everyone expected pork-knockers to act in a certain way, and I found myself living according to what people expected.

We lived in Elsa's brothel for a while, and after a few weeks I decided to buy a big house in a nice part of the city. Elsa introduced me to her solicitor, a brown man named De Freitas. The moment we shook hands and he led me into his office, he began spilling talk in my direction. He spoke so glibly you would have thought that the man had been brought up on birdseed.

"I know just the place for you, Mr. Smart. A man in your position needs a big house, not one of these newfangled ones that's bright outside and cramped inside, but an old one. The one I have in mind for you belonged to an Englishman." The solicitor shifted his spectacles up and down the bridge of a strong nose as he spoke. "It's a fine house, Mr. Smart. Wish I could buy it myself, but I can't afford that kind of money..."

"What kind of money, Mr. De Freitas?"

"Don't look so surprised, Mr. Smart, the house is going for next to nothing; it's just that I'm a poor man." I looked at the natural oil gleaming on his face, at the blur of his cunning eyes behind thick lenses, at the girth of his stomach, and I felt like laughing, but I kept a straight face and said:

"I'd like to see the house."

"Let me see." He looked up at the ceiling, showing a neck like a stretched concertina. "Would four o'clock be all right for you?"

"That would suit me fine," I said, listening to the clatter of typewriters in the adjoining room.

"I'll pick you up at Elsa's at four."

"Mind if I bring some friends with me?"

"Not a bit, Mr. Smart. Please yourself."

I returned to find Belle and Bullah in Elsa's front parlour, and they told me that Slackfoot, Elsa's man, had taken Tonic to the waterfront to see a British warship. Elsa's duties at the brothel usually kept her up all night and she slept until after midday. She was a small, highly-strung Portuguese in her mid-forties. Her skin was stretched over sharp bones and her hair dyed red and tied in a bun behind her head. Her black eyes were very bright, but there was something oily about them as if there was a store of oil under the flickering lids which lubricated her eyeballs; and when she spoke she jabbed her hands out at you. A maid brought her a jug of black coffee and she poured some into a small wooden cup.

"You see De Freitas?" she asked.

"Yes; he's taking me to see a house this afternoon."

"He sharp like tiger claw, so watch he, Shark."

"You don't think you should wait a bit, and settle up in you mind what you going to do before you buy big house?" Bullah asked, and I knew that they had discussed the matter while I was out. I resented this go-slow, cautious attitude of Bullah's. Belle did not say anything, but I could see it written all over her face that she agreed with him.

"I've only got one life to live and I'm going to live it as the spirit moves me, and I don't care what anybody thinks."

"Don't take me story to make vexation, Shark, 'cause me only talking to you like you was me son."

"I know you mean well, Bullah, but I've got a lot of things to work out in my mind. You know, every visit I pay to this city, it's like if I'm seeing it for the first time, and I've got to start all over again to arrange things in my mind so that I can get accustomed to the life here. I made a lot of plans when I was in the bush. I was going to do this and do the other, but now that I'm here all the plans don't sound good no more. Belle will keep on telling me to settle down in a village, but I want to see what city life is like. I never lived in a city; I just passed through."

"Me hope you don't live to curse the day you set foot in this place," Belle said, and Tonic and Slackfoot burst in just then, and they talked about the warship with its big-mouthed guns, and the way the white sailors polished the brass and scrubbed the decks.

"The girls should rake in some money tonight," Elsa said.

"Me better book one early," Bullah said. "Can't allow them white sailor to hog all we woman."

"Like you making up for you hermit life in the bush, old man," Belle said.

"Me still got a lot of juice store up in me back, Queen."

De Freitas came around later with a chauffeur-driven car, and he took us to see the house in Queenstown. It was a big white house, which looked like the doctor's mansion at Eccles. It had a front garden which was ringed with hibiscus hedges. There were two po-boy trees by the gate, and at the foot of the drive, a gnarled flambeau which shaded the front veranda from the afternoon sun.

"You like it, Mr. Smart?" De Freitas asked.

"Looks too big for a man without a family."

"You and the queen can fix that up quick," Bullah said. I noticed the neighbours peering from behind their Venetian blinds, and Belle said:

"Is so these Georgetown people stay, they want to see is which black man coming to buy the white man house. They does spend all they time bothering 'bout other people story."

I felt very proud entering that house, for there was I, a black man from a village, stepping into the shoes of the great ones. It was this feeling more than anything else that made me want to buy the house. Bullah and Belle looked frightened as they walked around the rooms, and in a way I understood their fear and shared some of it. They moved about quietly and spoke in whispers, while I raised my voice and put my feet down hard on the floorboards. But we were all conscious of the white man's presence. He had lived in this house and gone his way, but he had left a strange atmosphere behind him, forcing us to act as if he was listening to us all the time.

"How much you asking for the house, Mr. De Freitas?" Bullah asked, and once he started to talk business he sounded assured.

"It's a splendid property. Have you seen the lawns and tennis courts at the back?"

"How much, man? Don't worry with all that sweet-talk."

"Seven thousand."

"Them rafter must be line with gold."

"This is a house fit for a king. . . in the best district in the city. . . with the best of neighbours. . . ."

"Don't worry 'bout the neighbour," Belle said. "They don't help you pay for the house, and them me see peeping through they window at we don't look like the best of anything to me." We were standing in the centre of the drawing-room. Bullah left us and walked around the room very slowly. He walked close to the wall, and every couple of steps he stamped on the floor and thumped the wall hard until we could feel the house shaking.

"Three thousand five hundred and not a penny more," Bullah said. I kept out of the bargaining, because I saw that De Freitas had met his match in Bullah.

"Have a heart! You must live and let live."

"Me know that saying another way," Bullah said. "Leave and let live."

"Mister. . . ."

"Daniels is me name."

"Mr. Daniels, you're a hard man."

"That's right; come up the hard way from the gutter," Bullah said, and I thought I saw the solicitor's stomach quiver.

"Make it four, Mr. Daniels."

"Three thousand five is the best we can do. Shark didn't pick he money off a tree; he work like draught oxen for it." De Freitas adjusted his glasses, coughed several times and looked at us appealingly. Bullah examined the ceiling thoughtfully and said:

"Me see some water-stain up there, like the roof leaking."

"All right. I'll let Mr. Smart have the property for three thousand five hundred dollars."

"Now you talking sense," Bullah said. "It will just make the grade at that figure."

* * *

The living-room was sparingly furnished, but there was something wild and barbaric about it. I had bought the furniture for it myself. De Freitas had tried to sell me some of the Englishman's heavy mahogany tables, sideboards, cupboards, chairs, but I did not want any of it for the living-room. The bedrooms with their huge wardrobes and four-poster beds could house the white man's ghost. I wanted at least one room to belong to me. The first time I saw this room it looked like a twilight beach strewn with dead wood: everything about it was heavy, shadowy. It was as if the white man had been afraid of the colour and the sunshine, and because of this he made his house into a dark cave in which he could hide. I flung open the doors and windows to chase away the brooding that the white man had left in the living-room. I let in the sunshine and the violent colours in the garden. I had a builder come in and scrape off the dark stain from the floor so that the natural reddish-brown of the crabwood could blend with the pale blue walls. The chairs, tables, cabinets were all made of leopard wood and the dark brown spots against the bright yellow of the wood was strikingly vivid. To complete the furnishing of the living-room I put ocelot, monkey tail, red howler rugs, on the floor, and since the bamboo curtains between this room and the veranda were faded I had toucan and macaw feathers glued on to the bamboo in bright patterns.

At first Belle was overawed by the white man's furniture in our bedroom, and when I said that we should sell it, she said that it might bring us bad luck. One morning, however, she jumped out of bed so violently I thought she had gone mad. She flung all the windows open and abused the white man.

"Me didn't sleep at all last night," she said. "The white man ghost was prowling about the place whole night. Me see the man shadow outside the mosquito net, and he was watching at the two of we and shaking he head. Me sure the man jumbie living in that wardrobe."

"I told you to get rid of the thing."

"But is why you didn't build you own house?"

"Why do you always have to find some way of blaming me whenever anything goes wrong?"

"Me will go this afternoon and find an obeah-man who can drive 'way the white man spirit from the house."

"All those obeah-men are big scamps," I said, but underneath the bravado I thought that it was a good idea, and I was not going to discourage Belle too much. She was standing naked near the window and she suddenly changed the topic.

"I see that woman next door watching at me and cutting up she eye every time she see me. She better leave me 'lone or one of these days me will take a walk to she yard and tell she few things 'bout sheself." She looked as if she might have carried out the threat right then, so I hastily cut in.

"Belle," I said, "I told you I heard from Tanta Moore and Brother C.?"

"No; you en't tell me a thing 'bout that; you was too busy running up and down buying this and that for the house."

"They wrote thanking me for the money and said they didn't believe that I was a rich man until they read about me in the papers. Of course, old Tanta Moore can't read, so Brother C. must have told her about it. I want to send for them to come and spend some time with us. You will like them, Belle, and I know Bullah and Tonic will get along with them fine."

"Send for them, Shark. Will be good to have them in the house; then you can't make a big ass of youself. Me watch you going about you business, and is all right 'till stranger around; then you does start talk big and act foolish. Is why you don't act natural? You is a village boy, black as night; the white and the brown man shoes en't never going to fit you."

"One of these days you're going to go too far with me, Belle, and then there won't be any telling what might happen." I felt a sudden rage taking hold of me. I knew that I needed Belle. She had planted her feet in the village mud the first day she had started to walk, rooting herself on an earthy base for life, and because of this she could worship no false gods. I, on the other hand, took on and shed values and attitudes the way a lizard changes colour to merge with its environment. When I was in the bush I acted the part of a pork-knocker, and now that I was in the city I was acting the role of a town-man. Belle and Bullah were the only people who could break into the small enclosure of my fantasy and trample down the false gods, whoever they were for the moment. The difference between Belle and Bullah was that he always had more respect for my feelings. Belle had such a hatred for what was false, what did not ring absolutely true, that she often spoke her mind to me before she realised that what she was saying was pouring salt on a wound. She did not understand that I needed my enclosures of fantasy to keep me alive, and the money had provided me with a chance to widen these enclosures. Belle came and sat beside me, and she was suddenly tender in the way that only people who are strong of will and unusually robust can be:

"Me sorry if me hurt you, Shark, but you know how much me love you, and me can't stand by and see you digging trap for youself to fall in."

Bullah and I sat out on the veranda and watched Belle walk down the drive towards the front gate.

"Is where the queen going in this hot sun?" Bullah asked.

"She's going to hire an obeah-man to drive the white man's ghost out of the house; said she couldn't sleep last night."

"Me hope she get a good one."

"She says he's from Surinam, so he must be good."

"When me was a boy," Bullah said, "they had a Surinam obeah-man living in we village, and one day, a coolie woman chop up she husband after she find he two-timing she. The obeah-man name was Doorne, and he did like this gal, so he swear to put something on the judge so the gal can get off. Well, case come up, and the judge was a hard man; then suddenly when it was looking like things was going 'gainst the gal the judge take sick and dead. You should know that the next judge didn't take no chance: he let the gal go free as a heron, and after lil' while the gal marry Doorne."

The noonday sun was beating down on the white-marl street outside my gate, and the verging grass which was a soft green in the early mornings and late afternoons took on a neutral colour in the haze that simmered over it. A group of naked black children who had emerged from the alleyways between the big houses were tumbling in the grass, shouting and laughing, and my neighbour – a phantom woman always peering from behind Venetian blinds – sent her cook to drive them away. The cook was young and buxom, and when she spoke there was laughter in her voice.

"All you should be shamed of youself," she said, with arms akimbo and eyes dancing, "showing you nakedness to the backra people like this!" The children understood that the cook had a grumpy mistress and was doing her bidding. A few of the bigger boys saw the woman's shadow behind the slatted blinds, and they lifted up their penises and shot golden jets of urine at her until the shadow vanished.

"Come in here at once, Clysis!" a voice from the window said, and the cook adjusted her face before she went inside.

Bullah called out to the small-boys, "Come, boys. Me want a word with you!" A small black pod of life detached itself from the rest and came through the front gate sheepishly, while the others stood back waiting to see what would happen. The small-boy stopped at the foot of the front steps. He was so black that if you saw him on a dark night the only thing that would give him away would be the two white spots of his eyes when he opened them.

"Come on, boy. Nobody en't going to bite you!" Bullah said.

The child walked up the steps and I opened the door for him. The awe in his big eyes made me feel sorry that Bullah had called him in. The small-boy was an image of myself twenty-five years ago – this naked, black, potbellied scarecrow from the alleys and warrens which bordered on the big houses and yet were so far away. Only when a land breeze brought the stink from these foetid regions did the people in the big houses feel any discomfort over their existence.

"What's your name, boy?"

"Lion, boss."

"Who is you mother, boy?"

"Me mother name Bess, and she does wash clothes. . ." The small-boy was so nervous he wet himself and burst into tears.

"Is all right, chappie. Nobody en't going to harm you," Bullah said. "Look. Take this silver money and buy something for youself." He snatched the half-crown and darted through the door and down the drive. We watched him rejoin the others, saw them examine the money and bolt. I went back to my Berbice chair, but Bullah paced up and down.

"It en't right, you know, all this big house and shutting youself away. Me feel like me fall in a trap." Bullah was echoing my feelings, and I used words to cover up my uneasiness.

"I'm beginning to like it here. City life's taking hold of me. Some days I like to go by the market and wedge myself into the crowd so that I can drift along wherever the tide of sweating people carries me and become an ant like all the rest."

"Me don't know 'bout all them high-sounding reason. Me like the town for lil' while; me can play billiards, watch lil' cricket, and when night-time come, the whorehouse always got flesh to sell you. But me can't stay in town for long; me heart does sicken for the bush when me stay 'way couple month."

"By the way, Bullah, where's Tonic? I haven't seen the boy since yesterday."

"Is waiting me waiting for he to come back. Me going to show he who is man and who is boy in this house."

"City life's gone to his head, Bullah; you've got to give him reins to run."

"Me giving he rope to hang heself. All the boy asking for day after day is more and more money. From the time Tonic open he cross eye in the morning is, 'Bullah me want to buy this' and 'Bullah me want to go here', and once me give he the money then me eye en't lighting on he 'till he spend it all."

"That's him coming there now," I said, pointing down the drive. Tonic was wearing a cloth cap cocked at a rakish angle, a bright red shirt, sharkskin trousers and two-toned shoes, and his walk was a mixture of his bushman's shuffle and the jaunty swagger of the sweet-man of the streets and the waterfront.

Bullah took off his broad belt deliberately, and moved to the front door like a cat. As soon as Tonic entered he caught his arm in a cruel grip. Tonic's bravado gave way to dismay and fear and he tried to wrench himself free.

"Me tell you 'bout this staying out all night, boy!" He rained blows on Tonic's back and legs, but the boy never once cried out. His silence only seemed to anger Bullah more. "Me going to show you which of we is the man! After all the time me spend bringing you up, you going to end up knocking you body about with a lot of loose woman!"

"Skipper!" Tonic shouted, and Bullah came to himself and stared about him stupidly. "Skipper, you make it so that me got to leave you. Me meet a gal who me love, skipper, and me spending all me time with she. Me swear me telling you the truth, skipper; if me lie then the Lord strike me dead."

"Well, is why you didn't bring the gal round? If she is a decent gal, then nobody en't going be 'gainst she." Bullah knew that Tonic was lying, but he was trying to make-believe that the boy's story was true. He could not accept the fact that the pattern of discipline and authority which he had imposed on Tonic for fourteen years was breaking up, and he had no way of saving the situation except by using force. He pushed Tonic away violently and came over to me. For the first time since I had met Bullah he seemed at a loss to deal with a situation, and I felt sorry for him, for the hurt in his eyes was something I could not bear to look at.

"Bullah, man, you trouble is that you heart is too big. Let the boy go if he wants to; he'll regret it, but let him go just the same."

"The boy let me down bad, Shark, and the story hurt me. Is how after couple month in the city the boy can change so! Lord, when me think how he was good and quiet at Perenong me can hardly believe that he change so."

Tonic slunk off to the kitchen and Bullah followed him and I heard him saying:

"You don't have to come back to Perenong, boy, but if you decide to stay in the city, then you must take up a trade, motor mechanic or carpentering, something like that, 'cause you en't going have nobody in the world to look out for you if trouble or hard times catch you."

Belle returned with the obeah-man in the late afternoon. I told her that Tonic had walked out, and for a while she forgot about the white man's ghost so that she could console Bullah.

"That boy more treacherous than a snake, so is good that he pick up heself and gone before he heap trouble on everybody head. But people deceitful, eh! After all you do for that boy, Bullah! You was more than a father to he." The obeah-man sat himself down in a comfortable chair and helped himself to

Bullah's cigarettes. He rested a small black box on the arm of the chair and sat back, and although his body looked relaxed, his eyes were alert and cunning in his flat black face. I did not know how good an obeah-man he was, but he looked and acted the part so easily that I was prepared to believe in him, and I saw Belle and Bullah looking at him respectfully.

"We ready whenever you ready, Mr. Malo," Belle said, and the man crushed his cigarette out between his fingers, picked up his black box and stood up. He knew that we were watching his every move, but he didn't seem worried.

"Me got to walk 'round the house couple times to get the feel of the place," Malo said, and when I offered to show him around he said that he had to walk around on his own. He opened his black box and took out a cloth bag, and when he shook the bag it sounded as if it had bones in it. Walking around the room, he rattled the bones in the four corners. He did this with the gravity of a parson sprinkling holy water, and walked through the passage leading to the kitchen, leaving us standing where we were, caught in the spell of his black magic. It was a magic of the man himself; the softness of his movements, the way his dark face seemed to melt in the shadows of each corner, leaving only the luminous points of his eyes. We heard his catlike footsteps in the room above us, and when he returned to us he set about locking his black box very carefully. He said nothing, but we knew that he had trapped the white man's spirit. I thought I heard something fluttering inside the box.

"Work done now," Malo said, and suddenly the spell was broken, for he was hinting that it was time for him to go and he wanted his pay.

"Is how much you did say you was goin' charge?" Belle asked.

"Me did say five dollar, but the job was bigger than me thought, 'cause white man spirit harder to catch than black. Me got to charge you eight dollar now." I saw Malo's eyes taking in the furniture, the rugs, the polished floor and decided that even if he was a genuine obeah-man he was first of all a good business-man.

"Me will pay you seven dollar," Belle said, "and not a red cent extra," and from the fierceness with which she said this, I knew that she too was losing faith in Malo, and she was angry with herself for being taken in, rather than with him. Malo was quick to sense the change of mood and he collected his seven dollars and left.

"That nigger man smart," Bullah said, and he laughed so loudly that Malo must have heard him, but his laugh was not a happy one. "That son of a bitch proper smart!"

We did not live to regret Malo's visit, because Belle said that it felt easier walking around the house, and after a while we all felt as if the brooding that used to fill the rooms had disappeared. The few visitors we had noticed it too and commented on it.

* * *

Bullah paced the polished floor walking between the islands of rugs, and Belle shuffled and banged about in the kitchen, a clean kitchen, freshly painted, with new pots and pans on the white wooden shelves. Even the wood smoke from the big iron stove was clean and blue and fresh-scented. The sea breeze lifted the smoke over a dwarfed mango tree, over and above the dwarfed breadfruit tree with its large dark green leaves. From where I sat in the living-room I could look through the window and see the smoke floating away towards the high zinc fence behind the tennis lawns. The grass had grown tall on the lawns, for no one had tended them since the white man left. After a while I sat back in my Berbice chair and listened to carts rumbling by on the street, and a kiskadee calling its mate from the flambeaux tree. I remembered how I had shot one of these birds with a catapult when I was a boy in Mahaica. I had picked up the warm, crumpled bundle of brown and yellow feathers, and had felt no pity for the mate crying out its sorrow in the branches above me. I had walked away with the dead bird, and when its mate kept following me, I had shot it and taken the pair to Tanta Moore, but she had refused to cook them. She had said that they had worms in their heads.

"I was thinking of going to see the old people in Mahaica," I said.

"You should, Shark," Bullah said. "They was good to you."

"An even better idea is that I'll send for them to come and stay with me for a couple months."

"You think they will like that?"

"How do you mean, Bullah?" My eyes followed him as he continued pacing up and down.

"Me mean if the old people happy in they village, then why root them up and bring them to all this city noise and big house. You will just make them feel bad. Look at me. Me know this town long time, and yet when me come here me feeling like tiger on hot sand, and whole night me hearing the river and when me wake up in the morning me don't smell the dew nor me don't hear baboon shouting."

"We're just getting settled in, Bullah. You just wait until we start living, man."

"We getting funny weather these days, eh; one minute is sun-bright and the next minute the rain coming down," he said, and I knew that he had changed the conversation because he was sorry that he had told me about his homesickness for Perenong.

Raindrops drummed on the galvanised zinc roof, and I went to the front window to watch them tap-tapping on the roses and canna lilies and flambeaux blossoms.

Bullah joined Belle in the kitchen and I heard them talking and laughing.

"Come out and keep we company, Queen," Bullah said. "It en't good for two man to sit down and watch each other face whole day."

"Go 'long with you, Bullah Daniels! You got too much sweet talk in you mouth; them bright-gals better look out now that you'se in town."

"No bright gals for me, Queen, 'long as me can pay me dollar a time in Elsa whorehouse; that's good enough for me. Better man than me meet they Waterloo with sugar-tongue whore-in-disguise in this Georgetown. Me like the real thing, pay me money, collect me satisfaction and there the story end 'till next time."

"You make it sound like you buying vegetable in the market."

"Is same thing, Queen, food and woman; en't no difference."

"Belle," I said going to the kitchen door, "Belle, I'm going to hire a cook and a maid; you can't spend all your time sweating in the kitchen."

"Chu, cook and maid! Lord, is what me going to do then?"

"We've got to start living, gal, going about different places. Can't just pen ourselves up inside a house like poor people, gal."

"That's all well and good, Shark, but me don't want to sit around like no white woman. Sweat don't kill nobody unless they make it pile up inside them. You don't understand? You is me man and me want to make you happy in we house. You getting all kind of newfangled idea of late – you want buy motor car and dress up and go places. Chu, man, is what happening to you! Me is a black woman born and bred; en't no use forgetting where me come from."

CHAPTER TEN

PANCHO was the first person to really initiate me into the ways of the city. I met him the day I went to buy a car. He was standing outside the big garage gaffing with a group of loafers. The garage was near to Tiger Bay, a section of Georgetown which was popular with pork-knockers, pimps, whores and sailors. As soon as Pancho saw me he left his friends and walked up to me.

"Is long time me wanted to meet you, Ocean Shark," he said in such an easy, friendly way that for a moment I thought that we had met before.

"Your face looks familiar, but I don't remember you," I said, and he spat out the black sage stem he was chewing and laughed from deep in his belly. He was nearly a head shorter than me, but was well-built, and he had a bushman's loping walk.

"Me name is Pancho," he said, sticking out a thick hand, and I noticed that the palm was pink and the fingers short and blunt. Pancho looked as if he had come out of a cauldron of racial mixtures with a scalded brick-red complexion, and you could not tell what the mixtures were just by looking at him. His hair was brown and woolly, his eyes tilted upwards at the outer corners, and he squinted as if the sun was bothering him all the time. I shook his hand and thought that he would rejoin his friends, but he did not move from my side.

"You look like a bushman," I said, because I felt that if I made conversation he would tell me what he wanted from me sooner.

"Me born in the bush, skipper, but me grow up round here." He waved an arm towards Tiger Bay.

"I was going to look at cars," I said. "I want to buy one."

"Me know, skipper. That's why me join you, 'cause me know

more 'bout cars than Indian know 'bout tajah. Me chauffeur two white man and one brown man car already and when me hear that you come to town me say to meself, 'Ocean Shark must buy a motor and Pancho is the man to drive it for he,' so me was watching out for you, skipper, more than a month now."

"But I don't even know if I'm going to buy a car; I just came to look."

"You got to buy one, skipper; the black people expecting you to make a show, and if you go 'bout like ordinary man they goin' laugh at you and say you mean."

"I don't care what they say; they didn't help me to sweat myself out trying to find diamonds."

I bought the car and Pancho attached himself to me. He was the sort of person who made you do something, and after you had done it, you took all the credit for doing it because he wanted it that way. I took him home and Belle and Bullah looked him over. He met their doubtful looks with laughter. In a way they regarded him as a part of the car. They grumbled about the expense and accused me of acting like a white man, but they were proud of the new shiny monster. Once or twice I caught them gazing at the distorted reflection of their faces in the radiator. Looking at them I remembered the village children who used to gather around Dr. Ram's car. Since Pancho could drive and seemed to know all about the insides of the car he earned the respect of Bullah and my woman, Belle. He would have had a more difficult time becoming a part of the household if it had not been for the Ford coupé with its big brass headlamps and its glittering radiator. Pancho spent most of the day polishing the car, starting the engine and listening to it hum with a grave, knowing look on his face, or driving in and out of the drive. When he was tired he stretched out on the leather-upholstered seat with his new chauffeur's cap pulled over his eyes and slept. He was supposed to look after the garden and the lawns, but after a few weeks Belle hired an East Indian gardener because it did not seem right that Pancho, the chauffeur, should belittle himself in the neighbours' eyes. In the afternoons Pancho drove us along the old Dutch dyke outside the city, and every ride was an occasion for much honking of the horn and racing of the engine every time we passed a group of pedestrians. Pancho was bent on announcing to the whole city that we had the biggest and brightest car on the road, and sometimes pedestrians flashed us bright grins and waved and shouted us along in our triumph. The car seemed to crystallise everything that the sudden fortune in diamonds meant to me. I was soon driving myself with Pancho shouting warm-breathed instructions in my ear. I became so taken up with this new toy that at night I dreamt about long, burnt-brick roads rushing at me and trees, people, cattle flitting by as I careened across wide savannahs. Sometimes in my dreams the car would leap over the dyke and mow down the razor-grass on the seashore, and flocks of birds would scatter in sudden flight, puling and squawking and screaming.

I began to see less and less of Belle and Bullah as Pancho and I drove around the city visiting hotel bars and rum-shops just so that people should see us stepping in and out of the car. The two did not say anything, but I knew that they thought I was making a fool of myself. Belle showed that she wasn't happy by constantly reminding me of my promise to send for Tanta Moore and Brother C. I kept putting her off and saying week after week that I would send for them, but days were too exciting with me driving around to the bright spots dressed up in clothes cut by the most expensive tailors, and spending money as if it burnt my palm every time I touched a bank-note. I began to learn that money made the Georgetown folk colour-blind. If you spent enough of it they treated you like a white man, even if you were as black as the ace of spades. The moment you flashed out a wad of notes, eyes lighted up and you saw more teeth than pebbles on a beach. I kept my money in the Royal Bank, and one morning when I went to cash a cheque the white manager himself came out to shake my hand, and every two words it was Mr. Smart this, and Mr. Smart that, and I felt properly important and boasted about it long after.

One afternoon I went for a drive with Pancho sitting beside me with his cap over his eyes. He was still feeling bad after the pints of rum and whisky he drank the night before, and the sea breeze seemed to make him feel worse. I drove up Vlissingen Road past carriages, carts, and people walking as if they had lead in their limbs, because the hot sun had flogged all the energy out of their bodies, and now that it was cool, and the shadows stretched so far you could not see the end of them, they were going home to huts and hovels to nod over smoking charcoal fires and hear mosquitoes singing close to their ears. As I approached the dyke I heard the surf pounding up the beach. I parked the car under a flambeau tree when we were well outside the city. The dyke twisted like a huge stone snake beside the road and its verging grass. Beyond the dyke were thick growths of mangrove and courida, and I could hear the sea lapping at their roots. On the other side of the road were flooded savannahs with huts rising out of them like mounds raised by charcoal burners. The city and the country were close upon each other and yet they were separate worlds. Mahaica was only twenty miles away from Georgetown, but when I was a boy it could have been two thousand.

"Coming for a stroll, Pancho ?" I asked.

"No, skipper. Me will stay with the machine, thank you all the same. That liquor me drink last night heavy inside me head."

I walked along the top of the dyke past couples sitting close together facing the sea. The people of Georgetown were always looking towards the sea, turning their backs on a continent of swamp and forest. I saw curlews and pikers, crook-bills and sea geese flying low over a rim of amber foam which the surf pushed up a muddy beach. The crook-bills cried piercing alarms in the sunset, and the pikers and geese answered them. A black man was sitting on the dyke, hunched and gazing fixedly at the sea. He looked around as I approached and spoke to me.

"I see you're driving now," he said, nodding towards the car. His voice sounded dry and matter-of-fact, and the words he spoke could have been chipped off the tip of his tongue with a knife. "I saw you in the Napier Bar a couple of times, and De Freitas told me he had sold you a house." There was something dried up about this man, as if he had something knotted up inside his belly and he could not vomit it out. The way he tilted his head slightly, and beat his thick lips together as he spoke, reminded me of somebody, but I could not remember whom. "I'll join you for a stroll if you don't mind. My name's Kendall, George Kendall."

"I don't mind at all," I said. He was a powerfully built man. I always noticed the way a man rose to his feet from a sitting position; watching this single movement, I could detect if it was a townman, or a villager, or a bushman. Kendall hoisted himself up like a villager who was accustomed to squatting low on his haunches, to ploughing through mud and swamps, to carrying heavy loads on his back, and yet he spoke like a man from the city. We walked in silence for a while and then I asked:

"You from these parts, Mr. Kendall?"

"Call me George," he said.

"All right, George."

"I'm from the islands," he said. "Came here as a boy after my parents died, and grew up with a relative."

"I don't want to sound like if I'm rushing you, but what's your profession?"

"I'm a lawyer."

"I should have guessed it after you told me you were a friend of De Freitas."

"How are you liking it here, Aron?"

"Never lived in the city before, and I'm just settling down."

"Someone will have to launch you in the right circles, Aron. You're wasting your time around rum-shops and bars, man."

"They tell me black people don't make headway in this man's town, George."

"Not the barefoot ones," he said. "But look at me; I've managed. Came back from England five years ago, and now I've got a good practice and a seat in the Town Council."

"You're a big chibat," I said, and he laughed a kind of strangled laugh and said:

"You tag along with me, Aron, and I'll show you the kind of thing a black man can do with the kind of money they tell me you've got. What are you doing tonight, man?" I remembered that I had promised to drive Belle and Bullah to Elsa's house, and hesitated before I replied.

"Why?" I asked.

"I'm having a few friends round to my house. Why don't you come along?" I wanted to tell him that I would have to bring my woman and my best friend along with me, but I knew that he could not have them in his house. He must have known that they were staying with me, because there was not much that Georgetown people did not know about one another.

"What time can I come?"

"Come around eight-thirty. My house is on Brickdam, near the Law Courts; ask anyone and they'll direct you."

"What kind of clothes must I wear?"

"Just a suit and a tie." He examined me from head to foot. "Don't wear two-toned shoes; ordinary ones will do." I realised that I was betraying Belle and Bullah, and suddenly I felt angry with myself.

"What the hell does it matter what kind of shoes I wear?"

"As a matter of fact, Aron, you're rich enough to wear what you like and get away with it, but you asked my advice and I gave it."

The sun dipped behind the horizon quickly like a fire-plume woodpecker ducking its head in a river. On the way back to the car I wondered why Kendall was doing this for me. He didn't look like the kind of man who made friends just for friendship's sake. I felt in my heart that he was angling to lay hands on some of my money, but I believed that the money would last for ever and was prepared to take risks.

"Let me give you a lift home," I said.

"Thank you, but I've got my car parked further down."

"You know him?" I asked Pancho as we drove away.

"Everybody know Lawyer Kendall, skipper. He go 'way to England to study and when he come back he had a tongue like fire. He was hot to change everything, to put the white man in they place, and help poor people, 'till he fame spread and he start to make money and the more money he make the more he tongue cool off. . . and now he hustling like all the rest, drinking and whoring about and fathering bastard."

"You don't like him, Pancho?"

"Lord, skipper, who is me to like or not like the high-and-mighty? Me does play me game on the sideline, boss."

"I want you to drive me round to his place later on."

"The all of you, skipper?"

"No; just me."

Pancho fell silent as if he too, was bearing the weight of my betrayal.

"You might think I'm stupid, Pancho, but underneath it all I'm a fighter, pardner; come through all the hard knocks and toils by myself without anybody helping me."

"Me didn't say nothing, skipper."

"Say what you're thinking, man! Tell me how I let down the two people closer to me than the smell of my sweat. Go on, tell me!"

"You got to make you bed and lie on it, skipper." We drove across the islands of darkness between the street lights.

Groups of loudmouthed men were rolling dice on the pavements, street preachers were taking up their positions under the glare of paraffin lamps, sleepy cartmen were hunched behind plodding donkeys and mules as they made their way back to the villages after a day in the city, dogs were barking, the big houses in Queenstown were brightly lit, and as we drove by slowly we could hear the clinking of glasses, laughter and the hum of conversation.

Belle and Bullah were already seated at the table eating when we arrived home.

"Me didn't wait for you," Belle said, "'cause you is a man does keep all kind of irregular hour these days; en't no timing you comings and goings no more."

"We went for a drive along the sea wall, and I took a stroll and met a man named Kendall, and the two of us got talking and the sun drop down and the stars were winking in no time."

"You mean Lawyer Kendall?" Bullah asked.

"Yes. You know him?"

"Me know 'bout him. Me does hear 'bout everybody at Elsa house; that place does harbour more news than a paper. They say he is an up-and-coming smart-man. Nobody en't know where he come from, but they say he will take the nightgown off he mother."

"Black people can never say anything good about one of their own; they always have to scoop up mud and throw it around."

"Me don't know 'bout scooping up mud, but a lot of what you hear at Elsa true like gospel, and me should know," Belle said. "From what me hear 'bout that nigger-man Kendall me wouldn't trust he further than me can throw a mora tree."

"You coming round to Elsa with we?" Bullah asked.

"I'll take you there, but I can't stay."

"Is what come over you, Shark? Is why you acting so stranger like?" Belle asked, and the look in her eyes forced me to look down at my plate and the food had trouble getting down my throat. "Since you come to the city you only using me like a whore to sleep with when you feel like it. You talking different, you acting different, you dressing up like backra-man, and sporting 'bout the place and you treating me and Bullah like we is not you people."

The salt pork and rice I was eating suddenly tasted like ashes and I rushed to the kitchen window and spat it out. Pancho had put away the car and polished it, and was coming up the back steps.

"What happen, skipper?" I ran upstairs without answering. Belle came after me and found me lying face down on the bed.

"Me sorry me had to talk we story before other people, Shark, but me don't never get chance to talk to you alone. Shark, you losing youself in this white man city and me can help you if you 'low me to get close to you again."

"I'm sorry, Belle, sorry 'bout everything. I'm going to send Pancho for Tanta Moore and Brother C. tomorrow and next week I'm going to go and look for Dr. Ram and ask him if he wants to open a pharmacy with me."

"Why you don't go and bring the old people youself, Shark?"

"I don't want to go, Belle. I don't know why, but I can't face Mahaica right now; everything the place stands for has gone far away from me."

"All right; send Pancho for them." I remained with Belle that night, and tried to hold on to the smell and the feel and the rhythms of her, the way a man being swept towards the brink of a waterfall holds on to a rock. Our embraces were savagely urgent in a way that they had never been before. We laboured in an ague of passion until morning.

A hawker's high, lilting voice woke me up in the mid-morning. I got up, and, looking through the window, saw a black woman with a basket of fruit on her head, and she was singing out:

"Get you mango, sugar apple, sapodillas, soursop, star-apple and sweet jamoon!"

I went downstairs and found Bullah pacing up and down the living-room, and his eyes looked puffed, as if he had not slept well.

"Me glad you and the queen making another try of it," he said, and his words came out jerkily, charged with so much feeling that he struggled to utter them. I had come downstairs with an image of Belle, black and naked, still lingering in my mind. I could still see the midnight darkness of her against white sheets and I wondered why the image was so clear. It was as if my feeling for her had burnt itself out and my need for her body had lost all urgency. Bullah stopped his pacing and looked at me steadily, and the gleam in his eyes made me uncomfortable. Why was he so upset? I asked myself; and the answer came in a flash: he was in love with her and had been all along. When you discover something like this that has been right under your nose for years, a lot of past events suddenly form themselves into a pattern. Perhaps we had all been too close for me to have suspected that Bullah, the big father-man in my life, was in love with my woman. I knew that if I spoke to him at that moment I would betray my discovery, and was glad when Pancho came in and said:

"Boss, Lawyer Kendall send a small-boy 'round to say that he want to see you this morning urgent. He say he will be in he office 'till midday."

"Where's the small-boy, Pancho?"

"He downstairs by the car."

"I'll go and have a word with him." I nearly knocked over a big porcelain vase which Belle had planted in a corner of the dining-room. It was dark blue and stood about four feet high and I never found out why she had bought it, but of late she had taken to buying all kinds of fancy furnishings to fill up the big spaces in the rooms. I sent a message to Kendall to say that I would be over as soon as I finished breakfast.

Pancho fetched Brother C. and Tanta Moore in the late afternoon. They looked so old and decrepit, it was a pain to see them. Their old eyes measured me and probed into me. They did not seem to care about the big house at all; they only looked at me, and from the first instant of our reunion I knew that in their eyes I had not measured up to the man they had expected me to become, and I regretted sending for them. They took to Bullah and Belle and Pancho, but I was a stranger to them. When they talked to me it was as if they were speaking to the boy they had known in Mahaica and not to the man who had lost himself in the world outside their village. In many ways I had sent for them just so that I could find approval in their eyes. I wanted their blessing for all that I had achieved, but they withheld it from me. Brother C. was thin, grey, bent up like bush rope, but Tanta Moore had weathered the years better. Her face looked like a contour map of the Mazaruni foothills, and she had lost all but a few front teeth, but her back was still straight, her walk firm and her old eyes shone cunningly from their nest of crinkled flesh.

"You know how often me pray to the Lord asking He to spare me so that me can see you again, Aron?" she said.

"Boy, we talked about you so often your ears must have been buzzing all the time," Brother C. said. We sat and talked about old times while Belle, Bullah and Pancho listened. Tanta Moore reminded me about things I had said and done when I was a boy which I had long since forgotten, and Brother C. spoke about my grandparents. He spoke slowly, weighting his words, drawing a picture of the old people that brought them to life again. He wanted to show me how real they had been. In so many ways the fact that I had made a fortune did not matter to them. They could only see people against the background of work that they did, and they considered digging gold and diamonds out of the earth a lazy-man's job. If I had worked for a white or brown-skinned man for regular wages, or had set up a small business of my own they would have felt better.

"Your grandma and grandpa were good, God-fearing folk," Brother C. said, sitting back and sucking loudly at his clay pipe. "Your grandpa growed the biggest yams anybody ever growed on Mahaica land. Was a joy to see he carting he produce to the riverside market; some of the yams was big as a cow's head, and when old age hadn't filmed up he eyesight, they used to talk 'bout him up and down the coast 'cause he could shoot a humming bird out of the top of a full-grown coconut tree."

Tanta Moore interrupted him. Her hearing was not too good and she had caught a few words and thought he was talking about Gonzalez, the shopkeeper's son.

"The boy did go all the way to England and yet he come right back to the village and marry a girl from the coast."

"Did you ever hear any news about my mother?" I asked Brother C. He took his pipe out of his mouth and nodded.

"Her spirit went astray," he said. "Your papa, Joe Smart, Jesus rest his soul, was a man full of big-mouth laughing and talking, but he wasn't a fam'ly man, and your mama was an orchid woman and she never had a tree to twine around." They were tired after the journey and the talk trailed off. Brother C. sucked at his pipe and Tanta Moore nodded. A six o'clock bee was singing outside and the neighbour's dog was barking at a passerby. For the first time since I had moved into the big house it felt like home. A loud knocking at the door startled Tanta Moore awake, and Pancho went to see who it was. He returned quickly and whispered in my ear:

"Is Lawyer Kendall. He want to have a word with you." I found Kendall on the porch.

"I can't come in, old man. Just came to remind you that the party I'm giving in your honour is coming off tonight, so you've got to be there. This will be your real launching-out party, man."

"All right. I'll be there around half-past eight, and you don't have to tell me how to dress this time; I collected a new suit from the tailor today."

"Who have you got in there?" he asked, lowering his voice.

"Some old folks from the coast."

"I'll see you later then."

"Half-past eight."

"Is who that?" Belle asked after I had walked George to the gate and returned to the living room.

"The lawyer friend I told you 'bout."

"But is why he couldn't come in? Me suppose he too big-big to meet ordinary folk like we."

"He was in a hurry, Belle." She pouted and flounced away, and after a while I heard her banging about in the kitchen.

"The voice sound familiar," Tanta Moore said. "Was a hoy-poloy voice, but somehow like me hear it before."

"Everybody's voice does sound familiar to you, Tanta," Brother C. said. "One minute you saying that you hearing en't too right, and the next you talking 'bout how people voice sound familiar. When people get old like we, they does hear echo and it don't have to be nobody voice in particular; is just a lot of voice mixed up and echoing."

I offered Tanta Moore the room in which Belle and I slept, but she said it was too big, so we gave her the small bedroom over the kitchen. When I left her I heard her grumbling:

"Me must go back to me yard soon. Me too old to 'custom meself to all this newness." I looked in to see if Brother C. was all right. He had placed his clothes neatly on a chair by his bed and was looking at himself in the full-length wardrobe mirror.

"The Lord didn't mean for people to see they old age looking back at them like this," he said, and I had to stifle a laugh because he looked like one of the duppies the storytellers in the villages spoke about. He was wearing a red nightshirt and a baby flannel nightcap and his wrinkled black face was full of wonder.

"A white man used to own the house before I bought it," I said, and he muttered something about white people's ways being strange, and sat down on the edge of the bed.

"I was properly sorry when I heard that you left the doctor and you didn't even finish your pharmacy course, boy. The man came to see us afterwards and he said wasn't that you left, but was the way you left, that hurt him."

"Life with him was corseting up my days too much, Brother C., and I had to break out. I knew it was going to upset you and Tanta Moore, but I had to do it."

"You got time?" he asked and he fumbled in the pile of clothes looking for his clay pipe.

"I've got an hour or so before I go out," I said.

"Well, sit down, boy. I'm goin' tell you a story, and when I finish don't ask me what this mean or what that mean, 'cause you got to figure out what the story mean all by youself." He lit his pipe and puffed away at it. "Sit down," he said and I obeyed. "You don't read books no more," he said.

"I never had time after I left the doctor."

"Take 'way that light, boy; it hurting my old eyes," he said, and I took the paraffin lamp off its hook and went outside and hung it over the stairs. When I returned he had drawn his legs up under him, and was sitting in the middle of the bed.

"I know you dying to go out, but listen to this story well." There was the old authority in his voice, and once again I was a small-boy and he my teacher. "I heard this story from you grandpa when I was a boy. It come all the way from Africa and black people tongue keep it alive and fan it like fire that can never burn out. This is the story: In long-time-past-days there was a people peculiar unto themself, a people who could weight they foot down with stone and wait 'till the Lord deliver them from whatever trouble they was in. Now this people lived at the foot of a mountain which was shape like a woman breast with the nipple always in the cloud. And this chosen people live a long time in the shadow of the mountain, and time come when they had to chose a headman from 'mongst them, so they put they heads together and decide that all the strong-men in the tribe must climb up the mountain, and the one that climb highest must bring proof of the wonders that he see, and then he will be made headman. So the strong-men set out and them with weak limb and faint heart straggle behind, but the robust ones climb higher and higher until one young man reach highest of all. And he come down the mountain holding something in he hand, and when he reach the village square the folks gather 'round he, and they see that the thing he bring was a flower, and nobody never see a flower so beautiful, for it was bright and shapely and all who look at it had wonder-light in they eye. The people elect this man headman, and because he bring them the gift of beauty the Lord make he rule long, and He make them shape things in the image of the flower – all kinds of bright and beautiful things. And when this headman was called away, again the strong-men set out up the mountain, and one young man climb even higher than the first headman, and he come back and tell 'bout the wonders he see – the brightness, and the glory, and when he open he hand so them who gather 'round could see what he bring, he reveal a stone, and nobody never see stone so bright and beautiful and all the folks reach out and rub they hand over the curve of it, and the smoothness of it. The tribe make that young man headman and from that stone they learn the secret of work – how to sharpen the teeth of the plough, and the blade of the knife and how to edge all kinds of tools. And the time this headman rule pass quickly, 'cause everybody was busy, and the tribe spread out they farm right up to the bank of a river which used to tumble down from the mountain and out of the sky.

And when this headman die, for the third time the strong-men set out up the mountain and one of them was a dreaming, bright-eyed young man with a look of prophecy in he eye, and he climb so high that he loss 'way in the mist that does cover the mountain nipple. And when all the rest come back the folks ask:

"Where is the bright-eyed boy with the prophecy in he eye? and the men say:

"'He vanish in the mist and we 'fraid for he, but none of we had the strength to follow he.' And the folks wait and wait but the young man didn't come down from the mountain, and every day they post lookout to watch for he. The sun and moon lengthen many shadows, and the young man didn't come back, but the people keep hope 'live in they heart and they wouldn't give up. 'He must come back to we,' they keep saying.

"One day when the sun was hot and no wind was lying down and rolling on the grass, a woman who was washing clothes by the river see something coming down the mountain and she call out the whole village from they midday sleep in she excitement, and they all see this shadow-thing coming nearer parting the heat-haze, and the shadow take on the shape of a man and somebody shout,

"'Is he! He come back!' and the man come running down the mountain with he fist clench high above he head, and when he reach the village he run past the crowd of waiting people as if he didn't see them, and he would have run right through the village if he didn't trip on a piece of firewood and fall down. The folks gather 'round he when he fell, and he lie down on he face still clenching he fist, and somebody pry the man fingers open to see what he was holding in he hand. The crowd gasp, for the man hand was empty, he had no wonder to show them in it. They ask he many question, but he didn't answer, he just lie still where he fall breathing heavy. Some of the women run and bring kuru oil and anoint he and he open he eye and turn over. 'What happen, brother?' they ask all together, and he tell them that he climb up to the mist and over it 'till he did reach the top of the mountain, and suddenly the Lord send down a soft white thing like rain, and yet it wasn't rain 'cause it fall slow like leaf when there is no wind. It fall and flutter and spin, and some of it settle on he head and shoulders and into he hands, which he did open to catch it, and when he held it, one minute it was cold like a mountain pool and next minute it was like fire, and he catch a handful of it and press it hard in his hand. He set out down the mountain with this white and wondrous thing which sparkle jewels when the sun catch it, but the further down the mountain slope he reach, the less of it he had in his hand, and halfway down it vanish so that he only bring the memory of it with he. The light of prophecy shine in he eye and he tell the people that was God's gift that he was holding in his hand and the best of God's gift had to be something no eye can see . . . and the whole tribe believe and they make that young man headman over them."

"I never heard a story like that, Brother C.," I said. "I never heard a story like that in all my born days."

"Think on it," he said and he stretched out and prepared to sleep.

"Good night, Brother C. Sleep well!"

"Good night, boy!" I went to my room to get dressed and my head was dizzy with ideas knocking themselves together.

⋆ ⋆ ⋆

I took a shower, put on my new suit, a light grey tweed, and went downstairs. Belle and Bullah were still sitting at the table. The light from the living-room filtered through the bamboo curtains and barely touched their dark faces. I did not look either of them in the eye, but I could sense that Belle knew of Bullah's love for her. Somehow I felt angry with Bullah as if he had betrayed me. I was jealous of Belle, even though it was all over between us. The quietness between them with its suggestion of a complete understanding was something I could not bear.

"I'm going to a party that Kendall is giving in my honour," I said, hoping that this would goad Belle into answering me, but neither she nor Bullah said anything and I stomped out, slamming the door behind me.

Pancho was waiting for me, crouched over the wheel with the engine running.

"What the queen had to say, Skipper?" he asked.

"Nothing."

"That's bad, chief, bad when woman en't say nothing."

"I know, man."

"Since you got to face a showdown, you better line you stomach with rum tonight, boss. Have a good time, forget all you trouble, and when you come out in the cold morning air you will feel like a king."

There were cars and carriages outside Kendall's house. As I walked up the drive I heard a coachman asking Pancho:

"You skipper is Ocean Shark, the diamond king, eh?"

"Yes, pardner; that man got enough diamond to build a tower. He can buy out the whole lot inside there lock, stock and barrel."

I knocked at the door and Kendall opened it.

"Come in," he said. "The folks are bursting with curiosity to meet you, man." He led the way, and I noticed that his furniture was heavy, solid. The chairs, tables, sideboards, divans looked like those the white man had left in my house. I could not help thinking that George looked a stranger in his own house, and when he introduced me to his wife I was all the more convinced of this. She was a fat brown woman who never gave her tongue a rest, and everything she said made me feel that she wanted me to know that she was doing me a favour by having me in her house.

"I'm pleased to meet you, Misses Kendall," I said, squeezing her spongy hand as if I was testing for strength.

She winced slightly and withdrew her hand quickly, but her tongue was clacking all the time.

"We've heard a lot about you, Mr. Smart. Your name's all over the town, and the moment I heard about you I said to George, 'You must bring that Mr. Smart here and I don't mind what anybody says.' Didn't I, George?" She turned to her husband and flashed the kind of smile that made me feel that she loved herself very much.

"I'll introduce Aron around, dear," George said. "Remember your varicose veins." A gramophone was playing "Marchita" and a few couples were dancing. It was a stand-up party, and most of the guests were bunched together in little groups, talking and laughing the way people do when everybody knows everybody else, and they don't have to worry about what kind of impression they are making. I shook hands all around and the only person I knew apart from George was De Freitas. He was there with his wife, a narrow-chested, frail-looking Portuguese woman who looked as if you would have to cut down to the bone before you found any blood in her. De Freitas wanted everyone to know that we were friends, and he did more chattering than a monkey with a sick tail – Aron, this, and Aron, that. . . until George rescued me.

"Play cards ?" he asked, drawing me aside, and I barely heard him, for I was listening to the conversations around us, the talk about Town Council elections, horse-races, going to England on holiday, Government House parties. After the robust man-talk of the pork-knockers, and Bullah and Belle's easy loudmouthed talk and laughter, these polite exchanges made me uncomfortable.

"I need a few drinks," I said, and George led the way to the bar.

"You haven't said a word to anyone, Aron," he said.

"Haven't had a chance. I think about a lot of things to say, but when I listen to what everybody else is saying my talk just wouldn't fit in with theirs."

"Talk about yourself, man. They're just a pack of intellectually castrated people. They want somebody whose conversation moves from the waist down."

"George, you're a talk-man, eh. I can't keep up with you, man; you ate too much birdseed." I watched him knock back half a tumbler of whisky. He had been drinking steadily and his eyes were red and watery in his flat black face. Several couples were dancing and we turned around and watched them.

"Tell me something about yourself, George. Every time I hear about you they tell me a different story."

"I'm just a hustler, man, always was, knew what I wanted from the beginning and went after it."

"I wonder why I'm always thinking that I met you somewhere before. . ." He cut me short and said:

"I want you to meet that girl over there; she's the kind of gal you need to fancy up your big house. Doesn't matter if she's got nothing in her head." He took me across to the girl. Her name was Beryl Thompson. She had soft, bright eyes and was golden brown.

"Beryl wants to hear about your experiences in the bush," he said, and the young men standing around her drifted away. "Look after him; he's shy."

"But I'm shy too," she said, averting her eyes as quickly as a bird flashing across a shaft of sunlight. Because I was nervous, I talked and talked, and once when I told her about a man falling out of a tree the first time he heard a red howler roar she laughed and I liked the way her full lips curved around her white teeth, the way her eyes danced like a marmoset's.

"You haven't told me about yourself at all," I said.

"I haven't much to tell; not anything really; nothing ever happened to me."

"I'd like to see you tomorrow," I said.

"All right," she said, so quickly that I was surprised and flattered, but when I looked at her again I could see that she was shut up in a virginal pod, not knowing how beautiful she was, unaware of my lust for her.

"In the afternoon," I said; "about half-past five." George was heading our way and she said:

"I live in Raleigh Street, number five." Some of the guests were leaving and a surly young man came up and said:

"Beryl, your mother's going to blame me for keeping you out late."

"I must go, Mr. Smart. It was nice of you to ask me, Mr. Kendall." She sounded like a schoolgirl reciting a set piece. I shook her limp hand and watched her walk across the room.

"How old is she, George?"

"Twenty, and she's ripe for picking, man. She'll tell her mother about you and the old bitch will fasten her on to you so hard you'll have to tear flesh to break loose. The old woman's black, but she married an Englishman; used to be his servant. He left her a bit of money when he died, but she's still going to sell the girl to the highest bidder."

"You make it sound easy, man."

"It is easy when you've got the cash."

"I've got to go soon, George."

"Wait for a bit, man. I can't talk to my friends here; their brains have all been drowned in rum. You notice the way they keep looking at you? They hate you, man, every mother's son of them, the same way that the white man hates them. They feel it's a shame you should have all that money. They'll cringe and lick your boots while you've got it, and when it's gone they'll pass you on the street. Take a tip from me, Aron: make them kiss your arse while the going's good, plug up the hot holes between the women's legs, fill up their bellies; you can buy any of them, man, and when the reckoning comes you can have the last laugh. . . ."

"Lord, George; you hate them, eh!" I talked to him for a while longer, finished my drink and insisted that I had to go.

"Come around tomorrow night and we can play bridge or poker. You did say you can play, didn't you?"

"I used to play in the bush."

Mrs. Kendall took me aside when I went to say goodbye.

"George likes you," she said, "and I hope the Lord puts it into your heart to use a restraining influence on him." Her eyes searched out and found her husband at the bar. "He's in one of his moods tonight; the devil's got hold of him. What was he talking to you about?"

"Oh, nothing special; just the usual old-talk."

"When he's in one of his moods he tries to shame me before everybody, calls me names. Lord, it's a cross I have to bear! Jesus of Nazareth didn't have a heavier one!" She kept holding my hand as if this physical contact would help her to reach deeper into me for sympathy. "You will try and help to save a brother in Christ, won't you ?" I muttered something and freed my hand. Pancho was pacing the drive.

"Me don't think all is well on the home front, skipper."

"What you mean?"

"Well, boss, me drive past the house couple hour ago and me see like Bullah and the queen was moving out."

"You sure?"

"If me lie me die, skipper."

"I can't say that I wasn't expecting it, Pancho; it had to come about."

The two were still there when we returned home, Bullah looking sheepish and Belle bold-faced and brazen.

"The queen and me leaving for Perenong this very fore-day-morning," Bullah said, standing up and facing me as if he had thrown down a challenge. Pancho was standing in the shadows by the doorway and he cleared his throat loudly.

"Is so you leaving me, Bullah?" I was afraid of him, of his

strength. It wasn't only the power of his shoulders and fists that I respected, but I had relied on him to protect and sustain me so long, that the thought of his suddenly becoming my enemy made me feel lonely and exposed. I would have no one but Pancho to turn to if anything went wrong, for Brother C. and Tanta Moore were too old.

"You will ask me if me leaving you so, Shark? You who treat me like servant in you house? Bullah Daniels too old to 'low young man to look down they nose at he, pardner. How you treat the queen was you and she story, and me en't putting me mouth in that, but is meself me talking 'bout. Boy, me did love you like a son, me never had a bad wish for you in me mind, and me wanted to see you make a man of youself in the world. You got better education than either me or you papa and the Lord bless you with luck, but you taking the wrong road; me can tell you that, you en't acting right. Bright light and big talk can dazzle you too quick. Me know that you didn't have no mother to bring you up, but you had friend, close friend, and the queen, whatever you might say 'bout she, she was a good woman for you." I had no answer to all he said, and Belle said nothing, but I knew that she would never forgive me.

"I will come and see you off, Bullah," I said at last, still hoping that somehow, even though I had lost his respect, I could recapture something of the old relationship.

"Me think you better not, Shark. It won't look proper."

* * *

It was three o'clock in the morning and I did not feel like going to bed. Pancho's room was on the ground floor next to the garage, and when he heard the engine running he came out and said:

"Me coming with you, skipper; me thought the spirit move you to go out again, so me didn't undress." He climbed in beside me and we drove to Elsa's. We found Slackfoot in his corner away from the door. He limped towards us, grinning right across his face, so that I could see the deep lines curving around his wide mouth.

"Ocean Shark! Well strike me dead if is not the big chibat heself! Me was hearing 'bout you all over town and me thought you get too big for we here."

"Chu, man, Slackfoot, how can you say that?"

He cupped his hands and shouted upstairs,

"Elsa! E-l-s-a! Come and see who we got here, girl!" He had to shout above the orchestra, which was playing ragged, tired jazz.

"Shark, me en't see you long time, man," she said, coming halfway down the steps and leaning over the banister. "Aye, Pancho, you turn big chauffeur now, man!"

"Well I got to live, Elsa."

"Business sound bright," I said.

"Couple ships come in last night and the sailors take over the place. Them English sailor is trouble; they never got a penny, and after they gone, me have to send all me girls to the doctor."

"That is Mary," Elsa said when she saw me look up to listen to the woman who was singing with the band. "She got a voice sweet as a cooing dove." Mary was singing "Black is the colour of my true love's eyes" to a mob of drunken sailors and their cocoa-coloured partners.

"Play me some hot music, black boy," a sailor shouted, and the languid, lean saxophonist grinned. Mary sang in a swoon with hardly anyone listening to her. When she finished I saw Pancho helping her down from the stage, and afterwards they disappeared upstairs. A young sailor, with a boyish face rouged by sunburn and rum, embraced Elsa, and she pushed him away and cuffed him playfully. We sipped our drinks, listened to the music, and watched the sailors dance on legs which tangled like mangrove roots and did not seem to belong to anyone in particular. One black woman was holding her partner so that his feet never touched the floor.

"You mothering he, Hennie?" Elsa asked, and the sailor raised a blond head above a hillock of black bosom and said, slurring his words:

"I'm too drunk to stand on my own feet, and too polite to stand on the lady's."

"Me know that the queen leaving you to go back to Perenong with Bullah," Elsa said. "Is better like that."

"Yes; is better like that," I said.

"You didn't really know Belle, you know. She was a woman who take to whoring just so that plenty men can admire she; wasn't the money so much she was after, was the thing in a man eye that women does like to see. She and Bullah make a good pair, 'cause he getting old and he going to sit back and 'low all them pork-knocker to feast they eye on Belle, and he en't never going to be jealous. Bullah head fasten on too strong for anything to turn it now."

"I never really thought outright 'bout Belle like that, Elsa. I used to feel what you're telling me, but I never framed the feeling into a whole picture. I better go and call Pancho, because I want to go down to the stelling and see them go."

"Come again, Shark. Don't let high life lead you too far away from you old hang-out."

We drove through empty streets, waking the beggars on the pavements, and they cursed us so loudly that people opened windows and emptied chamber-pots on them. We mingled with the crowd by the stelling entrance and waited until Bullah walked up the gangway with Belle laughing and talking beside him. The sun rose above the mangrove by the river mouth and sea gulls swooped down to lip the river's fire.

"Well, skipper, you friend gone," Pancho said, but before I could answer him I caught a glimpse of Tonic a few yards away from us.

"Aye, aye, Tonic!" I called out. When he turned and saw me he dodged behind a woman with a basket on her head and vanished before I could follow him.

"Who was that, skipper?" Pancho asked.

"Bullah's pet boy whose eyes caught fire with town life."

"Oh, yes. You mean Tonic. Me know all 'bout he."

I suddenly felt tired and numb as we walked back to the car. I did not feel like facing Tanta Moore and Brother C., for they were bound to ask too many questions. I was hoping to escape them and to go straight to bed, but while we were putting the car away I heard them shuffling about in the living-room.

"Pancho, you go upstairs and use my room and let me sleep in yours. The way I feel now those old folks will be kinnah to me if I butt up with them."

"O.K. skipper. Me will tell them that me leave you at the lawyer house and you coming later."

★ ★ ★

I woke up with a rum-head and saw from the way the sun was slanting that it was afternoon. Tanta Moore was washing dishes in the kitchen and I heard her saying:

"But is so the boy will leave we whole day in the white man house! Lord, children can change eh. Aron was never a boy to do something like this. I hope nothing en't happen to he. You think he meet with accident, Brother C.?"

"You're always ready to pin accidents on people, Tanta. Don't worry; Aron will turn up."

"Me don't like what me hear 'bout that lawyer friend he take up with, like the boy keeping bad company. Me must talk to he."

"Don't say nothing to he, Tanta; the boy's smelling his sweat since God blessed him with all that money. . . ."

I went outside and held my head under the back-yard tap, and afterwards I walked upstairs feeling better. Tanta Moore started giving me a piece of her mind almost as soon as I had entered the living-room, but I did not attempt to defend myself. Brother C. never took his eyes off me, and Tanta went on and on.

I was thinking of getting dressed for my date with Beryl when Kendall came around. He was wearing a black velveteen jacket, a white cravat, striped trousers, and patent leather shoes, and the clothes sat uneasily on his massive frame. The jacket was too short, and his buttocks were threatening to burst out of the trousers.

"They tell me your friends have gone," he said.

"Tell me 'bout what you didn't hear, George."

"Who are the old folks you've got staying with you?"

"Come in and meet them," I said, but he hesitated, tapping one foot nervously on the threshold. "Come on in, man!" I led the way inside. Brother C. saw George first, and he gripped the arm of his Berbice chair so hard I saw the white knobs of his knuckles standing out.

"Is who?" Tanta Moore asked.

"It's my lawyer friend, Tanta. He's come to say howdy."

"Howdy, sir. Come near; let me see you face." She leaned forward and tilted her head sideways so that she could see George with her one good eye. The moment I saw George Kendall and Tanta Moore together I knew why he had looked so familiar the first time we met: George was her son, the boy who had run away from Mahaica years ago.

"What you say you name was?" she asked in a gasping voice as she fell backwards in the chair.

"George Kendall," he shouted, and Brother C. said quietly:

"You must pardon us, but you look like somebody we used to know a long time ago." For a moment I thought George was wavering, but he thrust his head forward and clenched his teeth so hard I could see two tight lumps where his jaws locked. I tried to imagine what the struggle to become a lawyer must have been like for him. This was the Brave-boy who had walked the twenty miles from Mahaica to the city and in this journey he had lost himself. He had become another person in his own fantasy, and for most of his grown-up life he had made himself into a make-believe person. The first time he visited me he must have known that his mother was staying with me, and he had returned to test if the phantom George Kendall was more real than the Brave-boy who had left Mahaica years ago.

"I came from the islands as a boy," George said, laughing as if the idea of his being somebody else was a joke. Tanta Moore knew, but she did not give her son away.

"Me hear plenty 'bout you, Lawyer Kendall," she said, and the words came out as if they were being torn out of her chest. "Them tell me that even the white man 'fraid for you tongue." He laughed a nervous, jerky laugh, and suddenly he turned around and walked away quickly. When I went to the porch he was already halfway up the drive. He climbed into his car and drove away as if a tiger was behind him. I did not hear what Pancho was saying from the bottom of the front steps because Tanta Moore was wailing the way village women do for the dead.

I visited Kendall later on, and the maid opened the door when I knocked. His wife had gone out, and he was alone in his spacious living-room. He had changed into a light grey suit and was sitting at a small card-table playing patience.

"Come on in, Aron. I've got some business to talk over with you, man. The wife's gone to visit her people and she won't be back for a while."

I was angry with him, not because he had betrayed his mother, cast her aside like a rice husk, but because it had frightened me to witness the betrayal. I saw that I too was walking the same trail.

"You could at least have hugged her against you. . . ."

"I want to talk some business with you." He kept fixing me with his sloe eyes. He was all locked up in himself and he was not even now going to give himself away to me.

"Jesus Christ, man, don't you have a heart!" I shouted. He looked away, and then continued his game of patience.

"Sit down and have a drink, Aron," he said, and I knew that he had built a barricade of make-believe around him which no one could ever break through. The maid brought out a tray with a cut-glass decanter of rum, a bowl of crushed ice, and glasses.

"What's the business you want to discuss with me, George?"

"It's a long story, but you'll get the point by the time I reach the end." He sat down on the edge of the chair, his shoulders arched and his head jutting forward. I was certain then that no matter how many lawyers you scraped off of George Kendall, you would never reach down to Brave-boy.

"It's like this," he continued. "The white men who rule us have power and money while all we have are illusions. Some of us, like my wife, carry a mountain of religion on our backs and others, like you and me, we know what our make-believe is about." He gestured with his hands as he spoke, showing thick, scrubbed palms. "We're all still slaves, every mother's son of us, but the damned funny thing about it is that we're our own slave-drivers. The white man is like a tiger orchid, high up, feeding on us, never sinking roots in the mud: he brings his orchid house from England and lives in it. He's leeching away our sap all the time, but he's so high up we don't even know or care for that matter. Most of us are in the mud trying to scrape it off our feet, but so many of us are trying we end up like a bunch of crabs – if one can't tear himself free, then none can. Ever seen crabs trying to get out of a barrel? Well that's how the whole lot of us act." It was not so much what he was saying that gripped me, it was the way he loaded every word with feeling, while his heavy, flat face looked like a devil mask, and his eyes like flame leaping out of a nest of hair and flesh. "I've got a scheme, man, a big scheme. I used to shout and rave against the white man, but after I went to England

and came back, I realised that he wanted us to do just that, for as long as we rave and blame everything on him we're admitting our slavery. If, for example, I say that you're to blame for everything that happens to me, then I'm admitting that I don't have a will of my own; I'm just a black boy in a circus jumping every time you crack the whip. As long as the white man doesn't allow us to admit that some misfortune is our own doing, or God's, then we're slaves, no matter how many Emancipation Acts they pass."

"But how are you planning to change this, George?"

"We need big money – not just for big money's sake – but because it will make us secure. Not us, the present generation, we'll never find out who we are, we're lost, man, but our children." He paused to pour himself another drink.

"I want to live good and I'm not worrying 'bout children."

"We've got plenty juice in our back yet and we can breed a flock of them, man. I've been planning this scheme I've got in my mind for years, man, and something good has just turned up – Whiting's Sawmill is up for sale and De Freitas and me have first option on buying it. We've got to raise a hundred thousand. If you put up thirty-five or forty thousand you'll be the biggest single shareholder, and we can raise the rest, fifteen thousand each and a mortgage on the balance. You see, both me and De Freitas are running for Town Council elections in a month's time, and with both of us in, we can collar all the municipal contracts." I could not fit all he told me into a pattern, but it sounded good. Once George started talking he could shadow-box with me the way a jaguar did with a bush rabbit.

"It's a lot of story you told me there, man, and I need time to think about it. One thing I know, and that is that I don't trust De Freitas further than I can throw a mora tree."

I trusted George, in spite of everything that had happened. I was proud of the way he had axed his way into high circles, the way he could talk the white man's talk and act like he owned the whole city.

"You and I are village boys, Aron, and we're making our way to the top, man. You don't think that I will let a city man do us out of anything? You couldn't believe that."

"I'll think it over, George. It's a gamble, man. If I do this thing I won't have much left."

"You don't understand what this will mean, Aron. We'll own half this city in ten years – a timber grant comes with the sawmill, seventeen square miles of forest – we'll own an empire, man."

"How soon will I have to decide?"

"Let me see. This is Wednesday. You've got to let me know by Saturday the latest." He knew that he had me when I stood up to go.

"I'll bring word by tomorrow," I said.

Pancho was waiting for me with the car.

"I've got to go to Raleigh Street and I'm late," I said, and he crouched over the wheel and careened through narrow streets scattering naked black children like birds. "You know anybody who got rich from timber, Pancho?"

"Me know one or two who get rich all right, but they didn't stay rich for long, skipper. Timber is a thing does make and break you quick."

"My luck's been good so far. I don't see why it shouldn't hold."

"Me don't know what you up to, skipper, but Lawyer Kendall is a man who can slide in and out where razor blade can't pass."

"Whatever they say 'bout him, Pancho, I think he'll act straight with me."

"You know you own story better than me, skipper."

"Pancho, what do people say about me?" I asked when he had slowed down before entering a main street.

"You know we folks, skipper; they never got a good word to say 'bout one of they own. They say you work obeah to get you money, that you sell you soul to the wendigo. Me does tell them that you is a hard man, that you got glue in you palm, me got to tell them so or they will flock round like locust to borrow money. Some of them does say you acting like white man and you don't have no use for black people."

"You know the Thompson family, Pancho?"

"Skipper, is who Pancho don't know in this man town! Old man Thompson was a Englishman and he eye catch fire on black woman flesh. He give up all he white friend to marry that black woman after she had a daughter by he, and when Mantop knock he down he left big property for the old woman." We stopped outside Beryl's house. It was a big, three-storeyed building with steps running slantwise across the front leading up to a small porch. The house looked white and clean in its dismal setting amidst unpainted tenements. It was late afternoon, and while the big houses along the street still caught the sun, the tenements were already melting into their pockets of shadow, and the men and women sitting on doorsteps were mingling with the dusk. This section of the city was wedged between the river and the sea, and had once been the site of a river-mouth fort. Far behind Beryl's house was the only relic of this fort, a watchtower from which flights of bats were pouring. I walked up the steps and knocked, and Beryl opened the door.

"Thought you weren't coming any more," she said, pouting. "Come in and meet my mother." The old black woman sat in a rocking chair in a corner of the front veranda, and the way she rested her hands on the arms reminded me of my grandmother. She was one of the shadow-mothers of Georgetown, keeping out of sight most of the time so that her fair-skinned daughter could make a good catch.

"This is Mr. Smart, Mother."

"You is a village boy?" she asked, turning her old condor eyes full on me.

"Yes, Mrs. Thompson – from Mahaica."

"Old Beauchamp pay for you schoolin', eh?"

"Yes, Mrs. Thompson."

"Me husband used to know old Beauchamp in the ole days. Lord rest his soul, he reach a sad end in that Berbice madhouse, they tell me; not a soul did turn up to he funeral."

"I didn't even know he was dead, Mrs. Thompson."

"Lord, boy, like you ungrateful to them that help you." I was about to defend myself when she added in a sharp, birdlike voice, "Stop this 'Mrs. Thompson' business and call me 'Mother'."

"All right, Mother."

"Take care of me Beryl; she is me one eye."

I was glad to escape her, because she had a way of sitting so still it made me feel uncomfortable. We drove past the watchtower and turned sharply into the road along the dyke. Two jetties, half a mile apart, stabbed into the incoming tide, forcing the sea to churn up golden foam in the afterglow. It was dark by the time we drove past Belair and left the city's winking lights behind us. Beryl had lost her shyness and she talked all the way. She said that she thought I had forgotten about our date, and when she saw the car stop and me come out of it, her heart had almost jumped out. I felt excited with this golden-brown girl beside me holding my hand and touching my ear with her breath. She looked so soft and delicate that I felt crude and ungainly. I knew that most of all I was going to enjoy showing her off, flaunting her in people's eyes, just as how George flaunted his brown-skinned wife. A black man could not be a success unless he had one of these brown dolls to offset his blackness.

Pancho parked the car in a grove of flambeau trees far in from the road. He got out and walked away, leaving us alone in the darkness. I held Beryl against me, and she responded in a dream-like terror, her body tensing and relaxing in spasms. She did not resist, although I knew that a part of her wanted to. I did not find any pleasure in her body as we laboured together, but I knew a wild delight in hurting her, subduing her, for without my money to act as a ladder she would have remained perched high above me, out of my reach. "You're hurting me! You're hurting me!" Her voice was wild as a sea bird's and she ripped at my chest with her nails. And when I would have released her at last, she clung to me, crying softly. The passion in her had been suppressed too long whilst her condor mother was waiting to strike the right bargain. I waited until she was calmer, then halloed for Pancho. His eyes did not give him away when he returned and saw Beryl patting and straightening out her dress, but I knew that he was sharing in my triumph.

On the way back Beryl sat close to me and begged me to keep my arm around her.

"You think I will get a baby, Aron?"

"I hope not, girl."

"But I want one. I want your baby, Aron!"

"That's small-girl talk, girl; a baby can cause no end of botheration."

"I wanted this to happen so much. You love me, Aron, even a little bit?"

"You're talking like a child, girl."

"You think I'm a bad girl for giving in so quickly?"

"They lock you up in a cage too long, girl, or you wouldn't ask a question like that."

"That night when you talked to me about the forest I could hardly sleep. I thought you were a real hero, Aron, not like the town-boys who come to take me out; they haven't done anything but go to college and parties and things."

"You're too young for me, girl. You're living in some dreaming heaven and you don't know what's happening around you."

I said goodbye to her at the foot of the steps and watched her walk up, patting her frock with one hand and waving with the other, "I should have met her long ago," I thought, "but the old mother would not have let me through her front door when I was just a black nobody." I watched her go inside and walked slowly back to the car.

"Skipper, you look more worried than a man who just murder he mother," Pancho said.

"I feel worse than that, Pancho."

"Skipper, you still soft-hearted! Suppose you did know how much story does go on in this Georgetown?"

"I was thinking about the mother; she knew what was going to happen."

"Don't tell me you need a prophet to tell you why, boss!"

* * *

Tanta Moore took to her bed for a few days, and when she got up she spent most of her time in the kitchen whining and becoming so crotchety that only Brother C. was able to deal with her. Pancho did not know what had happened, though he suspected that something was wrong and he tried hard to discover what it was. If the two old people had remained much longer he would have found out, for he had a good nose for scenting out trouble of any kind. But Brother C. insisted on taking her back to her yard in Mahaica.

"The old woman spirit will just sicken in all this strangeness, Shark; she too old and set in she ways to change now," he said, and so Pancho drove them back home. I did not go with them, because I did not want to see the village again. I was just beginning to wrap the feeling of the city around me, and the thought of returning to the mud-hole where I was born made me shy away. The last thing Brother C. said to me was:

"Don't forget the story I told you, Shark. Keep it in mind, and some day when you're up against it you'll see what I was driving at."

After they left, the emptiness of the big house pressed down on me like a fallen tree. The rooms were so quiet I could not bear the calm brooding that filled them. When Pancho was out I spent most of my time on the veranda watching the carts, cars, carriages, and pedestrians passing by. Midday was the loneliest time, because the white sun seemed to fasten itself to the sky roof, so that it could burn with concentrated fury. And the heat brought a heaviness and a hush with it, and even cartwheels rumbling on marl stones sounded muffled.

There was a new cook next door. My neighbour seemed to change them the way men changed singlets after walking in the hot sun. Since the buxom laughing one, who had been there when I had moved in, there had been three or four. The new cook had a son named Joshua who was always tumbling in the grass or popping his marmoset face over the fence. His skin could not stand the feel of clothes, and the mistress of the house was always complaining about Joshua's nakedness in her front garden.

I was waiting for Pancho one afternoon. He was due to take me to the sawmill with George and De Freitas. A sudden shower had come and gone, and when the sun burst out again the white marl street began breathing steam.

"Joshua, where you shirt boy?" the cook called out from behind the hibiscus hedge.

"Me lef' it under the house, Ma!" he answered, between bouts of laughter and tumbling.

"But this boy can't bear clothes on he back, eh! Come inside here, boy, before the mistress start complain 'bout you nakedness again."

"But me jus' started to play, Ma!"

"Come in, boy, before me pepper you skin!" The roses in my garden drooped, and the bright yellow veins on the croton leaves matched the colour of the kiskadee singing to its mate from a flambeaux tree.

Pancho arrived, and we picked up George and De Freitas and drove to the sawmill. It was a huge, low shed squatting on the mudflats of the Demerara River bank. The inside was dark but occasionally the fireman opened the boiler door and a tongue of flame flared out to brighten the gloom, showing a sudden picture of ant-like activity – boys filling baskets in saw pits above which giant saws pounded up and down, the fireman looking like a devil in hell as he stoked the furnace, women coming and going with baskets of shavings and wood-skin on their heads, foremen waving their arms about and shouting above the whine of the cross-cut saws. The manager, a small yellow man with a bouncing walk, came up and introduced himself and said that he was expecting us. His manner was humble and he was anxious to make a good impression. He showed us around, and when we came to the back of the mill where winchmen were piloting logs towards the saws, he pointed to a raft which was stranded on the mudflats tilting towards the swift, falling water. "Fifteen thousand dollars worth of timber," he said proudly, and I saw De Freitas crinkle his nostrils against the stench of the sling mud.

"I wouldn't want to work here," I said.

"You're going to own the place, man. Who is talking about working," De Freitas said, and his laugh rasped like a file on my nerves. There were hillocks of sawdust behind the shed, and I saw children scampering up and down them.

"You need more light in the building," I said to the manager.

"They cost money and the workers don't complain; they get accustomed to the dark," he said.

"You're looking at things from ground level, Aron; the higher you are the better it looks."

"This is the best sawmill on this side of the river," the manager said.

"How do you feel about it?" George asked on our way out.

"To tell you the truth, I felt a chill down my back the minute I set foot in that mill."

"But you're still coming in with us?"

"I promised, didn't I?"

"We must celebrate; a party tonight, and races on Monday."

"He'll need clothes for the races," De Freitas said. "Order an outfit from Agard's today, because we've got to make a show, will be good for the business. We'll hire a carriage and six white horses.

I thought of writing Bullah and asking his advice about the sawmill, but I was caught up in such a round of dancing, drinking, gambling, showing Beryl off, that my relationship with my old friend became too remote to even attempt re-establishing contact. All my life, before I burst into Georgetown with a sackful of diamonds, my feelings for darkness and light had been linked to a routine of work and a need for rest, but with nothing to do except to make the good times roll, time became a misty trail down which I stumbled wildly. My days merged one into the other, and the seasons within each day lost all meaning for me.

On the day of the races I returned home from an all-night party, had a shower, and started putting on the clothes which I had just collected from the tailor. Kendall and De Freitas arrived in the carriage before I was ready, and I looked through the window and waved to them. Pancho, who was equally at home as a chauffeur or a coachman, sat high, top-hatted, frock-coated, reining in six restless white horses, and behind him was a shrunken Portuguese footman in scarlet livery, brass buttons and sunflower yellow epaulets. The neighbours peered from behind jalousies waiting to see the richest black man in town step out. I examined myself in a full-sized mirror. I was going to make myself uncomfortable in the hot sun with four hundred dollars worth of clothes – a tail coat, a cravat white as tiger orchids with a diamond pin stuck in it, striped trousers, patent leather shoes, a silver-headed stick, white gloves and a grey top-hat – a tailor's dummy with a black face. A crowd had gathered around the carriage to give the diamond king a send-off – barefooted, sweaty men and women and naked children. I walked up the drive, slowed, and the crowd murmured approval. The footman jumped down nimbly, despite his aged look, and opened the carriage door with a flourish. We drove off to cheers and the explosion of Pancho's whip. We bumped and swayed past pushing, shuffling, laughing, sweating crowds, colourful and thick as wild flowers. It was a public holiday and everyone was heading for the racecourse on the edge of the city. The noonday was alive with dark faces, white teeth, and white eyes flashing in the sun. We passed troupes of masked dancers leaping and whirling and stamping in time to flutes and drums. The throngs of people thinned out as we approached Beryl's house on Raleigh Street, but the noise and the gaiety still pulsed and vibrated everywhere in the city.

Beryl came out flushed, her eyes bright as fireflies. She wore a silk dress of flamingo pink, a picture hat to match, and a dazzling parasol burst open like a morning glory over her as she reached the bottom of the steps. Drunken voices from the surrounding tenements shouted obscene compliments as I stepped forward and offered her my arm.

By the time we arrived at the racecourse the verging trees were already weighted down with a host of non-paying spectators nesting in the branches, and when a branch broke and sent a dozen men and boys headlong into the canal below, the waiting crowd outside the gates roared with laughter. People, thick as parasol ants, were herded towards a side gate by a tall Negro policeman who bellowed orders at them good-naturedly. The main gates swung open for us and the horses trotted towards the grandstand. Police stood at attention, and the conductor of the Militia Band raised his baton. The band struck up the National Anthem. The Portuguese footman performed his duty with a wide, yellow-toothed grin. I stepped out, bowed, and helped Beryl down. For a moment a hush settled over the racecourse as if the crowd was holding its breath. The music stopped suddenly, but a drummer-boy kept rattling his kettle drum. A flustered usher trotted out and led us to our seats, and Pancho's whip cracked loudly over the horses' heads, breaking the spell. There was a murmur, then a roar of shouting, cheering, laughing voices and I heard cries of:

"Ocean Shark, the diamond king! Ocean Shark! Ocean Shark!" I bowed low once more and sat down.

I was so excited during the rest of the afternoon that I moved about like a man with a high fever. People hailed me wherever I went, shook my hand, plied me with drink, toasted me and I played my part in the tinsel circus without knowing what I said or did, only conscious of Beryl holding on to my arm. Pancho told me after that we went to a fête and he had to carry me home limp as an empty sack.

* * *

I was dozing off on the veranda one afternoon, dreaming of galloping horses and crowds shouting my name, when Pancho shook me awake and said:

"Skipper, a woman say she want to see you."

"Who? Which woman?"

"She won't tell me she name, but she say she know you."

"Bring her in, Pancho!"

"Aron, you don't know me, boy?" A fat woman with bile-yellow eyes asked as she walked up to me.

"I just can't recollect seeing you before," I said.

"It's been a long time and a lot of water pass under the bridge." She sat down and her body creased her tight silk dress into folds. "It's Indra," she said. "You don't remember?" I saw not her, but the image of her mother, the gross, diabetic woman who used to hate me when I was Dr. Ram's servant.

"It's been a long time, Indra."

"You haven't changed much, Aron. You still look young."

"How is your father?"

"He's still at Maichony. You know, he never spoke a word about you after you left except once when he complained to me that it wasn't your going that hurt him, but was the way you left without a word. I read about you in the papers when they said that the Militia Band mistook you for the Governor." Her eyes took in the furniture, the polished floors, the rugs. "You're not still vexed with me, Aron?" she asked suddenly, "'Cause I was young and foolish?"

There used to be the same peevishness in her mother's voice, I thought.

"A lot happened since our Eccles days, Indra."

"You want anything, skipper?" Pancho asked. He had been standing near one of the French doors which opened from the living-room into the veranda.

"Bring some drinks," I said, and Indra laughed until her breasts trembled and tears ran down her cheeks, and I knew that it was her way of releasing pent-up emotions, so I waited until she calmed down again.

"I come to ask for your help, Aron, for old time's sake. My husband's in big trouble and my father won't do a thing to help.

I have five children and Papa's leaving all his money for them, but he won't let me have a penny."

"So you came to me for help. What about all your school friends, all the rich people you used to know?" She fidgeted in the cane chair, making it creak.

So this was the Indra I would have died for once, I thought, this shapeless pumpkin of a woman. I did not feel any bitterness towards her, but I realised that years in the forest had prevented me from feeling that I was growing older week by week. If I had remained in Mahaica I would have been able to see my own age in the people around me, but in the forest I had judged men by their stamina, their strength, their cunning. The weak ones died or drifted back to the coast. Indra, on the other hand, had been able to look at her five children and see herself grow older day by day.

"You think you can lend me a thousand dollars, Aron, not for my good-for-nothing husband or my broken-down self but for the children?"

"But why come to me?"

"I don't have anyone else to turn to; my friends are fair-weather friends."

"You wouldn't have helped me if I was in trouble."

"I will do anything, but lend me the money. We can draw up papers. I will pay you after the old man's death; he can't last much longer now; he's got bad kidneys and a bad heart." All the pride had gone out of her and I did not want to see her cringe any more.

"I'll lend you the money."

"Thank you, Aron, thank you, God will bless you, boy." Her hands felt like wet moss when they touched me. I wrote out a cheque and saw her to the garden gate. I felt her coming was a bad omen, and I did not want to see her again.

"Skipper, if everybody bring they trouble to you doorstep, them trouble will pile up like a mountain. That ole cow didn't have nothing to offer nohow."

"Can't you keep your big mouth out of other people's business, Pancho!"

"All right, boss. Is you funeral, not mine."

"Shut up, for God's sake, man!"

* * *

Pancho went to the Stabroek Market every morning to buy food and drink for the house. Because I was alone and a bachelor, George and De Freitas brought their friends and their women night after night. They kept the house lively with drunken talk and laughter, clinking glasses, and music from the gramophone they had encouraged me to buy. Pancho was never absent from these nightly sprees. Drink was a great leveller in Georgetown. Pancho, with his coarse habits and his loudmouthed, unbridled talk, was better suited for a rum-shop in Tiger Bay, but he was a great drinker with the capacity of a rum vat, and this made up for his social failings. Besides, he used his morning visits to the market to pick up the latest gossip about the high and mighty, and he was a good storyteller once he had downed a few drinks.

I soon grew tired of waking up when the sun was high and having to pick my way across rooms covered with broken glass, and having to face strangers with red eyes and mouths hanging open, while stale odours made it difficult for me to breathe in. Pancho was always able to drive most of the drunks home, but there were the odd ones who insisted on staying. Beryl visited me every evening, but her mother never allowed her to stay out later than nine o'clock, except on special occasions. The old woman knew that I was sleeping with her daughter but she did not mind once we kept up appearances. She was planning to trap me in marriage, and her peasant cunning and experience had taught her that sex was a habit which could cut deep, a need which could establish cravings like a drug. She knew that once the closeness of a woman's flesh had burnt its hot imprints into a man's heart, he could not face an empty bed night after night. Beryl often swore that she would stay the night, but the thought of her mother's anger always made her change her mind in the end. Beryl gave herself to me freely. During the time I met her she realised that her main talent lay in the delights her body gave. She was a hot-sun girl with a flyweight mind, and although she had been brought up on a diet of pretence and prudery, she knew instinctively how to bargain her curves and her colour. I liked having her around me, for she was good company. Her parakeet chatter about clothes, parties, her friends buzzed into one ear and out of the other. Underneath all this, however, was a feline cunning.

Her instincts about people were always sounder than my own, and there were times when I suspected that she knew me much better than I was willing to admit. She did not like George and De Freitas, and kept insisting that they were scheming against me. I often thought of marrying her, especially on nights when George and De Freitas did not visit me and Pancho went to Tiger Bay to gaff with his friends. On these occasions I would realise how much of a stranger I was in the city, and how necessary it was to have one person under my roof who could be absolutely loyal, who could act as a shield against the white marl jungle which began outside my front gate. But I never got to marrying Beryl, for I would start spreeing and spending with a new recklessness on the days following my lonely spells.

In order to fill up the gaps in the daytime I started visiting the sawmill. My share of the profits worked out to about five hundred dollars a month, and when I complained to George that it should be more he always had a host of excuses about how the workers were asking for more pay, or how this or that machine had to be repaired. They did not like my visiting the mill without them, but I told them that they had their offices, and Pancho his Tiger Bay friends, and I could not go on day after day watching my black face staring back at me from mirrors in an empty house, where a gramophone played the same records so often that I heard the music in my sleep.

I liked walking around the sawmill watching the fireman stoking the boiler whilst the sweat poured off him, the winchmen hauling logs up the river bank, old man Aldridge with hands like a crab's legs planing and grooving the boards, customers coming and going, and checkers and clerks strutting about with pencils stuck behind their ears, the manager bouncing back and forth wearing a straw hat which looked like a tent. The machines, fed by a heart of fire, seemed to have a life of their own as they pounded and hissed and whined, and somehow the noises they made seemed to echo my discontent. I met too many people to know anyone individually. George and De Freitas either visited me or took me out frequently, and often I took them home to their wives drunk and sleepy as mud. Mrs. Kendall always met me at the door, looking at me as if it was all my fault. One night Mrs.

Kendall's guests were still there when I dropped George off at the top of his drive. It was dark, and I waited until someone opened the door in answer to his loud pounding. After he entered there was a lot of screaming and bustling about, and from the street I could see that George was walking across his living-room without a piece of clothing on his massive black frame. Mrs. De Freitas, however, received the limp bundle of her husband resignedly; she never showed any emotion when I delivered him and she never said a word to me.

★ ★ ★

I left for the sawmill earlier than usual one morning. It was the rainy season and all over the city the ditches and drains were overflowing, and children were sailing paper boats in the muddy water. The sun was playing hide-and-seek with rainclouds, and I walked quickly to the mill during a bright interval. Pancho had used the car the night before and he had not returned. I knew that he would turn up around lunchtime, red-eyed and reeking of cheap highwine, and he would have a list of excuses a mile long. Old man Aldridge was standing at the saw mill gate sunning himself. He was tall and bent with high shoulders, long arms and big, gnarled hands. His dark-brown face could have been sculptured out of cured mora and the deep lines grooved into it with a chisel. He was a part-time street preacher, and I had often seen him at nights under the big flambeaux tree in the market square with a carbide lamp on the ground beside him, and a mongrel dog sleeping at his feet while he shouted hoarse damnation at the congregation of beggars and touts who had chosen to be entertained in this fashion. He kept very much to himself at the mill and seemed to be respected by his fellow workers and even the yellow-faced manager. And if he chose to break off in the middle of a job and to take some sun no one said anything to him.

He said "Morning, skipper," before I could open my mouth, and this took me by surprise, because it was usually I who greeted him first and got a gruff reply.

"Morning, Aldridge." I knew he wanted to talk to me and waited, watching the mule drays and donkey carts piled high with boards and planks filing out of the main entrance.

"Me had a bad dream last night, skipper." There were about

eighty workers at the sawmill and although I had spoken to many of them and knew a few of them by name, none of them had attracted me in the way that this inscrutable old man did, and looking at him at that moment I understood why; he was a man from the country and, like me, was out of place in the city. He had the fierce pride of a village elder, the certainty which comes with fighting against drought and flood, with seeing an image of yourself in the land.

"What kind of dream, Aldridge?"

"Me dream 'bout fire and blood, skipper."

"That's a bad dream; my grandma used to tell me that fire meant death and blood meant that the heart was going to be heavy with crying."

"Watch you step, skipper, 'cause is you friend you got to 'fraid more than enemy." He turned around abruptly and walked away.

The clerks in the small front office pored over their ledgers with devotion when they saw me, and the Manager came up and started telling me about a raft which had broken free from its mooring during the night.

"Five thousand dollars worth of timber," he said, "and the tug didn't take off after it 'till this morning. We just have to trust to luck." I left him and climbed up to the winchman's platform. The river was high and I heard the water slapping against the greenheart piles under me. The rain came down again, falling in slanting white sheets, and raindrops pounded against the wavelets on the river. I wondered why I had not seen George and De Freitas the night before. They had not visited me, and I had gone to the Jockey Club, Fung ke Fung's gambling salon, and Elsa's, looking for them without success. The droning of the rain on the low zinc roof sounded like the Grass Fall at Perenong. I watched Aldridge feeding boards to a cross-cut saw for a while. I was sure that he knew something about my partners which I should have known, but when I tried to talk to him he only grunted without turning to look at me.

I waited for the rain to stop and when it did not, took a cab home. Pancho was not there, and the house was damp and empty and looked as if it had not been lived in for years. I decided to go and look for Pancho. He would be somewhere in Tiger Bay spinning out ballads at the bars and brothels, and drinking himself into a stupor. The rain stopped suddenly and the late afternoon sun turned roadside ditches, and the pools that studded the city streets, all golden. I changed my mind about going to look for Pancho and sat out on the veranda. It was one of those days when I knew that something was going to happen. The night before I had dreamt about Christopher Columbus coming to my grandma's hut in Mahaica. And she had prepared a meal for him of white yams, eddoes, peas and rice, and just as we were all about to sit down to eat, Columbus complained that he had stomach ulcers and my grandma cut up some thin slices of roast beef for him, but as we were about to eat I woke up.

I heard a quick patter of feet on the drive and looked up to see Beryl hurrying towards me. From the way in which she held her head high and steady and pursed her lips, I knew that she was upset. She came in and sat down, and I asked her what was wrong three or four times before she answered.

"Mama says I mustn't see you any more," she said.

"But she couldn't just say that out of a clear blue sky; something must have happened."

"A lot happened since yesterday. . . ." She buried her head in her arms and started sobbing. "I told you not to trust them! I kept telling you, but you wouldn't listen!"

"Sweet-girl, don't fuss youself. Tell me what's wrong!" I knelt down beside her, and put an arm around her shoulders. "Don't fuss youself, sweet-girl!"

"I didn't tell you, but my periods were nearly a month overdue, and yesterday I went to the doctor and he said I was getting a baby."

"But what's there to worry about? You know I will stand by you. I'm not a wild beast."

"Is not the baby that's worrying me. . . You didn't hear the news that's all about town!"

"Which news? Tell me, girl. Don't just sit crying like a baby!"

"You two partners, Kendall and De Freitas, declare theyself bankrupt – they owe a lot of debt on the sawmill and they left you in the lurch to pay them. Is how much share you got in the mill?"

"I've got a one-third, share but the mill's working all right. I was there today."

"Lord, but you fool eh, Aron!" She brushed away her tears and held my face in her hands. "Is why you let them two trick you so, boy? I will tell you what happen. Mama hear the whole story: Kendall and De Freitas put you down for fifty-two per cent of the shares so that you could bear the brunt of whatever happen. . . the only reason that the white man did sell out and go 'way was because everything in the mill was so run down, the insurance people wouldn't even cover it. . . ."

"But they told me the place was insured!"

"Lord, you fool eh! You see the papers?"

"Come to think of it, they were always promising to show me, but they never did."

"Those two crooks really make a fool out of you; they didn't even put a penny of their own money in the mill, and not only that, they kept some of what you gave them and took out a seventy-five per cent mortgage. . . ."

"But how do you know all this, girl?"

"Mama heard. She hears everything; she can't read and write, but she's got a good business head – and just as she heard and I told her about the baby she said I can't marry you. 'You can't marry no black man who don't have a red cent to his name,' she said, and she went on saying 'bout how you not only poor and black now, but you stupid! She said you should have married me while you had the chance; then she would have helped you out with your business. . . . You don't see, Aron. She wants to tear us apart, and I love you, and I want to have the baby!"

So this was what old man Aldridge had been hinting at! How could I have trusted George when I had seen with my own eyes how the man had betrayed his own mother? I might have had luck, but I had worked hard for that money. Diamond mining was brute-work. The sweat which had bathed my claim at Perenong had come out of young sap, and now I was older and some of it had dried up. These thoughts ran through my mind and I was not conscious of Beryl holding my face in her hands. She broke out sobbing again and I cursed myself for being selfish. After all, she was one person who loved me and was loyal to me.

"Your mama can't stop us from getting married, girl. . . ."

"She swore she was going to, Aron. She said I must throw 'way the baby, and she arrange for it to be done already."

"Stay here with me. Don't go back home, 'cause if you go she'll work on you and make you change your mind."

I paced up and down the living-room while Beryl sat slumped in a chair. I did not want to believe all that she had told me, even though I knew that her story was true. Part of my disbelief came from not being able to realise all of a sudden what it was to be poor. I had made a fortune in diamonds, and all along I had been convinced that no matter how much I spent or what I did, the money would last for ever. The money had never really meant anything to me any more than it had meant anything to my father. I did not respect money in the way that George or Mr. Beauchamp respected it, because I was not a grabbing, acquisitive person by nature. Having it had given me a kind of sensuous pleasure in the same way that having Beryl did. I wanted to make sure that she had told me was true, but at the same time, by hanging around the house, I believed that some miracle would happen to save me.

Pancho returned home with a long face.

"Me hear what happen, skipper, and me hustle home. The talk 'bout you spreading 'round the town like fire. You think you will have to sell the car, skipper?"

"You heard anything 'bout those two crooks?" Beryl asked.

"Me hear that they catch boat for the Islands last night, Miss Beryl; they taking holiday 'till the trouble blow over."

"What are the people saying 'bout me, Pancho?"

"Boss, them en't blaming Lawyer Kendall and he friend; they blaming you. Is so black people stay, skipper."

"So they're blaming me, but they don't even know me. . . ."

"They know you, skipper; they don't have nothing to do but dip they tongue in other people story whole day – the higher monkey climb the more he expose heself."

"What are you going to do, Aron?" Beryl asked, and I resented her question because I did not want to face up to what I had to do. I was not frightened, but I wished that Bullah was around, for every time I had to do something in the city I felt like a man fighting against the wind, not seeing what I was struggling against and not knowing how to fight the forces I could not see. In the village or the forest it had always been a straight fight for survival against a primeval Nature while in the city a man was always coming up against institutions – laws which said one thing and meant another, a government which was like a body without a heart, for its heart had been cut out and buried under a mountain of paper. I paced up and down and heard the hard grinding creak of cartwheels on the streets. I stopped and looked out of the window, and saw swaying lanterns hanging from the axles of donkey carts and yellowing pools of water which the rains had left. A lamplighter set up his ladder against the lamppost opposite and touched the street-light with a point of flame. It flared out and made the wet leaves of a guinep tree sparkle. The city dogs began their barking and baying to a moon which showed a misty face behind thin, streaky clouds, and cocks cleared the hoarseness from their throats so that they could crow all night. Up and down the street the lights came on in houses, deepening shadows and brightening whatever was still wet – leaves and grass, and high front stairs into which feet had worn hollows. This was a street in the city where I had lived through hectic seasons, and yet I was more of a stranger in it than when my grandma had brought me on my first visit years ago.

"What are you going to do, Aron?" Beryl asked once more and she sounded hysterical.

"I don't know girl. I don't know."

"Sell out and head back for the bush, skipper," Pancho said. "Me will come with you."

"You can't go and leave me, Aron. Every time I leave you it does feel like tearing flesh apart. You can get a job and do your pharmacy again."

"Give me time to work this out, Beryl. . . I will get a lawyer. . . ."

"Going to lawyer now is going from Caesar to Caesar, skipper. En't no use doing that."

"You must tell me what you're going to do right now, Aron. I can't wait 'till tomorrow. I'm going back to my mama tonight and if I know that you want me and that you want us to get married and settle down, then I will set my heart against all that she tells me and she will come round to my way of thinking after a while. . . . But don't let me go like this, Aron, I beg you!"

"Stay with me now, Beryl. Don't go back! I feel in my bones that more trouble's coming, and if we're together – you and me and Pancho – we can fight if off."

"I've got to go, Aron. I can see it all over your face that you don't love me. You wouldn't ever love anybody but yourself. All along I made myself believe that after you got over your swell-headedness you would have loved me even a little bit. You helped me to grow up, Aron. You told me once that I was living in a private heaven. Well, I was, but I came down from it, and the coming down frighten me. You're surprised that I can talk like this, eh? Well, Mama was more surprise than you at the change in me."

"Beryl, you suddenly make me feel small, and I don't know what to say to you. One part of my mind's crying out for you, but the other part's shouting, 'Run away, Shark! Run 'way, boy!' 'cause that was what I always did when I saw trouble coming. I never faced up to any trouble in my whole life 'cause I found out that the country was big and it had a lot of space to run away and hide in. . . and yet it's only myself I'm running from, but even now I can't check up, call a halt, face the self I'm running from. I know what I should do. I should dig in, turn around and face all these people who going to laugh at me and make mirth at how two city men fool me. . . I should take you and the baby under my wing. . . but all this is only bigmouth talking. You know why this trouble catch me? You know, girl?"

"Don't run yourself down, Aron, 'cause enough people will do that for you!"

"I must tell you 'cause this is the first time I ever spoke to anyone from out of my heart. I always knew these things, but you helped me to see them clearer. . . . I never did any thing in my whole life 'cause all that came about since I was a small-boy just happened to me, and now that I have a chance to do something for myself I know what to, but I don't know how to do it."

Beryl stood up and straightened out her frock and I knew that if I let her go it would be all over with us, for her old condor mother was going to dip her tongue into the story, pile reproach on top of her head, force her to get rid of the baby, and drum a sense of guilt into her until she would not be able to see straight. Beryl knew it too and she lingered for a moment.

"I must go," she said wearily, and the next minute I heard Pancho starting the car and driving her away.

* * *

I should have left Georgetown immediately. Pancho had suggested that I cut my losses and pull out. I stayed to enjoy my downfall. I went back to the sawmill and the Manager treated me coolly as if I were a stranger, and when I asked for old man Aldridge they said that he had gone away and no one knew where. I went to George Kendall's house and his wife shut the door in my face. The only friends who welcomed me were Elsa and Slackfoot. The others passed me on the street, and the people who had acclaimed me at the races spat at me with looks when I walked in their midst. More and more I came to realise that I had never really lived in Georgetown. I had only inhabited a big house in the city for a season, the way a wild beast inhabits a lair in the forest and moves on. Every day letters came like leaves blown in by a high wind. They all contained bills, except one which came from Tanta Moore and Brother C.. They wrote to say that they still had some of the money I had given them and that I should come home and take over Brother C.'s pharmacy, but I did not want to do this.

I was left with a car and an empty shell of a house. Pancho had stored most of the furniture in a room in Elsa's house in case the bailiffs came. Once the rooms were emptied, the white man's spirit returned to brood over them. He could not wait for the strangers to move out.

One morning I was sitting on a rug in the middle of the living-room when there was a knock at the door.

"Come in!" I said without looking round.

"Shark!" It was Bullah. We faced each other across the empty room. Bullah looked older. His hair was streaked with grey, his eyes lacklustre and tired and the lines in his cheeks had deepened into rivulets. But he still had his barrel chest and booming voice.

"They tell me you was in trouble," he said.

"Who?"

"Pancho send me telegram. You can't get rid of you true friend just by getting poor, pardner. Eh, eh, man, is not like the old Shark, not to have talk in he mouth. You can't even say you glad to see me!"

"I'm glad to see you, Bullah," I said, and my eyes would not make four with his, because I knew that he would be seeing two generations of Smarts, father and son.

"You got anybody with you, boy?"

"Only Pancho, and he's gone to the market. All the other so-called friends I had wouldn't come near me any more."

Bullah's eyes roved from the bare walls across the dining-room to the kitchen and back to me.

"Me not vexed with you, Shark; me vex with meself. Me shouldn't have go 'way and lef' you to bear the strain alone."

"You did your best, Bullah."

Pancho came in with a basket of fruit and vegetables.

"Aye, aye, skipper. You come at last! Me know you was going to come." Pancho was one of those people who attached himself so close to you that you seldom thought of him as a person. All along I had taken him for granted, but seeing him with Bullah put him in a different light: the two of them were so strikingly dissimilar. Pancho belonged everywhere and nowhere, while Bullah was as solid as a boulder above the Grass Fall. This solidity of Bullah's made you believe that he never moved from one spot to another, but just carried his mass through space.

"Well, how the position stand, pardner?" Bullah asked and once more he was the businessman dealing with profit and loss. I pointed to the letters in the corner.

"Not so good, Bullah. So many debts that when I think 'bout them my head starts to spin." He gathered up the letters and stuffed them into his pockets.

"Bullah Daniels will be taking over from here," he said.

"Lord, skipper, this call for a drink," Pancho said, and he fished a bottle of rum out of the basket and passed it around. We sat on the floor and talked about the pork-knockers at Perenong and about my late father. No one mentioned Belle, although we all had her in mind. Afterwards I told Bullah about Beryl and the way her mother had banned me from seeing her after I lost my money.

"If she was any kind of woman she would 'ave find a way, no matter if she mother was bad like a dragon," he said.

"She's a good girl, Bullah, but that old queen's too much for her."

"If you feel that way, then go and see her. They can't shoot you, and when door slam in you face only lil' wind does tickle you eyelash, pardner."

"All right, Bullah. You come with me, eh."

"Yes, me will come. Can't lef' the gal with you child in she belly like that."

We drove towards Raleigh Street in the rain in the late afternoon, and the water running down the windscreen and the windows made the city look like if we were seeing it in a smudged mirror. Pancho drove slowly and leaned far forward, for the pits of darkness between the street lights made it difficult to tell what was street and what verging grass. I was grateful for the rain and the darkness, for the streets were deserted and there was no one to point and say: "There goes Ocean Shark. He make a mountain of money and now he don't have a red cent to he name!" When we parked outside Beryl's house I was sure that her mother was not at home, because I could see the old lady's empty rocking chair on the veranda. There was a yellow oblong of light shining from an upstairs window and every now and then a blob of blackness moved across the yellow light.

"Me want to see what this Beryl girl look like," Bullah said. "Come on, man. Like you frighten to face the trouble youself make!" We walked up the front steps and I knocked, and when there was no answer I knocked again, louder this time, and we were a long time standing in the rain before Ma Thompson opened the door.

"Is what you want, Mr. Smart?" she asked, holding a lantern up to our faces.

"I want to see Beryl," I said. "And this is my friend Bullah Daniels; he came along with me."

"You en't do enough to me Beryl, Mr. Man, you en't drag she name in the mud enough? You give she bastard pickny and now you come to make botheration! Let me tell you something. . ."

"Don't worry with all that, Mrs. Thompson – and me calling you Mistress because you old and me never meet you before. You hear what the young man say. He just want to see you daughter, that's all, and from what he tell me he got a right to see she. If this is a house and not a prison, then me don't see why he can't see the girl." The veins on Ma Thompson's stringy neck stood out, looking as if she had lizards breathing under her skin.

"If all you two don't fetch youself off me property me will call the police and put them on you!"

"Then call the police," I shouted, pushing past her.

"Come back, boy! Come back! Is where you going?"

"Beryl!" I called out. "Beryl!" There was no answer. I ran up to the top floor to the room with the light in it. I heard the shuffle of footsteps and a low moaning. The door was ajar and I rushed in. An old woman wearing a hat that looked like a squashed orchid backed away in a corner. Beryl was lying on a four-poster bed. Her eyes were big and staring, and her face pinched and yellowish. When I touched her, her skin was burning with fever. She was in a coma and didn't recognize me. I heard footsteps mounting the stairs and the rumble of Bullah's voice. I turned to the old lady in the corner, although I already guessed what had happened: they had tried to get rid of the baby and something had gone wrong.

"Don't look at me, mister. Me is a poor old woman trying to hustle a living. Me begging you, don't make trouble for me! The girl was coming round all right when things take a sudden turn and now is only God can help she. Me swear to you wasn't my fault at all at all!"

Bullah entered the room with Ma Thompson shuffling behind him. He took one look at Beryl and I saw from the expression on his face that he knew she was dying. Ma Thompson had broken down and the tears were running down her black, crinkled-up face. She no longer seemed to care that we were in the room or even to be conscious of our presence. There was a terrible silence in the house, for the rain had stopped drumming on the galvanised zinc roof. The crowing cocks and the barking dogs outside sounded remote and unearthly. Ma Thompson walked up and down the room slowly, silently, hugging herself and rocking from side to side. Death crept up on Beryl and passed through her like a breath of wind, and she did not struggle in the way the others I had seen die had done. I remembered that Woody Sam had once told me that there was no one word to explain a boatman's death; when they went down on the river the river folk would say that they had gone away. And the same thing had happened to Beryl; she had slipped away down a river of night. It was strange that in the midst of this tragedy I did not follow my own inclinations, which were to weep with self-pity, to throw myself on the girl's dead body and bawl aloud my sorrow. Instead my feelings adapted themselves to Bullah's. If he had wept I would have done so too. If he had cursed God and Ma Thompson and all the unknown forces which had schemed to ambush Beryl's young life, I would have echoed his abuse. But he remained a kindly old man who had seen so much that nothing surprised him any more.

Ma Thompson closed Beryl's eyes and put two pennies over them and the other old woman with the crushed orchid hat gathered up her instruments and put them into a worn leather bag.

"As me was telling you, Ma Thompson, there en't goin' be no trouble for nobody. Me doctor friend will sign the certificate and you can bury you one-child quiet like," she said. She was the first person to break a long silence, and her voice startled me with its dry, rattling, matter-of-factness. Ma Thompson walked out of the room and the way she moved you would have thought that she was groping through a maze of cobwebs. The crushed-orchid lady muttered something about not having been paid and followed her.

"We better go now," Bullah said, and he took my hand and led me out. We passed Ma Thompson sitting in her rocking-chair.

"If I can do anything, Ma Thompson. . ." I began, but the look in her old eyes made the words stick in my throat. She had turned her vision inwards, and I knew somehow that for the rest of her days she would only see images of Beryl alive and bright as a simitu blossom in morning sun. The tears still ran down her cheeks, trickling into deep creases, getting lost, then reappearing under her chin. She rocked back and forth, hugging her withered breasts as if she was nursing a baby, and suddenly the rocking stopped and she called out:

"Beryl! Beryl! How often me tell you that you mustn't play with them nigger yard children, girl! Come inside at once! Beryl, you hear me. The sun going to make you too black, girl!"

We left her sitting there and crept out.

★ ★ ★

Bullah set about fixing up my affairs, and it was not long before everything was in order. I ended up with nothing but the suit on my back, but my life was no longer corseted and I came as near to feeling happy as I had ever done in all my born days. I understood then why pork-knockers always came to the city, squandered their money and returned to the bush. They were men whose eyes had measured wide spaces of savannahs, forests and twilights under tall trees, whose energies were tuned to the rush of rivers and the race with the sun across seasons of every day. The city was a close place which had no answer to the needs within them. The tight charnel rows of houses and the mesh of streets, however, had the distant glitter of a carnival, and every now and then they came to join it like birds flying into a spider's web jewelled with dew, entangling themselves and bursting out.

We moved into a spare room in Elsa's brothel. Pancho brought along the car horn with him and polished the brass-work on it every morning. I wrote Indra asking her to repay the thousand dollars she had borrowed, but she never replied. Bullah staked me enough to buy supplies and equipment for a trip to the Cuyuni goldfields, and we left Georgetown for Bartica once more.

I saw Bullah off the night after we arrived in Bartica. He stood in the stern of a squat riverboat waving and shouting until the darkness left only his voice and the chugging of the engine. He was going back to Belle. Although he had never spoken a word about her, I could picture how she fitted into his life. He did not want love; he wanted a woman who could stir up echoes of his youth, and Belle fitted the bill. Bullah's life was an ordered flock of habits, thoughts, actions, which he shepherded through the years. I hated the disciplines his kind of life would have imposed on me, but I envied the security he enjoyed as a result of them. If you scraped Bullah with the sharp tooth of a rock you would never be able to wear away the layers of contentment around him.

Pancho and I settled down on the wharf beside our bales and boxes. Captain Rhodius was due to start for the Cuyuni at fore-day-morning and he and John Pye the bowman were trying to finish the rum in the Fire Plume Rum Shop.

"You take the change good, skipper," Pancho said, easing himself into a comfortable position on a piece of folded up tarpaulin, "like you en't sorry 'bout nothing."

"I'm sorry 'bout everything, Pancho, 'bout the girl, 'bout Bullah, 'bout all the time and money I wasted, but what's the use! Lord! If you ask me what I want to do now all I can tell you is that I want to strike it rich again." I stretched out and watched the stars and listened to the drunken voices in the town, and the water curling around the piles under us making a noise like the swish of a woman's skirt. Pancho fell asleep quickly, but sleep would not come to me. I remembered Brother C.'s story and tried to relate it to my life, but I could not. I went for a walk to the foot of Sorrow Hill and back, and foreday-morning caught me with my eyes wide open and my back propped up against a bale.

CHAPTER ELEVEN

IT was early morning, but the sun was already bright. A light wind had blown away the mist over the river. The dark water below the Kamaria rapids tugged angrily at rocks as if it would tear them loose and send them rolling towards the sea. This was the gateway to the Cuyuni gold-mines. I watched the water rushing by, and because I had just come from the city the rocks took on human shapes, they looked like dwarfs and giants, crawling infants, men and women and at times it seemed that it was not the river but these misshapen creatures that shouted and roared and hissed.

"Come and give a hand!" Captain Rhodius shouted, and John Pye threw me a towline. When I caught it, the rope felt wet and heavy in my hands. There were three pork-knockers in our party whom I had known at Perenong: Woody Sam, Barnes and English. They were not surprised to see me back. They had expected me to return in the same way that Rhodius and John Pye had, and if I had remained in Georgetown and become a solid citizen I would have let them down. A man was not supposed to have glue in his palms when he made money from gold or diamonds. The three had been drifting from camp to camp. Woody had run Bullah's shop, and when Bullah had come back without Tonic he had offered the old pork-knocker a small share in the business as a bait, but Woody was an itchy-footed man. The nomad in him could not bear the thought of being tied down.

"We going to sweat out all that bad city liquor now, Skipper," Pancho said as we began to haul the five-ton *Sun Girl* up the rapids. Twelve of us strained at the towlines and the boat inched along with the water bursting into foam around its bows. The sun climbed above the trees and because I had not felt it on my bare back for a long time I began to sing:

> "The mountain does sing at Arisa
> The river is king at Kamaria
> The sun jump up
> And the river jump down
> And the river-man shout,
> Oh, God, Sun King,
> Let me have me fling
> Let me have me fling. . ."

and the others joined in the chorus:

> "Oh, God, Sun King,
> Let me have me fling
> Let me shout and sing
> Let me growl and prowl 'til morning."

The singing made our labours easy, and it was not long before we came to a wall of falling water which was bypassed by a portage. We hauled the *Sun Girl* out of the water and pulled her across the portage on rollers. The rock surface was so hot I could smell the soles of my canvas shoes burning. Pancho and Woody were droughing the bales and boxes we had unloaded over to the camp site at the other end of the portage. They were bearing up so well that I could not show how the heat and the work were tiring me but I was dizzy with fatigue and at times I could not tell if it was men or rocks moving. River flies stung my eyeballs, redding them until I saw flaming stars. Out of the water the *Sun Girl* was a lame creature hunched on the slope of the portage, slipping and sliding on the rollers under her. During a rest interval at noonday I looked around me. It always took me a long time to realise that I was in a new place because my life had been so crowded with experience that as soon as I digested one I found myself in the midst of another. The reason for this was that what I saw was never as important as what I felt. I had to feel a place the way a bat felt darkness, and when I wrapped my feeling for a place around me it was the only time I felt safe. Everything that had happened in Georgetown meant little to me because my instincts never rooted me to the big house and the car, the crisscross of white marl streets and the row upon row of houses. On the other hand, my whole being came alive in the forest. The sight of the sun, white and molten in a wide sky, the big trees with no wind to breathe on them at midday, orchids and wild flowers on a rock-face, the sound of a river shouting quickened the flow of my blood and made my heart jump with excitement. At that moment, standing in the shade with the sweat pouring off me, the full realisation of my return to the forest dawned on me.

We knocked off at sunset and left the *Sun Girl* on the crest of a slope. I slung my hammock and eased myself into it while Pancho and Woody lit a fire. Rhodius kept walking back and forth as if he could not bear the feel of earth under his feet much longer. I saw a crescent patch of the sun as it lowered itself behind the trees and for an instant it looked like a wild beast, arched and indolent and ready to spring back into the sky. Night came and drowned the fragments of colour which glowed on the river and across the sky.

"Dinner ready, skipper!" Pancho called out. We sat around the bonfire with the others and ate, washing down the food with tea from big enamel cups.

"Tell me what happen since me see you last, Shark," Rhodius said picking his teeth with a wicked-looking black thorn. "Me hear lil' bit here and lil' bit there but you know how black people story contrary." English was plucking the bass chords of his guitar and he began to sing in a high sweet voice:

"Ocean Shark is king of men
Is king of men in Perenong. . ."

and one of the pork-knockers said:

"You live big, man, and you fly high, you make money talk and now you come back. En't one of we would 'ave done no different, man."

"You come back for good?" Ruction Daniel asked.

"None of we don't come back for good," Woody said, "but the bush does hold you jus' the same, man, and when it hold you it don't ever let you go."

It took us two days to haul the *Sun Girl* across the portage and when she dipped her bow into the river once more she shivered as if she was eager to contest every foot of the way to Warridi. We prepared to continue our journey at day-clean, rolling up the towlines and reloading the cargo. We had to stamp our feet and shake the dampness out of our limbs as we worked. Mist spiralled lazily upwards from the rocks like smoke from secret fires, and as the sun warmed us there was plenty of laughter and talk. Rhodius and John Pye bellowed orders good-naturedly. Pancho had risen early and gone hunting, and while I was preparing breakfast he returned with a bush hog.

"Got enough fresh meat to last we 'till we reach Arimu, skipper," he said, grinning. Pancho was always happy about little things that others never bothered about. Sometimes he reminded me of Santos, except that there was no envy or malice in him. When he was on the wagon he was the best companion a man could hope to have. As the weeks went by I realised that I had never really known him very well in the city. The moment we had left Bartica I had noticed a change coming over him; he became at once more relaxed and more alive. The rhythm of life in the forest was one that he could respond to like a dancer to a drum. Stripped of his town clothes and tanned a reddish brown by the sun, you knew at once that he was a river-man endowed with all the tension and the ease, the speed and the power of water running down from the mountains.

"Come on! All you like old whores at a christening!" Rhodius shouted, and we took our places aboard the *Sun Girl* and she chugged her way upriver with everyone in high spirits.

"Make it to Arawak by sundown!" Rhodius said, talking to the *Sun Girl* and we headed past rock walls where vines crisscrossed mossy surfaces and orchids and wild flowers striped and lightened the solid, dark green.

* * *

We set up camp near the mouth of the Arawak Creek and the Cuyuni River while Rhodius continued upriver towards Ikowan. Woody Sam, English and Ruction Daniel teamed up with Pancho and me. They said I had a lucky hand for finding gold and diamonds. The land at Arawak was thickly wooded with trees leaning over the two streams, and some of them dipping their branches into the quiet water. In the afternoons the massed green of the forest which verged on the river was dotted with the white and pink of cranes and herons, the blue-black of kingfishers and the brown of hannaquahs. Occasionally one of these birds dived after a fish and broke the glassy surface of the water. The claims in this district had not been worked for a long time and the campsite was thick with underbush and tall trees reaching for the sun.

The morning we started work I stood in the fretted twilight sharpening my axe blade while the others surveyed the claim and measured the distance to the creek. The wind brought their voices to me. Woody was saying that years ago he had worked a claim near Matope, a mile away and English, who had been a cane-cutter on the coast, was telling the story of how he had seduced a white overseer's wife. He had been telling this story since my Perenong days, but since then he had dressed it up with all kinds of new and imaginary incidents. As far as he was concerned, it was the only important event in his whole life.

"Is what you got that any white woman would want?" Daniel asked. "You don't look like no Romeo to me." The others laughed. They were bushmen and they did not like the loud-mouthed gaffers from the coast.

"What me go, Lord! You should ask the white woman 'cause once she taste the black sugar-stick the hubby had to send she back home and she swear she was goin' send for me."

"Is a case of luck beat handsome," Woody said.

From where I stood I could see the sunlight on the river. The gloom, the excess of life and decay around me made me feel that I was in a tomb preparing to cut my way out.

We spent weeks building huts and thatching them with turu palm leaves, working like ants under the big trees from fore-day-morning to sundown. The country was snake-infested, and at nights we had to put bowls of condensed milk outside the ring of the campfire's light to keep these reptiles away from the huts.

Hard work and heavy sleep dulled the memory of what had gone on before in my life. My existence was controlled by the demands on my energy that each day made and I had no time for dreams or regrets. When Pancho talked about Georgetown or Woody about Perenong these places seemed so remote to me that I could hardly believe that I had ever lived in them.

One morning Woody snatched up a young bushmaster snake and dashed its head against a tree. He could sniff around and tell you where a snake was lurking and he never made a mistake. In the evenings after work we bathed in a pool below the Matope Waterfall where the water was cool and clear and we were safe from cannibal fish and electric eels. It was the dry season and the sheet of water falling down the rock looked like a large glass window through which I could see the caves where flocks of starlings and bats lived.

It was too much to expect that five men could live in the close darkness of Arawak without somebody exploding. There was a heaviness about the place that oppressed your spirit so, that whenever you laughed you felt uneasy afterwards.

Pancho went hunting every morning and he seldom returned empty-handed. Sometimes I went with him and gathered pineapples and honey from the big-cupped flowers on the balsa trees. I had to go early for the honey because troops of monkeys would descend from the treetops, pick the flowers and drink from them as if they were goblets. I liked to watch Pancho standing still as a tree on a windless day while he called bush rabbits, turkeys, marudis. He knew the language of the forest creatures and would talk to them as if they were human. When he bagged his quota for the morning he would sing all the way back to camp or boast about past hunting exploits. He looked on the forest behind the Matope Falls as his private hunting grounds, and one morning when he caught English there with a shotgun the anger burst out of him like steam from a boiler.

"You notice anything, skipper?" he asked, and the fierceness of his tone surprised me for I had never seen him get angry before. English came towards us big and black and walking noisily.

"Me tell you don't set foot here with no gun in you hand!" Pancho shouted, and his neck was swollen and ropey and his whole body tense and ready to spring.

"Eh, eh, man. Nobody en't buy this bush yet," English said. "You looking for trouble, pardner."

"Trouble ? Me is a man who. . ."

"Stay away, me telling you!"

"All right, pardner, all right. Is why you frying up you fat so!"

"Just keep out, that's all! Me does share the game me hunt with everybody, and me swear if me catch you here again won't be no telling what will happen."

"Come on!" I said. "I can't hear the tinamous singing when the two of you start barking at each other." I put an arm around Pancho's shoulder and he relaxed.

"Pardner, me really thought you was vexed," English said, making such a wry face that we had to laugh. When the undergrowth was cleared we started to cut down the big trees around our huts. It was hard work, and after the first few days I had to lay off because of the blisters on my hands. Woody could wield an axe with the force of a cyclone and he exulted in his skill and strength as his axe blade bit into the tree trunk.

"Look alive!" he would shout. "Is what kind of young man we got today! All you making this work look hard." His muscles coiled and uncoiled as he worked. He was a short man with a small head, a thick neck, wide shoulders and stumpy legs.

"How do you do it, old man?" I asked one day as I watched him swinging his axe. He stopped for a moment, wiped the sweat from his brow with an old cap which always sat like an upturned bird's nest on his head and spat.

"Is the slave blood, skipper, the slave blood and a big heart."

"The old man tough like lignum vitae," Daniel said. He was tall and taciturn and had a way of breaking into sudden laughter; then he would laugh with his whole face, his eyes and his mouth and the row upon row of creases which dimpled his face.

"The other reason why me wear well is that me don't knock me body 'bout like all you young man," Woody said.

"Don't tell we that story, old man," Daniel said. "They tell me you can make the good times roll like fire when you get ready."

The big trees brought down dozens of smaller ones, and to see the sky widening day after day was like magic for it lifted the weight from our spirits. At night Daniel strummed his guitar under the low stars and English sang river chanties. This was to celebrate our bursting out of a twilight tomb under trees. Some of the creatures that lived in the treetops were killed, while others scurried to safety when the trees fell. Once I saw a three-toed sloth with a dead baby by its side. Its back was broken and its gentle eyes looked at me accusingly out of a thick nest of fur. They reminded me of the eyes of a child in pain. I fetched my gun and shot the crippled sloth.

The quiet of the Cuyuni always gave the impression that violence was lurking underneath, and you could never tell what form the violence would take. One afternoon a cloud like a bale of cotton-wool dipped in ink hid the sun and waracabras cried insistent warnings from the trees.

"Me don't like that cloud," Woody said. "If me know the Cuyuni at all, that is hurricane cloud."

We continued work watching the cloud swell until it blackened the whole sky. A wind stirred in the trees and made the still river shiver and ripple.

"Watch out! H-a-u-l a-b-o-u-t!" Daniel sang out, and we downed tools and hurried to the centre of the clearing. The wind gathered strength and suddenly it was ripping and roaring through the forest, scything down giant moras, greenhearts, aramatas. There was a crashing and a thundering and the earth trembled under us. Only the tail end of the high wind reached our camp, but it shredded and tore off the thatch and we had to lie flat to escape its buffetings. It all happened so swiftly that when the sun flared out and the clouds drifted away it was as if I had been day dreaming. But the hurricane had cut a lane through the trees a hundred yards wide and a mile long and for days after we were attacked by angry parasol ants.

"Won't be nothing to hunt for couple days," Pancho said. "Everything will be in hiding."

"You worrying 'bout hunting, pardner; you better thank God that He spare we," Woody said.

That night I lay in my hammock watching the stars through the holes the storm had torn in the thatch. Woody was in his hammock a foot away from me, while Daniel, Pancho and English were playing cards.

"You does never say nothing 'bout we Perenong days," Woody said, and I knew that he wanted to talk about Bullah and Belle. He had wanted to ever since we first arrived at Arawak, but I had never given him the chance.

"Life goes on, Woody, and what's happened, happened, man. I can't change anything now."

"When Bullah come back to Perenong with the queen you could 'ave knock me down with a feather, but old age does fuddle up we head. Why Bullah take up steady with woman at he-age only the Lord know. But he en't stupid 'cause he give the queen just so much reins and no more and she know that no matter how much man she eye want to light on she can't make wrong move with Bullah 'cause he is a tiger when he get vex. You should 'ave hear the talk round Perenong, skipper; all the pork-knockers say that you make deal with Bullah and he buy the queen off you. You know how black people tongue can mauvais langue them who they think flourishing too much."

"Bullah is my friend and he will always be my friend, and no woman won't change that."

"You know, since he take up with the queen, every day she looking more young while he hair getting white like tiger-beard orchid."

"One thing I know, Woody, I'm never going back to Perenong; that place bring me and me father too much bad luck."

⋆ ⋆ ⋆

We made a sluice box and installed it over a pit. After damming up the shallow creek, we dug two canals, one leading to the pithead and the other discharging from the pit to a point below the dam.

It was good to hear the pickaxes biting into sand and gravel again, to watch the sparks fly when you struck a rock. Woody, Daniel and English worked in the pit while Pancho and I did the washing. We watched the muddy ooze flowing past the riffles in the sluice box. In front of each riffle was a blob of quicksilver to trap any gold passing down, and every now and then we had to remove stones or branches when they stopped the flow.

We struck gold on the second day of opening the pit. I picked up the first nugget, rubbed it against a rock, held it up to the sun and shouted:

"Gold! Gold!" The others gathered around and the nugget passed from hand to hand.

"Lord, skipper, me never see man with luck like you!" Woody said. "Like me goin' make that trip to see me fam'ly after all."

"Is ten year me know you, Woody," Daniel said, "and since the first time me meet you been saying that."

"Me going this time, me tell you, me swear by sky and river!"

We broke a bottle of rum over the pit and with visions of mountains of nuggets before us we continued work. It was a good thing that we were not near to a big mining camp. Forty miles to the east of us was Ikowan and thirty miles down river, Kamaria. I knew that the pork-knockers would not stay long at Arawak even if they were making a fortune in gold. Just to have nuggets and gold-dust piling up in a canister was not their idea of living. I felt, however, that I could depend on them for a couple of months until the rainy season came.

⋆ ⋆ ⋆

Rhodius came to Arawak soon after the first rains. The pay had been steady, but not fabulous, and life had reduced itself to a dreary routine of work and sleep. Pancho and English had quarrelled several times, and when I heard them shouting at each other I knew that underneath the hard words was a need to let off steam and both were enjoying themselves. Rhodius, who often did a little business of his own on the side, sold the pork-knockers a few gallons of highwine at exorbitant prices and they were drunk all the way to Ikowan.

Ikowan was a settlement of rickety huts and plenty of mud and trampled grass. You only felt the sun when it was directly above you, for tall trees surrounded the huts and the yards and flung shadows across them most of the day.

My share of the gold worked out to about five hundred ounces, and after much haggling I sold it to Amagan, the shop-owner at Ikowan, for five thousand dollars. I don't know why I remained in this mud hole for two years when I had enough money to go where I liked, but when a man wants to make his own purgatory, not even his mother can stop him. During my two years at Ikowan my life lost all purpose. Perhaps it was that my life had to lose all purpose so that I could really come to terms with myself – who I was and what I was. Those two years at Ikowan were broken up into fragments of experience, none of them connected, none of them having any rhyme or reason. What had continuity during this time were the voices of Pancho, Woody and Daniel, voices trying to save me from myself; Pancho because he was loyal, and the others because they saw themselves in me and could not bear it. . . .

Hennie Bow-Wow was the ugliest woman between Roraima of the red rock and Orealla, Pomeroon and Akarai, but wherever she went she scattered sex around like molasses – thick and sticky and bittersweet.

Big Macey had a hut behind Amagan's shop. He loved food and drink and women above everything else in life and he found a pork-knocker's life a good one for indulging his passions. Hennie was my woman for a couple of months. I met her at the shop one day and she fixed me with a "come here" look and since that day she would not ease up her hold on me. Big Macey breezed in from Bartica and he wanted her so he challenged me to a crap game, winner take Hennie. Macey, blown out and large, with a shiny pate, looked as if he polished his head every morning, and when it was shiny sprinkled a few grains of salt and pepper on it. He sat facing me with his big stomach pressed against the edge of the table. The petrol lamp over us made the air hot and dry and I could hear Macey sucking the air up his immense nostrils. Hennie sat on a box away from us gripping a bottle of rum in one hand. The hut was small, and, smoky and Hennie's animal smell mingled with the alcoholic fumes. Macey slapped four hundred dollars down on the table and I matched it. Hennie smiled and leered at us through the smoke, ugly as a night of strife. Macey shook the dice in a small wooden cup and it chattered loudly. Hennie passed us cups of rum. She knew we were gambling for her and was pleased. Seven was the lucky number.

"Twenty dollars you don't throw seven!" I challenged Macey.

"Make it forty!" he said in a hoarse, jovial voice. My pile of dollars began to dwindle and Macey raked in the spoils, laughing and taunting me.

"Come on, Shark. You not playing! This is man-game, so prove youself!"

"I'll stake my last fifty-five on this one!"

"All right," he said, edging closer and pushing the table against me. "All right; me will bite at that one, pardner!" Suddenly Hennie had taken off her clothes and was sitting beside Macey rubbing her big, hanging breasts against the smooth of his bare shoulder. Macey breathed hard. I thought he was going to suck the dice up the dark tunnels of his nostrils. Hennie was using us like pawns in her own game. She wanted me to win and Macey to lose. Macey cupped one of her breasts in his hands and bit the nipple and she cuffed him and stood up.

"Let we go, sweet boy," she said, and I gathered up the loot while Macey laughed from deep inside his belly.

"I will get you yet, Hennie. Don't worry, gal. Shark won't want you for long!" he said.

Pancho and my three other conscience-men were waiting for me in the dark outside.

"But is why you wasting you time with this old bitch, skipper!"

"Lord, man can sink low, eh! To think that this is the same Ocean Shark me used to know at Perenong!"

"Skipper, leave that old, hard-faced harridan alone!"

"Go on!" I shouted. "For God's sake leave me alone!"

Hennie and I kept going steady even after she had become as repulsive as a snake in a mud-pit to me. One night I burst into the small hut I was sharing with her and found her in bed waiting for me and in a sudden rage I picked her up and threw her outside.

"You mad, Shark! You gone mad!" she bawled, and afterwards I heard her sobbing on the doorstep.

I woke up next morning and a mist was around my eyes like a bandage. One wall wobbled before me, flattened itself out and became solid. I reached out to touch the woman who I thought was beside me, but she was not there.

"Hennie!" I called. "Hennie!" Someone was sobbing outside. I jumped out of bed and opened the door and Hennie raised inflamed accusing eyes to me. I lifted her up and carried her inside, massaged her stiff limbs and coaxed her until she fell asleep.

Hennie moved in with Macey, and I can still hear the echo of his deep laughter.

In the midst of a drunken spree, with Amagan cursing me for wrecking his shop, I met Mabel Fox. She was a samba woman, all tenderness until you saw her claws. We teamed up for a season until she grew jealous of Madmus, my second string, but she was like a roadside melon, while Madmus was like a ripe fruit on a tree top. I went to Madmus down a moonlight trail where mosquitoes and an ooskudu owl sang me a love song and shadows were dark, navy-blue islands where fireflies danced. I lay in bed with Madmus and her warm breath and the snake-rhythms of her body were drowning me in a sweet river of night. Mabel flung the door open and tore us apart. The two ocelots, ignoring me, locked with each other – tearing, ripping, clawing. Neighbours heard the scuffling and the screams and claws encased themselves in women's sobs.

What Madmus had to offer was too good to let be and I sought her out again and again. Paris, a former lover came from upriver and caught her with Matabe, a sweet-man from the coast. Madmus and Matabe were together in a houseboat on the river and Paris went for them like a demon. They jumped overboard and swam away, but he paddled after them. He split Madmus' skull open with his prospecting knife, but Matabe escaped with one arm hanging on by the skin. The shadow of Madmus' death hung over me until Dearest arrived from Bartica. She was a brown girl with a wide mouth and dark eyes which never lighted on anything for long. I gave her silks and jewels and she purred her satisfaction in nights of labouring together.

"Leave them no-good whores alone, skipper!"

"You crawling low like a snake, boss!"

"Lord, is what you want to do, wreck you body?"

This was the chorus my conscience-men sang, the ballad they repeated in my ears time and again.

Dearest was two-timing me, but I never found out until I heard someone pounding at the door in the middle of the night, shouting, "Dearest, open the door! Me going to shoot that man you got there with you!" I scrambled out of bed and moved towards the back window, but Dearest, moving like a cat, whipped out a prospecting knife and blocked my way.

"If you move another inch I will chop you down like grass!" she hissed and I stood helpless between a man with a gun and a women with a knife. A cunning smile crept over Dearest's face. The pounding at the door grew louder, rocking the hut on its high stilts.

"Open or I will shoot me way in!" Dearest was satisfied that I would not try to escape and she left me and flung the door open.

"All right, Mr. Zacky. You got to shoot me first! Go on. Shoot if you call youself a man!" There was a long silence until Zacky spoke again, and all the anger had gone out of his voice:

"Ow, Dearest, me love you, gal. Is why you doing this to me?" His voice trailed off into sobs while a who-you bird sang its night song.

My conscience-men worked out a scheme to get me away from Ikowan. They spiked my highwine and bundled me aboard the *Sun Girl*, and when I woke up with humming birds in my head we were already nearing Arimu.

"How you feeling, skipper?" Pancho asked.

"Where's Woody?"

"He and he pardners stay back, they still got some money to blow out."

"Aye, Shark!" Rhodius called out. "Me thought you was finished, man; the way you was drinking and whoring about at Ikowan worry me. The last time me touch at Perenong me tell Bullah that he better come and get you out of that place before it was too late, but when Bullah did want to come the queen start to mutter that all of we got to make we bed and lie on it. She got it in for you, you know, Shark. She got it in for you proper, boy."

"They've all got it in for me, Rhodius. When I die they'll dance on my grave 'till they pound it flat. Why did you bother to drag me away from Ikowan, you and Pancho and whoever else worked out the scheme?"

"Me will tell you why, pardner. Bullah send me to bring you. He couldn't come heself 'cause he en't had nobody to run the shop for he."

"But how can he send for me when Belle's still with him?"

"You mean you en't hear the news yet?"

"What news?"

"You en't hear that the queen left the old man and gone back to whoring in Georgetown?"

"How did Bullah take it?"

"Me en't know the full story, but me think Bullah work it out that way after the queen eye start to rove. Me know that you did love the queen one time, skipper, but me see plenty in me time and a whore is a whore and will always be a whore. That's how the story does go."

CHAPTER TWELVE

I RETURNED to Perenong. The *Sun Girl* edged up to the landing at the foot of the high bluff of land and I saw Bullah coming down the front steps of the shop to greet me. It was late afternoon and powis and toucans were gathering in the tall trees beyond the hill to sleep. Nothing had changed except that the grass around the shop had grown waist high since Tonic had gone away.

"Me glad to see you, Shark," Bullah said. "Me was just beginning to wonder if you would come at all." I detected the loneliness in his voice; it was that strange loneliness of a man who was always doing good for others and always being betrayed. We embraced and I felt that I would never want to cut loose from Bullah again.

"Come on, Pancho," I said. "We're home, boy." Pancho grinned and slung the bundle with our belongings over his shoulder.

"This call for a drink," Rhodius said. "The trip from Kamakusa scrape me throat dry."

Bullah laughed as if he had just thrown off a heavy load.

"Well, come on in. What you waiting for?" he said. John Pye made fast the *Sun Girl* to the landing and we walked up the path to the shop.

"How she going?" Rhodius asked, leaning against the counter and swallowing his rum in big gulps.

"You can see for youself," Bullah said, taking in the empty shop with a sweep of his arm. "Business en't exactly jumping this way." He settled himself down on his high stool, sipped his drink, rolled it all over the inside of his mouth and swallowed it and I noticed that he had aged rapidly in the two years since I last saw him. His eyes had sunk deeper and there was an undertone of grey to his black skin, as if he powdered it with ashes.

"You know Kitchener?" He shot the question at Rhodius.

"You mean Ruben Kitchener? You mean that long man who does walk like he foot don't belong to he?"

"That very Kitchener. He look like when ugliness was sharing he bite off too much."

"Me know the man, Bullah; he got a difficult beauty."

"He making trouble for me, that man, that's why me glad Shark come. Me getting old now and me is not the fighter me used to be."

"Don't say that, Bullah. You still spry like a fighting cock, pardner," I said.

"This man, Kitchener, open a shop at Oronopai a month gone and he starting to smell he sweat. Me don't mind that he taking away lil' business from me, but the man trying to jump a claim topside of the Grass Fall, and Banner Baggert left me in charge of that claim."

"But is how he can do that, Bullah?" Pancho asked.

"Me coming to that part of the story, boy. It all start when the queen was with me, Kitch sweet-talk she and find out that the claim got gold like fire, and since Mark-a-Book gone the new Sergeant at Kamakusa backing up this robber-man."

I could hardly believe that this tired, peevish Bullah was the same man who had come to Georgetown to rescue me. It saddened me and at the same time made me feel good because it was the first time since I had met him that I could do something for him. He had always been a big father-man who I leaned on and depended on.

"Pancho and me can start work on the claim right away, and if the Mr. Kitchener sets his foot there he'll have to take on the all of us."

"You come home now, Shark. Lord! Hear how the man talking!" Rhodius said.

That homecoming was a new experience for me. Since I left Mahaica my life had run like a liana through forests of time without beginning or end, and now it was taking roots in the red earth and the sand at Perenong. Bullah had abandoned the cottage on the hill after Belle left and vines and creepers had overrun it and a tree had pushed through the centre of it, thrusting upwards until the roof sat on its branches like a hat. A few regular customers stuck by Bullah and came to the shop every night to drink and gaff and sweet-talk him into giving them credit. A man never really knows that he has changed until he sees the change reflected in other people's eyes, and I knew that I had grown up from the way Bullah would sit and look at me and smile to himself.

Pancho and I took over Tonic's room at the back of the shop and at nights I used to lie in bed for hours thinking about my boyhood in Mahaica, my days with Dr. Ram, my first trip to Perenong with Santos, the interlude with Belle, the tinsel glory I enjoyed in Georgetown, the disjointed nightmare at Ikowan. The people who had featured in these experiences talked to me and walked beside me, traitored me and laughed at me all over again, and their laughter echoed down all the rivers I had travelled.

★ ★ ★

We started work on Baggert's claim above the Grass Fall. The creek had overflowed during the rainy season, and when the flood water fell it had left a two-foot deposit of clay which the sun had cracked and hardened. It took us over two months to dig a pit and a tailrace and, because the creek was drying up, we had to groove the tailrace deep where it discharged. We widened the pit and worked downwards through hard alluvial clay and gravel until we found cool darkness and a layer of rock. It was quiet at the bottom of the pit with only Pancho and me working and every stroke of a criminelle, every thrust of a spade, was like a clap of thunder. We could not break through the rock and so we tunnelled horizontally along its surface. We worked on hands and knees, and if I arched my back upwards a few inches the gravel bruised my skin. We heaped the gravel into boxes, taking turns to carry it out of the darkness into the light at the pithead, and every trip I made I took the darkness with me, wrapped around my eyes, clinging to my limbs until the sun burned it away. The first day's gravel yielded an ounce of gold and the excitement I felt at seeing it made me break a long silence. I said:

"Pancho, this time I know what I want to do with the money I get, and nobody's going to vulture it off me, nobody. I'm going to buy land in Mahaica, a piece of land that will stretch from the sea to the forest and I'm going to grow coconuts and rice and ground provisions. I'm a village boy, and I know the land just like my grandpa knew it and wrestled with it all his life. . . ."

"But you can't leave Bullah, skipper."

"I thought about that, but he's getting old and weak and I can control him. I'm going to take old Bullah with me, and he and Tanta Moore and Brother C. can sit and gaff away their old age."

There was not much doing at the shop at nights except that old Percival, a drifter who was never returning to the coast, got drunk on a brew which he made from bark and cassava. One night Pancho sampled Percival's brew and he had to jump into the creek to cool off. He said it made him feel as if marabuntas were stinging his insides. Occasionally, Murray, a young claim-holder from near Oronopai, dropped in for a game of poker. Bullah did not like Murray, because he suspected that he was a friend of Kitch's and was spying on us. I tried to get Murray to work with us, but he took one look at the mine-shaft and the tailrace and said that there were easier ways of making money.

The dry weather held and we lengthened the mine until it took fifteen minutes to crawl to the pithead with a box of gravel. We had to use candles in the mine and huge, jumbie shadows danced on the walls every time we moved. I fastened my eyes on the vein of gold and worked in a fury. Mud caked on my body, weighted down and stiffened my eyelids and blocked my nostrils, and when I blew my nose echoes bounced around and lingered until they mingled with the tap-tapping of Pancho's pick. Sometimes I wondered what he was thinking, for I thought about all sorts of things: of Belle standing in the kitchen in Georgetown, legs wide apart and arms akimbo, of Tonic cocking his head to one side and looking at me with his cross eyes, of Brother C. sitting in his Berbice chair looking at the Mahaica River and telling me the story of how Drake sailed around the world, of the night my grandma put the curse on Uncle Richard, of Beryl begging me for a baby, of Dr. Ram watching the ants follow his wife's urine, of Santos telling me how Jordan was crucified – and always there was the thought of my father working in the darkness, not too far from where I was chasing a vein of gold, with his two hundred Chinese workers and Mr. Beauchamp striding up and down by the pithead. I was able to sort out the fragments from my past in the darkness of the mine, to give continuity to the story of my life.

After a while Pancho and I did not worry to sleep at the shop, but camped out on the mine site, and at nights we sat around a fire. The long spells underground dampened Pancho's spirits, and night after night he had no laughter, no jokes, no hunting stories to fill the long silences. He was part Indian and part Negro. Both the Indian and the Negro were forest people, but the former could match their moods to the brooding silence of a forest twilight, while the latter had an easy laughter to hide their sadness. Looking at Pancho night after night, I came to understand the things that bound us together very clearly. Ours had started out as a master-servant relationship, and he had kept it that way because in his heart he needed to be a servant.

One night I saw him crouching by the fire like a stone figure and I pitied him with the selfish pity of a man whose will had triumphed over the spirit of another.

"Pancho," I said, and he kept staring at the fire as if he knew that he would betray his need to live through me if our eyes made four. "Tell me 'bout the time you lived up the Demerara River as a boy."

"Skipper, is like if the dark of that mine scrape the words off me tongue. Me carrying that dark inside me belly and me can't root it out. To tell you the truth, boss, me 'fraid for that dark, you working like you got tiger behind you but all me want to do is to root that dark out me system."

"Chu, man. What you grumbling 'bout. We will fill up a canister with gold by the time the rains come. Twice I had luck and now this is my third and last toss. If I make a wrong move I know I'll never have another chance."

"Is not the gold bothering me, skipper; is the dark. Me don't like it; it does creep inside me flesh and bother me."

"If the dark is the only place with pay-dirt, pardner, then we've got to live in it and work in it. If Englishmen can come all the way from England to work gold and diamonds, why can't we?"

"Is all well and good for them, skipper; the white man eye catch fire for gold long time, gold is a thing they does eat like rice, and after all what is this gold – yellow dust and yellow brick. Me mama was an Indian woman and gold-fire never light in she eye nor in she people eye. If it wasn't for you, skipper, me would 'ave lef' the gold just where it born in the earth belly. Me like me hunting and me fishing, me walking through the bush whole day, and now and then me like a spell in town to gaff and drink with the boys. If all the folks in the world was like me, the gold and diamond would 'ave lef' jus' where they was borned 'cause when you take thing out the earth and you en't put nothing back the land and the river does claim sacrifice."

"I never heard you talk like this before, Pancho."

"Is the dark eating out me insides, skipper, making me think deep when me is a man don't like deep thinking, me like to go me way cool like a mountain pool, fast but not deep."

"So what you suggest we do, Pancho ?"

"Let we stay 'way from that dark lil' bit, skipper. Let we take walk by Sulpha Rose for couple days."

"All right. We'll lay off for a couple days."

★ ★ ★

We set out for Sulpha Rose when the sun was still fighting to bore through the morning mist. I had invited Bullah to come along, but he said that he was getting old; his body had beaten against too many years for him to take such a long walk through rough country. We travelled light, and I could barely keep up with Pancho; he moved like an ocelot ahead of me, arched and quick. When the sun patched the forest floor with shadows we had already reached the red-earth lands. It was a hot, dry day and the leaves only moved when birds or monkeys ruffled them.

"Good weather, skipper. Me like it like this when the earth feel hard and dry under me foot," Pancho said, and I noticed that his jauntiness had returned.

A rabbit bounded across our trail and Pancho vanished. I looked around and saw him pasted against a tree signalling me to follow suit.

"Something chasing that rabbit," he whispered, and he put the edge of a leaf to his lips and whistled in short, sharp fluting bursts. A jaguar parted the tall grass twenty feet away from us and looked around with green, malevolent eyes. We fired together and the big cat sprang and fell dead at our feet, and suddenly it looked small and crumpled, half the size it had been alive. I prodded the carcass while

Pancho held his gun at the ready, and when he was certain that it was dead he knelt down beside it and stroked the spotted coat as if he regretted killing this creature which was as bright as a flower and had the speed of the wind. He skinned the jaguar expertly, pried out the fangs and cut out the heart for roasting.

"Me bet you me will find that rabbit," he said. He got up and followed the rabbit's trail, and in a few minutes returned holding it by the legs.

"I didn't hear a shot," I said.

"Me find it in the hollow of a tree, dead with fright; once he look that big cat in the eye he didn't have a chance."

We were still on the move when the full moon came out. We wanted to take a stock of fresh meat back with us, and the moonlight season was a good one for hunting. The blue light came down to the forest floor in slanting shafts deepening shadows and gleaming on Pancho's bare shoulders.

"This is a place for bushmaster snake and we bound to meet up with couple of them, 'cause they like the moonlight," Pancho said. An ooskudu owl hooted and tinamous sang mating songs high above us.

"Look!" I said, pointing, but Pancho had already seen: two snakes were standing upright in a pool of moonlight coiled around each other.

"Two bushmaster cock fighting," Pancho said. "The she-snake must be watching on in the shadow; is the mating season." The snakes were not fighting, but dancing – coiling and uncoiling, parting and locking with each other. "That fight will go on for days and sometimes both of them does die and the she-snake does stand-by to see that nothing don't trouble she two dead lover-men, and sometimes she does dead with sorrowing."

We left the bushmasters to their fight, and as it grew later the moonlight brightened and our footsteps sounded loud on the dry leaves which the dew could not reach. One mad ooskudu owl kept hooting long after all the other creatures of the forest were asleep. We shot a pair of powis and two wild hogs. On our way back we passed the bushmasters still dancing. The female had come out of the shadows and was coiled up like a pile of thick wet rope near the fighters.

Moonlight turned the forest into an enchanted world. The dewdrops on the spider webs hung like stars above the trail and the air was fragrant with the smell of flowers and wild sage and locust gum.

We returned to camp in the early morning and I slept through to the afternoon. When I woke up my hammock was wet with perspiration. Pancho and Murray were playing cards under an Iowa tree. Murray saw me stir and shouted:

"Aye, aye, skipper, you wake up!" But I did not answer. I lay for a while watching the sunlight on the wings of river-flies as they buzzed around my head. The two came towards me and I got up and stirred the fire and poured creek water into a big iron pot which hung over it.

"I feel like some tea," I said.

"I wouldn't mind something to wash away the dust in me throat either," Murray said.

"Seen Bullah today?" I asked Murray.

"He down by the shop sunning heself, skipper."

"Boss," Pancho said, standing over me, and I looked up and thought that even in repose his face had a hunter's look, alert and listening. "Boss, Murray say he want to work with we, he say he think it over, and if we give he reasonable share he will help bring the gravel to the pithead."

"What happen, Murray, you changed your mind all of a sudden, man?"

"Well, is like this, Shark: me claim work out and playing card and beating me lip whole day don't put no food in me pot, man."

"This is brute-work, pardner; just take a look at the mine."

"Me en't fraid for hard work, me born and grow up with it, man."

"What kind of share you had in mind, man?"

"Since me come late will be all right with a one-sixth share."

"I will tell you tomorrow," I said, and we sipped our tea and poked the fire and watched the sun going down behind the trees. There was something final about the sunsets at Perenong. The whole forest waited for darkness and only after it came swiftly, pouncing on the dusk, did the six o'clock bees and the tinamous sing; and always flights of bats danced against the glowing sky until night merged with their black wings.

"I will come back at fore-day-morning," Murray said when he had finished his tea.

"What you think 'bout the offer?" Pancho asked as soon as the footsteps had died away.

"I don't like it, Pancho. That man's too close to Kitchener, and the two of them must be up to something. I never met Kitchener, but from what Bullah tells me about him I won't trust him."

"But two more hands can carry a lot of gravel to the pithead, skipper, and the rainy season coming. Me for one wouldn't mind the extra company, because you jaw does stay lock whole day sometimes."

"I'll take him on, Pancho, but these two eyes will never lose him."

"Boss, you don't trust nobody no more. . . ."

"Not even my mother with gold, pardner."

I went over to the shop that night and gaffed and drank with Bullah until late. Business was picking up since the news had gone abroad that I had struck it rich again. Bullah had a long talk with me.

"Shark," he said, "me glad you straighten out youself, boy, you still got a long way to go, but you come far already. You turn a man now and you get harder and nobody en't going to cheat you like Kendall and he sour-face Portuguese friend did do in Georgetown. Don't get too hard though, boy, and don't get too greedy, 'cause look at me; me got money and property and me en't got a chick or a chile to leave it for. Is only you me got, boy."

Three of us went down the mine next morning. Murray had come prepared to work, because he knew I could not afford to turn him down. I knew he had visited the mine while we were away and when he saw how much work we had done, he had decided that he had nothing to lose by teaming up with us. We lit our candles and started the long crawl. Drops of water glistened on the pitface and dripped on my bare back.

"All you do a properly big job here," Murray said, "just the sluice-box and the tailrace represent 'bout ten man work."

"Me done tell you that the skipper and me is not ordinary man," Pancho said.

Murray and Pancho talked all the time, and I was glad to be back in the dark, to feel the clay on my face and body hardening and pulling my skin tight. I worked on the mine face following the vein of gold while Pancho and Murray carried the boxes out and washed the gravel. I felt somehow that they had formed an alliance against me, and Pancho was doing this to protest against my greediness for more and more gold. I would listen to Murray's disembodied voice echoing through the mine and to Pancho's answering one. Murray was full of ballads about a girl he had left on the coast, and these made me remember Indra and Belle and Beryl and the whores at Ikowan, and for a moment I would stop work and lie flat on the damp gravel, and the cold water dripping on me felt like a woman's fingers. Murray was so black that when he came close to me to fetch a box of gravel his eyes looked like those of a fish peering out of dark water.

We came across a formation of gravel and rocks packed so tight we had to tunnel around it. Occasionally there were piles of decaying tree trunks, but these were soft as cardboard and easy to cut through. I cut through to a layer of sand and found some large nuggets, and I worked so concentratedly that I did not hear Pancho and Murray shouting at me. Pancho crept up behind me and clapped a hand on my shoulder.

"Skipper, skipper, you mad or what? Is dead you playing with; them nugget won't do you no good if couple ton of sand and rock make a hat to fit you head." I turned and blinked at him and wiped the caked mud and sand from my face. Pancho pulled me backwards and we had hardly covered ten yards when the roof of the mine fell in ahead of us, choking us with dust. I found myself laughing and shouting:

"Don't worry about me, pardner. If God himself blocked my way to those nuggets I'd throw Him aside. . . ." The dust choked back the other words.

When we came up from the mine that evening I noticed a ring around the moon and I said:

"We've got to work longer shifts; the rainy season's coming."

"Longer shift, skipper? We can't do more than we doing now,

we working from day-clean to night, is not steam we got in we vein; is blood like everybody else."

"You willing to work extra, Murray?"

"If you increase me share."

"I'll give you an extra half-share."

"A whole share; that is iron-man work and me can feel that sand resting on me lungs already."

"All right, man, a whole share."

"Me going to knock off as usual," Pancho said and because it was the first time he had rebelled against me I could not find words to answer him. It would have been all right if we had been alone, I would have laughed away his protest and promised him a trip to the city, but with Murray there enjoying the whole thing I knew that I had to even up scores.

Pancho and Murray stretched out in their hammocks as soon as we reached camp, but I sat by the fire. My shoes were soaked with dew from the grass along the trail and I took them off and held them so close to the flames that they began to steam.

"Pancho," I said, "I want to have a word with you, man."

He squared his shoulders and I could see them bulging through the close weave of the cotton twine.

"Skipper, we weary and me can't move." I went for him, almost knocking Murray out of his hammock.

"Watch out!" Murray said.

"You keep out of this," I said.

Pancho sat up looking at me with his sloe eyes, gauging how far I would go. I hit him full on the mouth and he made no attempt to defend himself: I struck him several times until he fell backwards with his mouth hanging open. I emptied a bucket of water over his head and he came to sputtering.

"All right," he said. "All right. I will work the extra time." Bullah walked into the camp just then and when he saw Pancho spitting blood and the angry look on my face he said:

"Me thought all you was big man, but like me make mistake 'cause all you acting like small-boys."

"The skipper nerve on edge these days, Bullah. Me just say couple word to he and he turn wild," Pancho said.

"Me en't going to dip me mouth in all you young people story, but me can tell you this, Shark: that gold you chasing kill plenty man before you. You can't finish all the gold in Perenong, Shark, if you dig from now 'till the carrion crow build nest."

"I'll stay with this mine 'till the first rains break, Bullah. You can't expect a man to leave off when he's finding nuggets like fire."

"Is up to you, boy, but me mind tell me that you playing with trouble. To tell you the truth, me don't like this underground mining and is the same way so me used to talk to Joe Smart, same way so, boy."

"Me feel like a drink," Murray said. "All this talk-talk don't get you nowhere."

Bullah, Murray and I walked down to the shop while Pancho remained in his hammock sulking.

"You hurt the man feeling," Bullah said, and I felt pretty bad and wanted to go back and make it up, but I was sure that Pancho would not be able to hold out and he would join us later. There was a big spree at the shop because the pork-knockers had drifted back from Oronopai, and they had brought women with them. These women usually came from Bartica with the rains, for the rainy season was the best time for vulturing the pork-knockers. Bullah was all smiles as he served drinks, broke up fights and hustled to and from the back room with bottles in his hand and under his arm. Woody Sam, Daniel and English breezed in near midnight looking as if they had never left Perenong, and Woody took his place behind the counter with Bullah. There were high bids for the women, although I thought that they did not have much to bid for. The spree lasted until morning, and when Murray and I staggered back to camp Pancho was not there. He had left with all his belongings – his hammock, his wareshi, his gun, his pots and pans. We went back to the shop to ask if anyone had seen him, but no one had. Bullah was sitting on the front steps watching the sun come up. He and his shop were like sweat to skin. You could not really appreciate the man he was until you saw him against the background of this institution he had created in the midst of the forest.

"Me can tell you why Pancho cut loose, boy," he said, slowly puffing away at his clay pipe. "That hunting trip you go on to

Sulpha Rose sicken he heart for the bush. Is funny with these bushman like Pancho or Tonic, they like the city or the deep bush, nothing in between. Is what use for a man like Pancho to make too much money? The money will just clip he wings. Like me was saying, Pancho heart sicken for the bush, and on top of that you hurt the man deep when you quarrel with he like you did, so he gather up he few things and go 'way."

"I will miss him, Bullah. You know, just when I thought he would never leave me he cut loose. Looks like I don't have luck with young people like myself." I left Bullah spinning dreams with the blue smoke from his clay pipe. Murray and I returned to work in the mine and all the time I expected to see Pancho's shadow dancing on the walls and to hear his voice echoing. Murray came for the boxes of gravel and the intervals between his coming and going seemed longer than usual. For the first time since I had started work underground I had a longing to leave the darkness, to feel the sunshine in my eyes, to let it burn away the weight of this darkness and the pressure of it from my temples.

"Skipper, some wind current twisting 'bout the mine and is not a good sign. Me candle blow out three times on me way to you." I continued chipping at the vein of gold, thinking that with luck the rains should hold for another week, wondering if I would be able to persuade Bullah to sell out and come with me to Mahaica. It had seemed easy when I first returned, because he had looked old and lonely, but of late he had been saying over and over again that he would stay in Perenong until they laid his bones under the big mora tree by the hill. I did not know if he meant it or if it had just been old man's talk, the dreaming about death long before it came.

"How does the sky look?" I asked Murray when he returned.

"Nothing but blue; not even a cloud as big as a penny."

Fifteen candles burned behind me with flames shaped like the petals of a tiger-beard orchid, and it was comforting to look back and see them.

Whenever I thought of Pancho I realised that I had only seen flashes of his real self. I could understand Kendall and Belle, Uncle Richard and Santos – they were village folk like me who had left the land and lost themselves – but Pancho could drift in and out of any situation and come out without scars. He was a nomad who carried all of his life around with him and he could move from place to place without leaving any traces.

I heard Murray shouting from the pithead, and when I looked back all the candles had gone out except one and the flame from it was leaning away as if a wind was pressing against it, and at the same time I felt a trickle of sand on my back. I crawled towards the candle like a snake, but just as I picked it up a rush of wind extinguished it. I heard Murray shouting.

"Hurry, Shark! Oh, God, hurry, man!" There was a dull thud and I had to shut my eyes and hold my nose against the dust and suddenly it felt as if a tree had fallen across my legs. I lay face down on the mine floor and could not move.

"Shark! Oh, God, Shark!" Murray shouted and his voice drummed against the walls and echoed back and forth. I felt a numbness creeping up, past my knees to my thighs and suddenly there was a hard stab of pain.

★ ★ ★

I woke up with the sun in my eyes, and when I tried to move the pain thrust upwards from my legs and stuck forks into my spine. I heard voices, Bullah and Woody and Daniel. One minute the voices were clear and individual, and the next they were mingled and drawn out and they got mixed up with other voices. Bullah knelt beside me and put his thick dry hand on my forehead.

"Boy, you make me old heart jump and rumble this day."

"Bullah," I said, "what's happened, pardner?"

"You get injure bad, Shark, and we got to take you down to the coast." It was not his words that cleared my mind: it was the pain; it burst all over me. I tried to roll over, but strong hands pinned me down.

"I want to know what's happened. Don't hide anything from me."

"You legs get crush below the knee and we had to cut one off."

"Raise me up and let me see them!"

★ ★ ★

I saw the sun moving across the treetops ahead of us. Rhodius shouted something to John Pye and Bullah bent over and said,

"You doin' fine, pardner," and he fixed the tarpaulin around me. I closed my eyes and listened to the river and I remembered the night when Rhodius had told me about the voices under the river. I listened, and all I heard was a single voice – Brother C.'s – and he was telling me the story of the men who had gone up the mountain, and he kept repeating the last part of the story:

"When they open he hand it was empty and they keep asking he, 'How is it that you come back and you en't bring no wondrous thing to show we? How is it?. . . how is it?. . ."

THE END

ABOUT THE AUTHOR

Jan Rynveld Carew was born in 1920 in the village of Agricola in Berbice, Guyana. When he left Guyana in 1945 to pursue his education he began what he described as 'endless journeyings' that involved periods in the UK, North and South America, Africa and Asia. He lived in Jamaica between 1962-66 with his then wife Sylvia Wynter, moving to Canada for some years before settling in the USA. He taught at Northwestern University and at Princeton and was at the heart of developments in African American studies.

His first two novels, *Black Midas* and *The Wild Coast*, were both published in 1958, both set in Guyana. *The Last Barbarian*, set in Harlem, USA was published in 1961, and *Moscow is Not My Mecca*, published in 1964 (also as *A Green Winter*) took a Caribbean student to disillusion in Soviet Russia. Jan Carew has written several books for children, a number of plays, and a collection of poems.

In his retirement to Kentucky, Jan Carew has resumed his old love of painting.

ABOUT PEEPAL TREE PRESS

Peepal Tree Press has been decolonising bookshelves since 1985 with our focus on Caribbean and Black British writing. We are a wholly independent publisher and part of the Arts Council of England's national portfolio since 2015. In 2024, we established a partnership with HopeRoad Publishing.

Peepal Tree's list features fiction, poetry and non-fiction, including academic texts and creative memoirs. By the end of 2024, we will have published 490 books by 320 different authors, including those published in our anthologies. Most of our titles remain in print. Our books have won the Costa Prize, T.S. Eliot, Forward, OCM Bocas, Guyana and Casa de las Americas prizes.

From the beginning, women and LGBTI authors have been fully represented in our lists. We have focused on the new by publishing many first-time authors and have restored to print important Caribbean books in all genres in our Caribbean Classics Series. We have also published overlooked material from the past as a way of challenging received ideas about the Caribbean canon.

We see decolonisation as about overthrowing and repairing oppressive, economically exploitative and racist power relationships. Many of our books explore the halting, difficult process of overcoming four hundred years of colonialism in the Caribbean in the post-independence period. But we also see decolonisation as needing to happen in Britain. We are committed to ending British amnesia over the destructiveness of empire and colonialism, including our role in the irreparable damage of nearly three centuries of slavery , and promoting an understanding of how Britain's long relationship with the Caribbean has contributed to the making of British society in ways that persist into the present. As a publisher, we have taken a stand on supporting Palestinian rights for freedom from a colonial occupation and denial of statehood.

We hope that you enjoyed reading this book as much as we did publishing it. Your purchase supports writers to flourish. Keep in touch with our newsletter at https://www.peepaltreepress.com/subscribe, and discover all our books at www.peepaltreepress.com, and join us on social media @peepaltreepress